"Unhand me!" Emmeline tried, futilely, to escape.

"Not just yet, Emma. First we are going to talk."

"Emmeline."

Jamie turned her and sat her down on one muscular thigh. "That name does not suit you. 'Tis too formal and stuffy for a lady with your spirit and passion."

Emmeline's mouth gaped open. She snapped it shut. "You know naught about me," she sputtered.

"You forget, I've sampled that fire you seem so determined to hide." He glanced briefly at her mouth, a subtle reminder of the devastating kiss they'd shared. When his gaze returned to hers, its intensity was anything but subtle. Blatant desire flared in that single midnight eye.

Emmeline gasped sharply as an answering heat streaked through her. It sank deep, touching some hidden core of herself. Like a sleeping dragon, the seed unfurled again, spreading the flames. "Nay," she whispered, denying the rush of sensation....

Dear Reader,

With this month's *Knights Divided*, Suzanne Barclay again returns to her award-winning Sommerville Brothers series. Emmeline Spencer kidnaps Jamie Harcourt, believing that he is responsible for the death of her sister, but the innocent Jamie escapes, turning the tables on her and bringing Emmeline along as his captive. Don't miss this exciting story where lovers must battle evil before they find true happiness.

On the trail of a gang of female outlaws. Federal Marshal Clay Chandler doesn't realize that he's falling in love with their leader in Judith Stacy's heartwarming Western, *Outlaw Love*. Haunted by their pasts, a gambler and a nobleman's daughter turn to each other for protection against falling in love in Nina Beaumont's new book, *Surrender the Heart*. And in *Bogus Bride*, by Australian Emily French, spirited Caitlin Parr must convince her new husband that although he had intended to marry her sister, she is his true soul mate.

Whatever your taste in reading, we hope you'll find a story written just for you between the covers of a Harlequin Historical novel. Keep a lookout for all four titles wherever Harlequin Historicals are sold.

Sincerely,

Tracy Farrell,
Senior Editor

Please address questions and book requests to:
Harlequin Reader Service
U.S.: 3010 Walden Ave., P.O. Box 1325, Buffalo, NY 14269
Canadian: P.O. Box 609, Fort Erie, Ont. L2A 5X3

Suzanne Barclay

Knights Divided

Harlequin Books

TORONTO • NEW YORK • LONDON
AMSTERDAM • PARIS • SYDNEY • HAMBURG
STOCKHOLM • ATHENS • TOKYO • MILAN
MADRID • WARSAW • BUDAPEST • AUCKLAND

ISBN 0-373-28959-6

KNIGHTS DIVIDED

Copyright © 1997 by Carol Suzanne Backus

This edition published by arrangement with Harlequin Books S.A.

® and TM are trademarks of the publisher. Trademarks indicated with ® are registered in the United States Patent and Trademark Office, the Canadian Trade Marks Office and in other countries.

Printed in U.S.A.

Books by Suzanne Barclay

SUZANNE BARCLAY

has been an avid reader since she was very young; her mother claims Suzanne could read and recite "The Night Before Christmas" on her first birthday! Not surprisingly, history was her favorite subject in school and historical novels are her number-one reading choice. The house she shares with her husband and their two dogs is set on fifty-five acres of New York State's wine-growing region. When she's not writing, the author makes fine furniture and carpets in miniature.

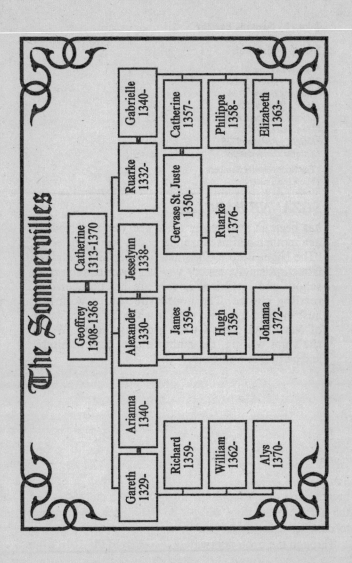

The Sommervilles

Geoffrey 1308-1368 — **Catherine 1313-1370**

Children:
- Gareth 1329-
- Alexander 1330-
- Jesselynn 1338-
- Ruarke 1332- — Gabrielle 1340-

Arianna 1340- (with Gareth 1329-)

Gareth 1329- children:
- Richard 1359-
- William 1362-
- Alys 1370-

Alexander 1330- children:
- James 1359-
- Hugh 1359-
- Johanna 1372-

Jesselynn 1338- — Gervase St. Juste 1350-
- Ruarke 1376-

Ruarke 1332- & Gabrielle 1340- children:
- Catherine 1357-
- Philippa 1358-
- Elizabeth 1363-

Prologue

Derry, England
September 4, 1386

"Mistress? There's soldiers come into the shop asking for ye," Peter whispered from the door of the workroom.

Emmeline started, scattering the costly saffron threads she'd been transferring to a parchment packet for a customer. "Did they say what they wanted?"

Her apprentice shook his head so violently blond hair whipped across his fear-filled eyes. "Th-they s-said they had to tell ye something."

Something bad. "Did they mention Cedric?"

"Nay, 'twas ye they asked for, not yer sire."

"I see." Drat. Six months ago she'd nearly lost the shop paying up his gambling debts, and he'd promised...Emmeline sighed. She'd learned early that Cedric le Trompour's promises were seldom more than a puff of breath. And that usually stinking with sour ale. What had the old reprobate done now? And how much was it going to cost her to extricate him?

Through the open doorway that separated the shop from

the back room where she stored the more costly herbs and made creams from her mother's recipes, Emmeline glimpsed the three men who'd invaded her establishment. Two were obviously soldiers, hard-faced men in dark livery with watchful eyes and huge swords.

The third stranger was a rumpled little man who prowled the shop's interior, poking a pudgy finger into the bunches of dried herbs with the air of complete absorption. His face was round and wrinkled as the old-fashioned brown gown he wore. A rim of frizzy gray hair lapped at the edges of his bald pate like moss on a shiny rock. He didn't look like the sort of man who'd demand she sell the apothecary shop she'd inherited from her mother just to satisfy a drunken old fool's gaming debts.

Emmeline drew in a steadying breath. "I'll see what they want. Please finish packaging this saffron for Dame Wentworth, Peter, and mind no more than three threads per packet."

"Mistress..." Peter caught at the sleeve of her gown, his thin fingers stark against the brown wool. "Let me go with ye. If there's trouble, I can help."

Despite her trepidation, Emmeline smiled. Though he was only three and ten, Peter was a good lad and likely to make a fine apothecary. Providing she didn't lose the shop before his training was completed. "I'll be fine."

"I beg ye leave the door open," he whispered as she left the workroom. "If they threaten ye, I'll come running." And he would, too. They were closer than apprentice and mistress, more like the only family either of them had. Peter was an orphan, and Emmeline nearly so. Her mother had died a year ago after a long illness, and her father...well, Cedric had been dead to Emmeline ever since she'd found out what he was.

More to salve Peter's pride than out of any actual fear, Emmeline left the door ajar and stepped into the store. The soldiers tensed; the little man looked up. His eyes were brown, large and sleepy-looking in the gentle folds of his face. He resembled an old hound roused from his warm spot by the fire.

That comfortable comparison gave her the courage to answer his sad little smile with a tentative one of her own. "May I help you?" she inquired past the lump in her throat.

"Mistress Emmeline Spencer?" he inquired, bowing from the hips, for his belly precluded anything else. "I am Sir Thomas Burton, come up from London to speak with you on a matter of some—" his fleshy features tightened "—some delicacy."

"London." Emmeline's heart sank. Whatever trouble Cedric had gotten into would be expensive. "What has he done?"

"Who?"

"My…father," she admitted. "Cedric le Trompour."

"Le Trompour is your father?" Sir Thomas pursed his lips. "I had not realized he had chil…oh." A flush stained his jowls as he made the obvious leap.

"My sister and I are Cedric's natural daughters." A prettied-up way of saying they were bastards.

Sir Thomas coughed. "Then Alford is your grandfather." At her nod, his frown deepened. "I wished I had known. I'd have taken my news to Cedric, or to Old Alford."

"Grandfather disowned Cedric years ago and won't give you a farthing to repay his debts." She, however, was more vulnerable. Though he'd failed to wed her mother, Cedric was her father, and could dispose of her as he wished. Thus far, she'd managed to forestall any marriage plans by keeping him in coin.

"I am no usurer come to collect my due." His gray

brows knit together. "I hate to presume on your hospitality, but is there a place where we might speak in private?"

"In private?" Belatedly Emmeline looked out the large window that faced Market Street. Bunches of dried herbs, rosemary, thyme and mint hung from the open shutters. The wide sill formed a counter on which sat baskets of pepper, black and white, both ready to be weighed up for sale. Most days she had a modest flow of customers. Today the opening was crammed with people absently fingering the merchandise while staring at the unfolding drama.

Emmeline felt the color rise in her face. No matter how hard she worked to erase the stains of her own past and the continuing stigma of Cedric's debauchery, she was ever the object of the town's pity, scorn and ridicule.

"My men could give your apprentice a hand in closing the shop," Sir Thomas suggested.

Oh, it must be very bad. Emmeline's fists clenched a little tighter in the folds of her gown as she called, "Peter."

The boy popped out of the storeroom like a rock launched from a catapult. Brandishing the large pestle she used to crush peppercorns, he flew at Sir Thomas.

"Peter!" Emmeline grabbed her protector by the arm before the blow landed. "Please, do not hold this against him."

"On the contrary. I find his defense of his mistress quite a tribute in this day of deceit, murder and betrayal," Sir Thomas said so forcefully Emmeline wondered who or what he was.

She found out soon enough. Leaving Peter to deal with the flood of customers—under the watchful eye of the two soldiers—she led the way up the stairs to the small solar.

"Er, can I offer you wine?" Emmeline asked, not at all used to entertaining men. Cedric's perfidy had made her distrust men, and she avoided them as much as possible, except for Toby, who'd been with the family forever, and Peter, who was just a lad.

"'Tis most kind," Sir Thomas said. "We've had a long, dusty ride." The sturdy chair by the hearth, the best piece of furniture she'd inherited from her mother, creaked as he lowered his bulk into it. "But only if you'll join me."

Stiff with dread, Emmeline forced herself to walk to the side table and fill the two cups that stood next to the pitcher. Her neck prickled, but when she turned, Sir Thomas was looking around the room, not at her. No doubt gauging the worth of the furnishings. She wished she'd never brought him up here to see the few things she'd thus far managed to keep. The trestle table and stools her great-grandfather had made, the tapestry and pair of silver plates.

Angry now at her own helplessness, she thrust the crockery cup at her visitor. He accepted it with a gracious smile, then gestured to the smaller chair that had been her mother's. "Won't you sit?" he asked.

Nay. She wanted to stamp and scream and throw things. She wanted to kick the stools and hurl the plates against the whitewashed walls. Impotent rage warred with her mother's strictures. "You have a strong will, Emmeline," she used to say. "Use it to overcome the base emotions you inherited from Cedric."

Emmeline's fingers knotted behind her back. "If you will kindly state your business, sir."

"Mayhap we should send for your father."

"Ha! So this does concern him." Inside her, something cracked. Like a kettle set too long to fire, her anger boiled over. "This time I will not pay. I don't care if you throw him in debtor's prison. I don't care if you—"

"I spoke truly when I said I haven't come to collect money," Sir Thomas said gently. "It…it is about your sister."

"Celia?" Her anger evaporated. "What has happened now?"

"Now? Has she been having trouble of some sort?"

All her life. Beautiful Celia with the laughing eyes and insatiable appetite for self-indulgence inherited from their sire. She was Emmeline's opposite in all things—pretty, popular, irresponsible. Though their mother had constantly harped about her younger sister's frivolous ways, Emmeline loved her dearly.

"Not trouble, exactly," Emmeline said. "But sorrow, surely. Two years ago she wed Roger de Vienne." Proving herself as susceptible to a rogue as their mother had been, but he'd given Celia the one thing she wanted more than anything, a chance to leave Derry for the gaiety of life in London. The prize had not come without a heavy price. "Roger was killed six months ago." Run through by a husband who'd returned home at a most unexpected and inopportune moment. Celia had retired to Derry briefly till the scandal had died down, but declared she couldn't work in the apothecary or bury herself in the country. "Is it money?" Like Cedric, Celia never seemed to have enough.

"Nay." Sir Thomas set aside his cup and scrubbed a hand over his face, rearranging the fleshy folds into a mask of regret. "I am so sorry to bring you this news, but your sister is dead."

"Dead!" The air whooshed out of her lungs, taking with it the starch in her knees. She sank into the chair. Tears blurred her vision; a dozen questions whirled in her brain. "H-how?"

"She was murdered," Sir Thomas said softly. He handed her a linen handkerchief and went on, the explanation falling like hot acid on her aching heart. Two weeks ago, Celia's maid had gone to awaken her mistress and found her dead. "I apologize for the delay, but it took me that long to conclude my investigation and locate you...through some letters in her possession."

Emmeline battled her tears. "H-how did she die?"

"She was strangled."

"Strangled?" Emmeline's throat contracted. "By a thief?"

"No one had forced their way in, and naught was missing. Nor did Lily see anyone, for Mistress Celia had sent her off to bed. Despite the late hour, Lily says she was expecting a visitor."

"A lover who killed Celia in a passionate rage."

"Do you have proof of that?"

"Nay." She was appalled she'd spoken aloud. "I am given to fanciful musings, I fear." She'd tried so hard to break herself of such nonsense, to be practical and logical like her mama. But Cedric came from a long line of minstrels, and the urge to weave romantic tales seemed to be bred into her.

Sir Thomas nodded. "Small wonder. The minstrels fill women's heads with songs of love and passion. Actually, we do believe Celia's visitor was a lover. She had undressed and donned her bed robe. Do you know if she was involved with someone?"

"I had a letter from Ce-Celia a month ago. She mentioned a man." Emmeline rushed to unlock the chest where she kept her receipts and papers. A rare letter from Celia was tucked along the side. As she took it out, she saw the ledger wedged into the corner, and a pang of guilt went through her. It contained the verses she'd penned in secret. With her mother gone, there was no longer any reason to hide them, but it seemed unfaithful to Mama's memory to flaunt a skill she'd detested.

Emmeline returned to the chair and unrolled the letter. Celia's scrawl was as erratic and impetuous as her personality. *Oh, Celia, I shall miss you so.* Tears blurred her

vision. She blinked them back. A Spencer did not cry in
public. "'I have met the most...'" She squinted. "'Wonderful,' I think this says. 'Wonderful man. Lord Jamie
Har...Har-something.'"

"Harcourt." Sir Thomas grunted in what sounded like
disgust.

"What is it? Do you know him?"

"Aye, and I've questioned him, too. I said naught before
because I did not want to put words into your mouth, but
Lily said Mistress Celia was having an affair with Lord
Jamie. Though she was not certain 'twas he your sister
expected that fateful night. Do you know how long she'd
been involved with him?"

"I—I don't. Celia seldom wrote or came to Derry, and
I...I never cared for the city, so I didn't visit her." Reaction trembled through her. "I should have. I should
have—"

"Humph. No sense flaying yourself over that, mistress.
What else does she say about James Harcourt?"

Emmeline looked down, frowning. "'He owns a
ship...and is always sailing off on some...adventure or
another, but when he comes back this time, I'm certain
he'll wed me.'"

"Humph."

"I take it Lord Jamie is not the marrying sort."

"He's said to have been through more women than three
men."

Emmeline wasn't surprised. Like mother, like daughter.
"Do you have any proof he killed her?"

"Nay," he said slowly. "But there's one more thing
you should know. Lily suspected your sister was carrying
a child. Though Lady Celia hadn't named the father—"

"My God! Celia tried to use the child to force him to
wed her and he...he killed her."

"We cannot know that," he said gently. "Lord Jamie was out to sea when your sister was killed."

"Then he had her killed."

"Of that, I've no proof."

"But…you mean he'll go free? He'll get away with murder?"

He sighed. "Without proof, my hands are tied. 'Tis possible she was also, er, involved with another," he murmured.

Emmeline stiffened. "My sister was not like that."

"Life in London is more, er, free than it is here."

"Bother that. What about justice? Does Celia go unavenged?"

"I cannot prosecute a man like Lord Jamie, a wealthy lord from a powerful family whose friends number among them John, Duke of Lancaster, without proof."

Emmeline's chest tightened, and with it, her resolve. Sir Thomas's hands might be tied, but hers weren't. She didn't know how, just yet, but one way or another, she'd prove this James Harcourt had murdered Celia and make certain he was punished.

Chapter One

Harte Court
September 18, 1386

It was dark by the time Jamie Harcourt drew rein at the crest of the knoll. Not that he needed the light to guide him, for this was the land of his birth. He'd explored these fields and forests from the time he could walk, and every square inch was indelibly engraved on his mind.

Yet a thrill went through him as he looked across to the keep built high on the opposing bluff. Harte Court was as vast as a small city, its four sturdy towers and countless dependencies tucked safely behind twelve-foot-thick walls. Fierce and intimidating, some called it the impregnable fortress, but to him it was home. Or had been once.

Home. A pang of longing struck him, swift, sharp and totally unexpected. After seven years in exile, he'd hoped he'd gotten over his attachment to this place. Now he knew he never would. As the eldest son, Harte Court was his birthright, yet he could never claim it. The familiar bitterness rose up inside him. Impatiently he shoved it away. His time here was short, too short for useless regrets.

"No sense borrowing trouble when we've plenty enough, eh lad?" He patted Neptune's glossy black neck and kneed the stallion back onto the road. The air smelled sweet indeed to a nose more used to the tang of the sea. 'Twas fragrant with the mingled scent of ripe wheat and the wildflowers nodding in the hedgerows separating the fields into neat squares. Prosperous and well tended, he mused. There seemed to be more cultivated land than he recalled from his youth, but then, he'd been more interested in chasing the maids and learning to wield a sword than overseeing the estate that would one day be his.

Now he could not afford to care.

Resolutely pinning his gaze to the ribbon of dusty road, he thought instead of the things he must do after he'd paid his duty call. Return to London. Meet with Harry. Sail quickly back to Cornwall. Tight schedule. No time for lagging or sentimentality.

"Who goes there?" demanded a gruff voice.

Jamie looked up, startled to find the moment he'd been anticipating and dreading was nearly at hand. The drawbridge had been lowered over the moat, but was manned by a guard of twenty. Not surprising in these troubled times. "Jamie Harcourt, come to bid my mother well on her name day."

"The hell ye say." A stout soldier in Harcourt green and gold strode forward and held a torch aloft. "Jesu, it is ye."

Jamie laughed. "I know. George of Walken, is it not?"

"Ye've a good memory, milord." The old warrior grinned. "Yer sire said ye'd come to honor yer lady mother, but—"

"No one thought I'd dare show my scarred face."

George looked at the patch covering the ruins of Jamie's left eye, then away. "There was some who thought ye'd not come...considering that murder business, but I wagered on ye.''

The reference to Celia made his stomach lurch. Would that mistake haunt him, as well? "How much did you win?"

"A pound, all told." George chuckled. "New men. They don't know ye as well as I do." His smile dimmed. "I was always sure ye'd be back. I just didn't know 'twould be so long."

"Ah, well, black sheep are never certain whether they're welcome or not," Jamie replied with a cheeky grin.

"Ye were never that," George said stoutly. "Just a high-spirited lad who pulled his share of pranks, ran off to sea and found he liked the adventuring life better than all this."

A few pranks...like getting himself maimed, his brother crippled and breaking his parents' hearts. How he wished he could go back and live his life over, but that was impossible. "Fortunately my brother isn't cursed with my wild nature."

"Sir Hugh's been a fine lord in yer stead. Fair and honest and as hard a worker as any under him. But...but he can never be the warrior ye are. What if we are invaded by the French?"

"I doubt the French will come, but if they do, good old Hugh will do what's needful. He always rises to the occasion."

"Aye, that he does." George glanced at the patch again, no doubt recalling the day that had changed Hugh's and Jamie's lives forever. "Ye just missed him, rode down to settle some trouble in the village not half an hour past. I could send someone to—"

Jamie shook his head. "Unless Hugh has changed greatly, he'd not thank either of us for dragging him from his duty for so frivolous a thing as greeting his errant twin.

I'm certain he'll return before I leave. Thanks for wagering on me, George.'' For believing in me where others have not, Jamie thought to himself.

Kneeing Neptune into a trot, Jamie passed under the teeth of the portcullis and up the road that cut through the outer bailey. Here were the barracks for the soldiers, the stables and the training field. A wave of nostalgia assailed him as he recalled the many hours spent in the tiltyard learning to wield a sword under his father's exacting eye. The memory was tainted by the fierce competitiveness between himself and Hugh, the strife that had ended in a blood-spattered glade seven years ago.

Look ahead...never back, he warned himself.

All hope of slipping within, seeing his mother and leaving without causing a stir vanished when he rode through the gatehouse and into the inner ward. The courtyard was washed bright as day by the hundred torches fixed to the massive stone towers and packed with those who'd come to celebrate the forty-third anniversary of Lady Jesselynn's birth. From inside drifted the sounds of music, laughter and general merrymaking.

The ringing of Neptune's shod hooves on the cobblestones brought several heads around. The crowd in the courtyard fell silent quickly, as though they'd all been struck mute at once.

'''Pon my word. 'Tis young Jamie,'' a man exclaimed.

His name riffled through the crowd like an ill wind. Men's eyes widened, their mouths twisted over words he'd heard before: Ingrate. Brigand. Wastrel. Murderer. The older women flinched and crossed themselves; the younger ones giggled and stared.

''*Dieu*, he's a handsome one,'' said a blonde upholstered in red silk. She appraised him as greedily as she might a slice of beef.

''Too rough. Too dangerous,'' hissed her companion.

Beneath her elaborate headdress, the blonde's eyes sparkled with a lustfulness he'd had directed at him by women from the time he sprouted a beard. "I certainly hope so." She sauntered over, laid a hand on his hose-clad knee and gazed up at him through kohl-darkened lashes. "Did you really lose your eye battling the pirates?" she purred.

Jamie grinned, tempted to oblige her by lifting the black leather triangle. That's what they wanted...men and women alike...a peek under his patch. Well, jaded ladies like this one wanted a bit more, a quick tumble to judge for themselves if he was as dangerous as he looked, as hedonistic as his reputation. Many's the time he'd been only too happy to oblige. But not tonight. "Not pirates, milady," he replied, cool but courteous. "I fear the story is far less colorful." Far more tragic.

"A jealous woman, then?" she asked archly, wetting her lips, clearly not discouraged by his lack of warmth. "I know I'd not take kindly to sharing you." Leaning forward, she pressed her ample bosom against his leg, giving him an unimpeded view of the charms spilling over the bodice of her low-cut cotehardie.

Jamie groaned inwardly and struggled against the nature with which he'd been blessed—or cursed, depending on your view. Women fascinated him. They were soft, fragile and endlessly pleasurable creatures. Coy, seductive packages whose silken wrappings he could no more resist exploring than he could stop breathing. Since that near disaster with Celia, he had been celibate as a monk. His life was currently dangerous enough without added complications. "Another time," he said gallantly. "I must first seek out my lady mother."

"Have you come back to stay?" asked a tall man. Though older and grayer, Jamie recognized Gilbert Thurlow, chief of his father's vassals. Gilbert had often criticized Jamie's wild ways and doubtless preferred Hugh's stable hands at the helm. With Gilbert stood several other Harcourt retainers, faces equally concerned as they waited for his response.

"I fear I cannot stay," Jamie said. The sigh of relief that went through the group confirmed the difficult decision he'd made seven years ago. They were better off without him. "You'll excuse me if I don't linger, but I am anxious to see my parents." He inclined his head cordially, winked at the blonde, because old habits die hard, and wheeled Neptune toward the stables.

Grinning over the whispers he'd left in his wake, as usual, he dismounted and tossed his horse's reins to the stable boy along with a penny. "We've had a long ride. See he gets a rubdown and an extra measure of oats, lad."

The boy stared at Jamie. "Ye are Lord Jamie. I've heard tell of ye. Are ye truly a pirate, milord?" he whispered.

Jamie grinned. "Aye, that and more. What's your name, lad?"

"Rob. I'm George of Walken's son. Please, milord, take me with ye when ye leave."

"Pirating's a hard life, Rob."

"I don't care," the boy said passionately. "'Tis deadly boring duty here, and I've wanted to go to sea ever since I went with yer sire to London harbor and stepped aboard his ship."

Jamie knew the feeling well. He'd been smitten when he was five and his father had taken him on a short voyage aboard *The Sommerville Star.* Later, when he'd run off to sea, his father had understood...up to a point. "You need to grow some before you're big enough and strong enough to manage the sails," Jamie said gently. He didn't want to pinch Rob's pride, but he was not taking him into harm's way. And that's exactly where his own ship, *Harcourt's Lady,* was sailing.

"I could be yer cabin boy till I'm grown."

"I already have a lad to serve me, but we'll talk of this again next time I come home."

"Promise?"

Jamie nodded. Another lie. When he returned, 'twould be for burial in the family plot. Presuming traitors were allowed such privileges. "Saddle my horse after you've rubbed him down and leave him just inside the stable in case I must leave quickly."

The last was no whim. It was as deeply ingrained a habit as sitting with his face to the door and back to the wall, or sleeping in his clothes with his sword to hand. A sad commentary on what his life had become. But more often than not a man did not choose the path he trod; it chose him. Just a little longer, he told himself. A month or so and he'd be free of this terrible responsibility. Free to get on with his own life.

And then what? mocked a harsh voice.

He knew nothing else but death and deception. Where did spies and murderers go when they gave up the craft? *To hell.* The now-familiar weariness crept in to weigh on his spirit and conscience. He pushed it away, having neither time nor patience for self-pity. He'd wallowed in both the year he'd lost his eye, and nearly himself. Never again, he'd vowed when his father had succeeded in hauling him back from the brink of self-destruction. Squaring his shoulders, he started for the house.

"Lady Jesselynn's greetin' her guests in the gardens, sir," Rob said. "Just follow that path 'round the back."

"I remember." Only too well. Jamie strode down the walk that ran alongside the manor. On one side it was bordered by the stone keep, on the other by the gardens put in by his Aunt Gaby, because his mother preferred managing the estate to domestic tasks. So why couldn't she understand why he preferred the sea to land? Because she knew it for a lie. Much as he loved sailing, he'd have stayed here if he could. But that was impossible.

Jamie rounded the corner of the castle and stopped, every muscle in his body tensing. Damn, half of London was here. The crush was too much even for the vast hall, and tables had been set about in the grassy verge between the blocks of flowers and trees. Laughing and drinking, the noble lords and ladies milled about before the stately old manor. Torches stuck in rings in the old stone walls shimmered on costly silken gowns and the precious gems banding them at throat and hip.

No expense had been spared, it seemed. To one side, a pair of sweaty-faced boys turned an oxen over a blazing fire. Platters of roasted game, pink salmon and a dozen accompaniments he recognized as his mother's favorites crowded the long tables. Musicians played in the shadow of a pin oak tree for a line of merry dancers. Maids bearing heavy trays worked the crowd, making certain no ale cup or wine goblet went empty.

Footsteps behind him brought Jamie around. In one swift move he drew the knife from his belt and crouched to repel an attack.

"We've had our differences, but I hoped it hadn't come to this," drawled the voice that had dispelled his childhood fears.

"Papa." Jamie sheathed his blade and straightened. Uncertain what to do, he stood still, struggling not to squirm beneath the piercing scrutiny of midnight eyes so like his own.

Time had laced silver hair at his father's temples and etched deep lines around his mouth. Or was his own behavior responsible for his father's air of weary resignation, Jamie wondered. An apology bumped against the lump in his throat. But what could he say that would make up for all he'd done.

"I prayed you'd come," his father said.

"I...I shouldn't have, I suppose," Jamie murmured. "I'd hate to taint you with my trouble."

"Nonsense." The fire that never quite left Alex's eyes flared. "You were acquitted of that girl's murder."

That wasn't the trouble he'd meant. Strong was the urge to unburden himself to the one person who might understand what he was doing and why. The need for caution kept him silent.

"Is it my imagination, or does this gaiety seem a bit frantic?" Jamie asked, smoothly changing the subject. He was good at that, so good at lies and evasion it was sometimes hard to separate them from the truth.

His father glared at the nobles, most of whom were friends and acquaintances of long standing. "They've gone mad. The whole damned country's hysterical with fear of this rumored French invasion. They say Charles has mustered thirty thousand men."

"And is reportedly readying a transport of near twelve hundred ships to bring them here." Jamie had seen both the soldiers and ships for himself. But of course, 'twould be treason to admit as much.

"Two days ago the king ordered London's suburbs demolished."

Jamie gasped. "Why? Has he gone truly mad?"

"Oxford thought 'twould make the city easier to defend." Alex shook his head. "I do not agree, but 'tis fruitless to oppose the king or his ministers. They are so anxious to find someone on whom to blame the excesses and stupidity which has landed us in these dire straits that they lash out at any who disagree with them. Walter Dunwell is a case in point. He converted his coin to jewels and tried to flee to the safety of Italy with them sewed into his tunic. He was arrested in Dover, charged with treason, and hanged before his family's eyes."

Jamie felt the noose tightening around his own neck. "London buzzed with talk of it when I landed a few weeks ago." He'd barely paid them any mind, for he'd had troubles of his own. Sir Thomas Burton had met him on the docks with the news of Celia's death and a lot of tricky questions. Damn but that had been a close brush with disaster. If not for his loyal crew—

"Nor is Walter the only one who has panicked. Those who have not succeeded in leaving are spending their money like...like sailors come ashore on their first liberty."

"In case there is no tomorrow."

"Aye. Fools. They'd do better to fortify their castles and hold up in them to resist the invaders."

Jamie winced, imagining hordes of blood-crazed French troops battering down the gates of Harte Court and slaying those dearer to him than his own life. "Richard and his advisors are not fit to rule," he said in a hoarse whisper.

"I agree they've brought much of this trouble upon us, but the French have taken advantage of Richard's weaknesses and now have us in a stranglehold." Which was true enough. Last year King Charles had captured Bruges and confiscated the goods of English merchants there, effectively cutting off the wool trade that was a main source of royal revenue. A new wool staple had been established at Middleburg, but profits were slim because the ships had to sail in armed convoys to protect them from French privateers. "The royal treasury is so depleted it cannot fund foreign mercenaries to protect us, and we nobles have been taxed to the limit." Alex sighed. "No one disputes the fact Richard has been a disappointment. He's headstrong, capricious and—"

"Irresponsible. Oxford and the other greedy fops he's surrounded himself with since he cast off his uncle's good counsel will be the ruin of us all. They are the true traitors."

"None would dare say so. Oxford stands so high in Richard's favor he has only to whisper a thing in the royal ear and it is done. John of Gaunt alone had the power and courage to speak out against them. 'Tis a pity he picked these perilous times to go to Spain and press his claim to his father-in-law's throne."

"Lancaster chose it apurpose," Jamie said. "He has been so vocal in his censure of his Richard's actions he feared the king would give in to Oxford's urgings and put him in the Tower."

"Are you still close with Lancaster and his brood?"

Closer than ever, but that would only hurt the father from whom he'd become estranged. Jamie had been fostered into the royal duke's household at age nine, and a valuable, if sometimes dangerous, association it had turned out to be. "His Grace asked me to provision his ships for the voyage to Castile, and Harry and I hunted together a few months ago."

"You'd best be careful how you go. There are some who'd like to see Lancaster or young Henry of Bolingbroke on the throne in place of Richard."

And Jamie was one of them. "Enough of this war talk."

The militant light faded from Alex's eyes, replaced by quiet joy. "Aye, I'm glad you've come home, Jamie. Your mother has been worried about you." He grinned ruefully. "As have I."

"I can only stay a short time," Jamie murmured, not wanting to raise any false expectations.

"But if there is trouble, we'll need every fighting man."

"I've never stayed away from a battle in my life," Jamie exclaimed. "But the attack will come from the sea, and I can best serve England from aboard the *Lady*." If it came to that.

His father nodded. "I suppose there is truth in that, still..." He sighed. "Though you're a grown man, I hate having you off fighting where I cannot defend you if need be."

Jamie longed for the days when his problems were simple enough to be solved by his father's strong arm and sage advice. He was on his own in this, vulnerable as a fly on a whitewashed wall. If he was caught, he'd die a traitor's death, and no one, not even his powerful foster father, would step in to save him.

So he must not fail.

"I may not have you standing behind me, Papa, but I have the skills and training you drubbed into my thick skull."

Alex laughed. "'Twas not easy to teach a lad who thought he already knew it all."

"Shall we see if we can find Mama. I've a gift for her...a dagger from the East that I think will take her fancy." He was adept at knowing what women liked, especially his mother, whose tastes ran to practical things, not pretty baubles.

"Your presence is the best gift she could have." He draped an arm over Jamie's shoulder and together they worked their way around the fringes of the crowd. "Hugh should be back soon."

Jamie stiffened instinctively, but his father only held tighter to him.

"You are both grown, now. Let there be peace between you."

"Of course," Jamie said, but he knew he and his twin could never live in harmony. There was too much between them. Blood and betrayal. Guilt and remorse. "I know it hurts you that we always fought when you and your brothers were so close, but Hugh and I are so different." Hugh, the stuffy prig, Jamie the hellion.

"Aye, Hugh was ever quiet and serious—"

Cold, remote and sanctimonious.

"And you a hellion bent on mischief," Alex added. "'Twas evident from the first night. We'd put you together in the one cradle because we hadn't known we'd be needing two. When you awoke, you howled for attention. Hugh just lay there, quietly waiting his turn."

Jamie laughed. "Mama said I'd inherited your temper, curiosity and thirst for adventure."

"Ha! Speaks the woman who pitched a kettle at me when she saw me talking...only talking, mind you...with another woman. At least I learned to control my temper. And taught you the same."

"Lessons that stand me in good stead, else I'd have shoved Hugh's teeth down his throat every time he tattled on me."

"Which was often and with good cause, you rascal. Ah, there are your mother, uncles and aunts." Alex veered toward a fivesome standing beneath the spreading branches of an old oak.

How handsome they are, Jamie thought with a spurt of pride. Light from a nearby torch played softly on the fair hair of the two tall men, Ruarke, youngest but bigger and more thickly muscled. Gareth, the eldest Sommerville and now earl, and the smiling faces of the three petite women, his mother and aunts, Gabrielle and Arianna. Though Alex had also been born a Sommerville, he'd changed his name to Harcourt when he'd wed Jesselynn, last of that line, so her name wouldn't die out. The minstrels had devoted many a verse to that romantic gesture.

"Let the French come!" Uncle Ruarke roared in a voice that in his day had urged men to victory against the French, making him the hero of Poitiers and the scourge of the Continent. "My men are well trained. They'll not take Wilton whilst I live."

Aunt Gaby clutched at his sleeve. "Oh, Ruarke. 'Tis been years since you've fought. Is there no other way?"

"Nay!" her husband shouted. "Do you impinge my skills?"

"No one doubts your strength," soothed Gareth. "But the French number thirty thousand. How many can you field?"

"Two thousand, twice that with your men and Alex's. And there are at least ten other nobles who can muster a like force."

"Too little. Too late." Gareth shook his head. "Mayhap the king is right to try and solve this by treaty."

"Treaty!" Ruarke's roar shook the branches overhead and caused heads to turn the length of the garden. "That effeminate little brat will lose his crown and his head if he trusts Charles. Curse the Earl of Oxford and the other greedy—"

"Hush," Gareth interjected. "Do you want to be arrested?"

"'Tis good to see you've not grown soft with age, Uncle," Jamie called before the man dug himself in any deeper.

All five whipped around. Their mouths fell open, then lifted into smiles of welcome as they rushed to him with glad cries.

"You are well come, lad." Uncle Ruarke lifted him off the ground in a rib-cracking hug, then passed him down the line of grinning Sommervilles, their cheeks wet with happy tears.

Lastly he came to his mother. "Happy Birthday, Mama."

Jesselynn Harcourt's green eyes filled with the ghosts he knew he'd put there. But they were chased away by delight. "Oh, Jamie... I thought... I feared..." She opened her arms.

"I'm fine, Mama. He bent to bury his nose in the veil that hid her wild red hair. She still smelled the same, like lavender, like home, but the fragility of her body startled him. Either he had grown or she had shrunk. Before he could voice his fears, his father's muscular arms enveloped them. For several moments Jamie stood there, soaking up the balm of their unspoken love, then a shriek rent the air and a solid body collided with his back.

"Jamie! You wretch." Despite the harsh words, slender arms encircled his waist and clung. "Why did you not write you were coming?" wailed a muffled voice. A fist slammed into his ribs.

Grunting, Jamie released his mother and twisted about to plant a kiss on the red curls that barely reached his breastbone. "You've grown, bratling, but you're still a heathen."

"I was ten and five last birthday and know how to act the lady when I choose." Johanna was a miniature of their mother, with flaming hair, brilliant green eyes and a wayward nature that made Jamie seem tame by comparison. Their mother had lost two other children before delivering Johanna, so she was doubly precious to them all. And spoiled. "I'm old enough to be betrothed," she added loftily.

"Perish the thought," Jamie teased, though the idea of his darling Jo wed to some man was intolerable. "Who'd have you?"

"Lots of people. I'm an heiress, you know."

Jamie glanced at his father. "You haven't—"

"Nay, I haven't." Alex exclaimed. "I'm never going to part with her." He ruffled her curls. "No man is good enough for my little princess."

Agreed, Jamie thought. Despite the differences in the sexes and ages, he and Jo were as close as he and Hugh should have been. There was always a letter from Jo waiting when he put into port, and she'd come to London a few times with their parents to see him. Hugh had never come, of course, claiming pressing work on the estate as an excuse, whilst Jamie pleaded a busy schedule as the reason he didn't travel to Harte Court. "More like, no man is fool enough to undertake to discipline her as we never could."

Jo snorted. "If I have to become a prissy mouse like Willa in order to catch a husband, I'll never wed."

"Who is Willa?"

"Willa Neville. Hugh's betrothed."

"This is news."

"The contracts were signed only last week," Alex explained. "Though they won't be wed till she is sixteen."

Jamie smiled. "Is she beautiful and well dowered?"

"She has her father's hawk beak and is so homely she'd not get a husband if she weren't a great heiress," Jo muttered.

"That is no way to speak about your new sister," her mother chided. "Willa is only eleven. She may…grow into her features."

"She is Lord Matthew Neville's only child," Alex hastened to add. "His lands border Harte Court on the north and on the east, those of Austen Heath, the keep we gave to Hugh."

"Trust Hugh to take a wife who will increase the family fortunes," Jamie said more sharply than he'd intended.

"At least he is marrying," Aunt Gaby said pointedly.

"I am certain my parents are glad Hugh thinks with his mind and not his—"

"James Harcourt!" Jesselynn exclaimed.

"I beg pardon, Aunt Gaby." Jamie bowed stiffly. Jesu, even when Hugh wasn't present there was trouble between them.

"I think they deserve each other." Jo wrinkled her nose. "Willa is as dull and serious as Hugh."

"Your brother carries a heavy load of responsibilities," Jesselynn said, but she looked at Jamie, silently reminding him the burdens Hugh shouldered should have been Jamie's.

I cannot, Jamie cried, staring into his mother's hurt-filled eyes and wishing things didn't have to be this way.

Johanna broke the tension by plucking on his sleeve. "How long can you stay?" she demanded.

Another unwelcome question. Over the guests' laughter and jesting, he heard the minstrels strike up a sprightly tune. "Long enough to dance with you, brat."

Catching hold of her hands, Jamie tugged his sister toward the couples forming up for the next set. As they passed by the minstrels in their red and gold tunics, he realized one of them, the one glancing over her shoulder to speak with the leader, was a woman. 'Twas not unheard of, merely unusual, especially since their badges identified them as members of the Golden Wait of Harrowgate, the professional troupe employed by the city of London. 'Twas a source of great pride and prestige to be a member of the group founded by the legendary Alford le Trompour.

Out of long-standing habit, Jamie looked the woman over a second time. She was tall, her figure unfortunately obscured by the concealing folds of the simple woolen gown that fell from shoulders to hem without a belt to cinch it in. He noted she was not wearing the badge. A substitute called to fill in for an ailing player? If so, she was not much skilled, for the instrument she held was the bells.

"Jamie?" Jo asked, plucking at his sleeve.

"Hmm. I am waiting for the music to begin," he said without looking away from the girl. Not beautiful, he mused, studying her profile. But pretty. Her dark hair had

been skinned back into a single braid, exposing her high
forehead, slim nose and determined chin. At the moment,
said chin was thrust out in a manner reminiscent of Jo in
a fury, and her cheeks were flushed. Ah, a lass with fire.
He liked that.

Jamie redirected his gaze to the source of her anger, a
bull of a man with black hair and coarse, florid features.
He mistrusted the man on sight. The bastard's lips moved
as he took the girl to task for something. In one hand, he
held a trumpet, the other beat the air as he made his point.

The girl lifted her chin further and countered with a
remark that turned her opponent's face purple.

He is going to hit her.

Without waiting to confirm the hunch, Jamie dashed
across the intervening space, shoving people from his path.
But he was too late. Just as he leapt over the wooden rail
separating the minstrels from the dancers, the brute lashed
out with one massive paw, and the girl went down in a
heap.

"Bastard!" Jamie launched himself at the man. The impact of flesh hitting flesh drove the air from his lungs and
toppled them both to the ground. Jamie came out on top.
Conscious that the man outweighed him by several stone,
he got his hands around his opponent's fleshy throat and
braced for a fight. But the man lay beneath him like a dead
fish, gasping for breath and moaning piteously. "Do you
yield," Jamie rasped.

"Aye…" the man said, choking. "P-please do not strike
my mouth. I…the horn."

Thoroughly disgusted by this craven display, Jamie
lifted himself off the man and sat back on his haunches.
"See you never strike her again." Speaking of which, he
turned his head and found the girl sitting on the ground a
foot away, her eyes round as serving platters, one hand on
her cheek. He crawled over to her. "Are you all right?"

She nodded mutely.

"Let me see." He took her hand to move it aside, and something ruffled through him. A shock of awareness, a feeling of being connected. His gaze locked on hers, and for an instant the noise and lights faded away. "Wh-who are you?" he whispered, because the air had been punched from his body by whatever was happening to him...to them.

"Em...Emmeline." She sounded as dazed as he.

"Emmeline." He savored the taste of it on his tongue.

"Jamie!" His father grabbed hold of his shoulder, breaking the spell. "What happened?"

"I was rescuing the fair Emmeline from yon brute." Jamie gave her his most dazzling smile. The one that caused ladies to melt at his feet. This lady looked cold as the North Sea in December. "You've not asked, but I will tell you 'tis Jamie Harcourt you have to thank for saving you."

Emmeline pulled free of his grasp. "I know who you are." She glared at him with such hatred she stole his breath for the second time that night. Scrambling to her feet, she speared him with one last, damning glance and dashed off into the crowd that had assembled around the musicians.

"What is going on?" his father demanded.

Damned if I know, Jamie thought, staring at the place where the mysterious Emmeline had disappeared. But he meant to find out. No woman ran away from him.

Chapter Two

James Harcourt was here! Her desperate gamble had paid off.

Emmeline hurried through the crowd in search of Toby to tell him the news. He'd come disguised as the minstrels' groom and should be near the stables, but in her haste, she got hopelessly lost in the gardens. Dazed and winded, she sank down on a small, secluded bench to catch her breath and get her bearings.

James Harcourt had actually come to his mother's birthday fete. Proving, she supposed, that there was a speck of decency in even the most evil of men. *He charged in to rescue you from Uncle Markham,* a sly voice reminded her.

Ha! Such an unprovoked attack proved Lord James was a man of violent temper and ungoverned impulses. Unprovoked? Well, he couldn't know her foolish taunts had goaded her father's brother into slapping her. She should have known better than to try the patience of one who had not only disliked her because he hated her father but was jealous of her talent, as well.

Poor Markham, her arrival in London a week ago had set his well-ordered world on its ear. She'd arrived on the doorstep of her estranged grandfather, half expecting to be tossed out. Fortunately Alford le Trompour was not one to bear a grudge. He'd made her welcome and even cried over Celia's death, despite the fact that she'd spurned his offers of friendship years ago. A stiffness in his limbs prevented Old Alford from getting about easily, so he'd turned the running of the Wait over to Markham, his younger son, but he still taught a few pupils.

"None of them is as gifted as you, my dear," he'd told her as they chatted in his private chamber over a cup of wine. High praise from the man whose musical skills had made him a legend among players and leader of the famous Golden Wait of Harrowgate, the minstrel band chartered by the city.

"Thank you, sir." She'd smiled briefly, recalling the magical summer when her father's parents had come to Oxford to meet the children Cedric had never told them about. Small wonder, since his alliance with their mother had been a lie and a sin. When he'd wed her, Cedric had neglected to mention the wife he already had. 'Twas not until Olivia found out about them and followed him to Derry that Cedric's sins had been revealed.

Cedric's parents had been anxious to meet their only grandchildren, but embittered by Cedric's betrayal, her mother had refused the old couple's overtures of peace. Curious as she was to know her grandparents, Emmeline wouldn't have defied her mother if not for the lute. The one her father had brought her; the only gift he'd ever given her. Gift, ha! It turned out the lute was a priceless antique Cedric had stolen from his father. Alford recognized the instrument as he was leaving her mother's apothecary shop, but told her she might keep it.

Emmeline had felt bound to return the lute and sneaked out to the inn where Alford and his wife were staying.

Alford had coaxed her into playing a song for him and then another. Her talent, raw and unformed, as he called it, had so impressed him he'd not only insisted she keep the lute but offered to teach her. Torn between loyalty to her mother and a soul-deep longing to make music, Emmeline had agreed. The lessons, given in secret, had opened up a whole new world for her, but the glimpse of heaven had cost her dearly. She'd deceived her mother and finally ended up hurting her nearly as much as Cedric had.

"I am sorry I could not come to London with you after that summer," she told Alford. "But Mama collapsed, and…"

"You could not leave her." He patted her shoulder with a gnarled hand. "You are far more loyal than your father. It's been years since Cedric has crossed our threshold."

Nay, I am no better than my father. Out of selfishness, she'd deceived her mother and broken her heart. And she'd failed Celia, too, but she was trying so hard to make amends. "I have come to London to learn what I can of Lord James Harcourt."

"I know of him. He was often at court, being a member of John of Gaunt's household. A handsome young man and much favored by the ladies, as was his father, Lord Alexander, who was accounted a rake in his day."

Like father, like son. She explained how Sir Thomas's hands were tied by Harcourt's connections and his men's testimony. Alford had immediately sent out inquiries, but they'd found naught to link James to Celia's murder. Elusive and mysterious were two descriptions applied to the wayward Harcourt heir. He'd always had a penchant for adventure, and rumor linked him to smuggling and other illegal activities. But 'twas speculation without a shred of proof. Adding to her frustration had been the disappearance of Celia's maid. Lily had gone off a week ago, taking with her Celia's few pieces of plate and the small silver brooch Emmeline had given Celia. They'd not been taken by the murderer, for Sir Thomas had listed them on his inventory of Celia's possessions. None of Alford's contacts had been able to find Lily. The silly girl was probably hiding somewhere, afraid she'd be arrested for thievery. Emmeline didn't care about the pin, all she wanted was answers. And to make James Harcourt pay.

"Ah, there you are," murmured a deep voice.

Emmeline gasped as the object of her speculation plopped down onto the bench beside her. She would have leapt up and run off, but he was sitting on the edge of her gown.

"Stay," he commanded when she tried to wriggle free. "Why did you run away?" He stared at her intently from that single, black eye of his. Torchlight filtering in through the bushes limned his ruggedly handsome features, high cheekbones, sensual mouth and strong jaw. Even sitting still, there was a vitality about him that commanded attention. An aura of power, leashed at the moment but likely to explode as it had when he'd attacked her uncle. She'd been right to think him dangerous.

"I—I was afraid."

"Of me." He managed to look as guileless as a schoolboy.

Fraud. "You hit Markham, and 'tis said you killed a girl."

"Your uncle is a fool and a bully. He deserved a few bruises for hitting you."

"He was wroth at me because my grandfather insisted I be allowed to play with the Wait." That much was true. When Alford had heard about the party, he'd been certain James would attend and had forced Markham to bring her.

Her indignation at being relegated to playing the bells had precipitated the slap.

"Is Alford le Trompour your grandfather?"

"Aye, he is. I'm surprised you know of him."

"He is a minstrel without equal. As a lad I sat enraptured whenever he came to play for King Edward. I longed to make music as he did." He gazed at his wide, callused hands lying palm up on his muscular thighs. "You'd think I had ten thumbs so poorly do I play. 'Tis not fair, for I always know all the words."

"Grandfather says it is a talent you are either born with, or not." Unfortunately she'd gotten the gift from Cedric, along with other, less pleasant, traits.

"What is your special talent?" He watched her as though her answer were the most important thing in the world to him. His regard, his attention, were too flattering to deny.

"The lute."

"Yet you play the bells today."

"Aye. 'Twas the source of the argument and the slap. Markham does not think me good enough to play with them because I am neither a trained harpist nor a member of the Wait. I am only here because—" She stopped, aghast to realize she'd been about to spill her plans for revenge to Celia's murderer. What kind of wizard was he to make her so quickly forget her goals?

"What is it? Did the slap cause your head to ache?"

"Nay. Aye." Emmeline put a hand to her temple. Damn, he was the most confounding man. "Why did you come to my aid?"

He grinned and laid a hand over his heart. "I am the most chivalrous of men. If I see a maiden in distress, I must ride to her rescue like the knights in the ancient ballads."

"Humph."

"Not even a hint of a smile to reward my foolishness? You are far too serious, my lovely little harpist." He leaned closer, his face so near it filled her vision. "Damn." Gently grasping her chin, he tilted it toward the light. "He marked you." His thumb barely grazed her cheek. "I should have been quicker."

Light as the touch was, it sent an odd tingle streaking down her neck, leaving gooseflesh behind. His fingers were so warm, his expression so full of concern she felt herself being drawn in, drowning in the depths of his dark, compassionate gaze.

Shivering, Emmeline struggled back from the edge of disaster. Pulling her chin from his hold, she said, "Please…"

"Your head aches. Small wonder." Quick as lightning, his hands slid around to the nape of her neck and attacked her braid.

"Wait! What are you doing." She leaned away. Or tried to, but only succeeded in getting her hair pulled. "Ouch!"

"Hold still." He was nimble and knowledgeable. In seconds he had her braid undone. "There." He tunneled his fingers into her hair at her temples and gently massaged her scalp.

It felt so good a moan escaped her throat.

"See. Is that not better?" he murmured. His fingers slid in farther, tracing circles on the sides and back of her head.

More than better. 'Twas magic, pure and simple. Her mind ceased to function. Her eyes drifted shut; her head fell back into the supporting cradle of his hands, her entire being focused on the wondrous sensations created by his touch. Exciting little ripples radiated down her spine. Deep inside her, something ruffled, like a flower unfurling beneath the warmth of the sun.

"Your hair is beautiful," he murmured, his voice blending with her drifting senses. "Dark and soft as finest silk." His breath fanned her ear as he leaned close. "And it smells of flowers. I'd like to see it spread across my pillow."

"Mmm," she said from her cloud.

"But not here. My ship's in London harbor...we sail on the tide. Will you come away with me, my lady fair? And all the wonders of love's pleasures will we explore."

"Mmm...what?" Emmeline's eyes flew open as his words penetrated her haze. A pirate stared back at her, a cocky smile on his lips, his single eye smoldering with the sort of fire she'd avoided all her life. "Sweet Mary!" She yelped, jumped back and yelped again as a few hairs remained in his grasp.

"Don't be alarmed." His grin was a pale blur in the dimness. "I realize we've only know each other a short time, but I believe in plain speaking. I want you, and I think you feel the same."

Emmeline gaped at him a moment before finding her tongue. "How...how can you think I'd agree to such a thing? Is it because I am only a common minstrel and you think—"

"There is naught common about you, Emma. What I feel for you is most uncommon, I assure you."

"Oh, they were right. You are a rogue and a scoundrel." And a murderer. It occurred to her that he had taken control of her inquisition. And he'd never denied killing poor Celia. Cheeks hot with shame and fury, she leapt from the bench. "You...you..."

"Easy, I meant no offense." He stood, taking her shoulders in a painless but unbreakable grip.

Determined not to show weakness by struggling, she

glared at him. "How could I not be offended by so low an offer?"

"My aim was just the opposite," His gaze, warm and appreciative, moved over her face. He towered head and shoulders above her, sun-streaked blond hair gleaming like a beacon in the gloom. Even with the eye patch, he was a handsome man, his deeply tanned face set off by a blue velvet doublet that gave him the flash of a songbird. "I meant to laud you, to cosset you and please you. 'Twould be good between us...I feel it." His seductive mouth hiked up in one corner as though he knew something no one else did, a secret that would bring her untold pleasure if only she would come away with him. 'Twas a tempting offer, especially embodied by an elegant, dangerous man. The lure of exploring such a mystery was a siren's call to which countless women had harkened...including her sister.

Sobering thought, that. Beneath his smooth demeanor and sleek finery, he was as ruthless as a hunting hawk. "Your interest is not returned," she said coldly. "Kindly unhand me."

His smile fled. "Why? I know when a woman is interested in—"

"You, sir, are a lecher...a conceited lecher. I'd not share a cup of wine with you, much less a bed." She tore herself from his grip, picked up her skirts and fled into the night.

Stunned, Jamie listened to her footsteps on the gravel path. What the hell? He had not mistaken the intense connection, the awareness that had flowed like a molten river between them.

"My compliments on the lady's taste, whoever she was," grated an all-too-familiar voice. Giles Cadwell strolled out of the darkness.

"What are you doing here?" Jamie demanded.

"I came with my lord of Oxford." He was Oxford's

tool, a shrewd, ambitious man who would go to any lengths to serve his powerful master. His comely features and courtly polish belied a genius for cruelty, which Oxford exploited. A dangerous enemy, indeed, Jamie thought as Giles's malevolent gaze cut to the path Emmeline had taken. "An interesting piece, lovely hair. Mayhap she'll find me more to her taste."

Jamie schooled his face to betray none of the possessiveness raging inside him. "Only if she has a preference for snakes."

Giles's hand went to his sword hilt. "Name the time."

Anytime, but Jamie could ill afford to kill Oxford's man and land himself in trouble with the crown. "I'd not want to bloody your fashionable new garments." He looked Giles up and down. His close-fitting green doublet was cut so scandalously short it revealed the tops of his golden trunk hose and the padded, bejeweled codpiece. The church called such displays sinful. Jamie thought it boastful for a man to wander about with his private parts decked out like a Fleet Street whore.

"I'd be happy to strip them off," Giles said. Though he looked the fop, he was a dangerous man.

They'd been enemies since their days as pages to rival lords, Jamie with Lancaster, Giles with Oxford. But it wasn't only political. Giles had a mean streak, a penchant for abusing defenseless creatures, that Jamie found abhorrent. They'd crossed words and swords several times when Jamie had stepped in to protect some hapless victim. But tonight Jamie had to protect himself and his mission. "I'd not want to ruin my mother's fete."

"Ever the gallant. I'd forgotten how solicitous you are of women…except for poor Celia."

Jamie's hand fell to his sword hilt. "Careful, Giles…"

"I meant that the girl might still be alive had she not shunned me and gone off with you that night."

The breath caught in Jamie's chest; his mind whirled. If not for Giles, Jamie never would have met Celia or bedded her. Had the whole thing been staged by Giles in hopes he might use Celia to spy on Jamie? "Are you saying you killed Celia because she had the good sense to reject your advances?"

"Of course not." Giles looked more amused than affronted. "I was not even in London that night."

"Nor was I," Jamie growled.

"Hmm. Your men say you were aboard ship bound for Calais, but they'd tell the sheriff whatever you bid them. I, on the other hand, was with His Majesty's court in Lincoln...in full view of a hundred noble witnesses."

Jamie crossed his arms and silently counted to ten...his father's technique for controlling a hot temper. "Have you proof I was not aboard the *Lady,* or is this just idle talk?"

"I have no proof...yet. But I know you are up to something. I mean to find out where you keep sneaking off to."

Jamie's blood ran cold. Damn. Did Giles know about the ships, or was he merely grasping at straws, trying to bring him down while Lancaster was too faraway to help? If they succeeded, they'd ruin more than they guessed. Stiff as he was, he managed to shrug. "Just a bit of honest trade."

Giles snorted. "I think you're trading with the French. I've men searching the most likely ports. I'll catch you."

Damn. Was he looking as far as Cornwall? "Oxford would be the one to know about such things. Is his man, Roger Salisbury, not negotiating a treaty with the French?"

"King Richard is exploring all means of preventing

war," Giles said hotly. "If a peaceful settlement could be arranged, 'twould be our salvation."

"Or our ruin. King Charles would use the treaty as an excuse to gobble us up without having to wage a war."

Giles's lip curled. "Brigands such as you would not understand a pledge made between honorable men."

Jamie glared back to hide the fact he was shaken by Giles's astute guesses. "You wouldn't know an honorable man if he came up and bit you in the arse." He watched anger flare in Giles's face. "Charming as it has been to cross words with you, if not swords, Giles, I must attend my lady mother." Jamie walked away, as though dismissing the man as harmless when the truth was just the opposite. Giles was a danger to his plans. It had been a mistake to come here, a weakness to want to see his parents one last time...just in case things turned sour.

"Do ye still want to go through with this?" Toby asked.

Emmeline nodded, hoping the shadows in this corner of the stable hid her flushed cheeks. She'd rebraided her hair, but her emotions were still in turmoil. "I know he's guilty. He sidestepped the question when I asked if he'd killed her."

"Jesu, Mary and Joseph...ye cannot accuse a murderer—"

"Oh, I—I worked it into the conversation so it didn't sound that way. He didn't answer. You'll never guess what he did."

"What?"

"He..." Emmeline sucked back the rest of her words. How could she explain to Toby that she had turned out to be as weak as Celia where this man was concerned? "He attacked Markham for slapping me."

"Markham slapped ye?" Toby's fists clenched.

Emmeline grabbed hold of Toby's hand. "'Twas only a slap, and I provoked him with my demands to play his lute." See where her thirst to display her talent had gotten her? Her mother had been right, emotions were a bad thing. Twice tonight an excess of emotions had gotten her into trouble.

"I don't care if Cedric did try to steal the Wait from him, Markham's got no cause to take his grievances out on ye."

"Life is rarely fair. And Cedric's antics would try a saint. Now, how are we going to capture Lord Jamie? Oh." She straightened on the cask she was using for a stool. "I should have gone with him as he asked. 'Twould have been easy to—"

"Gone where?"

"Er, never mind that. I think I know how we can take him."

He had tarried too long. Jamie strode quickly down the path toward the stables. Already the moon rode high in the starry black sky, and he'd have to set a merciless pace if he hoped to reach London before the tide turned. But his heart wouldn't let him go till he'd danced with Jo, his mother and his aunts, and talked defensive strategy with his father and uncles. He'd left behind a few tears and lies that tweaked his conscience, but he could not even hint at the desperate odds he faced.

As he rounded the keep, he spied someone walking toward him. Hugh! 'Twas like gazing into a mirror. Except that his twin didn't have an eye patch. Hugh's scars were more easily hidden.

"Jamie." Hugh stopped a few feet away, his glance going first to that damned patch. "You are looking well."

So formal. So cold, but that was Hugh for you. Ice to Jamie's fire.

"And your limp is scarcely noticeable."

Hugh glowered. "Only you would be crass enough to mention my crippled leg at all."

"Why, when I am responsible for it? I thought we'd agreed I am crass and low." They stared at each other like rival dogs sizing each other up, except they knew each other's strengths and weaknesses all too well. He'd forgotten how eerie it was to look into a face so like his own, yet not. The absence of the black patch wasn't the only difference. Though Hugh was tanned from riding over the estate, his skin lacked the burnished glow Jamie had acquired from years at sea. Hugh's chin was a little softer, no doubt because he'd stuck it out less often than Jamie had his. And his eyes were colder, his mouth unsmiling.

"You've come home, then," Hugh said.

"But not to stay, so you can lower your hackles."

"Harte Court is yours, after all."

"True, but you'd not be pleased if I did decide to claim the estate you've sweated over these past years."

"'Tis yours by right of birth." He looked grim, yet determined to do the honorable thing and step aside, if that's what Jamie wanted. Hugh had not changed one whit.

"If not by deed." Jamie held up his hand to forestall Hugh's rebuttal, the bitterness so acrid he nearly choked. "I have not returned to take up the mantle I tossed you when I rode away."

"I do not understand how you can turn your back on this."

Because I owe you. The silence deepened.

"Where are you bound this time?" Hugh asked at length.

"To sea. I'm patrolling the coast in hopes of encountering French spies." That, at least, was the truth.

"If the king succeeds in negotiating a peace treaty, such measures won't be necessary."

Jamie snorted. "The treaty could be a trap."

"I...I agree 'tis risky to trust the French," Hugh said slowly. "But surely the hope of peace is better than war. Harte Court does not lie very far north of London and would doubtless be pillaged by the French if they invaded."

"I would hate to see that happen, but—"

"I've done all I can to keep us safe," Hugh said earnestly, and began detailing all the precautions he'd taken, from building new storage buildings inside the castle walls to hold more foodstuffs to arming and training the villeins to defend the lands around Harte Court.

Jamie could well imagine similar efforts going on throughout the country. The knowledge that such measures would, at best, only slow the advance of the well-armed French, strengthened his determination to see his own plans through. "You are a fool to trust the French to negotiate in good faith."

Hugh stiffened. "How like you to want a war. To you, life is one long adventure. You were always charging into danger."

"And dragging you after me." Jamie fingered the patch. If he hadn't gotten angry, hadn't issued that stupid challenge, neither of them would have been maimed. "You saved my life that day."

Hugh looked away, a muscle in his jaw jumping. "If I'd been closer...if I hadn't hesitated."

"You saved my life," Jamie repeated, conscious this was the first time they'd discussed the fateful attack that had changed their lives so drastically. "And I know you'll do your best for Harte Court." He smoothly changed the subject. "I understand you are to be congratulated on your future marriage."

Hugh shrugged. "'Tis an advantageous match. Did Papa tell you she is Neville's daughter, and her lands—"

"Bother her lands, do you love her?"

"Love?" Hugh blinked. "What has that to do with it?"

"Everything."

"To you, mayhap," Hugh said stiffly. "You've fallen in love with every girl you saw from the time you were ten and five."

"Ten and three," Jamie amended, chuckling. "'Twas the rope dancer at the London fair, and she taught me such wonders."

"You've lusted after low women ever since." Hugh's lip curled. "'Twas your duty to wed well and breed up heirs."

Jo was right, their brother was a sanctimonious prig. "You are my heir, Hugh, and I'm well pleased to keep things that way." His throat tightened as he realized this might be the last time he saw his family. "Take care of things here," he said hoarsely. "If Harte Court is threatened and you need me, send word to the Killigrews at Arwenack in Cornwall." 'Twas as much of his whereabouts as he dared give out. Only a few people knew where he was and, of those, even fewer knew what he was really about. "Tanner, my agent at the docks, can dispatch a ship."

"Do you really think the French will come?"

"'Tis the moment they've waited for. A chance to repay us for the humiliating defeats they suffered at the hands of King Edward and The Black Prince. So long as they believe we are weak and vulnerable, they will come." And we may all die. 'Twas his last chance to wipe clean the slate. Jamie turned to face his twin. "I want you to know that I tried to sign my inheritance over to you, but the estate is entailed to the eldest, and there was naught I could do. 'Tis not fair. You should have Harte Court," Jamie muttered. "Jesu, you've worked hard to make it prosperous."

"Life is not always fair," Hugh muttered. "I will have a fine estate when I wed Willa."

But it wouldn't be Harte Court. "I'm sorry. I shouldn't have brought it up."

"'Tis all right." Hugh cleared his throat, a sure sign he had something to say. Something he deemed unpleasant. "I...we were upset when we heard you'd been accused of murdering that woman. I abandoned work on the west walls and rode with Mama and Papa to London to support you, but we arrived to learn you'd been cleared and had returned to your ship."

"Sir Thomas had naught against me save the maid's word her mistress had been expecting a man that night. Lily never actually saw who did visit poor Celia, but it wasn't me. I was aboard the *Lady* at the time, and my men bore out my story."

"I should have known you would come out on top...you always do. Did you know her...Mistress Celia, I mean."

Jamie nodded. "Aye, but not well."

"She was very beautiful. The sort of woman you like."

Celia had been vain, stupid and shallow, but Jamie wasn't one to speak ill of a lady. Especially a dead one. "Aye."

"I heard she loved you."

"Who said that?"

A shadow passed over Hugh's face, gone so briefly it

might have been a trick of the light. "'Twas the talk at court."

"Since when are you a courtier?"

"Even crippled second sons are welcomed at court."

"I did not mean you weren't welcome there. 'Tis a surpris—"

"Aye, I'm sure you are astounded anyone could enjoy spending time with me. Icicle, is that not what you and Jo call me?"

Jamie flinched. "I am sorry that my biting wit wounded you. Despite our differences, I think you are a good man, Hugh. A better man than I." He deeply regretted the gulf between them caused by his youthful pranks and mockery.

Hugh looked even more ill at ease.

"Lord Jamie," called a soft voice. The overblown blonde hurried along the path toward them. "Have you a moment?"

Jamie gazed down into naughty eyes and wished they moved him half as much as Emmeline's sober ones had. Ah, well, a man could not have everything. "Sorry, I must be going."

"Let me come with you." She pressed against him.

"Impossible, I'm afraid," Jamie said with no real regret.

Hugh cleared his throat and bowed stiffly. "If you'll excuse me, I should be getting back to Mama's party."

"Hugh, please take Lady…"

"Chantal," the blonde replied.

"Of course. Please take Lady Chantal back to the—"

"I want to go with you." Chantal pouted prettily.

"She obviously prefers you." Hugh sounded petulant, too.

Jamie had no time to humor either of them. "Well, we don't always get what we want." He bowed over Chantal's white hand, gallantly lied about seeing her in London and hurried away. "Thanks for everything, Hugh," he called over his shoulder.

The nape of his neck began to prickle as he reached the stable. The courtyard was deserted, Rob nowhere in sight. Jamie paused at the stable door, acutely aware he'd be silhouetted in the opening when he entered to retrieve Neptune. An inviting target if someone waited within.

His ears and eyes strained to pick out any hint of trouble lurking in the dimness. All was quiet save for the low, contented sounds of horses dozing or chewing. Reassured but still vigilant, he stepped within. The new straw crunched beneath his boots, and he cursed his father's fastidiousness. Had the straw been old and wet, his movements would have been soundless.

Neptune was saddled and waiting in the first stall. Nerves taut, Jamie reached for the reins and prepared to swing into the saddle. Straw rustled to his left. Quick as lightning, Jamie dove to his right, drawing his sword in the same practiced move and raising it to counter an attack.

"Sweet Mary," gasped a soft voice.

Jamie stared up the length of naked steel into Emmeline's pale, shocked face. "Emma, what are you doing here?"

"Emmeline," she replied. "Waiting for you."

"For me?" he echoed.

She nodded, her eyes huge, her fingers pleating her skirts.

"Is Markham after you?" Jamie leapt up, wrapped an arm around her and scanned the darkened stables for her uncle.

"What? Nay." She looked even more uneasy, and shudders rippled from her body into his, tearing at him.

"Easy, sweetling." He drew her closer. "Tell me what troubles you, and I'll deal with it."

"I...oh, this is so difficult." She looked up at him, her lips set in a grim line.

He had a sudden urge to kiss her and soften her mouth, bend her to his will. *Not now, you randy wretch.* "Tell me," he coaxed.

"I will go with you."

"With me?"

She nodded. Her slender throat worked as she swallowed, the gulp audible in the silent stables. "If...if you still want me."

Want was a feeble word to describe the thrill that shot through him. Anticipation. Triumph. He hid both. 'Twas not chivalrous to gloat. "Of course I do, but what changed your mind? You were so, er, vocal in rejecting me earlier."

She looked away, then up at him, not through her lashes as a practiced flirt might, but openly, directly. "I am afraid."

"Of Markham," he guessed. At her nod, he sighed. "Well, at least I am accounted the lesser of two evils. You were supposed to smile at that," he added when she didn't.

"I have not had much to smile about lately, milord."

"None of that formality if we are to be, er, traveling companions." He wondered if she meant to share his bed, then dismissed the notion as unworthy of a white knight. "Have you a horse?" he asked.

She let go the breath she'd been holding, the sound even louder than her gulp had been...and more touching. "Aye, but I fear the poor old thing will not keep up with this fine beast."

"I could take you up with me if you'd prefer."

"Would you mind?"

"Mind cuddling you on my lap all the way to London? I should say not." He waggled his brows in a mock leer that never failed to make the ladies giggle.

Emma, or Emmeline as she preferred, blinked like a solemn little owl, then nodded. "Let us be about it," she said grimly.

Damn. She really did see him as the lesser of two evils. If matters had not changed between them by the time they reached London, he'd take her directly to her grandfather's house. 'Twas likely for the best anyway. Though she stirred him as no woman had in years, taking her to Cornwall with him would be lunacy.

As he swung up behind her and put his arm around Emma to grasp the reins, Jamie's good intentions faltered. That voluminous gown of hers concealed a delightfully slender, supple body. The poker stiffness of her spine as she held herself away from him only heightened his interest. What would it take to get her to relax and lean against him?

The good-natured ribbing of George and the other guards at the front gate did not aid Jamie's seduction. He deflected their jests gruffly and nudged Neptune into a ground-eating gallop that spirited them out of earshot as quickly as possible. "Sorry about that," he murmured, slowing as they cleared the drawbridge.

"Why? Th-they were right in what they said. You are taking me with you so you...so we..." Her voice trailed off.

"Only if you want to, Emma."

"Emmeline." Her back was stiffer than ever. "'Tis what you do with your women, is it not? Take them to some tavern or mayhap in their own homes and...and..."

"Only if they are willing." A new idea intruded. "Emma... Emmeline, have you ever been with a man?"

"Of course I have. D-dozens of them."

Liar. Sweet, prickly little liar. He was stricken by absurdly conflicting urges to ravish and protect her. He was glad the distance she'd put between them would keep her ignorant of the effect she was having on his wayward body, which had already decided what it would prefer to do.

They rode along the moon-washed road in a tense silence, their only contact the brush of his forearm against her waist as he held the reins. She was shivering, dammit. Hoping it was from the chilly night air, he pulled his cloak from the roll behind the saddle and draped it over her shoulder.

"Wh-what are you doing?"

"You are cold. Since you refuse to share the heat of my body, I'm gallantly giving you my cloak."

"Oh. Thank you." Grudging words.

"What do you do in London?" he asked politely.

"Do?"

"You said you were not a member of the Wait. Are you your grandfather's chatelaine? I recall his wife died years ago."

"Oh. Aye, she did."

"I am sorry. I didn't mean to make you more unhappy by bringing up her death. Were you very close?"

"Nay. I—I was estranged from my grandparents until recently…because of my father, Cedric, Markham's older brother."

"Did he inherit leadership of the Wait, then?"

"Nay." Short, curt and angry.

Jamie didn't ask why. He knew full well elder sons sometimes did not follow in their father's footsteps. "What does he do?"

"He lies and breaks hearts."

Damn. He could feel her pain and longed to ease it, but she'd take naught from him, certainly not pity or comfort.

"Could we stop?" she asked suddenly.

Jamie started and looked around. They'd reached the tumble of rocks and trees that marked the base of the next ridge. "I cannot leave you here, Emmeline. If you want to go back—"

"Nay, I need to get down for a moment." Her voice dropped to a miserable whisper. "I—I should have visited the garderobe before we left, but did not, and now I have to—"

"Certainly." Jamie eyed the thick woods and giant boulders. A fine spot for an ambush. "But not here. Up on the ridge—"

"I need to get down now."

Jamie sighed, dismounted and lifted her to the ground. She darted away into the brush. "Call if you need me."

Almost immediately he heard a grunt and a thud.

"Emma?" He drew his sword and started forward. "What is it?"

"I—I fell...I think I've broken my ankle."

"Don't try to get up." Sheathing his blade, he stepped into the woods. 'Twas dark as the inside of a pocket. "Where are you?"

"Here," she called from his right.

He turned, tripped over something and pitched forward. As he brought up his hands to break his fall, something slammed into the back of his head. Pain exploded and black dots danced before his eyes. He fought it, fought to stay conscious, but the darkness sucked him down, down....

Chapter Three

"Lord Giles, what a surprise to find you here."

Giles turned away from trying to decide which of the guests he might use to spy on Jamie and started. "Oh, Lord Hugh, for a moment I thought 'twas your brother."

"I do not see how. His patch is most distinctive."

Giles ground his teeth together. Cold, haughty bastard. Though they'd only met a few times at court, he disliked Hugh nearly as much as his twin. "Ah, you are the one with the lame leg, are you not?" he sneered, pleased to see Hugh flush. "I recall both afflictions were the result of the same incident."

Hugh's gaze turned even frostier. "Why are you here?"

So, he was as loath to discuss the event as Jamie. Interesting. Giles had heard they'd been set upon by brigands and nearly killed, but there was something else. Something in Hugh's expression when he mentioned Jamie that made Giles's heart leap. Anger. Jealousy. Did Hugh dislike his brother? If so, Hugh might prove useful. "I could say I was here to honor your mother," Giles said, smiling now, "but the truth is, I came to spy on your brother."

"What has he done now?" Hugh grumbled.

Fascinating. "The Earl of Oxford has appointed me—"

"I am well aware you are Robert de Vere's hireling, so you needn't wrap this up in fine linen. What has Jamie done now that will again stain our family name and wound our parents?"

"We think he and Lancaster's son are involved in something."

"Of course they are. Jamie fostered in Lancaster's household. He and Henry of Bolingbroke are close as brothers."

"What are they up to?"

"I am the last man Jamie would take into his confidence," Hugh growled.

Better and better. "You two are not close, then?"

"'Tis a fine jest that we are identical in looks, yet under the skin we are completely different. Except, of course, that we are both scarred...in our own way," he added bitterly.

"Jamie and I never dealt well together. I did not enjoy being the brunt of his sharp tongue," Giles said on a hunch.

Hugh snapped up the bait, his manner softening as he nodded. "I suffered the same fate till he went to Lancaster's."

"It cannot have been easy being Jamie's brother."

"You are a master of understatement. He was always first in everything, swordplay, wrestling, running, swimming and, of course, women." A muscle worked in Hugh's jaw, and his eyes burned with the fire of past grudges. "The victories came so easily to him, yet they meant naught. Even Harte Court, an estate any man would give his soul to possess... Jamie turned his back on it and went off adventuring."

Giles smiled inwardly. He was the son of a simple knight, but he'd risen to the right hand of a powerful earl by exploiting others' weaknesses. Each man had his price, and Hugh had just declared his. *Harte Court.* Now he saw how he might fan Hugh's resentment into the fires of Jamie's destruction. "You should have been the first-born...not him."

"Aye." Hugh shifted his weight off his left leg and grimaced. "Jamie does not appreciate what he has."

Giles looked around the crowded garden, then drew Hugh onto one of the shadowy paths. Lowering his voice to a conspiratorial whisper, he said, "Oxford agrees with you. Your brother is not only unworthy of the high station he holds, he is a danger to England. We think..." Giles cast about for a suitably nefarious crime. "We think he is plotting against the crown."

Hugh's lips thinned. "I knew he'd go too far one day. It's the Lancasters, is it not?"

Oh, this was too good to be true. "Has he said something?"

Hugh shook his head. "I told you he'd not confide in me."

"Quite so. Then what makes you mention Lancaster?"

"Jamie's thick with them, and the duke has been vocal in his criticism of the king. If Lancaster decided he'd make a better king than Richard, Jamie would be certain to support him."

Giles nearly wept with joy. Though he doubted Lancaster was plotting to usurp his nephew's throne, he did agree with Oxford's suspicions that the duke, Bolingbroke and Jamie were working secretly to thwart Oxford's peace treaty with the French. 'Twas Giles's job to uncover their scheme before they ruined the agreement that would make Oxford the most powerful man in England...and fill Giles's own pocket with gold.

Carefully he began to reel in the fish he'd unexpectedly

netted. "We must have proof. Do you know where Jamie has gone?"

"Well…" Hugh looked uneasy. "He said he was patrolling the Cornish coast to keep watch for French ships."

Cornwall. They'd not looked so far afield. He'd dispatch men there at once. "That area is ripe with smugglers."

"Smuggling. I'd not thought of that," Hugh murmured. "But 'tis far more likely he'd be trading in stolen goods and evading the king's tax collectors than that he'd actually try to overthrow the crown."

Pity, Giles thought. The penalty for treason was much stiffer. "Well, I must return to London. If you hear anything you think the king should know, please contact me at once. His Majesty is lavish with his gifts to those who aid him. Who knows, you might be rewarded with an estate as fine as your brother's."

The grinding of Hugh's teeth was audible. "I shall see what I can discover."

I am certain you will.

Jamie awoke to shadows and a wretched pounding in his head. The rest of his body was so stiff and sore he wondered if he'd been beaten. Where was he? The last thing he remembered was tripping over a rope. Giles! Giles had captured him?

Terror drove out the pain. Had he talked? Then he remembered Emma, and an agonized moan clawed its way out of his chest.

"Ye're awake," said a coarse feminine voice. A cup pressed against his lips. But when he tried to lift his head, hot pain tore through it. "Easy, don't try to move. Just open yer mouth."

He obeyed, sighing as something cool slid down to ease the wool from his parched throat. Sweet wine laced with herbs. No dungeon fare this. Opening his eye, he focused on his nursemaid, an older woman in clean home-spun. She offered him the cup again, and he drank, a dozen questions whirling dizzily in his mind. When she took the cup away, he asked the uppermost one. "Emma?"

"If ye're meaning Mistress Emmeline, she's sleeping."

"Safe?" At her nod, he took heart. "Where am I? How long have I been here?"

"Two days."

"Can't stay." Jamie tried to sit up. There was a loud clanking noise, and something caught at his wrists and ankles. That was nothing to the agony in his head. Fighting to stay conscious, he lay still. When the worst of the pain had passed, he rolled his good eye toward the maid. "Have I bedded down in the scullery with the pots and pans?" He smiled faintly.

"Nay…" She frowned.

The pounding in his head disoriented him. "Then where am I?"

"'Tis not for me to say."

"Is he giving you a hard time?" asked a familiar voice. Emma's face appeared above him in the gloom.

"Emma." The relief at seeing her was almost as diz-zying as his headache. "How is your ankle?"

"Fine. Go up and break your fast, Molly. I'll sit with him."

Jamie smiled as he watched Emma primly tuck her skirts about her and take the stool Molly had vacated. "I fear I failed miserably at rescuing you and am now in your debt. What happened? My limbs feel like they're made of lead."

"I expect that's the chains," she said flatly.

Chains? Teeth clenched against the pain, Jamie lifted his head just far enough to survey his body. His bare feet stuck out of the end of a coarse blanket, shackled at the

ankles. "What the hell?" His wrists were chained, too.
Belatedly his dazed brain fit the pieces together, the thin
pallet on the floor, the meanness of the stone walls, the
dank smell of earth and straw. "Giles Cadwell's dungeon?" he croaked.

"My storeroom," she countered. "You are my prisoner."

"Yours, but why? Did Giles put you up to this?"

"No one employed me to imprison you. I have my
own—"

"How much to release me. That is what this is about,
is it not? Ransom," he added when she still didn't catch
his meaning.

"Certainly not." She seemed affronted. "I want justice."

"Because I tried to seduce you?"

"Not for myself, for my sister. Celia is...was my sister."

Good God! "Impossible. You don't look anything
like—"

"I am aware I am no beauty, but she was my sister."

"I didn't kill her," Jamie exclaimed.

"So you told Sir Thomas, but we do not believe that."
Her expression tightened. "He explained that his hands are
tied—" her gaze flickered to his bound wrist, a half smile
hinting at wry humor he'd have appreciated at another time
"—by your alibi and your family's prestige. I, however,
am not so constrained."

"What do you hope to gain by this insane—?"

"Your confession."

"For something I didn't do?"

Emmeline glared at him, disgust mingling with disbelief. "You had been my sister's lover for several
months—"

"Once! I took her to bed only once. And rued the episode almost the moment it was over."

"So naturally when she told you she was pregnant, you—"

"Pregnant! That's impossible."

"You refused to marry her, and—"

"She never told me she was pregnant."

"And when she persisted, mayhap even threatened to drag your precious family name into the mud, you killed her."

"I did not!"

The door to the room flew open, hitting the wall with enough force to make the room tremble. A large, sturdy man strode in. "Do ye need help, mistress?"

"Nay. Toby, could you hear us upstairs in the shop?"

Shop? Jamie's eyes widened. A shop meant people. If—

"Not a whisper," Toby said. "This room's hollowed out of solid stone. Ye could scream your lungs out down here, and no one would hear ye." As he spoke, the big man grinned and fingered the knife in his belt. "Mistress Emmeline's got some odd notion of wringing a confession from ye. Me, I'd as leave slit yer gullet for what ye did."

"I did not kill Celia," Jamie said, enunciating every word as though speaking to backward children. Or lunatics, which he very much feared they were. "I was only with her the once, and that five months ago," he protested. "If she was carrying my child, she'd have contacted me."

"Her maid claims you were a frequent visitor this summer."

"Impossible. Bring her here. Let her say so to my—"

"Lily is not available. But according to Sir Thomas, the neighbors saw a man of your description enter my sister's house on several nights over the past months."

"It was not me. There is another man, a knight with a grudge against me and your sister. Giles is tall and blond, like me, and he knew your sister."

"Celia wrote and mentioned you...by name. She said she loved you. She hoped you'd wed her. My poor, trusting sister."

Jamie groaned. None of this made any sense. It must be some diabolical scheme of Giles's to get rid of him. "You have my word as a knight and a gentleman that I did not murder your sister. Please, release me. I must return to my ship."

"You'll stay till I have your confession."

"Nay! I have to be in Cornwall by Wednesday," he exclaimed.

"Well, your latest doxie will just have to wait."

"This isn't about some woman." He choked back his anger. "'Tis a matter of import to the whole country," he risked adding.

"And I'm the queen of England." Her lips thinned. "You men are all alike, full of lies and deceit."

Jamie cut her off with a string of creative curses garnered from ten years at sea. He strained and thrashed against the chains, but they didn't give an inch.

"You will cease spewing such filth."

"Want I should gag him?" Toby asked eagerly.

"Nay. We will remove ourselves from earshot." Emmeline stood and glared down at him, her arms crossed over her chest. The gesture was robbed of its militancy by the way the plain brown cloth molded to her surprisingly generous breasts.

Jamie was in no mood to appreciate the sight. "I'll take you with me, and Toby, too, if it would make you feel safer." Lies and more lies. He couldn't afford to have anyone witness his meeting with DeGrys. But he was desperate enough to promise anything to get away.

"As if I'd trust you." Her lips curled. "You'll find I'm not the gullible fool my sister was where men are concerned."

"Nay, I'd say you've shriveled into a vengeful prune because no man would have you," he snapped.

"I thank God I am not a target for every puffed-up male who fancies himself nature's gift to women." She marched out, head held high as a queen, the faithful Toby close on her heels.

"Damn you, let me out!" Jamie shouted at the top of his voice.

"Not till you confess," Emmeline snapped. She punctuated the statement by slamming the door.

"But I'm innocent," Jamie shouted.

"Men are born guilty" came the muted response.

"Come back here." But beyond the door, all was quiet. She'd left him here. *Bloody left him here.* Enraged, he tugged on the chains till the rusted cuffs bit into his wrist and ankles.

"Damn. Damn!" Seething with impotent rage, he closed his eyes. If he wasn't there when DeGrys landed, months of planning, hundreds of pounds in bribes would be wasted. Worse, he might not get another chance to act.

All because of one puny woman's misguided sense of justice. A niggle of respect for her boldness and loyalty worked its way past his anger. Jamie shook it away and set his mind on the only course open to him.

Escape.

By fair means or foul, he had to get out of here.

"What do ye mean ye can only give me a pound for this." Lily picked up the brooch and shook it in the old man's face. "'Tis solid silver, and my lady set great store by it."

"The unicorn design is unique, I grant. But it has no gemstones, and the silver's not of the best quality," the pawnbroker insisted. "Mayhap it had sentimental meaning to her."

Lily sighed glumly. "Aye, her sister, Mistress Emmeline, gave it to her. My lady sold off the pieces her husband had given her after he died...so as she could buy new gowns and such and go to court to find another. Husband, that is." She stared into the old man's crafty eyes, trying to gauge his honesty.

The pawnbroker was licensed, she'd asked to see the parchment. Though the words made no sense, the seal was that of London's mayor. And the broker was hardly skulking in an alleyway. He'd set up his table outside a fine inn a block from the tavern in which she'd found work serving at table. It was early evening, and there were few about to see her barter the trinkets she'd taken when she'd left Lady Celia's house. Not that she felt guilty. 'Twas her due. She'd been cast into the streets with no reference to help her get another post, and Lady Celia had owed her a quarter's wages.

"Make up yer mind," the pawnbroker grumbled.

Lily sighed. "I'll take the pound ye offered for the plate, but I'll keep the brooch." Mayhap she'd find a way to return it to Mistress Emmeline. She carefully tucked it and the coins the broker gave her into the pouch behind her belt. The cutpurses weren't getting what little she had.

Lily headed off in the direction of the tavern. She hadn't eaten anything since last night and hoped the cook would give her a good price on whatever was left over from the—

"Lily?" inquired a deep voice.

She whirled and saw a man behind her. He wore a long,

fur-trimmed cloak, the cowl pulled forward to obscure his face. "Wh-what?" She backed away, eyes darting about for an escape route.

"Easy. I mean you no harm." He took a step toward her. The door of a nearby inn opened, sending a brief flood of yellow light over his face.

All she saw was the patch...a slash of black over his left eye. It was *him*. The dark pirate who'd been Lady Celia's lover.

"Oh, God." She'd known he'd find her. Sobbing, she put up a hand to ward him off. "What...what do ye want?"

"Only to make certain you are all right. You disappeared so abruptly, I feared you'd seen Celia's killer and he'd found you."

"Nay. I...I didn't see anything that night."

"Really?" His single eye glittered in the shadows of his cowl, slithering over her like a snake's.

She shivered, wondering how her gay, frivolous lady could have loved such a dark lord. Lily had never been this close to him before. He'd always come at night, mysterious and secretive as a wraith, and gone directly to Lady Celia's chamber. Once or twice Lily had brought them refreshments, but always her lady had taken the tray at the door. She knew who he was, of course. Lord Jamie Harcourt. "Really, milord. I was in my room...sleeping."

"You didn't hear or see anything?"

Voices, arguing. They'd wakened her, alarmed her enough so she'd crept up the stairs to her lady's chamber to investigate. She shook her head. "Nay."

"Pity, if you had, you might have seen her killer." The very silkiness of his voice raised her hackles.

Jesus, Mary and Joseph, had he done it? Had he been in London? In Lady Celia's chamber, instead of out to sea? Lily was taking no chances. She had survived for years on her wits; she hoped they'd save her now. "I'm a sound sleeper."

The lie stuck in her throat, clogged by the memory of what she'd seen when she'd crept up the stairs and peeked through the keyhole...her poor lady lying on the floor, sightless eyes staring at the ceiling. Lily had known Lady Celia was dead, but she'd started to go to her anyway. A sound had stopped her.

A rasping sob. The harsh breathing of someone else in that chamber. An instant later, a shadow had fallen across Lady Celia's face. A man's hand had reached out to touch her face.

Lily hadn't waited to see anything more. She'd fled down the stairs and out the back door. Clad only in her shift, she'd cowered in the privy till dawn when the cook had came out and rousted her from her hiding place. Lily had been tempted to pack and run, but she'd been more afraid of being accused of the lady's murder herself than that the murderer would guess she'd seen him. It seemed she'd made a tragic mistake.

"Why did you leave Celia's?" Lord Jamie asked.

She itched to run, but he was too close. The street was empty except for a drunk snoring in the gutter. "To find work."

"Of course. I'd not thought of that. Poor Ceila was fond of you, she'd be saddened to know you'd been forced to earn your way serving in a tavern."

"Y-ye know where I work?"

The cowl bobbed as he nodded. "If you'll come with me, I may be able to find something better for you on my estate. My sister has reached the age where she needs a good lady's maid."

Lily debated, caution warring with practicality. Maid to a wealthy young lady. If she was wrong about him, if he wasn't the one, she'd be throwing away an opportunity to better herself.

"What is it? Why do you hesitate?" He took a step closer, and this time she didn't flee. "You know, don't you?" Before his question had scarcely registered, his hands flashed out from beneath the cloak and grabbed her shoulders.

"Please, milord, ye're hurting me." She tried to twist free, but his fingers sank into her flesh like talons.

"You saw me, didn't you?" He gave her a little shake.

It jarred her brain, and the pieces fell horribly into place. "Oh, God! It was ye."

"It was me." He sounded sad. "I'm sorry, Lily. Celia's death was a tragic accident. But yours...I'm sorry."

"Wait. I didn't see anything. I heard voices and came to the door. I saw she was dead, but not who'd done it. I didn't know."

"Then I am doubly sorry. But I couldn't take the chance that you'd left Celia's because you knew something and would eventually tell." He spun on his heel, tripping over a pile of garbage as he carried her deeper into the stinking black alley.

She opened her mouth to scream, but it was too late even for that. He cut off the sound and her breath with a wide, icy hand.

Chapter Four

"Why do ye not let me get rid of him for ye?" Toby asked as they trudged up the steps from the cellar.

"I do not want the death of an innocent man on my conscience," Emmeline said indignantly.

Toby snorted. "So, he's charmed ye into changing yer mind."

"Nay, he has not."

"Has not what?" Molly asked as they emerged into the small room at the back of the house that served as a kitchen.

"Made me change my mind about him." But he'd shaken her resolve and a good deal more. To hide her confusion, Emmeline walked over and poked at the pottage simmering in a pot suspended over the fire. Behind her, she heard Toby bolt the trapdoor and slide the woven mat and worktable over it. "I do want him to pay for what he's done," she said, half to herself.

Yet she felt a qualm when she relived their ambush in that little glade: the swiftness with which Jamie had charged to the rescue when he'd thought she'd hurt her ankle, followed by a curse as he tripped over Toby's rope, and the ground-shaking thud of his big body hitting the dirt...the rocks. One of them had gashed open his skull and rendered him senseless during the long journey home in her grandfather's wagon. They'd stanched the bleeding, of course, and she'd stitched the wound after the three of them had wrestled his deadweight down the cellar steps, but—

"Ye're certain he's guilty?" Molly asked.

"Aye." Calmer now, Emmeline turned to her servants. "Well, he's surely the greatest rogue and womanizer ever born. Why, he reminds me of that little brown man we saw at the fair, the one who coaxed the snakes from a basket and held them in thrall with the power of his music. Lord Jamie's magic is in his words. They flow smooth and free as warm oil, slipping around every question I ask. But when he said he was not in London the night Celia died, there was something in his eyes...his eye. I know he was lying. I know it. Is it so wrong to want him punished?"

"Of course not," Toby and Molly said in unison. They'd been with her family forever and would support her no matter what.

"But he's a tough one, make no mistake," Toby added. "A man doesn't lose an eye or get the kind of scars he bears on his body by being a coward."

"Scars?" Emmeline said faintly.

"Aye. When I removed his clothes for ye, I saw someone had taken the hide from his back. 'Twas years ago, but—"

"Oh, dear," Emmeline murmured. She had no qualms about imprisoning him, but if he didn't confess, would she have the stomach to apply physical pressure? "He's anxious to be free and about important business in Cornwall. Mayhap if we just wait—"

"Mistress! Come quick!" Peter catapulted into the

room, eyes agog. "'Tis Sir Cedric. He's here. In your so-lar."

"Father?" Emmeline gasped, forgetting she hadn't called Cedric that since the day she'd discovered the truth about her parents' marriage. Or non-marriage. "Why?" But she knew why. There was only one reason why Cedric came visiting. Money.

She found him seated in her chair before the hearth, swilling the expensive Burgundy from her only glass goblet. Swine! "How much do you want this time?" Emmeline demanded.

Cedric turned, the handsome features he'd passed along to Celia blurred by drink and hard living. "What a way to greet your father." The sensual mouth that had cajoled her mother into trusting him now turned down in perpetual dissatisfaction.

"Why lie to ourselves, *Cedric*. Money, or your constant lack thereof, is the only reason you seek me out."

"Tut-tut, my dear. Such cynicism is why you've reached the age of two and twenty and are unwed."

"Is it?" She glared at him, seeing through the veneer of polish to the soft, weak core. The only reason he hadn't wed her to someone was because he didn't want to lose the profits from the shop, which would go to her new husband. The gross unfairness of the whole thing made her furious. Her mother had left the shop to her. She ran a successful business and was a member of the guild in her own right. But simply by virtue of the fact he was her father, Cedric had control over her life. If he received a lucrative offer, he could marry her to the worst dog in all Christendom and no one would say him nay.

Emmeline curled her hands into fists. Men! A pox on all of them. "Why have you come?"

"Actually, I have got myself in rather a fix." Cedric

sighed, an affectation that always preceded a particularly huge demand. His smooth, supple fingers lazily stroked the arm of the chair. Minstrel's hands, capable of coaxing a tune from harp or trumpet, but he had wasted his talent.

Jamie's palms were callused, the backs sprinkled with the same fair hair that swirled over his chest. The capable hands and taut muscles of a man who worked for a living. Or wanted to impress a woman when he undressed for her, a sly voice taunted.

"...could use the money, but what I really need is a place to stay," Cedric was saying.

"Stay?" Emmeline gaped. "Here? Now?"

"Why not?" One sand brow rose. His bloodshot green eyes grew frankly speculative. "Never say you've got yourself a lover hid in the cellar and don't want your dear father around."

Emmeline knew him well. One hint he was onto the truth, and he'd pick at her like a dog on a bone. "Ha! As if I'd let a man into my house much less my life," she snapped.

"Did Margaret and I set such a poor example of wedded life?"

"Wedded, ha! 'Tis called bigamy, and you are lucky Mama was too ashamed to report you to the church."

He flushed and dragged the lank blond hair away from his face. "I was happy with Maggie as I never could be with the wife my father foisted on me." He glanced sidelong at Emmeline. "Your mother gave me love and children. We were happy here."

"Until she found out how you'd betrayed her."

"I loved her," Cedric whined.

"You used her." Margaret Spencer, plain only daughter of a wealthy spice merchant with lofty aspirations. He'd been thrilled to wed his daughter to the son of a noble family. But Cedric's title had been as false as the rest of his story. Emmeline had been twelve and Celia ten when the truth came out. They were bastards, daughters of a glib-tongued rogue with a wife in London. He'd run through his wife's money and been cast out of the Golden Wait for stealing their instruments and selling them. "All you ever wanted was the money from the shop to augment what you earned when you played in Grandfather's Wait."

"He never paid me what I was worth."

"So you stole their instruments and sold them…except for the lute, which you gave me as a gift." Alford had found out, of course, and ordered Cedric to leave London or face arrest. Cedric's wife, Olivia, had decided to follow him to Derry and discovered his guilty secret. "Your lies ruined our lives."

"I did not mean to. I loved your mother. I would have married her if I could have shed Olivia."

"Liar. You did not care one whit for our pain and shame so long as you had what you wanted. You cheated us all, Cedric." Tears welled, blurring her vision. She turned away to pour herself a cup of wine, unwilling to let him know his betrayal still had the power to hurt her.

"Celia forgave me. I went to see her in London, and she—"

"Don't you speak to me of her," she said, rounding on him. "If you hadn't filled her head full of tales of the splendor of court life, she never would have eloped with Roger de Vienne."

"Roger made her laugh. He helped her escape from the dull—"

"He was a scoundrel. If he hadn't taken her to London, she never would have gotten herself killed by James Harcourt."

"Celia hated being stuck in this dreary town as much

as I—what's that? I thought Harcourt had been cleared of her murder.''

Drat her hasty tongue. "So I heard."

"Pity, I'd like to see her murderer caught."

"But not enough to bestir yourself to pursue the matter?"

"Lord Jamie has an alibi."

"Hmm. So I've been told."

"You are up to something. I know that mulish look of yours."

"What could I, a poor apothecary, do against such a man?"

"That has not kept you from tackling lost causes in the past." He stared at her intently, then settled back in the chair, stretching his feet toward the fire. "But this is beyond even your stubbornness." There were holes in the heels of his hose but he looked about as movable as a rock.

She couldn't afford to let him stay. "How much do you need?"

Cedric pursed his lips, but she saw the triumph edging them. "Ten pounds would see me out of debt."

"Ten! What did you buy, half of London?"

"Nay. 'Twas a scheme gone bad, naught more."

"You have more schemes than a dog has fleas, and they always go bad. I don't have much, but I'll give you some of the precious spices, saffron and cinnamon, which you can sell in London."

The crafty old devil shook his head. "I could not take your trade goods. I'll just bide here till you have the coin."

"I don't have that much profit in a year."

"I don't mind rusticating a bit. London has grown tedious."

Dangerous, more like. But naught short of a fire would

drive him away. "I'll tell Molly you're staying, but I'll not give up my bed. You can sleep in the workroom with Peter."

"A pallet here in the solar would be warmer."

"I'm certain it would be, but I'll not spend my nights listening to you snore." Her chamber adjoined the solar. If he slept there he'd see her coming and going from the storeroom.

"Very well." Having gotten most of what he wanted, and doubtless smelling secrets in the air, Cedric smiled. It was the same, unabashedly roguish grin that Jamie Harcourt had worn when he attempted to seduce her.

Damn both men, Emmeline thought as she stamped off to inform her cohorts in crime that fate had added a new wrinkle to her own already precarious scheme.

The candle had long since gutted when Jamie heard the key scrape in the lock. As the door eased open, he closed his eye against the blinding flood of light and breathed a silent prayer of thanks. Lying alone in the dark with naught but pain and the prospect of his failed plans for company had been a humbling experience. He'd been afraid they'd leave him here to die.

Jamie opened his eye. The fact that they'd left the patch on his left one gave him a measure of comfort. He hated exposing the worst of his scars to others. Especially Emma, for some reason. "I thought you'd decided to starve me to death."

Toby ducked into the cell, a tray in his hands, a chamber pot dangling from one stubby finger. "Serve ye right if she did. Us waiting on the murdering scum like he was royalty."

"That's enough, Toby." Emmeline followed him in, carrying linens and a candle. "Set the things there." She jerked her chin toward a table in the corner. Above it hung shelving loaded with crocks. Jamie had tried and failed to reach it, thinking to break a pot and fashion a weapon. "Then go out and lock the door."

"I'm not leaving ye in here alone with him."

Emmeline sighed, and Jamie noted with grim glee the lines of fatigue bracketing her mouth. "He's chained to the wall and cannot hurt me. I need you to stand lookout."

For whom? They'd not done that before. Was there someone about? Customers in the shop, mayhap? Jamie's dulled hopes flared, but he kept his expression bland as he watched Toby go.

When the door closed, Emmeline moved in, stopping short of Jamie's feet. Her gaze went to the linen wrapped around his head. The candlelight picked out the green flecks in her hazel eyes, making them glow like gemstones. "There's blood on the bandage. I warned you not to move about or you'd reopen the wound."

"What did you hit me with, a sword?"

"You cracked your head on a rock when you fell."

"Tripped...over a rope, I think, coming to your aid."

Her gaze dropped. "I do not normally resort to trickery."

"Really? Your cry of pain sounded authentic," he taunted.

She flushed, her expression remorseful. "I had to—"

"So, you believe the end justifies the means?"

"Only in this case." She set the candle down and knelt to rummage through her supplies for a roll of linen and a small knife. "I'm going to cut away the old bandage. If you attempt to take the knife, I'll stick it in you. Is that clear?"

"Very. Never argue with a wench wielding a blade. If

you think I'm guilty, why did you not kill me in that glade?"

"I want justice."

"Ah, a kidnapper with scruples."

Her brows jammed together. "If you do not stop trying to bait me, I may be forced to bend my morals."

"And cheat yourself of torturing me?"

"I am not torturing you."

"What else would you call leaving an injured man in this dank cellar with a host of hungry rats?"

"Rats!" She pulled her skirts close and gazed into the shadows. "I don't believe you." An obliging vermin chose that moment to streak toward the table, likely drawn by the smell of his supper. Emmeline shrieked, leapt up and shooed it away.

"If you rattle your chains at them, it keeps them at bay."

Emmeline looked disconcerted as she set the food down at his right side. "I'm sorry, I didn't..." She blinked and glared at him. "Why am I apologizing to you?"

"Mayhap because you realize you are wrong to hold me here like this. Sir Thomas has already cleared me of the charges."

"He no more believes in your innocence than I do."

"Is he in this with you?" When she shook her head, his temper boiled over. "Idiot woman. What do you hope to prove by this? Don't you realize that a confession obtained under such conditions would carry no weight with the courts?"

"It will." Her face was so close to his he noticed the freckles on her nose. They made her look younger, more vulnerable. "When your sailors hear you have been arrested and are unable to coerce them, they will tell the truth, too. They'll tell Sir Thomas you weren't aboard your ship that night.''

How could she know that? Jamie groaned inwardly. Damn. Most of his men had been with him for years; they'd lie for him till the bitter end. But all it would take is one mistake to bring this whole scheme down. ''I have no time for this,'' he snapped. ''Look, I have vital business elsewhere. I'll do anything you say, if you'll let—''

''Will you confess?''

''To a crime I didn't commit? Certainly not.''

''Why? If such a confession is worthless, why not admit—''

''I may be many things, mistress, but I am not a cold-blooded murderer of women, and naught will get me to say so.''

''Then I guess you are stuck here.'' She uncorked a flask and dabbed a vile-smelling potion on his wound. It burned like fire.

Jamie yelped and flinched away, setting his chains to rattling. ''You will rue the day you did this,'' he said through his clenched teeth. Though he'd left a trail of broken hearts behind him, he'd never consciously harmed a woman before. But he'd make an exception for this one.

''Did you say something similar to Celia?'' she asked.

Jamie swore vilely, but took no pleasure in her shocked gasp. He wanted more. He wanted her to pay for ambushing him and endangering his plans. But most of all, for making him want her, then deceiving him. ''I never harmed your sister. Nor any other woman. I like women, and they like me.''

She snorted in disgust. ''I despise you.'' Fire bloomed in her cheeks, transforming her face, making it glow from within. Untapped passion trapped in a nun's icy reserve.

The impact of her unconscious appeal caught Jamie like

a mailed fist to the gut. The desire had blazed between them from the first. He'd admitted as much to her, and she'd used it to entrap him. No one used him.

Jamie struck with the swiftness that made him an excellent swordsman. Chains rattling, he snagged her around the waist and dragged her across his body. The impact caused the air to whoosh from her lungs and sent pain jarring through his head. He was too angry to care. There was enough play in the chain for him to roll over, trapping her beneath him. He had a moment to savor her panicky expression before she opened her mouth to scream.

"Nay." He sealed her mouth shut with his own. Her silent cry vibrated against his lips, sent a shudder through his body.

Triumph. He might be chained, but she was powerless in the grip of his superior strength. His to do with as he would. He took ruthless advantage of her weakness. Driven by endless hours of impotent rage and savage frustration, he seared her flesh with his, determined to lesson her.

She whimpered. The tiny sound, more felt than heard, slipped past his fury to touch on his worst fear. That one day, if he wasn't careful, the dark side of his nature would break the leash of his iron will. Nay, he wouldn't let it. Digging deep, he found the patience to gentle his hold on her and set his mouth to apologize. In that instant, everything changed. The kiss intended to punish took on a life of its own.

Her cry of distress became a soft sigh, her hands ceased to claw at his arms. Beneath the persuasive pressure of his mouth, hers turned pliant. He'd been right to judge her inexperienced, but her untutored responses sent a shaft of lust arrowing down to his groin. How easy it would be to forget his anger and lose himself in her.

Lifting his head, he stared into her flushed face. Passion transformed her, heightened her beauty. Her lips were wet, swollen, her pupils dilated and dazed. A feeling of intense male satisfaction filled him. "Emma, unchain me."

"Wh-what?" She blinked, passion fading, awareness returning. With a gasp of outrage, she began to thrash.

"Damn. Hold still...argh," he cried when a blow caught him in the ribs. He loosened his grip, setting her free.

Emmeline scrambled from under him and huddled in the corner, struggling to gather her scattered wits. How could she have let him kiss her? She should have screamed the moment he'd grabbed her, instead she'd...she'd...

Nay. Don't think of it. Nearly sobbing with reaction, she scrubbed a hand across her lips, but the taste of him lingered. She had to get away, had to wash the feel of him from her skin. Legs trembling, she got to her feet, walked to the door and called for Toby to let her out. The moment the door opened, she brushed past her startled servant and bolted for the stairs. "See he's locked in," she called in a voice she didn't recognize.

As the door clanked shut again, Jamie sighed and lowered his head to the floor. Damn. How had he lost control of the situation? He had her in his grasp. He could have put his hands around her slender throat and threatened to strangle her if she didn't release him. Instead, he'd...

He'd kissed her and lost himself totally.

Damn. That hadn't happened to him...ever. He'd been with more women than he could count, most of them more beautiful than Mistress Emmeline Spencer, and kept his wits intact. Why her? Because she was different. He'd sensed it the moment they met, and every exchange between them since had strengthened the notion.

Forcing his eyes open, he tried to plan his next move.

His eyes caught the dull glint of metal on the floor. The knife. In her haste to leave, Emmeline had dropped it. Mayhap he hadn't blundered so badly after all, Jamie thought as he retrieved the weapon. Not large enough to kill, but just the right size to pick the locks on his shackles.

Jamie levered himself into a sitting position and was immediately swamped by dizziness. As he sagged against the wall the press of cold stone against his bare back had the rousing effect of a lash. He didn't have much time. Convincing Mistress Emmeline of his innocence was a lost cause. Nor could he count on the slim hope of rescue. Harry would worry when he didn't arrive as expected at the Hound and Stag and send word to the ship. But they'd never think to look for him so far from London.

He spent what remained of the night kicking away curious rats, plotting his escape and devising exquisite tortures with which to repay Mistress Emmeline for daring to kidnap him.

Chapter Five

"Ah, Lord Hugh, thank you for coming." Robert de Vere, Earl of Oxford strode around the ornate desk in his withdrawing room and motioned his guest into a chair by the hearth. "Can I offer you wine, food?"

Hugh sat stiffly. "Your message said the matter was urgent."

The man was a prig, just as Giles had said, but a valuable one, so Oxford swallowed his ire. "So it is, but there is no reason why we cannot observe the amenities till Giles joins us."

"I did not mean to snap," Hugh replied. "'Tis harvest time and I am needed on the estate."

"Your brother's estate?" Oxford asked smoothly.

Hugh flushed and took the proffered cup of wine. "Aye, Harte Court will belong to him when my father dies, may that day be long in coming, but Jamie has not the inclination to manage it."

"He is fortunate his brother is willing to run it for him." Oxford took the other chair and stretched his legs toward the hearth, where a small fire sought to drive the dampness from the stone tower. "You are identical...except for the eye."

"Outwardly, we are."

"Hmm." Oxford sipped his wine. "It must be tedious to so resemble a man with such an unsavory reputation. Are you ever subjected to abuse by those who mistake you for him?"

Hugh tensed. "What makes you ask that?"

"Idle curiosity, naught more," the earl murmured. "I have heard much good about you, a capable landlord and dutiful son, 'tis said Harte Court prospers under your—"

"If you've called me here to extract some new tax, I must say we have naught till after the harvest is in."

"That was not my intention at all," Oxford said, bristling at the man's sharp tone. "I but made polite conversation till—"

The door opened and Giles strode in, followed by Sir Thomas Burton, looking even more rumpled than usual. Oxford would have liked to replace the old fool with one of his own men, but Sir Thomas held office at the behest of London's mayor, and the city aldermen brooked no interference...royal or otherwise...in the administration of their city.

Oxford stood and made the introductions, noting the way Hugh started when he learned Sir Thomas was the sheriff.

"What is it? What has happened?" Hugh set his cup down so quickly wine sloshed over the rim and onto the table.

Sir Thomas smiled genially. "Rest easy, my lord, I've not come to arrest you." He accepted a cup from Giles and drained it before lowering his bulk into the very chair Oxford usually sat in. "I fear my title makes even the innocent uneasy."

Peeved, Oxford took the chair Giles was about to sit in

and snapped, "Lord Hugh is pressed for time. If you'd tell him…"

"Of course." Sir Thomas's expression turned suitably grave. "I fear there has been another murder."

"Murder!" Hugh's face turned pasty white. "Wh-who?"

"Lily…Celia de Vienne's maid," Giles replied.

Hugh's eyes were black as two burnt holes. "How?"

"Strangled." Sir Thomas supplied.

"Dieu," Hugh breathed. "Do you have any idea who?"

Sir Thomas shook his head. "None, except that it was likely the same man who murdered Lady Celia. There are similarities between the two murders," he added.

"What kind of similarities?" Hugh asked faintly.

"I am not at liberty to release that information."

"I see. But…but why would anyone want to kill the maid?"

"To silence her. Mayhap she knew more than she told me," Sir Thomas said. "And was trying to blackmail the killer."

Hugh blinked, reached for the cup and drained it. "If I am not a suspect, then why have you called me here, my lords?"

"Because Jamie likely killed her," Giles snapped.

Oxford wanted to cuff him. The fool was so intent on his personal dislike of Jamie, he was blind to all else. "When we heard about the murder, I naturally offered Sir Thomas my support with the investigation," the earl said smoothly. "Giles recalled your saying Jamie was bound for Cornwall. We thought you might know where he was going and when he left."

Hugh nodded slowly. "He said he was sailing that night. The night of my mother's fete."

"His ship is still in London harbor," Sir Thomas said.

"He could have gone by land, I suppose," Hugh muttered, absently, as though his mind was only half on the question.

Oxford nearly groaned aloud in frustration. He didn't know if Jamie had murdered the maid, nor did he care, but it had seemed a perfect way to finally get that slippery eel into prison where Oxford could interrogate him about Lancaster's plans.

"Well, I suppose that is that." Sir Thomas huffed out of the chair. "You will let me know if you hear from your brother."

"Of course." Looking visibly relieved, Hugh stood also and made to follow the sheriff from the room.

Oxford was not yet ready to admit defeat. "A moment, Lord Hugh," he called.

"What?" Hugh poised at the door like a deer about to bolt.

Oxford stalked closer, noting that Hugh did not have his brother's boldness, his strength of character. Of the two, he decided he actually preferred Jamie, even though the man was a thorn in his side. "You did not say where Jamie was bound."

"Nay, I did not." Hugh met him stare for stare.

"Do you know?"

"I have a way to contact him in an emergency."

"I fear your brother may be involved in something nearly as serious as murder," the earl began.

"Giles mentioned smuggling," Hugh replied. "Is there proof?"

Oxford noted the hope in the young man's eyes and knew Giles had been right about the animosity between the twins. "Not yet. By coincidence, the king has given me a task to undertake for him in Cornwall. Giles sails for there today. If you were to give him Jamie's whereabouts, go with him, help him catch and arrest these smugglers, the crown would be…grateful.''

"How grateful?" Hugh asked bluntly.

Oxford nearly laughed aloud. "You may name your own price. Anything short of the throne or my earldom. Harte Court could be yours," he added.

"I will need to think it over," Hugh murmured.

"You have an hour," Giles interjected. "If Jamie has indeed gone overland, he may already be there…somewhere. Cornwall is a large area to search, and I do not have much time."

Hugh nodded. "I will let you know what I decide. 'Tis not every day a man is asked to betray his brother."

"Or offered the richest estate in England," Oxford added.

Despite a nearly sleepless night, Emmeline was up at dawn, harried by the long list of tasks she'd compiled to keep her mind from the problems she couldn't fix. She broke her fast on ale and Molly's brown bread while she took stock of the business transacted while she was in London. Peter had neatly recorded each sale in Emmeline's ledger. Comparing what had been sold against her stock, she hastily wrote out a list of those herbs and spices that would need replenishing.

The kitchen herbs like sweet basil and thyme were not in great demand this time of year, for they were ready to harvest in the small gardens behind many of Derry's homes. The imported spices, black and white pepper, cumin, coriander and nutmeg were always popular, thus Emmeline's mother had taught her to keep a goodly supply on hand. Thinking of the bags and crocks below in the locked storeroom reminded her of her prisoner.

How fared he this morning? Did his wound still bleed?

Had he become fevered? She should have gone down and tended him herself this morn. Sending Molly and Toby in her stead had been an unprecedented cowardly act. She always faced up to her responsibilities. Always. The more distasteful she found a deed, the quicker she was to take it on. To prove she was not her father's daughter. She was good, and—

Good, ha! She'd kidnapped a man and was holding him prisoner. The enormity of her crime had kept her tossing all night. She, who had always prided herself on her honor and honesty, had committed so many sins the priest would have her reciting the rosary for the rest of her life.

"Mistress?" Peter stuck his head into the room. "There's a Lady Ella without asking for your rosewater cream. I told her we had none to hand, and she insisted on speaking with you."

Emmeline blinked and took down the appropriate crock from the shelf above her worktable. She'd made up a full batch of the cream before leaving for London; now the jar was nearly empty. "Drat. I'd best come and see if I can send some to her later."

She rose and walked quickly into the shop. Sunlight streamed in through the open front window onto the counter behind which she or Peter stood to weigh purchases. From there they could also watch over the bundles of herbs displayed on the trestle table outside the shop. Crocks and baskets on the counter held the more fragile items—dried marigold, chamomile and lavender flowers, seeds of anise, cumin and fennel.

Lady Ella waited outside on a milk-white mare, flanked by no less than five liveried retainers. The costly fabric of her dark blue gown reinforced the impression of wealth; her cold expression warned she'd be haughty and difficult.

Emmeline sighed. Though her mother had never minded

it, she resented having to bow and scrape to ill-mannered nobles. Money and lofty bloodlines did not give people the right to snap and cuff at those in the lower classes. Or to murder them. Nay, she must stop thinking about Jamie, or she'd go mad. Pasting on a smile, she curtsied. "How may I serve you, my lady?"

The lady glared down her nose as she might at a bug. "Lady Helena de Boise praised your rosewater cream. As I was in the area, I thought to try some, but he says there is none."

"That particular cream is quite popular with those desiring to soften their skin," Emmeline said, noting the dry patches on the lady's high cheekbones. "I could send some to your lodgings."

"I leave for home in two days," the lady said curtly. "And I wouldn't purchase that which I hadn't tried first."

"Nor would I want you to." Emmeline's mind whirred. If the woman liked the cream, she'd purchase a large supply to take with her. And pay in coins. Which might be used to get rid of Cedric. "I do have a small bit left, if milady would like a sample," she said in her most servile voice. "I will make up more today, and have it ready by this evening. You have only to send word you would like some and it can be packaged for travel."

The lady frowned, clearly surprised by the unusual offer. "I suppose I could, but I have other errands to attend."

"Ah, but none so important as guarding milady's natural beauty from the elements," Emmeline purred, hating every word. She felt as deceitful as…nay, she'd not think of him. "'Twill take me only a moment." She ran inside, hastily scooped the cream into a small pot and returned with it wrapped in a leather pouch.

Lady Ella looked at the offering, sniffed and motioned for her maid to take it. *Ingrate.*

"I wish you good day," Emmeline murmured, curtsying.

"I'll send word if 'tis satisfactory." Nose in the air, Lady Ella wheeled her mount and spurred off, heedless of the pedestrians scrambling to get out of her way.

Emmeline turned toward the shop and found her way blocked by Cedric. In his hands, he held a small, leather-bound ledger. "Where did you get that?" she demanded, making a grab for it.

He held it away. "I found it in the bottom of a chest."

"How dare you go through my private papers."

"A daughter should not keep secrets from her father."

"Thief! You were looking for money." She tried again, but he held the book over his head like a child playing Keep Away.

"Actually, the verse is quite good. I'd not have credited you with having such a romantic nature. You were always such a serious child, always frowning and working."

"Not always. But I found little to laugh about after my twelfth year."

"'Twas not my fault Olivia followed me."

Emmeline kicked him in the shins, and snatched the book away when he grunted and lowered his hands. Stuffing it into the waistband of her skirt, she glared at him. "Do not meddle further in my business or I will have Toby bar you from my home."

Cedric scowled. "You will be glad I did when you hear what I have discovered. Your maid is stealing from you."

"Molly? She's as loyal to me as she was to Mama."

"Small wonder we never had any money, then. No telling how long the wench has been at her dirty tricks." He leaned closer, the sour wine on his breath making her eyes water. "She's come back from the market with twice what's needed to feed us. Doubtless she sells the extra food and lines her pockets.''

Emmeline knew exactly where that food was going. ''I—I'll have word with her, but I'm certain 'tis just that you are here and she didn't want you to go hungry.''

''Bah. That bitch has always hated me. She'd be only too happy to watch me starve.'' He scowled. ''She's made up a tray of food, too. Are you planning to eat in the shop or in your room?''

Emmeline suppressed a groan. ''Why don't you take a cup of wine before dinner, and I'll have a word with Molly.'' She forced herself to walk calmly to the kitchen. There she found Molly sweating over a pot of jugged hare. On the table sat the tray holding a single bowl and a hunk of bread. ''Oh, Molly…''

''What?'' She turned, face red, spoon dripping gravy.

Emmeline sank onto the bench beside the table. ''The tray. Cedric saw it and began asking questions.''

''Oh, dear. I—I never thought…what did ye say?''

''I lied, of course. I'm getting quite good at it.'' Her voice caught. ''*Dieu,* but I hate this. The lies, the fear of discovery.'' The seductive attraction of the tiger she'd caged in her cellar. ''It all started so simply. I'd hold him, he'd confess, Sir Thomas would arrest him. Now everything is so complicated. He is not at all what I expected, and I—I am so confused.''

''There, there.'' Molly patted her shoulder.

''What will I do if he doesn't confess? I dare not release him. God knows what he'd do. Burn the shop…kill us all…''

''Mayhap ye could appeal to Sir Thomas.''

''Tell the sheriff of London that I kidnapped the son of a noble family, the nephew of an earl?''

''Well…'' Molly straightened. ''It's early days, yet, and

he's that anxious to be released. When Toby and I took him his vitals this morn, he offered us money if we'd let him loose.''

"Where would he get money?" Toby had searched his person and the leather pack on his saddle for incriminating evidence before stabling the stallion with the blacksmith at the edge of town.

"Dunno. We refused, of course, but that didn't stop the man from insisting he was being kept from important business. Toby thinks he's expecting a shipment of smuggled goods. Too bad it isn't a hanging offense, or ye could let him go and arrange to have him caught for that at least.''

"'Tis a thought, but I won't rest easy and neither, I think, will poor Celia, till he's tried for her murder. Hide the tray till after we've dined. Mayhap Cedric will be deep in his cups by then and I'll go below to see Harcourt for myself.''

Emmeline dragged herself back up to the solar and endured a seemingly endless meal with Cedric. His interest in the food seemed perfunctory, his hooded gaze too sharp for her comfort. For once she actually urged him to swill her best wine, hoping he'd drink himself senseless. She breathed a sigh of relief when he pushed aside his empty bowl and retreated to the hearth with what remained of the bottle. Still she didn't stir from the table till his head dropped to his chest and his snores filled the sunny chamber.

Emmeline was absurdly glad Molly had insisted on carrying the tray for her. 'Twas lowering to admit she needed a buffer between herself and a man, but after the way she'd acted...she shuddered as the shameful memory resurfaced. With it came a fire in her blood and that horrible melting sensation in her belly. Passion. She'd read countless verses on romance, even penned a few of her own in secret. But they were tales of a gallant knight's courtly devotion to his lady, not the fevered gropings of a one-eyed rogue.

She shivered again. The cellar seemed especially oppressive, the darkness swallowing up the light from the torch she held aloft. Her hand shook slightly as she bent to unlock the door. As she pushed it open, she heard a furtive rustling and hesitated, recalling the vermin he'd complained of this morn.

"I'll go first if ye like, mistress," Molly murmured.

"Nay." Determined to show no weakness before him, she swept into the room. Her steps faltered when she saw how still he lay beneath the blanket. His head was turned away from her; rusty smudges edged the metal cuffs on his wrists and ankles. Blood. Her soft cry echoed off the stone walls as she hurried over to kneel beside him. "Oh, dear." She reached out—

He rose like a hungry trout, grabbed her shoulders and flung her onto her back so quickly she barely had time to gasp. As the clatter of chains died away, Emmeline found herself once again pinned to the floor beneath his considerable weight.

"Mistress!" Molly shrieked. The tray crashed onto the hard-packed earth.

"Back," Jamie warned. Something cold pressed against Emmeline's throat. "I'd hate to mar such delicate flesh, but…"

"Run for help!" Emmeline cried.

"Move and she dies," Jamie countered. He watched the maid sidle into the corner and sit where he'd commanded, all-too aware of the woman lying beneath him. Her heart beat against his like the wings of a trapped bird. She was softer than he remembered. More womanly. Chilled from countless hours on the icy floor, his body soaked the heat from hers like a greedy sponge. She felt good, so damned good he was loath to move.

"Do you intend to crush me to death?" she snapped.

Jamie grinned. "Ah, but what a pleasurable way to go. *La petite mort*, the French call it."

"Is that all you ever think of?"

"Given our positions, 'tis difficult to think of anything else. Still I am pressed for time." He levered himself onto his knees, straddling her waist and keeping the blade near her throat. It was white and smooth, he noted, the beat of her pulse frantic in the hollow. Her fear sickened him. "I do not like to threaten you, but nothing I say will convince you I didn't kill Celia, and I cannot linger here."

"Your attack on me strengthens my belief in your guilt."

"Jesu, but you are the most stubborn of women."

"I want justice."

"You have it, then, for I am not guilty."

"You are a skilled liar, sir, and I despise you." Her mouth flattened into a thin line, but he recalled all-too vividly how full and ripe those lips had felt beneath his own. She was such an intriguing contradiction, a cool, self-possessed woman who seemed unaware of her own passionate nature. Would that he could be the one to awaken her. Impossible.

"Fascinating as this has been, I fear I must be on my way." Snatching up the nearest cuff, Jamie shackled her wrist.

"I will follow you," she warned. Though she sprawled before him like a slave, her expression blazed pure defiance. And a will he'd do well not to underestimate.

"Not if I lock you in and take the key."

She stared at him in dawning horror. "You'd leave us here?"

"Aye," he replied, ignoring the tug of her fear. "Mayhap a few days in the dark with the rats will convince you to leave the matter of judging a man's guilt to the officers of the court." He climbed to his feet, swayed and steadied himself on the wall. The weakness was due to inactivity and loss of blood, but he wasn't fevered, thank God. For which he had the apothecary to thank. What manner of woman carefully stitched and tended the wound of a man she believed had killed her beloved sister?

"I will find a way to follow you."

Jamie sighed and raked a filthy hand though his equally disreputable hair. "Now I really will have to lock you up."

"Lock who up?" asked a voice from the doorway.

Jamie whirled, the ridiculously small eating knife in his hand, just as a skinny man ducked into the room. "Who the hell are you?" Jamie demanded.

"I'm Emmeline's father. Who are you and what is…?"

"Run, Cedric!" Emmeline cried. "Get out and lock the door."

Cedric leapt like a scalded cat and was out the door before Jamie could plunge across the room. The grating of the key in the lock said the old man was as quick with his hands as his feet.

Cursing under his breath, Jamie tried the latch anyway. It held fast. "I've got your daughter and her maid in here."

"Never mind us," Emmeline shouted. "Run for the soldiers."

"Shut up!" Jamie snarled, torn between stuffing a rag in her mouth and battering down the door with his bare fists.

"Who the hell is he?" Cedric's muffled voice inquired.

Emmeline shouted, "James Harcourt…Celia's murderer."

"I am not. I'm innocent." Jamie and Emmeline glared

at each other across the room, while the maid sat goggle-
eyed as a spectator at a bearbaiting. Ignoring the women,
Jamie turned his attention to getting out. "I wasn't even
in London when Celia died. Sir Thomas Burton himself
investigated and cleared me. But I cannot make this stubborn woman believe me."

"She is stubborn," Cedric allowed. "Does she have
proof?"

"Not a shred."

"He was seeing Celia. She was carrying his child,
he—"

"Lies!" Jamie cried. Frustration made him clench his
teeth so hard his jaw ached. Damn. Had he not lingered
to trade insults with Emmeline he'd have been out before
Cedric arrived. Then he recalled a few words Molly and
Toby had exchanged when they'd brought him his morning
meal.

"Poor Emmeline is always miserable when Cedric
shows up. He knows she doesn't want him here, but he
says he can't leave till he has ten pounds," Molly had
said, giving Jamie the impression Cedric was a creditor or
a difficult customer.

Jamie didn't have ten pounds with him, but he did have
six gold florins, three hidden in each boot. Emergency
funds. And this was clearly an emergency. The boots were
on the worktable with his neatly folded tunic. He retrieved
them, startled to note they'd been washed. Of his chain
mail, there was no sign. Likely it was with Neptune. He'd
need to find the stallion, but first things first. "I'd pay you
well if you'd release me, Cedric."

"Nay!" Emmeline exclaimed.

There was a slight pause, then Cedric showed he was
far less honorable than his daughter. "How much?"

It took only moments to strike a deal, but as he walked

out of the storeroom, Jamie had more respect for the loudly raging Mistress Emmeline than for her greedy father. "I am sorry," he called to her over his shoulder.

"Not as sorry as you are going to be," Emmeline shouted.

Self-preservation made him turn back and lock the door before going in search of his stallion.

Chapter Six

Jamie and Cedric were both long gone by the time Toby returned from his errand and released Emmeline and Molly from the storeroom. By then, Emmeline's anger had burned down to red-hot coals, and a plan had solidified in her mind.

"But ye can't go after him!" Molly cried.

"I can and I will." Emmeline shimmied into a pair of Peter's hose, then pulled on his second-best tunic. The former was too small, the latter too large. Which was all to the good, for the knee-length folds hid the curves the hose defined. "What do you think? Will I pass as a boy?"

"Not in a hundred years," Molly snapped.

Emmeline sighed and hugged the woman who had been both maid and mentor to her after her mother died. "I know you have only my welfare at heart, but please don't fight me on this. We cannot give up now just because Cedric sold us out. I will take Toby with me. We may reach London ahead of Harcourt for we'll be riding that great beast of his, and he has only Cedric's sorry nag." She was glad now that she'd had the foresight to stable the stallion with the smith to avoid raising questions.

"How will ye know where to go?" Molly asked after Toby had gone to retrieve the horse.

"Grandfather's men learned much about James's habits." She knew what inns he frequented, the name of his factor and the name of his ship, as well. She'd find him.

"But what will we tell the customers?"

"That I have gone to buy spices so that they might have the freshest available," Emmeline said. "Now braid my hair as tight as you can and pin it under Peter's cap." Molly was right, she thought, glancing at the swell of her breasts beneath the tunic. She'd not pass for a boy, but as they'd be traveling swiftly and mostly at night, no one would look too closely at her.

Emmeline's step was light, her spirit fired by the righteousness of her cause as she mounted behind Toby. But an hour of bouncing over the rutted roads dimmed her enthusiasm. Merciful heavens but she'd be lucky if she could walk by the time they arrived in London. As it happened, her fears were well justified. When Toby drew rein before the Hound and Stag some six hours later, Emmeline slid from the saddle and collapsed in an ignominious heap in the crowded courtyard of the inn.

"Lord. I should have listened to Molly and left ye at home," Toby muttered. "Here, let me carry ye inside."

"Nay. 'Twould draw more attention," she whispered, conscious of the curious stares they were already getting. Just her luck, the evening was warm and half the city seemed to be crowded into the inn's cobbled courtyard. Smoky torches had been set around the perimeter. The flickering light reflected on knots of men who stood about drinking and joking. One nearby patron made a ribald comment about her likely relationship with Toby. The others laughed and turned away.

"Give me a hand up," Emmeline said. "I'll be fine

once I've moved about a bit." She had to be, because there was nowhere to hide. Her abused muscles protested as Toby hauled her to her feet. She groaned and covertly rubbed her prickling backside.

The stable man materialized beside Toby and demanded, "What's the likes of ye doing with such a fine beast?"

Physical discomfort forgotten, Emmeline nudged Toby, who promptly repeated his rehearsed speech. "Milord's ship is due in any day. He sent word we was to meet him here with his—"

"Right. There's no room inside at present, what with the crowd come for the cockfight, but I can put him in the lean-to out back till the morrow when this lot leaves."

Toby nodded, gave the man a coin for the stallion's care and herded Emmeline toward the inn.

"Ye won't be finding any rooms, neither," the groom called after them. "Not till tomorrow."

"We can bed down with the horse for one night," Toby replied, though in truth they had no intention of staying. This was the inn James Harcourt was known to frequent and a good place to leave the horse, who would only be a hindrance on the crowded streets if they needed to expand their search to another tavern.

As they reached the front of the inn, a young woman burst from the shadows at the corner of the building. The bodice of her gown was ripped, exposing one bare breast; her hair was loose and tangled. A man hurtled after her, grabbing at her skirts.

"Get away! Let me go," she cried.

"Not till I've got what ye promised me." He grabbed the girl and tossed her over his shoulder.

"I didn't...I'm not a whore." The woman glanced around wildly, fists flailing at the man's back. "Let me go!"

The men who bothered to turn around looked frankly envious. Several were apparently friends of the captor, for they shouted encouragement and offered to help him with his prize.

"Toby." Emmeline tugged on his sleeve. "We've got to help."

"Nay." He covered her hand with his. "It pains me to say this, but there's too many of them. Even did we get her away from the bastard, we'd never escape his friends." He swore as the girl was carried off through the cheering throng.

Emmeline leaned her forehead against the solid mass of his arm. She felt sick inside, sick with loathing for men in general and for the vulnerability of women. She wasn't aware of moving, yet when she raised her head she saw Toby had maneuvered them into the shadows, out of the way of the milling crowd and, hopefully, out of sight.

"We should leave," he said hoarsely.

She shook her head. "I—I am fine. It just unnerved me to see her treated so and know we dared not help."

"'Tis at times like these I'm not proud to be a man. Mayhap if I went after them…"

This time Emmeline restrained him. "Nay. You are right. It would be hopeless and only end up with both of us hurt."

Toby sighed and looked around. "Don't see how we'll spot Harcourt in this press," he grumbled.

"He's taller than most of these men," Emmeline replied absently, up on her toes and scanning the crowd. "And that eye patch of his makes him noticeable."

"Aye, and unforgettable. What say we step inside and see if the innkeeper recalls seeing him?"

Emmeline hesitated. What if her disguise didn't stand

up under the light inside? The idea of being caught and abducted like that poor girl made her skin crawl.

"Wait here where 'tis safe," Toby said as though he'd read her mind. "I'll nip in quick and careful. Be back in a flash."

She hated letting Toby go alone, but if there was trouble, it could cost them both dearly. So she crouched where he instructed, behind a thick yew bush, her back to the inn, body as cold as the stone wall she leaned against. The seconds seemed to drag by. Tension drew her nerves tight as a harp string. At any moment, she expected someone to broach her hiding place and drag her off to be ravished.

The arrival of several horses scattered her thoughts.

"Wait here while I see if my friend has yet arrived." The voice was deep, smooth and vibrant with authority.

"Aye, milord."

Some peer of the realm come to watch the cockfights, no doubt. Curious, Emmeline peered gingerly from her bower. Ten men had ridden in and now sat to her left, at the edge of the crowd. Odd they had not dismounted. They were plainly dressed, but their alertness fairly screamed "soldier" as did the long swords at their sides and the glint of mail beneath their dark tunics. As she puzzled over this, one of the men tossed the reins of his mount to another and walked toward the inn. He was not overly tall, but had the arrogant bearing of a prince.

His path took him beneath one of the torches, and she saw he was younger than she'd thought. Twenty, mayhap, his red hair and beard cropped close. His eyes, a startling blue against his tanned face. 'Twas Henry Bolingbroke, the Earl of Derby. Her grandfather had pointed him out to her one day on a London street and mentioned the rumors he was after his cousin's throne.

Emmeline straightened, senses tingling. Some instinct

hinted this man could be here to meet James Harcourt. The notion grew when instead of entering the inn, the earl turned right just short of her position and took the path that led between the inn and the stables. Should she follow? Or wait for Toby and possibly risk losing her quarry? The debate was a short one.

Jamie waited until his contact had walked by the back of the stables before he stepped onto the path. "Harry?"

Henry of Bolingbrook whirled, one hand drawing his sword. "Jamie!" he whispered. Resheathing his weapon, he clasped Jamie in a rib-crunching hug, then stepped back and continued in a hoarse rasp, "By God, when you didn't show up as expected, I was afraid Oxford had arrested you. I rowed out to the *Lady,* and Captain Donaldson said you'd gone to your parents'. We sent a man to Harte Court, and he brought word you'd left with a woman. Damn, how could you endanger our mission for a bit of pleasure?"

"I didn't go willingly, and it was no pleasure." Jamie's gut burned with latent fury. "It took a while to extricate myself from the situation. I was afraid you'd not still be waiting."

"Well, when we heard about the woman, I figured you would show up eventually. I came back last night, waited an hour then left. If you hadn't come tonight, Donaldson was going to send men into London to search for you." He eyed Jamie's wrinkled, stained clothes. "You look as though you've been beset by brigands. Are you certain this has naught to do with our plans?"

"Aye. I'm positive of it."

"That's a relief." Henry, Earl of Derby and eldest of John of Gaunt's vast brood, sighed. "Jesu, but I wish Papa had not gone off and left us with this impossible scheme of his."

"Having second thoughts?"

"Nay, I've reached third or fourth. And you? You are the one whose neck is stretched out the farthest."

Jamie put a hand to his throat and groaned. "Could you not have found a more delicate way to phrase that?"

Harry chuckled. "You know I am better with a sword than with words." True, he was a skilled warrior like his father, but he'd also inherited Lancaster's wit, cunning and ambitious nature. He'd make a far better king than his cousin Richard.

"All the time we spent listening to Geoffrey recite his verse and none of it rubbed off on you?" Chaucer had also been attached to Lancaster's household, his poetry and translations of French verse such as "The Romance of the Rose" meant to round out the courtly education of the boys fostered there.

"I am content to leave such pursuits to rogues like you, who employ poor Geoffrey's art to seduce the ladies." Henry's mocking grin robbed the words of their sting, then he sobered. "Oxford suspects something. He has had men watching my house."

"And Giles Cadwell came uninvited to my mother's birthday fete. He accused me of smuggling and said he has men searching the coast for proof."

"Do they know about the ships, do you think?"

"Not yet," Jamie said. "But we must be very careful."

"Aye. Which brings us to your rendezvous with Simon DeGrys. Has it been compromised by this delay?"

"Not if I can reach Cornwall in two days' time." He looked up at the starless sky and smelled the rain in the heavy air. "There's a storm brewing, but I think we can outrun it if we sail on the evening tide instead of waiting till morn."

"Sail at night? Isn't that dangerous?"

"Let us say it takes guts and experience. My crew and I have plenty of both...and a powerful reason to take the risk."

A sound came from somewhere on the far side of the barn.

One of your men? Jamie asked with a look.

Harry shook his head, eyes popping with apprehension.

Keep talking, Jamie mouthed. He moved to the corner of the building and crouched beside the wagon parked there. The sounds from the inn intruded faintly, mingling with Harry's litany of nonsense about the fall weather. He ignored both and fancied he heard the catch of soft, frantic breathing in the shadows. Someone *was* watching them.

Drawing the blade from his boot, Jamie slipped under the wagon, then stopped, senses alert, muscles tensed to spring the moment he was certain...ah, there it was. A furtive movement in the blackness; a sob scarcely above a whisper. Soundless as the night, he launched himself at the spy. He had a brief glimpse of a pale face and wide eyes before their bodies collided.

The impact drew a faint "oof" from the would-be attacker. Then an even softer cry of alarm. It was muffled as Jamie's hand instinctively closed over the man's mouth. The bastard's head hit the ground with a thunk, and his struggles stilled.

"Serves you right," Jamie growled, sitting up.

"Jamie?" Harry called softly.

"I have him," Jamie whispered. "He's knocked himself out, thank God. Leave as quick as you can."

"But I have nine men with me, we could—"

"Nay. You know it's imperative your involvement be kept secret." Jamie hoisted the limp bundle over his shoulder and trotted out to face his accomplice. "I'll take him out to the *Lady* and question him in private there. It'll provide excellent cover. The first mate returning with a drunken crewman.'' He readjusted the burden. ''By the heft of him, he's just a lad.''

''Children make the most dangerous spies,'' Harry said ominously. ''No one suspects them.''

''Agreed,'' Jamie murmured. The lad's limp form weighed heavily on his conscience. Damn. Who had sent this child on such a risky mission? ''I'll see he's in no position to jeopardize our plans.''

''I like it no more than you, but needs must.'' Harry laid a hand on Jamie's other shoulder and squeezed gently. ''Thank you, my friend. 'Tis a perilous course we've set ourselves on, but I know you've the courage and cleverness to see it through.''

Jamie dredged up a smile. ''I pray you are right. Things were dicey enough without this delay. If I am not there to greet him, DeGrys may lose what little guts he possesses and run back to France with his tail betwixt his legs.'' He turned to leave, then looked back. ''If aught should happen to me, would you find some way to tell my family...'' What? That he regretted not being the son and brother he should have been.

The lines in Harry's face deepened, and his massive shoulders sagged. ''I owe you that and more, but you know what would happen if anyone learned what we were about.''

Heads would roll...quite literally. Jamie grimaced. ''Just tell them that I did love them, and my last thoughts were of them.''

''Jamie...'' Harry held out a hand. ''If you've any doubts...if you are afraid...''

''I've doubts and fears aplenty.'' But he was in too deep, had been from the first moment Lancaster had approached him with this plan. And he knew too much. They could no more let him walk away from this than Harry could stand at the top of the White Tower and scream the truth aloud for all of London to hear. "'Tis what keeps my wits sharp," Jamie added with a mocking grin. "I'll not let your father down, and we will win." They had to, because to lose would cost them all their lives.

Raising a hand in silent pledge, Jamie turned and walked away into the night. He knew every back alley and used these mean streets to reach the harbor in record time. His nostrils were filled with the stench of rotting garbage, his spirits depressed by the squalor of the closely packed tenements. The stink of fish was almost welcome.

The body on his shoulder showed signs of life, twitching a bit as Jamie crossed the docks and descended the stone steps to the beach. He tightened his grip and quickened his pace toward the end of the quay. When he saw the boat drawn up on the rocky beach, he breathed a sigh of relief. Trust Donaldson to follow orders to the letter.

"Evening, lads," Jamie drawled, grinning as the five men who'd been lounging in the boat leapt up.

"Milord!" They clustered around him like eager pups.

"God, ye gave us a turn," Red Ranold exclaimed. "What's that ye're carrying?"

"Likely a lass." Alain MacNab jabbed Ranold in the ribs and winked broadly. "Told ye that's what had delayed him."

"Nay, 'tis not a woman. It's a spy I..." He tensed as the bundle on his shoulder shifted. "Explanations'll wait till we're aboard ship."

Alain nodded. "We'll have to hurry if we're to catch the tide. Donaldson's had us waiting here every night. He said if ye didna come tonight, we'd miss the rendezvous with the Frenchman." He reached to take the lad from Jamie, but the bundle suddenly exploded into a welter of milling limbs. A foot in the gut felled Alain, and the lad tumbled to the ground between them.

Clearly stunned, the boy lay on his back, eyes open, gasping for breath. Even in this dim light, he looked...

Jamie swore and went down on one knee, recognition bolting through him with stunning intensity. "By all that's holy, what in the hell are you doing here?"

Emmeline Spencer groaned softly. Welling tears magnified the frightened eyes she turned on him. "Traitor," she croaked. "You're not only a murderer, you're a traitor to the crown, you and Henry of Bolingbroke."

Traitor. Jamie sat back on his heels. Any doubts he might have had about the little spy having seen him with Harry vanished under her accusation. He shook his head slowly, regretfully, then looked up at Alain. "Bind her. She goes with us."

Chapter Seven

She was going to die.

Emmeline sagged against the rough plank door of the master cabin, terrified but too exhausted, in mind and body, to move.

"I'll be back," Jamie had growled before locking her in.

Back to kill her.

He'd wanted to strangle her. His intent had been clear in the fierceness of his expression when she'd mentioned Bolingbroke. When was she going to learn to keep her mouth shut? The only reason he hadn't killed her on the beach, she reasoned, was because it would be so much easier to dispose of her at sea.

Emmeline's empty belly rolled up into her throat. Then she realized it was the sway of the ship, moving beneath her feet. They were sailing.

Her instinct for survival drove her into action. Fighting the pitch of the ship, she groped her way around her tiny prison. Her luxurious prison. Harcourt's love of fine things was evident in the intricately carved desk that occupied one corner and the velvet-draped bunk that filled the other. 'Twas a satyr's bed. No surprise. What shocked her was the prick of jealousy she felt at imagining his big, tanned body tangling with another woman's.

Disconcerted, she turned away. Matching curtains were drawn over the wall beside the bed, but only one upper section of the mullioned window they covered opened. The urge to break the glass and jump died aborning; she couldn't swim. Still she stared longingly at the phosphorescent wake. If worse came to worst...

The grating of the key in the lock brought her around just as her nemesis strolled in. He'd changed into fresh tunic and hose but still wore the same grim expression.

"Thinking of jumping?" he drawled.

Emmeline trembled but stood her ground. "'Twould likely save you a bit of trouble. So I won't. Anything to inconvenience you."

"You are more than an inconvenience." He crossed to her, his presence filling the cabin, his intensity sucking the air from it. He stopped so close the toes of his boots nudged the tips of hers. "Why in God's name didn't you stay at home? And how did you happen to be at the Hound?"

"'Twas not by chance. I know you often stay there." His mouth gaped with such satisfying astonishment she had to add a few other details. "With the help of Grandfather's contacts, I learned much about your habits. Men like you take no notice of tradesmen and servants coming and going," she said scathingly. "But they see much, and you stick out, even in a crowded city like London." She gazed pointedly at the patch over his eye.

"Damn," he breathed, shaking his head. It wasn't a curse, more like admiration. Nay, she must be mistaken. She'd caused him no end of trouble. He smiled ruefully. "You've the makings of a good spy. Pity you could not have put your cleverness to a safer use. How much did you overhear?''

"Enough to know you and Bolingbroke are up to something. Grandfather says he aspires to Richard's throne. I hope they catch you. I'd very much like to see you drawn and quartered.''

"Ah, bloodthirsty to the end. I admire your tenacity, if not your forbearance. 'Tis not wise to tell your enemy all you know of him." He gave her a roguish smile. The one that made her pulse hitch despite her immunity to his kind. "Turn around.''

"Would you strangle me with a smile on your lips?''

"What better way to go? Easy, do not tremble." He touched a finger to her nose. "Your poor opinion of me cut deep, and I but sought to make you squirm. Ungallant, but then... I only want to see if your head was gashed when it struck the ground.''

"Oh." Dizzy with relief, she turned, but the feel of his fingers sliding along her scalp was torture of another sort. A syrupy warmth drifted down her neck; she wanted to lean back and give herself over to his caress. "Can you not hurry?''

"You've a knot. Does this hurt?" He touched her gently.

Emmeline jerked. "Of course it does.''

He backed her up a few steps, sat on the edge of the bunk and examined her head again. "Poor Emma.''

"Emmeline.''

"Hmm." From a drawer beneath the bunk, he produced a cloth and a leather flask with which he moistened it. "This may sting.''

"Ouch!" She tried to escape, but he held her fast in the vee of his powerful legs. "What was that... liquid fire?''

"Nearly. 'Tis whiskey... from Scotland. Good for

cleansing a man inside or out. I do not think 'twill require stitching.''

"Pity, I'm certain you'd enjoy sticking a needle in me."

"A needle...nay, though there are other things I'd rather—''

"Unhand me!" She tried, futilely, to escape.

"Not just yet, Emma. First we are going to talk."

"Emmeline."

He turned her and sat her down on one muscular thigh. "That name does not suit you. 'Tis too formal and stuffy for a lady with your spirit and passion."

Emmeline's mouth gaped open. She snapped it shut. "You know naught about me," she sputtered.

"You forget, I've sampled that fire you seem so determined to hide." He glanced briefly at her mouth, a subtle reminder of the devastating kiss they'd shared. When his gaze returned to hers, its intensity was anything but subtle. Blatant desire flared in that single midnight eye.

Emmeline gasped sharply as an answering heat streaked through her. It sank deep, warming some hidden core of herself she'd been blissfully unaware existed until he touched her. Like a sleeping dragon, the seed unfurled again, spreading the flames. "Nay," she whispered, denying the rush of sensation. The feelings she hadn't wanted to have for any man, but especially for him.

"Aye." He lifted a lock of hair and rubbed it between his fingers. "Fine and silky," he murmured. "But strong, like you. Had I realized there was so much red mixed in with the brown, I'd have known you'd be trouble. *Red of head, fiery of heart.*"

Emmeline put up a hand to hold him off, but instead her fingers clung to the wool stretched taut across his chest. Beneath her palm, his heart thundered to the same wild, staccato beat as her own. "I am not like that."

"Aye, you are, and we both know it." He caught hold of her shoulders and drew her closer, trapping her hands between them. His expression as he looked down at her was as anguished as her own rioting emotions.

"What is happening?" she cried.

"We are," he said simply.

Emmeline didn't even pretend to misunderstand what he meant. Trembling, she fought for her sanity, her soul. From the time she'd been old enough to understand the hold Cedric had over her mother, she'd been determined to steer clear of that trap. "Nay, she whispered. "It cannot be. I…you…I do not even like you."

He sighed and bent his head. For one horrified moment she feared he meant to kiss her. But he only rested his forehead against hers. "I know. This is all wrong. We are wrong. I thought I could ignore it, but you had to follow me. When I saw you lying there on the beach…bloody hell! Why couldn't you have stayed safe at home?" His cry seemed to come from the heart, and it pierced hers to the quick. "Damn." He sighed. The tremors that shook him hinted at some intense struggle.

She understood it, for the same battle was being waged inside her. She could not, would not succumb to the lure that had been woman's undoing since the time of Eve. To think she had almost weakened, and toward him. He who was her enemy. Goaded by fear and anger, she fought back. "You mistake the matter. The passion that fires me is hatred. Doubtless you cannot conceive of a woman who fails to fall into your arms at first sight, but know this. I'd rather die than be anywhere near Celia's murderer."

He stiffened and drew back so their gazes met, locked.

"I did not kill her." Laying a hand on his heart, he added, "'If I do lie to you in this, / I pray to Mars to so repay me / That shame and death may befall me, and death / Strike down my family in that same breath.'"

Emmeline stared at him. "I know that verse. I've heard it, or something very like it, before."

"I altered it a bit to suit this occasion, but 'twas composed by a man who lived in Lancaster's household where I fostered. Geoffrey Chaucer. Do you know of him?"

She nodded and finished the stanza. "'And that my soul after death may go / And wander nightly to and fro, / And may I forever bear a traitor's name.'"

"You've read him."

"Aye." Emmeline frowned, unable to believe he had met Chaucer. "My grandfather gave me two of his works. *The Legend of Good Women*." That was the source of the verse he had quoted. "And *The Book of the Duchess*."

"What of romances, do you care for them?"

Emmeline flushed, thinking of the poems she'd written so long ago, emotional verses chronicling the most impossible of fantasies...the love of a gallant, honorable hero for his ladylove. "I—I like those about King Arthur."

He reached again into the drawer and brought out a slim, leather-bound volume. "Here is something you'll not have read. The author is anonymous, but the verses might amuse you."

She looked at the book, then up at him. They were so close she could see the laugh lines crinkling the corners of his good eye and the leather grain on the patch over the left. The contrast was apt, for he seemed to be two men. "I gather this means you aren't going to kill me immediately."

He grinned. "Not immediately."

"Then release me, I swear I won't tell anyone..."

"Ah, I fear I cannot do that, Emma."

"Emmeline. You cannot just change my name."

He chuckled. "Why not, you've slurred mine?"

"Are you never serious?"

"Seldom. Do you never laugh, never make a jest?"

"Seldom."

He laughed again, the rich sound vibrating down her spine like a delicate caress. "We shall have to change that, then."

"You could not." As she tore her gaze from his mesmerizing one, reality intruded. She sat on his knee like a doxy, his hand stroking her back. He'd done it again, made her forget who and what he was. "Oh!" She jumped up and backed toward the door. "Please, you must let me go."

He stood, all traces of laughter fading. "I regret that I cannot. You know too much."

"But I—I have a shop to run, people who depend on me. Toby and Molly will worry about me."

"You should have thought of that before you undertook the mad scheme to follow me. 'Twould seem our roles are reversed, but I have given you a far more comfortable prison than you gave me. I will even leave the light so you'll not have to endure the dark as I did." He gestured toward the tall metal cylinder on the desk. One side was made of thin horn, allowing light from the candle inside to illuminate the room. "The flame is contained and the lantern bolted to the desk, but if the weather turns rough, you should extinguish it."

As the door closed behind him, her knees failed and she sank onto the edge of the bunk. "Sweet Mary. What have I done?" she whispered. Would she ever see her home or Molly and Toby again?

Jamie closed the door behind him, then turned away before he relented and let her go. Much as he hated holding her against her will, she'd seen him with Harry. That in itself was dangerous to both of them, and he could not trust her to keep silent.

The stiffening breeze drove thoughts of Emma from his mind. While he'd been battling one kind of storm, another had been brewing outside. Thick clouds rolled overhead, so close they obscured the top of the mast. Sailors slipped in and out of the mist, tying down the sails. The rumble of thunder propelled Jamie down the stairs from the after-castle to the main deck, where Donaldson met him.

"Looks like we're in for a bit of a blow." The Scots captain's burr had thickened with concern.

"I'll lend a hand with the helm." Jamie ducked under the aftercastle. It was constructed in two tiers, with the lower one providing shelter for the cog's helmsman while he manned the rudder that guided the ship. The upper level held a small quarterdeck and the cabin he'd just left. Jamie spared a brief thought for the woman he'd locked in there. If they couldn't outrace the storm, she was in for a rough maiden voyage. The two words so aptly described his prickly lady that he smiled.

"Grinnin' down the devil, milord?" the helmsman asked.

Jamie blinked, then shook away the image of Emma as he'd last seen her, terrified but too proud and stubborn to show it. He must be insane to want her. Was it only the thrill of the chase that made her seem more desirable than any other woman he'd met? He couldn't afford to find out. "Aye, Sim, you know me, ever one to laugh in the face of danger."

There was no time for teasing after that. The wind abruptly picked up, raising the sea from a chop to a stomach-lurching roll. The *Lady* bobbed about like a cork in a briskly boiling pot. Together, Sim and Jamie battled to keep the tiller steady and the ship plowing straight into the menacing waves. If she turned sideways, she'd founder and capsize. As the night wore on, the storm intensified. Rain pelted the decks, turning them so slick and treacherous the men tied ropes about their waists to keep them from slipping overboard if they fell. Lightning raked the sky, illuminating their struggles in stark, frantic vignettes. More than one man turned to prayer, and Jamie began to wonder if he'd tried the Lord's grace once too often.

He was leaning against the wall of the aftercastle, spelled at the helm by Alain, when a thud sounded above them. Alarmed looks were exchanged. Had the mast split and come down? A scream rose above the pounding rain. A woman's scream.

Emma!

Jamie tore out of the aftercastle and up the stairs just as a slender body slid across the quarterdeck. Mouth wide, hands and arms grasping futilely for purchase on the slick planks, Emma was headed toward the rail. Shouting her name, he flung himself into her path. As they collided, he wrapped one arm around her waist, drawing her into the curve of his body and twisting so his back, not hers, struck the rail.

The impact drove the air from his lungs; pain lanced through his body and black spots blotted out his sight. Fighting to stay conscious, he reviewed his options. He couldn't get them to safety before the ship tilted the other way, sending them back across the deck and likely off the other side. He struggled to get his right arm around the spindle and hung onto it and Emma for dear life. What seemed like hours later, but was really only moments, he guessed, Donaldson reached them.

It took five men, tied securely to one another in a human chain of sorts, to get Jamie and Emma into the cabin.

"Och, ye're enough to turn a man's hair white, laddie," Donaldson grumbled when they were safe. "Ye could have let her go and saved yerself a lot of trouble."

Laid out on his back and gasping like a beached cod, Jamie looked at the bedraggled woman a hand's span away. By the lantern's dim light, he saw her clothes were plastered to her body; her hair clung wetly to her cheeks, black against her bloodless skin. "Likely you're right," he murmured. But he couldn't have let her wash overboard any more than he could lie there nursing his own hurts when she clearly needed help.

"Can you manage without me whilst I get her out of these wet clothes and see that she's all right?" Jamie asked, making certain the patch was secure before sitting up.

Donaldson shook his head and muttered something about hot-blooded young fools. "Aye. This storm's about blown itself out by my reckoning. Tend her, then look to getting yerself dry and warm. I'll call if we've need of ye."

When the door had closed behind his captain, Jamie crawled over to Emma and felt for a pulse. Her skin was cold as ice, the blood beating sluggishly under his fingers. Her eyes opened, black with fear. "A-are we dead?"

He managed a rusty chuckle. "Nay, but 'twas a near thing."

"I su-suppose y-you expect me t-to th-thank you," she said through chattering teeth.

"Nay. I know better than that." He dragged a blanket off the bunk and wrapped it around her despite her feeble attempts to fend him off. "Lie still while I get you out of these wet things or you may yet die of the ague."

"D-don't want your help."

"I know." He bracketed both her icy wrists in one hand and reached under the blanket with the other to strip her. "For the moment, you have no say in the matter. Save your strength to fight off the cold," he added in a gentler voice. "Time enough to hate me again tomorrow when you're stronger."

"I'm strong now," she said, but the effort drained her. Her lashes drifted down, and her head lolled to one side.

"Damn." Jamie flung aside the blanket and tested her pulse again. Slow but steady. Mayhap it was better if she was unconscious while he stripped her bare, even though he was in no condition to be tempted by Circe herself. When he finally managed to wrestle Emma's limp body out of the clinging garments, he discovered that fatigue and numbing cold had not rendered him immune to the lure of her surprisingly lovely body.

She was not for him. She despised him.

But he could change that. There was a connection between them that defied reason and logic…and Emma's hatred.

He'd felt the passion flare in her when they'd kissed and knew he had the skill to fan the flames into a wildfire. He wanted more. He wanted to win her trust…and her heart.

And then what? If he won her, he was doomed to hurt her.

Emmeline floated on a warm, furry cloud. There were things she should be up and doing, but she was loath to leave this cozy nest. Purring contentedly, she arched her back and burrowed deeper.

A rough groan vibrated against her ear. "Don't move."

Her eyes flew open and focused on her pillow. A naked, bronze chest. "Sweet Mary!" She tried to roll away, but her hair was caught, and a heavy log pinned her legs to the mattress.

"Please...I beg you do not move."

She tilted her head, gazed up past a darkly stubbled chin to a horribly familiar sight. A black eye patch. "James?"

"What is left of me."

"Where are we? What is going on? Why am I abed with you?"

"We were sleeping. And there's only one bed."

"A gentleman would have let me have it."

"I am dying, and she gives lessons in chivalry."

"Why are you dying?" she asked suspiciously.

"My back. It feels as though I broke it."

"Oh." Emmeline licked her lips and tasted brine. Memories resurfaced: opening the cabin door and being snatched up by the storm, the slide across the deck, the hard grip of James's arms, the sickening crunch as they hit the rail. He'd broken his back trying to help her. "I'm sorry I left the cabin. I feared the ship would sink, and I'd be trapped within."

"I'm sorry you were afraid," he murmured. Belatedly she realized there was a layer of blankets between them. He had played the gentleman, and he had saved her from drowning.

"'Tis I who am sorry. Is your back truly broken?"

"It feels like it."

"Oh. What can I do to help?"

"A drink would be most welcome...my throat is parched."

"Of course." Emmeline drew her hair out from beneath his bare shoulder and glanced about. Lemony sunshine flooded in through the window, washing over mellow wood planking and a tangled pile of linen towels.

"There's a jug of water on the floor beside the desk."

"I see it." She sat, groaning as her own muscles, abused by the long ride and the slide across the deck, protested. The blanket fell away, revealing her bare breasts. Gasping, she snatched the blanket back up. "Where are my clothes?"

"Drying in the sun with mine."

"I do not recall undressing."

"You had fainted. Could you get the water?" His gaze was perfectly bland.

"I cannot get up without my clothes."

"Wrap the blanket around you like a toga."

"A what?"

"A garment such as the ancient Romans wore. Wrap it around under your arms, then tuck the edge in your lovely bosom."

"My…oh! You *did* undress me!"

"Easy. 'Twas dark and, gallant soul that I am, I kept the blanket over you while I took off your wet things." For once, he sounded serious and sincere.

"Well, 'tis light, now. Close your eyes."

"Eye," he amended, and complied.

How could he be so casual about such a dreadful wound? He must be mad. Emmeline watched him closely as she rose, wrapped the blanket about her and got the jug. He directed her to cups in a desk drawer. She filled one and carried it to him. When she sat on the bunk, the edge of the blanket threatened to pull free. Anchoring it against her chest with one hand, she put the cup to his lips. Water ran down his cheeks and into the pillow.

He smiled up at her helplessly.

Emmeline sighed, let go the blanket and lifted his head. His hair was thick and wavy, a warm brown streaked with sunshine. An odd feeling thrilled through her as she watched him drink. He was her enemy, and yet… She felt connected to him. "More?" she asked when he'd emptied the cup.

"Nay. Thank you."

"Is there anything else you need? Anything I can do?"

"Several things come to mind," he teased. "But my back..."

"I could look at it."

"Do you have a potion to cure me?"

Not if it truly was broken. "Do you think you could turn over, or should I call one of the men?"

"For another such smile, I'd turn handsprings."

His bravery made her smile.

"If I'd known this is what it would take to coax a smile from you, I'd have gotten myself injured ere now."

"This is no jesting matter."

"Indeed. It hurts like hell. If you'll help me onto my belly, you can have your wicked way with me."

Emmeline looked askance at his bare body above the blanket, broad tanned chest, lightly furred with golden hair, wide shoulders and thickly corded arms. Nowhere could she grab hold of him without touching naked male flesh. Steeling herself, she laid her hands on his upper arms. 'Twas like picking up a lighted coal, hot and jolting. She gasped; her fingers tightened but scarcely made a dent in his rock-hard muscles.

Let go. Let go, common sense screamed. But she was powerless to comply.

Dazzled, she raised her eyes and realized he'd felt it, too. His single dark eye reflected her own dawning awareness. "Jamie?"

His smile was crooked, touching. "I think you'd better roll me over before we do something you'll regret."

Emmeline swallowed and nodded mutely. It took surprisingly little effort on her part to get him over, but he groaned mightily. As he flopped onto his stomach, the blanket parted, revealing his back, bare above the linen drawers he wore. "Sweet Mary." She gaped at the livid bruises coloring him from shoulder blades to waist. "'Tis awful. And what are these white lines?"

He glanced over his shoulder. "Souvenirs of my brief stay aboard a Spanish galleon. The lashes hurt, but…here, what is this? Don't weep for me, Emma. I will live."

Emmeline swallowed and wiped furiously at her cheeks. "Of course you will," she said, but the tears continued to fall.

"Shh. I cannot bear to have you cry over a few old scars and some new bruises." He levered himself up on one elbow and gently brushed the tears away.

Mesmerized, she stared at him. His expression was gentle, devoid of teasing or mockery, his gaze lit by the compassion she should be showing him. "Oh, Jamie, I wish there was something I could do to…" She blinked. "How is it you can sit up if your back is broken?"

"It feels broken."

"You…you wretch. It isn't broken."

"You are disappointed I'm not crippled for life?"

"Nay, of course not. But…"

"'Twould it have served me right for what you think I did?"

"Of course not."

"Ah, now you are not being entirely truthful, Emma. You do not know what to make of me. Part of you wants me to be guilty because I am a rogue and a wastrel and also because it would absolve your conscience of Celia's murder."

"My conscience?"

"You are the responsible sort, like Hugh. The two of you feel obliged to take on the world's ills. When something goes wrong, you agonize over what you could have or should have done to prevent it—'' he fingered the eye patch, his expression grim ''—even if you did all you could.''

Emmeline stared at him. ''Who is Hugh? Did he have something to do with the loss of your eye?''

''Hugh is my twin...my perfect brother. But we are not discussing my relationship with my twin. We are discussing you.''

''You are discussing me,'' she retorted. ''And I care no more to have you picking at my past than you obviously do.''

''Fair enough.'' He tossed the blanket aside and climbed gingerly from the bunk, giving her a heart-stopping glimpse of his lower body, the drawers riding precariously low on lean hips, the material clinging to every—

Emmeline gasped and turned away, but the image of his tall, lithe figure and bulging muscles was burned into her brain.

''You need not shrink back in maidenly disgust,'' he drawled. ''I will leave you in peace. But whilst you are reflecting on my supposed crimes, consider whether a man who is capable of choking a woman to death would not also have killed the nosy sister who impugned, kidnapped and generally harassed him.''

Emmeline spun toward him, keeping her gaze safely on his face. ''I suppose you expect me to thank you for last night.''

His expression changed, the anger replaced by a more dangerous light. Desire. '''Tis not your thanks I want, Emma,'' he said silkily.

''You...you are toying with me, trying to confuse me and make me forget why I hate you.''

''Do you? Do you really hate me?'' He crossed the few

steps to the door, movements slow and stiff, so unlike his usual cat's grace she knew he was in pain. One hand on the latch, he turned and murmured, "Search your own heart for the answers. The truth about me lies there." He left, closing the door quietly behind him and leaving her with her thoughts.

Emmeline stared at the door, mind awhirl. Who was he really?

Chapter Eight

Clad once more in Peter's clothes, Emmeline knelt on the window seat, nose pressed to the mullioned panes. The ship had anchored in a small bay, but night had fallen, and all she could see was her own reflection. She stared at it and tried to ignore the rustling sounds from behind her as James dressed to go ashore. 'Twas unnerving to share close quarters with a man. Nay, any other man she could have ignored, but not him. Some fault in her nature urged her to glance over her shoulder and peek at his bare chest. Surely it wasn't as fascinating as she remembered.

Emmeline moved her head and discovered something truly horrible. She could see his reflection in the glass, clad only in formfitting black hose, a matching tunic dangling from one hand. His chest was even broader than she'd remembered, tapering down to a narrow waist and hips. He was as trim and lithe as the huge cat she'd seen in the king's menagerie.

He looked up suddenly. "What do you see?"

"I..." Mouth dry as dust, she looked away. "Naught now, 'tis too dark. But what I saw before the sun set did not look promising. A narrow beach set below steep rock cliffs. A forest so thick it formed a wall of green, and nary a hint of a town or another ship in any direction. Where are we?"

"Cornwall," he replied.

She thought a moment, then whispered, "Camelot."

"Some think this was Arthur's kingdom. Have you read *Mort d'Arthur*?"

"I've heard of it." Excitement spun her about, only to find he now stood but a hand's span away. "Oh." She tried to back up, but the window seat blocked her retreat.

"Easy." He gripped her elbow to steady her. "You have naught to fear from me. We shall have to find you a copy of it."

"Lord James…"

"Jamie, if you cannot bring yourself to call me something more intimate."

"More intimate…?"

"Hmm. I've given the matter some thought today." He released her and pulled on the tunic. "You've gotten yourself into a bit of a tricky situation," he said as his head emerged from the neck hole, hair ruffled but eye patch in place. Did he glue it on? "The only solution is to pretend you are my mistress."

"Your what?" Stunned, she sat on the bench.

"Mistress. 'Twill be an act." He grinned. "Unless, of course, you'd like to make me the happiest man—"

"I'd like to make you a eunuch. Failing that, I'd rather be home in Derry in my own bed. Mistress, of all the mad—"

"Emma." He knelt at her feet and enveloped her icy hands in his warm ones. "You cannot know…and I am not at liberty to tell you…what trouble you've embroiled yourself in. My partners—"

"Bolingbroke and your cohorts in crime, you mean."

She wrenched free of him, stood and stepped around him as she might a pile of filth.

He rose slowly but made no attempt to corner her. "You are mistaken about my meeting with Bolingbroke. Henry has naught to do with what brought me to Cornwall. He is my foster brother and was worried when I disappeared after my mother's fete. The Killigrews of Arwenack, with whom we will be staying, are another matter. They are smugglers and do not take kindly to spies."

"Ha! I knew something illegal brought you here. I will not stay with a band of thieves and smugglers. I insist on staying aboard ship."

He sighed. "Emma, Emma, I regret you have no say in this."

The cabin door flew open and a bear of a man stamped in. She had a brief impression of flowing black hair and rippling muscles before the newcomer grabbed Jamie and thumped him on the back.

Jamie yelped and jumped away like a scalded cat. "Mind my back, you heathen."

"Grown soft in London town, have you? Or did some irate husband catch you where you shouldn't have been and slice you up?" the bear asked, teeth white against his bushy beard.

"I was rescuing a lady, Bran," Jamie said.

"Lady?" The bear swung his head toward the corner where she lurked and looked Emmeline up and down. His scowl deepened. "Damn, you jeopardized our plans for another of your whores."

"Careful how you speak of my betrothed."

"Betrothed!" Emmeline cried, but the sound was drowned out by the bear's shout. He ranted and cursed in a tongue that sounded much like that spoken by the Welsh merchants.

"Enough!" Jamie snapped. "Whatever you may think of my timing in this, you will treat Emma with the respect she is due. She was forced to flee in disguise—" he added, gesturing at her boy's garb "—because her father is against the match."

"He is not the only one," Emmeline said with asperity.

"Poor love." Jamie hugged her so tightly she could scarcely breathe, much less voice her objections. "I know you are tired and frightened, but we'll be ashore soon."

Bran glared at her with open hostility. "You should never have brought this outlander here."

"I'm sorry, Bran," Jamie said gently. "But 'twas needful. She is not like Rosalind, she is kind—"

"Do not mention that bitch's name in my hearing." Bran scowled at Emmeline, then turned on his heel. "I will await you on deck...where the air is cleaner."

The slamming of the door behind him broke her trance. She wriggled free of Jamie's grip and turned on him. "I do not know what you hope to gain by this...this..."

"I am trying to save your life."

She snorted. "More like, you want a convenient bedmate."

"Convenient, ha! There is naught convenient about you."

"Then let me go."

"Think, Emma." He gave her a little shake. "This reckless obsession of yours has landed you in more trouble than you can possibly comprehend. Knowing how I'd feel if the person I *thought* had murdered my brother went unpunished, I've tried to make excuses for your damnable actions. And I've treated you far better than you deserve, considering all you've put at risk, but I cannot let you go free to spill what you know."

"I swear I will not tell anyone anything," she whispered.

"Unfortunately, my enemies would not ask what you knew, they would demand...in a most unpleasant manner."

"Sir Thomas Burton? He'd never torture me."

"Nay, but the Earl of Oxford and his cronies would cut out your heart to get what they want." His hands gentled, stroking her upper arms. His gaze was calm, yet compelling. "Emma, I swear on my mother's soul I did not kill Celia. And I am doing my damnedest to see you do not end up feeding the fish in Fal Bay. But you must help yourself by keeping your mouth closed and doing as I say."

"Y-you would really kill me in cold blood?" she asked.

"I would not willingly harm you in any way, but I...and those with me...must do whatever is needful to see our plans succeed."

The knot of fear in her belly tightened. "C-could you not leave me aboard ship?"

"Nay. The *Lady* sails on the tide, and I'd not trust you to remain aboard once she reached her next port of call. For good or ill, you must stay with me till this thing is finished."

"How long till your ill-gotten goods are come?"

"Three weeks, four at the most."

"So long?" Her heart sank.

"I like it no more than you do, but needs must."

Emmeline hesitated, confused anew by this complex man. "If I am such a trial, why didn't you let me wash overboard yestereve?"

"You know the answer to that." In his gaze flickered the ghosts of what had passed between them before. Needs and yearnings that defied their tangled relationship.

"It...it must have been instinct."

"An instinct as old as time," he said cryptically. "What say you, will you accompany me?"

She filled her aching lungs, then released the air slowly. "It seems I have no choice. Why did you say we were betrothed?"

"I cannot picture you as any man's mistress."

Because she was too virtuous? Or not pretty enough? "I will not sleep with you."

A cynical smile twisted his mouth. "I'd not ask it of you." His eye twinkled briefly. "Tempting as the notion is."

A pang gripped her chest. It was not desire or longing. She wouldn't let it be. But this time with him had showed her an unexpectedly gentle side of Jamie. She had a hard time imagining a man who quoted verse and rescued damsels in distress capable of murder. He was too soft, too pleasure loving. She picked up the book of verse he'd offered her and took it with her.

"Are they smugglers?" Emma asked as Jamie helped her out of the small boat that had brought them ashore.

He gazed at the ten swarthy Cornishmen who waited for them on the beach. Ten good men in mail shirts and boiled leather vests who'd put their lives and the lives of their loved ones in jeopardy for him. "They are a good deal more than that."

"Oh." She sniffed, doubtless to let him know she wasn't intimidated, but he felt her hand tremble in his.

"All will be well if you do as I bid," he murmured.

"Following men's dictates has never been my strong suit."

"Not just any man." In the light of half a dozen smoky

torches, his face glowed with devilry. "Your betrothed husband."

"Do not suppose to use this pretense to rule me."

"I?" His wounded air was ruined by the dazzling smile he gave her before turning to his men. "Lads...I'd present to you my betrothed wife. The Lady Emma."

"Wife?" they exclaimed in a startled chorus.

"Never thought to see the day," muttered one man.

"The women'll be sorry to hear this."

"We'll be kept busy consoling them," another chortled.

"Did you have someone waiting for you?" Emmeline asked.

"Does the notion make you jealous?" he teased.

"Hardly. I wondered if there was any hope she might claw out your eyes for having arrived with another woman."

"Eye," he replied.

"I'm sorry. You...you seem so unaware of your eye, that I sometimes forget and make a thoughtless comment."

"Apology accepted, for I know how stingily you bestow them." She was wrong about the eye. The lack of it hindered him in battle, and for every person who found his piratical look fascinating, there were two who were repelled. He was glad she didn't seem to be one of them. "Come, my lady, your mount awaits." He led her forward and lifted her into the saddle of a shaggy Cornish pony.

"You expect me to ride alone?" His brave lady looked faint.

"Alas, I fear you'll have to. These beasts are stronger than they look, but I don't think it fair to make one carry both of us." He swung up onto his own horse and looped the reins of hers in his hand. "I'll lead him and keep you close."

She nodded, eyes huge in her pallid face, her hands twice as white where they gripped the saddlebow.

Emmeline was oddly glad of his presence as they entered the woods. She'd often ventured into the forests near Derry to gather herbs, but this was different. The trail up the mountain was narrow and winding, the brush close on both sides, the trees curving inward at the tops to form a leafy green tunnel. Small wonder Cornwall had proved so difficult for William the Conqueror to subdue. An entire army could stand a few feet off the path and not be seen. Or a person bent on escape.

She glanced about, wondering if she could get away.

"The woods are deadly if you don't know your way."

"Better that than what awaits me at this Arwenack."

"'Tis a gracious home, and Lord Petrok, Bran's father, a gentle man. I'll expect you to behave yourself accordingly. If you've a mind to take your anger out on me, wait till we're private in our chamber."

"Our chamber? Betrothed couples don't share a room."

"We will. I'm not letting you out of my sight."

There was a nasty thought. Come bedtime, she and Jamie would be shut up together in one room. What would happen? If he tried to touch her, would she resist? Or would she melt as she'd done the last time he kissed her? Suddenly the enormity of her situation came crashing down on her, making her shiver. She was surrounded by smugglers, enacting a false betrothal to a man who might not be a murderer, but who was a danger to her nonetheless.

"Cold or afraid?" Jamie asked.

"B-both."

"I am sorry, Emma."

"'Tis my own fault, I know, but—"

A hoarse scream ripped through the night. Suddenly the woods were alive with men and horses.

"Ambush!" Jamie shouted. "Douse the torches." The flaming brands were thrown to the ground but they continued to flicker, casting an orange glow over a scene straight from hell. Arrows flew at them from the darkness, dealing death and mayhem. Men cried out; horses shrieked and plunged.

Emma sat frozen in place, numb with horror. A hand clutched at her waist. She screamed and beat at it.

"Easy. 'Tis Jamie." He hauled her from the saddle and carried her the few feet to a mound of huge boulders. "Get into the rocks and stay hidden. Use this if you have to." He thrust a knife hilt into her hand, kissed her quick and was gone.

Emma scuttled behind a rock and leaned against the cold stone. Until now, she'd never thought herself a coward, but to die like this, alone in the dark. She closed her eyes and shuddered, afraid, so afraid. But she soon discovered that listening to the grunts, groans and grating of steel was worse than watching. Worse than that was the sickly fear that Jamie would come to some harm. She shouldn't care, but she did. So she crept back around, just enough to see...

Only one of the torches yet burned, and it was hard to spot Jamie in the knots of men who writhed in combat, swords flashing and grating against each other. Then she spied him only a few feet away, battling two men at once. Two. Her heart slammed into her ribs. He fought daringly, brilliantly, his movements nearly too quick to follow. His left side was toward her, and he swung his head from side to side as he parried and thrust. How odd. Then she realized it was because he could not see out of that eye. He was partly blind, vulnerable in a way she'd never guessed before because he always seemed invincible.

Oh, Jamie. She climbed to her feet, silently urging him on. So intent was she on the battle that she didn't see the man on the ground until he crawled into her line of vision. He was clearly wounded and hitched himself along with his left arm. He seemed to be making for Jamie. Seeking help?

Emmeline stepped from her shelter. "You there, come this way and I'll tend you," she called. "Do not distract Jamie…"

Despite the noise of the battle, Jamie heard her and turned his head toward her. The man on the ground sat up and drew back his hand. Something long and slender glittered in it.

"Jamie! Beware! He has a knife!" Emmeline started forward but knew she'd never reach him in time. Her fist clenched on the solid haft in her hand. Jamie's knife. She threw it more out of frustration than an intent to kill. Which was a good thing, for it clattered uselessly to the ground.

Jamie's aim was truer. He sent his blade flying into his assailant's neck, then spun toward the two he'd been fighting. Bran and another man had already taken up the battle and were winning. "Take them alive," Jamie shouted, then he raced across to her. "I told you to stay down." He led her back behind the rocks and sat beside her. "Why did you come out?"

"I was worried about—"

"I am sorry you were afraid, but 'tis nearly over."

Emmeline didn't correct his assumption, annoyed at herself for worrying about him. To think she'd thought him soft and pleasure loving. "Who were they? Rival smugglers?"

"I doubt it…they fought like outlanders. Men not from these parts," he explained. "With any luck, we'll take a few to Arwenack with us and learn who sent them and why." His hair was disheveled, his face grimy but flushed with excitement. He looked like a lad, winded from a day's hard play. Except his sword was real, as was the blood staining it.

Emmeline shuddered, unnerved by the violence and by her own part in it. She'd thrown a knife at a man.

"Do not fall apart now, brave lady."

"I didn't feel very brave."

"You did well." He looked around the rock and stood. "My thanks for your timely warning," he said softly. "Stay here till I'm certain there's no more danger, and I'll soon have you safely inside Arwenack's gates."

Arwenack proved to be a surprise. Emmeline had expected a cluster of hovels such as those on the outskirts of London. Her first impression was of a high stone wall broken by a wooden gate reinforced with bands of beaten metal. Then she looked, really looked at the twin towers on either side of the gate. Metal poles jutted out from each. From one dangled a body. A dead body.

Emmeline gasped then gagged and looked away.

"A spy," Bran snarled. "Caught him sneaking about Penryn, asking questions about us. Bet he was running with this same bunch." He jerked his stubbled chin toward the two prisoners, bound and carried on wooden poles like roe deer.

"Barbarians." Emmeline squeezed her eyes shut.

"Easy." Jamie drew her back against his chest. He'd insisted she ride with him, and now she was grateful. How safe she felt, held tight in his arms. 'Twas nonsense, of course, for he was her enemy, but just now it didn't seem so. "We cannot let them go. They wounded three Killigrews and they threaten our plans."

"Are your smuggled goods worth so many lives?" she asked.

"They are," he said, an odd tightness in his voice. "You will be safe if you keep to the castle and to our story."

"As if I would betroth myself to someone like you," Emmeline snapped, exhausted, frightened and heartsick. "I was wrong to think you too soft to commit murder."

"I do what is necessary," he said quietly.

Including kill her if she was a threat? She had to get away, but she could barely sit up, much less run. She closed her eyes and dug deep for the strength to endure. She felt his thigh muscles tense beneath her bottom as he nudged the horse forward, but she didn't open her eyes again till she heard Bran call a halt. Cautiously lifting one lid, she saw an immense stone tower with mullioned windows and a covered stairway leading up from the courtyard to the first story. It was far smaller than Harte Court, which was the finest castle she'd ever seen, but prosperous looking.

Clearly smuggling paid well.

The doors of the dependency buildings flanking the tower flew open, disgorging a horde of people. They were simply dressed in dark wool unadorned by embroidery or jewels. They chanted Jamie's name, welcoming him like a conquering hero or a favorite son. He acknowledged them all, calling each person by name. Their boisterous shouts turned to cries of pain and rage when they saw the wounded. And the prisoners.

For an instant, Emmeline feared they'd hang the two men out of hand, but a tall man strode out of the crowd and restored order. "We'll be questioning them, as Jamie says."

"Then we'll be hanging them, brother mine," Bran

added before he and a group of men dragged the prisoners away.

"My thanks, Colan," Jamie said as he dismounted and lifted Emmeline to the ground. "Feelings are running high."

"Hmm. I've a bone of my own to pick with you," Colan grumbled. His resemblance to Bran was striking. Though Colan was a bit less burly and a lot less volatile. "You're so late I'd begun to fear Oxford's men had gotten hold of you."

"Nothing so dire...I've brought someone with me." He drew Emmeline out from his shadow. "Colan Killigrew, may I present Lady Emma, my betrothed."

"Betrothed!" Colan exclaimed, his cry echoed by those who hadn't gone with Bran and the prisoners, or to tend the wounded.

"Aye." Jamie grinned and put a proprietary arm around Emmeline. "Her father opposes the match, so I stole her away."

Colan frowned. "Hell of a time to go courting."

"Jamie, thank God!" The crowd parted for a young woman. She was plump yet very pretty, her braided hair and twinkling eyes as black as night. "I feared you'd run afoul of the law."

His mistress? Emmeline wondered, cringing inside at the prospect of yet another traumatic scene.

Jamie bent over the woman's hand, then performed the introductions. "Mariot, may I present to you Lady Emma, late of London, and my wife to be. Emma, this is Lady Mariot Killigrew, wife to Colan and chatelaine of Arwenack."

Emmeline inclined her head, as much to acknowledge her hostess as to hide her flushed cheeks. It was one thing to discuss playing the part of his betrothed, quite another to carry out the role under the aristocratic nose of this lady. Despite her simple clothes, Mariot was clearly a lady. Her next words proved her to be a gentle one.

"Wife!" Mariot fairly beamed. "My dear, you are most well come." Tisking loudly, she berated James for dragging poor Emma about without a cloak or a proper mount. And exposing her to the horrors of a battle. "I'd expected better from a man such as yourself, Jamie. Come with me, Lady Emma, if I may call you that, and I'll arrange for a bath, fresh clothes and food. Can you walk so far as the keep, or should Jamie carry you?"

"I'll walk!"

"Poor love," Jamie said smoothly, his hand caressing her shoulder. "I know you're exhausted and frightened. But we are truly safe here." Providing she did as she was told, his piercing gaze warned. "If you could find a chamber for us, and mayhap something more suitable for her to wear. We were caught in a storm and Emma's clothes were lost overboard, and herself very nearly with them."

"Of course, your wife is more than welcome to whatever we have," Mariot said, smiling warmly.

"Betrothed...not wife," Emmeline amended. "A bath and food would be most welcome." Still she found it impossible to relax as she followed her hostess through the crowd of curious Killigrews and up the wooden stairs to the first story. When she reached the top and looked back, she realized Jamie had not accompanied them. Instead, he strode off toward the stables with Colan.

The sight of their heads, one fair, one black, bent together in whispered conversation fairly screamed conspiracy. A reminder that Jamie was in league with these people in some risky, illegal business. She was the outsider, a threat to them and they to her. She remembered, too, that though she had vowed to maintain the fiction they were betrothed, she had not promised she wouldn't try to escape. That reminder sent a warm glow to chase out the block of ice in her chest.

"She what?" Colan cried.

"Hush. Keep your voice down." Jamie glanced around, but the two of them were alone on the parapet atop Arwenack tower.

"'Tis true she recognized Harry, but she doesn't know what is really going on. She thinks we are smugglers."

Colan grunted, resting his arms on the merlon. "'Twas a close thing. If you'd not escaped in time—"

"Aye." If not for Cedric's greed, their plans would have been ruined. "Feeling as she does about avenging her sister, I could not leave Emma behind to tell what she knew."

"Of course. Nor could you harm her," Colan added. Their sharp wits and deep sense of honor had made the two men friends from their first meeting. They were closer to each other than to their blood brothers. "But your wife..." He chuckled. "She does not look like the sort of woman you favor."

"Nay, she doesn't." But Jamie knew looks could be deceiving. For all she was no great beauty, Emma roused something in him no other woman ever had. Something deep, profound and singular. Something he dared not explore or expose. "The only way I got her to agree to this was by hinting you Killigrews were a wild, vicious bunch. The dead body decorating your front gate lent credence to my tale." He raised a questioning eyebrow.

"Oxford's man. He's been traveling about, asking a lot of questions about you. Seems Oxford's curious about your habits."

"Do they know about the fleet?"

"This one didn't. He was only told to find out where you were and what you were doing in Cornwall."

"We are safe, for the moment, then." Jamie looked out over the dark woods toward the secret harbor. It was hidden by the hills, a small inlet where the Carnon River emptied into Carrick Roads, known only to a few locals. Here they were building ships, while French spies watched the port of Fowey from which the Fowey Gallants sailed regularly to harass Calais.

Bran and Colan were jointly overseeing the project, but Colan was unaware of their real purpose or of the building methods his brother's crew was employing...on Jamie's orders. Much as he hated keeping Colan in the dark, it was necessary. If things went ill and his plans were discovered, Colan's outrage over Jamie's treachery would convince everyone he was a traitor.

Rumors of the ships had reached Charles VI, and he had agents looking everywhere for proof England really was preparing to counter his invasion force. Now it seemed Oxford was on their trail, as well, though he did not yet know what he was looking for. If they were found out, Oxford would be as anxious as the French to wipe out the fleet because it jeopardized his lucrative peace treaty. "How did Oxford know to come here?" Jamie asked.

"None of our men talked, I'd swear it. But the man we hanged tried to follow a few of the workmen to the harbor. We've doubled the patrols and put a vanguard on each work party. I wonder if the men who ambushed you tonight were Oxford's or Charles's?"

"Bran will soon find out." Jamie's gut twitched as he considered what was taking place in the dungeons. "Thank God he has the stomach for it, because I never did."

"What of the girl...your betrothed?" Colan muttered.

"Can we trust her to keep silent about what she sees and hears?"

"I wish to God I knew," Jamie mused. Then he smiled ruefully. "Since I don't, I shall just have to keep her close at hand." A prospect he relished more than was wise...for either of them.

Chapter Nine

The sun poked its head over the horizon, ending what was probably the longest night in Emmeline's memory. But the coming of dawn didn't end the misery or the waiting.

"I thought I might find you up." Mariot peered around the chamber door. "I didn't want to knock in case you'd somehow gotten to sleep. May I come in?"

"Of course." Emmeline tightened the belt on her borrowed bed robe and pasted on a smile. "I was just watching the sunrise."

"Hmm. I doubt you got any more sleep than I did." Mariot pushed open the door and waved in a pair of servants. The aroma of fresh bread rose from the covered trays they carried. "But standing with our eyes glued to the gate and our hearts pounding with fear will not bring our men back safe or any sooner." To the servants, she said, "Please set the food on the table, then you may break your own fasts. We will serve ourselves."

"I am not worried." 'Twould be God's justice if James died chasing down the rest of the men who'd ambushed them.

"Ha! Your eyes are as dark with fear as my own."

"Sleeplessness." Emmeline hurried over to help her hostess uncover the food, glad of the diversion. "I'm not very hungry."

Mariot smiled knowingly, but accepted the change of topic. "Nor am I, but 'tis not only from worry." She laid a hand on her flat belly and sat in one of the chairs. "I am with child."

"Oh, how wonderful." Emmeline sat, too.

"More so than you can know. Last year I lost a babe. I was only three months gone," she added in response to Emmeline's murmur of sympathy. "But I cried pails of tears nonetheless."

Emmeline nodded, asked a few gentle questions and discovered this pregnancy was in its fourth month. "Mayhap all will be well, this time." She fell into her customary role, suggesting a few potions that might ease the nausea and strengthen the womb.

"How come you to know so much about childbearing?"

"I am an apothecary."

"How wonderful to have such a skill." Mariot proved to be such an interested listener, Emmeline found herself opening up in a way she never had before. Mariot scowled over Cedric's perfidy and cheered Emmeline's courage in running the shop her mother had left her. "But Jamie is not like Cedric," Mariot said.

"He is a rogue and a consummate liar. He can twist words to suit him as skillfully as a tumbler does his body."

Mariot frowned. "If you feel so strongly against him, how do you come to be betrothed to him?"

Drat. Mariot had befriended her, but she was a Killigrew by marriage. "Our relationship is very...complex. Part of me is held in thrall by his charm, the other is skeptical of him."

"I felt much the same about Colan when he was courting me. The Killigrews are loud, boisterous and rowdy as a litter of pups, while my family is quiet and serious. We were so different, I did not think I could be happy with him, no matter how desirable I found him, er, physically," she mumbled.

"Exactly. Jamie is never serious or responsible. And this smuggling business goes against every principle I hold dear. To cheat and steal..." She clapped a hand over her mouth. "Oh, I didn't mean to smear your family with the same tarred brush."

"Cornishmen don't see smuggling in a bad light. We are simple, honest folk. Hard-pressed to make a living from the land, we've turned to the sea for fish and for commerce. True, there is no tax collected on what we trade, but whom does that cheat? Only the king, who would use the coin to buy rich luxuries for himself and his favorites whilst our children went cold and hungry."

"I had never thought of it that way." Emmeline paused to sip the ale Mariot had poured for them. "But what of the man who was hanged? And the others who attacked us last night? Surely such wars between rival factions are wrong."

"Those men were not rivals," Mariot exclaimed. "They are spies, sent to locate the harbor and burn the fleet the men are building to repulse the French."

"A fleet to repel the invasion?" Emmeline breathed.

Now it was Mariot who covered her mouth, eyes round with horror. "Oh, I've said too much. Colan and Jamie will skin me."

"'Tis wonderful. The whole country is hysterical with fear. Why have the people not been told we have ships to defend us?"

"Because if the French find out what Jamie and the others were doing, they would come and burn the ships."

"Jamie is a part of this?"

"'Twas his idea, and he was charged with overseeing the project...along with the Killigrews and the Cornishmen who work night and day to complete the ships," Mariot said proudly. "But..." Her smile faltered. "You must not say I told you."

"I will forget you mentioned it." But how could she? Now she understood why he'd been so frantic to escape from her cellar. Why hadn't he told her? Because she wouldn't have believed him, then. And now... She thought back over all that had happened since she'd kidnapped him. He'd been furious with her, yet not once had he harmed her physically. Nay, he'd twice saved her life.

Silently Emmeline weighed Jamie's actions against the words in Celia's letter. Something was wrong...horribly wrong, but she didn't know who to believe, her sister or a roguish womanizer.

Loud shouts echoed up from the courtyard, followed by the creaking groan of the drawbridge being lowered.

"They are back." Mariot rushed to the window with Emmeline right behind her. "Oh, there are wounded."

"Where is Jamie?" What if he'd been killed and she never had a chance to admit she might have misjudged him? Then she spotted him in the middle of the filthy, tattered column. His head was down, his tunic red with blood. "He's hurt. Oh, God, he's hurt." She bolted from the room without a backward glance, took the narrow, winding stairs at a reckless clip and emerged into the courtyard just as the men were dismounting.

All was chaos. The stone walls rang with the sounds of Killigrew men shouting the details of their adventure while the women cried over their hurts. The castle dogs ran in circles, yapping and snapping at the heels of the horses, who shied away from the groomsmen and threatened to trample the warriors who'd survived the expedition. So thick was the press that Emmeline couldn't even see Jamie.

"Jamie!" she screamed, and began to elbow her way through the crowd. "Jamie!"

"Here." The throng parted, and there he was. Battered and bloody, one hand braced on Bran's shoulder.

Sweet Mary, he was weak from loss of blood. "Oh, Jamie." She swayed herself, then rallied. "Don't just stand there letting him bleed to death, you dolt, carry him within," she snapped at Bran.

"Just a minute," the Cornishman growled.

"He may not have a minute. Take his shoulders. You there!" She snagged the arm of a burly trooper. "Take his legs...and mind you don't bump him. Oh, mayhap we should lay him on the ground and get a litter."

"I can walk," Jamie said quietly.

"Save me from prideful men! You will lose what little blood you have left if you try to walk—"

"Emma." Jamie let go of Bran and took her hand, his grip surprisingly strong for a dying man. "Most of the blood is someone else's...several men's, in fact."

"You are not wounded?"

"Well..." He grinned, his teeth white against his filthy face. "I've a gash in my side that may need a stitch or two, and someone laid a mighty stroke across my back. It may be broken."

Emmeline wanted to hit him for worrying her so. Instead she did something even more shocking. She laughed. 'Twas a rusty sound, yet it felt good. In the past few days, her feelings toward Jamie had swung back and forth, veering between hatred, desire and suspicion.

Jamie might be a rogue, but he was also a brave, honorable man bent on saving his country. If he had murderous tendencies, he'd surely have killed her for causing him so much trouble. It must be as Jamie said, that poor Celia had been murdered by this Giles Cadwell. She laughed again, this time in relief.

"Emma?" Now he looked worried.

"She's giddy, I think," Mariot said. "She was up all night."

"Waiting for me." Jamie smiled. "I may faint after all."

"Don't you dare. I'm not carrying you up the stairs," Bran grumbled. But he looked at Emmeline with a bit less hostility.

"Inside, all of you," Mariot said in that low yet firm voice of hers. "There's a hot meal waiting in the hall."

"Ah, small wonder I wed you a week after meeting you," Colan said, looping an arm over her shoulder. "I knew you were just what was needed to take this rowdy bunch in hand."

Emmeline smiled at them and looked away. 'Twas then she realized she'd come down wearing only her shift and robe, which gaped open at the neck to reveal the upper swell of her breasts. "Oh." She drew the throat closed.

"I cannot think of a more welcome sight to come home to," Jamie said. "But I'd not have this pack of lustful Killigrews ogling my woman. Let us go within." He held out a hand, then scowled. "I'm no fit escort. I stink of blood and sweat."

"Come by in a good cause." Emmeline took his hand.

"Emma...? First laughter, now you praise me for fighting. What has caused this transformation?"

"Mayhap your charm has swayed me."

He frowned, then shrugged. "Who am I to complain. Lead on, my lady, but slowly, I fear I am none too spry."

"Lean on me." Emmeline put her arm around him, but her shoulder did not reach his armpit. "I'm too short."

"You are just right." He cuddled her close and kissed the top of her head.

"None of that, milord. Remember you are a wounded man. Once you are bathed and stitched up, you must rest."

"I'm sure to heal faster if you lie with me."

"Incorrigible," she replied.

"So I've been told. Interested in trying to reform me?"

Emmeline gazed up at him. Beneath the dirt and gore, he was ashen with fatigue, yet his step was firm. The lines bracketing his mouth betrayed the pain he hid with his banter. Why did he not want her to know he was brave and honorable? "I do not think you'd require as much of that as you'd have the world believe."

He sobered. "Do not fool yourself into thinking I am a good man. I'll break your heart as I have the others who loved me."

"I am safe, then, for I could never love you."

I could never love you.

Emma's words haunted Jamie all through the day. They hovered in the back of his mind while he reviewed the lists of materials needed to complete the ships. They gnawed on him while he and the Killigrews set a patrol to watch for any other spies Oxford might send. They taunted him as he finalized the strategy for the last step in his plan. The crucial meeting with DeGrys.

'Twas best she not love him, of course, but the ache of loss was sharper than the pain of the sword slice Emma had cleansed and stitched that morn. As he escorted her into the hall that night, he couldn't stop wishing things were different.

"You look very pretty tonight." Jamie's gaze swept over the green gown she wore, lingering on the provocative thrust of her breasts. "That color brings out the green in your eyes."

"'Tis the finest thing I've ever worn." She sat on the bench he'd pulled out for her and petted the velvet surcoat worn over an under tunic of gold silk. "I hope it doesn't get soiled or torn in this crush."

Jamie stepped over the bench and sat. "Finding the Killigrews a bit much?" Dinner was an unusually boisterous event, with spirits running high after the rout of the spies.

"They certainly are loud," Emma shouted over the din.

The Killigrews didn't stand on ceremony, so there was no high table. He and Emma sat at a trestle table near the door, thigh to thigh with the Cornishmen and women. Leaning close, he whispered in her ear, "My family is nearly as rowdy when they have something to celebrate. If they intimidate you, we could repair to our room."

She glanced up at him through her lashes, eyes glinting with wry humor. "That sounds even more intimidating."

Emma flirting? The notion was as sweet as the lavender that clung to her hair. "I promise to be on my good behavior," he replied, captivated by this new boldness of hers.

"Then why bother to be private?"

"Emma!"

Her smile fled. "I shocked you."

"You delight me." He put his arm around her and kissed her temple, where her pulse beat too quickly. "And surprise me."

"I—I am not usually like this." She looked down, her fingers crumbling the edge of the manchet bread trencher they shared. "Mother would be appalled to see me laughing and flirting."

A strict mother and a wastrel for a father. Small wonder she seldom laughed. Jamie wanted to make it up to her.

He wanted to court her and spoil her and teach her to enjoy life. And then what? *Leave before you hurt her.* But he couldn't. He told himself he played the ardent, attentive swain to uphold the fiction of their betrothal. 'Twas selfishness. He wanted her. Badly. "How could she fault you for being rendered giddy by my charm?"

"Your charm? Conceited oaf." She smiled, revealing the dimples she'd been hiding. She looked young, carefree and enchanting. The woman she might have become had fate not burdened her with heavy responsibilities and a wretched father. "I am giddy with *relief,* I expected Arwenack would be a cluster of filthy hovels inhabited by wild animals. Instead, they set a fine table and are as entertaining as a troop of traveling players."

He grinned back. "Isolated the Killigrews may be, but they are not uncivilized."

"Nay." Her gaze swept the hall, from the fresh rushes on the floor to the sturdy trestle tables lined with cheerful Killigrews to the whitewashed walls hung with colorful tapestries. "I've never been in so grand a place. The hall where the Peppers' Guild holds their annual Michaelmas feast is possibly as large, but not half so finely furnished. And the food..." She looked down at their trencher, heaped with the delicacies he'd selected for them. From the sea, fresh salmon in lemon sauce, shad roe and pink mussels in wine and garlic. From the flocks on the inland moors, roasted lamb sauced with rosemary and chicken stuffed with wild mushrooms. "Mariot said she'd ordered a special dinner in honor of your safe return, but I had no idea there'd be so much."

Their differences struck him anew. She had led the simple life of a merchant, he the privileged one of money and power. His sire and grandsire had been advisors to old Edward III. As Lancaster's foster son, Jamie had gone to court when he was only seven, and dined there countless times since. While Arwenack was a fine keep, it was half the size and grandeur of Harte Court. The reminder she was not of his world was but one more reason why a relationship between them was impossible. To cover his bleakness, he teased, "So much food, or so much noise?"

She laughed. "Both, I guess. 'Tis a wonderful banquet they've put on in your honor. They...they much respect you."

"Which must surely make you think them poor judges of a man's character," he replied dryly.

"Nay, well, not entirely. That is..."

Hope swelled in his chest. "Never say you believe in me?"

"I...guess I do. Your reputation and the fact you had been involved with Celia, led me to believe you guilty, but if you were a murderer, you'd surely have killed me for meddling in your business—twice." She smiled ruefully. "Now I'm sorry I kidnapped you and caused you so much trouble."

Jamie grinned. "Apology accepted. After meeting Cedric, I can see why you distrust men."

"You are not like him."

Nay, he betrayed his wife and daughters; I betray an entire nation. "I will be glad if you no longer think me a murderer, but do not make of me a hero, either."

"You are." Emmeline looked across the table and caught Mariot's warning glance. Though she ached to tell him how proud she was of his project, she respected her vow to Mariot. Mayhap he'd tell her on his own. "You saved me from drowning."

"At great personal cost." He arched his back and groaned.

"Fie, sir, you are delicate as a wee boy."

"He is not." A freckle-faced lad pushed in between them. "Jamie's the bravest and strongest man in the world."

"My thanks, sir, but who are you?" Jamie asked of the boy.

"It's me...Enyon. Enyon Killigrew."

"Truly?" Jamie winked at Emmeline and pretended to study the boy. "Why you're a head taller than my friend Enyon."

"I grew." The youngest Killigrew stood even straighter. "And I'm a page now in Sir Morley Nash's household. He said I might visit home, and I've just ridden in this very minute."

Jamie leaned closer. "Why, 'tis you. Turn about so I can see you better. Is that a sword you carry?"

"Aye." Enyon's black eyes glowed as his hand came to rest on the hilt. "'Tis a wooden one, but ever so sharp. Want to see?" He drew the weapon, nearly striking Emmeline in the shoulder.

She gasped and ducked; Jamie leapt up, grabbed hold of Enyon's arm and got the blade back under control.

"Have a care!" Jamie exclaimed.

"Enyon!" Petrok, patriarch of the Killigrews, jumped up from his place beside Colan and glared at his youngest son. "How many times have I warned ye—"

"I am all right, really," Emmeline said quickly.

Petrok strode around the table, his salt-and-pepper hair flying about his angry red face. "I see Nash has had no better luck controlling yer impetuous nature than I had. Remember what we said last time? Yer sword." He held out a wide, scarred hand.

Enyon's lower lip wobbled, but he withdrew the sword from its leather scabbard and handed it, hilt first, to his father.

"Now apologize to Jamie's lady," his father ordered.

"That isn't necessary…" Emmeline began, but Jamie silenced her with a shake of his head.

"I'm sorry," Enyon mumbled, head down.

"Accepted," she said readily. "But—"

"I've a mind to get in some sword practice while I'm here," Jamie said into the strained silence. "If Enyon was to work with me and prove he'd learned the proper handling of his blade, might he have it back?"

"Ye spoil the lad," Petrok grumbled.

"Don't we all," Jamie replied cheerfully. He and Enyon regarded Petrok with identical hopeful expressions.

"Oh, very well," Petrok growled. "But—"

"You can set the rules and conditions," Jamie cried. Seizing the grinning Enyon by the waist, he hoisted the boy onto his shoulders. "Let us see if we can find David and the others and get up a game of tourney. Or are you grown too old for that?"

"Nay," Enyon crowed, fairly bouncing on Jamie's shoulders.

Jamie winced. "Have a care, there. I'm a mite bruised just now," he added as he adjusted his burden.

"In a battle?" Enyon asked breathlessly.

"Aye." Jamie winked at Emmeline and walked away. "My opponent was eight feet tall and as strong as an ox. I barely escaped with my parts still attached." His voice faded as he headed down the aisle between the tables, but Enyon's laughter rose above the din.

"I should have beaten him more," Petrok muttered as he sank onto the bench beside her.

"Which one of them?" Emmeline asked.

Petrok threw back his head and roared till his eyes watered. "Ah, that's a good one, milady," he said after a moment, wiping the tears on his sleeve. "I can see yer beauty wasn't the only reason why young Jamie stole ye away from yer father.''

If you only knew. "Hmm," Emmeline said noncommittally, uncomfortable to be entertaining the giant who'd sired Bran, Colan and Enyon. Across the way, Mariot and Colan were deep in conversation, and she was loath to interrupt the private words and warm glances they exchanged.

"Mariot's been a godsend," Petrok murmured.

Emmeline nodded, thinking of all the lady had done to befriend her. "She made me most welcome and seems a capable chatelaine for one so young."

"Aye." Petrok's eyes glazed, filled with some terrible anguish. "She had the running of this place and the managing of us thrust upon her when my wife suddenly...died."

The pause hinted at things better left unsaid. "I am so sorry to hear of your loss," Emmeline murmured. "My mother died last year and left to me the management of her apothecary shop."

Petrok nodded. "I can see why Mariot took to ye so quickly, then, for ye've much in common."

"Mmm." In truth, they were little alike, she and the lady of Arwenack. The running of a large estate, the ordering of meals and managing of the legions of servants it took to keep such a castle going was as foreign to Emmeline as...as the wild Cornish woods she'd glimpsed from her chamber window. She felt a sudden wave of longing for home. She missed Peter, Toby and Molly. She missed her neat little shop with its familiar mingling of pungent herbs. She even missed the things she disliked, the early-morning shouts of tradesmen hawking their wares, the noise and the stench of too many people crowded together in the narrow streets.

A whoop of laughter cut through her brooding, and she looked up to see a space had been cleared along one wall of the hall. An avid group of spectators rimmed the area. At either end of it stood a man with a boy astride his shoulders. One of the pairs was Jamie and Enyon. At a signal from Bran, Jamie and the other man ran at each other, neighing and prancing like stallions. As they passed, their riders batted at each other with the sticks they held.

"Isn't that dangerous?" Emmeline asked over the crowd noise.

"Their lances are well padded with wool," Petrok replied.

The sight of Jamie galloping about the hall with young Enyon on his shoulders made something catch in Emmeline's chest. Her heart leapt, then beat faster, her spirits soaring with it as she watched the men and boys at their play. Their faces were flushed, their mouths wide with taunts and laughter. Everyone was laughing. Even the servants had stopped clearing away the remnants of the meal to cheer on their favorite.

"It does my heart good to see him like this," Petrok said softly. "For he was such a quiet, hurt thing when he came to us. So troubled I never thought to see him smile again."

"Enyon?"

"Jamie."

"Jamie?" Jamie the rogue? Jamie the man who laughed or teased or mocked most everything?

"Aye. He had run away from home and got as far as Penryn before he took sick from cold and lack of food. The townspeople brought him here. My Kayla sent word to his family that he was safe and nursed him back to health. But even after his body healed, 'twas clear his mind was not at peace."

"He ran away from a life of plenty? Why? What happened?"

"Ye'll have to ask him."

"Was that…was that after he'd lost his eye?"

"Aye. That was part of it." He looked again at the gamboling man. "As to why he ran away. Jamie didn't confide the whole of it to me. I only know it was something to do with his brother. He is a complex man, our Jamie. And a brave one. But then, I expect you already know all these things."

Nay, but she was coming to.

"He's returned our care a hundredfold," Petrok continued. "Had it not been for Jamie's encouragement, Enyon might not be alive today. He was with his mother when she was attacked and blamed himself for failing to save her. Nothing we said relieved his guilt, and I feared he'd grieve himself to death. Jamie's kindness and understanding brought him back."

Because Jamie had his own burden of guilt. She knew that instinctively.

"You have been good for Jamie, too. I've never seen him so protective of a woman." Petrok heaved his bulk from the bench and bid her good sleep before wandering off.

Was Jamie protective of her? Or worried she'd betray his secrets? Suddenly she hoped for the former.

Jamie ambled over with Enyon bouncing along beside him. They were both flushed with victory.

"Did you win?" Emmeline asked.

"Barely." Jamie flexed his shoulders. "I'm getting too old for such sport." He picked up his cup and drained it.

"You are not. Jamie's the strongest…the quickest." Enyon leaned his elbows on the table, eyes shiny with adoration.

"Not to mention charming, loyal and kind," she added.

"If you don't, I will," Jamie quipped.

Emmeline laughed. "And above all, modest."

Enyon frowned. "Such modesty would be false, for Jamie knows he is the best knight alive."

"How much did you pay this lad?" Emmeline asked.

"I promised him my horse and half my kingdom if he but convinced you of my worthiness to be your own true knight."

Emmeline started. "I recall that phrase from the book of verses you lent me."

"Ah, you read them. What did you think."

"I liked the romances, and the epic battle was very stirring. But the one about the knight whose thoughtlessness results in his brother's death and his own exile...'twas so sad I could not finish it. Are they some of Chaucer's early work?"

"Nay, they were penned by a man of far less talent."

"I disagree," Emmeline replied, but before she could elaborate, Mariot called to her.

"Lady Emma...would you favor us with a tune?"

"Oh, I...I couldn't."

"Now you are being falsely modest," Mariot chided. "You played the lute most prettily for me this afternoon."

"We've a talented minstrel in our midst," Jamie said. "Her grandfather is the founder of the Golden Wait of Harrowgate."

The Killigrews looked unimpressed, but Mariot clapped her hands. "Why did you not tell me? They are the musicians employed by London to play at the fetes," she explained to Petrok.

Emmeline protested, "I am not a member."

"She played with them at my mother's birthday celebration."

"I will play," Emmeline said, glaring at him. "But only if Jamie agrees to sing with me."

"Sing…me?" he exclaimed.

"You told me you know the words to the ballads."

"And so I do." He stood and held out his hand.

As she took it, Emmeline felt a thrill of excitement, mixed with a dash of apprehension, a sense of embarking on a scandalous adventure, though they traveled no farther than the pair of chairs in the center of the hall.

"You are pale as a virgin bride," he murmured. "Why so nervous? You must have performed a hundred times."

"Actually." Emmeline licked her lips. "Actually your mother's fete was my first. Mama didn't approve of music, not after she found out about Cedric."

"She forbade you to play?"

"Or even read the verses."

He cursed under his breath, then his expression softened. "Then we must make tonight memorable." He swept her into her chair with a bow that brought female sighs of envy.

Uncertain how to respond to his gallantry, Emmeline busied herself tightening the lute's catgut strings. "I—I am ready," she whispered, conscious they were the focus of all eyes. The hall was silent for the first time all evening. Even the men dicing before the hearth had left their game to draw near. "Why don't you choose something they'd like," she added.

Poor little Emma, trying so hard to be prim and proper when her soul yearned to soar. "Why don't I choose something you'd like." Jamie named a popular romantic ballad and waited while she played the introductory chords, her eyes closed, her lips parted as the music transported her. *Dieu, she is beautiful.* The desire that surged through him roughed his voice as he matched the tune she played to words he'd written himself.

Emmeline's head snapped up, scarcely able to credit her ears. It was Jamie, the same man she'd fought with, argued with and laughed with. He sat beside her, his gaze full on her, as though he sang to her alone. Never had she heard anything to equal the power of his singing. Deep and stirring, Jamie's voice poured over her, through her. Her breath caught in her lungs. The words of duty and daring took on a new and more profound meaning. When he flowed smoothly into another song, she followed. He sang of love, and she believed. He sang of betrayal, and her eyes filled with tears for the doomed knight and his lady.

There was complete silence when his last words died away, the boisterous Killigrews held in thrall by his performance. Then the hall erupted in cheers and foot stamping.

"That was wonderful," Emmeline leaned close to say.

Jamie grinned and ducked his head. "I take that as a great compliment from a trained minstrel such as yourself."

"I am an apothecary."

"Because that was what your mother expected of you. At heart, you are a musician, a teller of tales, a weaver of magic."

How could he know that? Emmeline wondered.

"Give us another song. Another song!" chanted the crowd.

Jamie shook his head and stood, taking Emmeline's hand and raising her to stand beside him. "No more this evening." The announcement drew a chorus of complaints, which he ended with, "Enough, you greedy children. My lady is weary and would seek her bed." A few catcalls greeted that. He silenced them with a glare, inclined his head and led her from the hall like a prince making a grand exit.

The door closed behind them, shutting out the noise and light. By contrast, the passageway was blessedly dark and silent. Emmeline paused to draw a breath of cool, quiet air.

"Come to bed, love. You are tired, and I need to make an early start tomorrow morn," Jamie murmured.

Emmeline nodded, still under the spell he'd cast with his voice. "If I can walk so far."

"Allow me, my lady." He swung her up in his arms and headed for the stairs.

"Jamie! Have a care for your wound." She tried to wriggle free. He held her with ridiculous ease.

"The day I am too feeble to carry you, is the day they will bury me. Say it again," he demanded as he climbed the stairs.

"Have a care fo—"

"Nay, my name. Hearing you say it is like music to my ears."

"Jamie." She looked up into his face, draped in shadows for there were only a few torches in the upper hallway. His smile was a wicked blur in the night, his arms strong and muscular. A thrill went through her. "'Tis a bit romantic to be swept off to bed by a handsome pirate who can sing like a nightingale."

"I am your dearest dream, your secret fantasy come true."

Emmeline's heart lurched. "What makes you say that?"

His smile faltered so briefly it might have been her imagination or a shadow. "I saw it in your eyes. When you look at me like that—" he shifted her slightly, lifted the latch and kicked the door open with his toe "—I want to lock us up together and throw away the key."

"And then what?" 'Twas insane to ask.

"Then you would make my fantasies come true." He set her on her feet, his hands on her shoulders to steady her, or so she thought until he lowered his head. His mouth touched hers, light as the brush of a butterfly's wings.

It was wonderful. It wasn't nearly enough. Emmeline swayed, hands splayed on his chest. He was warm, so warm her fingers were singed through the layers of wool. The thunder of his heart against her palms hiked her own pulse. Wordlessly, wantonly, she offered her mouth up to him. "Jamie..."

He groaned, the sound low and tight as the tension building inside her. Inside them. His mouth slanted across hers, sealing their lips together, robbing her of breath and sense.

Emmeline didn't think at all. She only felt. His lips were firm, unyielding, branding her with a kiss that tasted of passion too long denied, his and hers. Terrified it would consume her, she whimpered. The pressure of his mouth gentled instantly, lips that had lately bruised brushing over hers in a silent apology. The tenderness was nearly her undoing. It had been so long since anyone had held her, cherished her. Moaning softly, she parted her lips to the persuasive questing of his tongue.

A growl rumbled through his chest as his tongue swept in to conquer the hidden recesses of her mouth. He tasted of wine and desire. She savored both along with the rough texture of his tongue as it coaxed hers into an intricate game of give and take that left her breathless. Dimly she felt his arms tighten around her, lifting her so their bodies meshed together. His sheer size, the feel of his taut muscles against her softness, thrilled her. Groaning, she tried to wriggle closer.

The feel of Emma catching fire in his arms ripped at

Jamie's control. Never had a woman fitted him so perfectly. He ran his hands down her back, stroking and caressing, wanting more. Not to take, but to give. To show her what love could be like between them. Love?

Aye, love. Jamie wrenched his mouth free, gasping for breath. "Emma. Oh, Emma, I love y—"

She stared up at him, eyes dazed with passion. "Wh-what?"

What had he said? God, he had no right to love her, no right to ask her to love him in return. His past was dark and twisted, his present dangerous and his future...didn't exist.

Somehow he dredged up a smile. For once, it felt stiff. "I want you in my bed, Emma." That at least was the truth.

She drew in a quick breath. "Oh, Jamie," she whispered.

Jamie blinked. He'd expected her outrage to save them both. "This is where you denounce me as a rogue and slap my face."

"Oh." She studied him closely, too closely. "You are still, and probably always will be, a rogue. But an honorable one."

He wanted to hold her, but let go and walked to the hearth. "I told you not to make of me a hero."

"Your deeds do that for you."

She believed in him. His heart stopped, then began to pound with possibilities. Somehow he'd have to keep his distance from her. "You may have the bed, I will make a pallet on the floor."

"Ever the gallant knight."

"I am not." Listening to the rustle of clothes and the creak of the ropes supporting the mattress, Jamie slouched deeper into the chair. If he'd been a man given to drinking, he'd have poured down enough to guarantee oblivion. But his first bout of drinking had ended so disastrously it had been his last.

It was going to be a very long night.

Chapter Ten

"Why ever would you not want Emma and me to go with you to Penryn?" Mariot asked the next morning.

"Emmeline does not care for riding," Jamie replied stiffly.

"Only because I have no experience." Emmeline had not missed his scowl or the use of her whole name. Both part of his plan to discourage her from going along to this Penryn. The shipyard must be nearby, and he didn't trust her with that secret.

How that hurt. After last night...the song, the kiss, the regret in his expression as he'd sent her off to bed alone...she'd fallen asleep dreaming there was something special between them. She'd been disappointed to find him gone from his pallet by the fire when she awoke, but the way his face had lit up when she entered the hall to break her fast had made her heart soar with hope. Now he wanted to shut her out of his life.

Emmeline refused to let him. In her mind's eye she pictured them, standing atop a hill, gazing at a harbor bristling with tall masts. She'd hug Jamie and tell him how much she respected what he was doing for their country. He would kiss her and tell her how much he wanted her. Emmeline's heart lurched, then steadied as she glanced up and saw him watching her with a mixture of longing and pain.

The longing, she understood, the pain...? When she won his trust, he'd share that with her, too. An incredible warmth swept through her. It felt so good, she had to smile. "You will teach me, won't you, Jamie?"

"Wh-what?" stammered the man with the golden tongue. He turned red and she guessed his dreams were not as pure as hers. The notion was frightening...and exciting.

"Why, to ride, of course," Emmeline said.

Colan said something to Mariot in Cornish that made her gasp and poke him in the ribs. Jamie turned purple.

Emmeline's smile deepened. "Please...I will not cause any trouble," she said. How odd their positions were reversed, and she was trying to win his trust. "I should like to buy a gown or some cloth to make one. You did say we'd be here a few weeks, and I can't keep borrowing Mariot's."

"Certainly you can," Colan interjected. "She won't be able to wear most of them till after the babe's born."

Mariot stamped on his toe. "Are you saying I am fat?"

"Nay." Colan jumped about holding his left foot.

"Oh, do not be so mean as to deny us an outing," Mariot begged. "You will likely be all day at the shipyard."

"Shipyard?" Emmeline looked to Jamie, hoping he'd take her into his confidence.

"I need to order a refitting of the *Lady*," he grumbled.

Emmeline knew it for a lie and rejoiced. Not because he'd lied—she must cure him of that—but because she was learning to read him. Learning to respect and value him. She no longer had any doubts that he was innocent of murder.

"Penryn is not much of a town," Jamie told her.

"I do not care. I hunger for fresh air and a vista beyond these walls."

"Let her take a turn in the garden," Bran grumbled.

Jamie groaned and scrubbed a hand over his face. "The shipyard is a rough place. I cannot take you there."

"Leave Emmeline and me in Penryn whilst you ride on to the harbor," Mariot proposed. "We can buy what we need, and you can return for us on your way back through."

"I cannot leave you alone in town!" Colan exclaimed.

"Of course not," Mariot soothed. "We will have a guard of any number you want, and Papa will stay with us, will you not?"

Petrok roused from staring into the fire, an occupation that had consumed much of his time since the death of his beloved Kayla. "I would do it gladly, if 'twould please ye, my dear."

"Oh, thank you, milord. 'Twill only take me a moment to change into something more suitable." Emmeline hiked up her skirts and raced off before Jamie could find another impediment.

He followed a few moments later, entering their chamber just as the maid finished slipping a sturdy brown gown over Emmeline's head. "I'll see to her laces, Eda, isn't it?" he muttered.

The maid flushed, obviously pleased he'd remembered her name. "As ye say, milord." Dropping a curtsy, she left.

"Wait," Emmeline called, but too late.

"Afraid I've come to beat you into submission?"

"Nay, you would not." Emmeline cocked her head, searching his face in a pale morning light and seeing so much she'd missed before. Courage, honor, compassion.

"You might try to coerce or manipulate me into doing your will, but you'd no more harm me than you'd...you'd beat wee Enyon."

"Ah, the lady thinks she has my measure." Expression grim, he stepped behind her and began doing up her gown. "You are mistaken, I am the same rogue who tried to seduce you at my mother's fete. The same man you thought murdered Celia."

Emmeline jerked free of his grasp and spun. "You told me you were innocent—over and over again. Your words and your deeds have finally convinced me. Is that not what you wanted?"

"Aye," he growled. "But..." He exhaled and absently touched the patch, a habit when he was troubled. "I always end up hurting those who believe in me. I do not want to hurt you, Emma."

He was hurting. She felt it. "You won't," she said softly. *You are far too good a man for that. Even if you refuse to see that.* Again she wondered why. Did it have something to do with the way he'd lost his eye? "If you'll finish lacing me up." She turned, lifting the braid out of the way.

He hesitated. "Promise you will not try to escape."

"Why would I want to do that?"

"To return to your shop and your people."

Emmeline sighed. "I miss Toby, Molly and Peter, and I regret they are worrying about me when I am perfectly fine." Better than she'd been in years, mayhap ever. "But you said I must stay here till your business is finished, so..." She shrugged. Three weeks, four, mayhap. Once it had seemed a lifetime, now it seemed too short a time to have with Jamie. If he didn't learn to trust her, it might be all they ever had.

"As long as you vow not to do anything foolish." Jamie

concentrated on doing up the laces that molded the gown to her body. The linen under tunic prevented him from touching her skin, but he could feel its seductive warmth on the backs of his fingers as he tied the leather strips. The memory of how good she'd felt in his arms had kept him tossing on his pallet much of the night. Sleeplessness did not improve his mood, but it was wrong to take it out on Emma. "There, you are done."

"Thank you." She smiled at him over her shoulder. For a woman who hadn't smiled at all when they'd first met, she'd perfected it quickly. One quirk of that soft mouth of hers turned his heart to mush and his lower body to iron. God help him if she ever realized what power she wielded.

"Here." He loosened the strings on the pouch at his belt and withdrew a few coins. "If that is not enough to buy what you need, mayhap Mariot will extend credit till—"

"Nay. It makes me feel like a…a kept woman."

"'Tis my fault you need the garments." He braced for further arguments. She gave him none, merely smiled again and took the coins. Why this change in attitude? Was she hoping to lull him into relaxing his vigilance so she could escape? The idea of Emma wandering through the hostile countryside made his gut roll.

"Are we ready, then?" she asked brightly.

He could not quash her enthusiasm. "Aye. Let me give you my cloak. The morning air is damp and chill." He opened the chest he'd brought from the ship. On top was a roll of parchment. "What is this?"

"'Tis mine." Emma reached for it, but he held it away.

"What is it?" he asked again, yet he didn't unroll it.

"A…a verse I was working on."

He was sore tempted to look at it, but her guarded, defiant expression stopped him. "May I read it when it's done?"

"I—I do not know."

Curse her parents. "I would deem it a great honor." Bowing, he proffered the roll.

"Thank you." She clutched it to her chest.

"You may keep it in the chest with my books if you like. I'll not read it unless you give me leave."

She fixed him with her solemn, piercing gaze, the one that saw through mockery and pretext. "Truly?"

"On my honor." He touched her cheek. "There are some things I cannot tell you, but I will not lie to you about any matter that is between us."

"All right." Emmeline handed the roll back to him. "Would you keep this safe for me?"

Her trust warmed him clear through. He still wasn't certain what he'd done to earn it, but relished it all the same. "I will guard it with my life."

The town of Penryn had been built atop a ridge overlooking the Penryn River estuary. A tortuous maze of crooked streets spilled down the hill to the water's edge, abutted by gray buildings fashioned of granite from the nearby quarries.

"The Killigrews hauled stone from there to build Arwenack," Mariot told Emmeline as their horses negotiated the steep grade from the main street to the riverfront.

Emmeline nodded, grateful for Mariot's friendship. The girl had kept up a running commentary from the moment they'd ridden out of Arwenack's gates. The four-mile trip had taken twice as long as might be expected because the wooded trail snaked up and down the faces of countless gullies and along the crests of several steep gorges. A mile into the trip, Emmeline had ruefully admitted Jamie's assessment of the land was correct. If she'd still been bent on escape, she'd never have made it alone.

"Are you tired?" Mariot asked. The two of them rode together in the center of the well-armed column.

"Nay," Emmeline said quickly, conscious Jamie had turned to watch her from his place at the front of the column. "Well, my rump is a bit sore. But what of you?"

"I am fine. Both the babe and my belly are quiet this morn…thanks to the potions you brewed for me."

Bran rode up beside them, his scowl darker than ever. "No talking," he whispered. "The sound of voices travels far."

Both women nodded, chastened, but when he had once again fallen in behind them, Mariot made a face. Emmeline bit her lip to keep from giggling. Actually, Bran's surliness was no laughing matter. Poor man, he bore a heavy burden. Against his father's advice, Bran had wed an outlander, who had betrayed them to their enemies. Colan had discovered Rosalind's perfidy in time to summon help, but Kayla had been killed and Enyon wounded in the subsequent battle to regain Arwenack.

What of the incident that had cost Jamie his eye, Emmeline wondered. Would he ever tell her about that?

"See there," Mariot whispered. "Is it not grand?"

Emmeline shook off her dark thoughts as they reached the bottom of the hill. Here the street widened, bordered on one side by shops and open stalls selling merchandise of every sort imaginable. Across the street was the stone seawall, and beyond, wooden docks piled high with crates and barrels. The area teemed with people: servants doing the marketing, burgers' wives buying trinkets and draymen hauling cargo to and fro.

"I hope you do not find it small and poor compared

with the London markets," Mariot said, chewing on her lower lip.

"Nay. 'Tis friendlier. Less...less overwhelming."

Mariot beamed, then looked away as Colan maneuvered his horse alongside hers and bent to speak with her.

"That was kindly said," Jamie remarked.

Emmeline whirled to find him standing at her right stirrup. Even though she sat above him, he still radiated a unique brand of power and vitality that made her feel vulnerable yet protected at the same time. "I like Mariot very much."

"And she you." He smiled, his gaze moving over her face in a caress that was nearly palpable. "Let me help you down." He lifted her to the ground with effortless grace, his hands lingering on her waist, his gaze burning with silent hunger.

The air backed up in her lungs; her heart beat so fast she feared it would fly out of her body.

"I confess I thought it too dangerous to bring you here, but I am glad, now." He tucked a stray lock of hair behind her ear, making the skin tingle. "The fresh air has put roses in your cheeks, and made your eyes twinkle like stars."

'Twas his nearness. "It has also restored the silk in your tongue," she teased.

He chuckled. "Your beauty does that, my lady."

"Fie, sir, for so flattering me. I have a silvered mirror and know the face reflected there is no thing of beauty."

"Not so. I have only one eye, but I find your slender grace, sleek chestnut hair and changeable eyes more appealing than the plump blondes the balladeers laud in their verse."

His compliments went to her head faster than strong wine. No one had ever found anything about her beautiful.

Unconsciously she stepped closer, her mouth raised for the kiss she knew he wanted as much as she did.

"Emma." He lowered his head, blocking out the sun. His lips brushed across hers, once, twice, then they settled over hers, and the rest of the world vanished.

She became a creature of sensation, relishing the taste and feel of his mouth, the subtle slide of his tongue coaxing hers into foray after foray, the fresh scent of soap and man, the delicious glide of his hands on her back as they drew her up against the hard planes of his body. The rapid thud of his heart matched her own ragged pulse; the heat of his body warmed her through their layers of clothing. She could stay here forever.

All too soon he raised his head. "You are potent as Scots whiskey, Emma. One sip, and I forget myself." His voice was low and tight as the tension coiled inside her.

"I am glad you are no longer wroth with me," she said.

"Never that, sweetling. I only wanted to keep you safe."

"I feel safe when I'm with you."

He grinned crookedly. "If you knew what kissing you makes me feel like doing, you'd not feel so safe."

"Indeed." She gazed through her lashes in a challenge as old as Eve. "That does depend on one's view of safety."

"Emma." Her name came out a groan. He leaned his forehead against hers. "I am no good for you."

"Jamie!" exclaimed a harsh, grating voice.

Emmeline turned toward the newcomer and got a decided shock. Beside them stood a man who was Jamie's mirror image, except he had two good eyes.

"Hugh!" Jamie cried. Naked pain mingled with his surprise. "What are you doing here? Is aught wrong at home? Mama? Papa?"

"All is well." Hugh looked as grim as death's messenger. "Or as well as can be expected with the harvest to gather and steps taken to repulse an invasion." He flung the words as though Jamie were somehow responsible for the ripe crops and the French.

"Then why—?"

"I came to warn you that Giles Cadwell sailed for Cornwall."

"Giles, here? Do you know why?"

"Officially, he is going to Truro to collect the Stannary Tax on the tin for the king…at Oxford's behest."

"Unofficially?"

Hugh looked around at the circle of curious Killigrews, and at Emmeline, who still stood beside Jamie. "'Tis a private matter." He glanced at Jamie's eye patch, then away.

Jamie touched the leather, as though receiving a silent message from his brother. "Will it keep an hour or two? I have pressing business just now. If you'll wait and return with us to Arwenack, we can speak there."

Hugh nodded but didn't look at all pleased. "I am sorry my appearance here has angered you, but I sought only to help."

"I am certain you did." Jamie's bland reply did not mask the strain between the two.

How sad. Emmeline looked from Hugh's cool, remote expression to Jamie's shuttered one. What secrets did they hide? What had caused this breach, and how could she heal it? Celia's death had taught her life was too short to be wasted on feuding. She regretted they hadn't been closer. And didn't want Jamie to feel the same if something happened to Hugh.

"…and this is Emma Spencer," Jamie was saying.

Emmeline shook off her brooding and curtsied to Hugh. "I am pleased to meet you, milord."

Hugh inclined his head briefly, coolly. Doubtless he thought she was his brother's mistress.

"Emma is my betrothed," Jamie added.

"Betrothed?" Hugh cried.

"Aye." Did she imagine the defensiveness in Jamie's voice?

"This is...sudden."

Jamie put an arm around her. A gesture of affection or a warning? "She kidnapped me."

"How...unusual."

Jamie grinned. "Aye, she is that." He dropped a kiss on Emmeline's mouth, but the heat of his flesh didn't chase the chill from hers. "I will be back as quick as I can. Mind you wait here and do not get into too much trouble."

"I've been caring for myself for years."

"But that was before you met me." He whirled away and mounted before she could think of a suitable rejoinder. "I'll be back as quick as I can, Hugh," he called over his shoulder.

"I can scarcely credit it...Jamie betrothed," Hugh muttered, staring after him.

Emmeline blinked, realizing that sometime between last night, when Jamie had sung to her, and this morn she'd forgotten the betrothal was a sham.

"Do you think Giles is just here to collect the taxes on the tin?" Bran asked as they rode out of Penryn.

"If so, 'tis the most incredibly bad coincidence that he should arrive now."

"I never believed in coincidences, either." Bran looked back at Colan, who brought up the rear. "Is it still tonight?"

"I've had no word to the contrary."

"You should let me and some of the men come with you. What if DeGrys betrays you?" Bran whispered.

"He won't. He needs me."

"I do not like it. What if something goes wrong? What if you are caught?" Bran grumbled.

"I won't be." He couldn't afford to be, not now when he'd just found Emma and there was a reason to hope for more happiness than he'd ever thought possible. But Jamie knew hope was fragile and life all-too dangerous. "If I am, we'd best hope 'tis after I've met DeGrys, not before."

They crested the hill then, and the trail widened enough for Colan to ride with them. "What is Giles really doing here?" he asked at once. "Do you think Oxford knows about the shipyard? Should we double the guards around the harbor?"

"Nay," Jamie said more sharply than he intended. There were already enough patrols to make sneaking up on the harbor risky. He debated telling Colan about the meeting with DeGrys, but the fewer who knew, the better.

"Mayhap we should capture Giles and his men," Colan said. "We could detain them till it's safe."

"And bring Oxford sniffing around here looking for his thugs?" Jamie shook his head. "Nay, we will go on as we have." By the time they reached the hidden harbor, his teeth hurt from grinding them together. Of all the damned luck to have both Giles and Hugh here. What had happened to send Hugh searching for him?

Part of his anxiety was jealousy, Jamie ruefully admitted. His brother was so like Emma in attitude he feared she'd prefer Hugh to him. The idea of returning to find they'd become friends burned in his gut.

They broke clear of the woods just then, and all three

drew rein to gaze at the harbor far below, its smooth blue surface dotted with ships in various stages of completion.

"You've accomplished much while I was gone," Jamie said.

"The men have worked like demons." Colan's eyes shone with pride. "Still I wish we had more time. I know we agreed to finish as many hulls as possible and then go back to build the decks and aftercastles, but…" He swore and scrubbed a hand over his weary features. "They are so vulnerable right now. If the French found the harbor, we'd not be able to sail all of them to safety."

"If the enemy controlled the hills," Jamie interjected. The passageway between the harbor and the estuary leading out into the sea was so narrow a few archers on the hills could rain death and destruction down on the ships as they passed. "Which the French will never do. The Danes, Vikings, Romans and William's Normans all tried and failed. The French could not land a sizable enough force to take the bay without every Cornishman from here to Penzance mobilizing to drive them off."

"I suppose you are right." Colan looked at the harbor. "But we've worked so hard, and these ships may be our only bulwark against another conquest of England."

"Aye, they are." *But not in the way you think, my friend.* Jamie wanted to tell Colan the truth, but knew he dared not. "I am more worried about Oxford," he said, shifting in the saddle. "Lancaster is certain he means to force through a treaty with the French that will put him in power. If Oxford learns about the fleet, he'll destroy it."

"I say we get rid of Giles," Bran growled.

"I don't think we need go that far." Jamie grinned. "There's five and twenty miles of rough country between here and Truro, and Giles'll be kept busy there." The Stannary Charter of 1201 that extended to Cornish tin miners the rights of free men had also established a system by which the tin they streamed from the rivers was stamped and the tax on it paid every half year. "The tinners are a drunken, lawless breed who'll not give up their gain willingly. Giles will have his hands full."

By the time they returned to Penryn, Jamie had nearly convinced himself that all would be well. Giles would stay in Truro, Hugh would not long remain away from Harte Court. Everything was going to be just fine.

His first hint that he'd deluded himself came when they reached the Hawk and Hart tavern and found Hugh had escorted the women back to Arwenack. Damn, had Emmeline been so taken with his brother she hadn't even cared to wait for him?

In a foul mood, Jamie spurred his horse for the castle.

Chapter Eleven

"Do you need help?" a familiar voice inquired.

"Jamie!" Emmeline spun away from the pot she'd been stirring over the fire, "I'm so glad you've..." She stopped when she saw who stood in the doorway of the solar. "Oh, 'tis you, Lord Hugh."

"Women are usually disappointed when they find 'tis me and not my brother," he muttered.

"I did not mean...that is, I am not disappointed, but I've put Mariot to bed." The poor girl had fainted before the tailor's stall, and they'd brought her back to Penryn in a litter. "She must stay quiet, and asked me to run the household for her, but I've no experience in such things. Not that the maids would follow my orders if I knew what to say. They are so worried about Mariot they do naught but cry and wring their hands. I—I thought Jamie would know what to do."

"Jamie, see to some domestic matters?" Hugh strolled over to the hearth, his freshly scrubbed face and clean clothes making her aware of her tangled hair and dusty skirts. "He will not even manage his own estates. I fear he is not interested in anything but fighting, sailing and wenching."

Emmeline flinched at the last. "He would help me."

"Your loyalty does you credit. I hope he appreciates it."

"He does," Emmeline snapped, worried about Mariot and in no mood to listen to Hugh's carping. "I know you do not approve of me, but that is no reason to go looking for faults in Jamie."

"I've never needed to. He has them aplenty." Hugh studied her a moment. "But I should not take my wrath at him out on you. I do not disapprove of you," he added. "Indeed, I am pleased he has decided to wed, and you seem a most sensible girl, not at all the frivolous sort he usually consorts with. I was impressed with the way you reacted when Lady Mariot took ill. Lord Petrok was no help, and we might still be milling about in Penryn had you not taken charge. Though my parents would have preferred he wed an heiress with land and money, you have much to recommend you."

How cleverly he'd managed to insult and praise her at the same time. "Thank you, I think."

"Not at all." He gave no sign he'd even heard her little jest. Jamie would have grinned and teased her. "I have some skill at managing an estate. If you like, I will go down and set the servants to their tasks."

"It might be best…if we hope to dine today," she added with a smile. That, too, went over Hugh's head, and she keenly missed Jamie's sense of humor.

"I'll see there is dinner," he said so grimly she felt obliged to move the potion off the fire and follow him. He set such a brisk pace she had to lift her skirts and run down the steps to keep up.

The great hall was crowded with Killigrews. Abnormally quiet Killigrews. They huddled together in small groups, the men bleak faced and worried, the maids red eyed from weeping. The moment they spotted Emmeline, they came to life. Surging forward, they cried out for news of their mistress.

"Silence!" Hugh bellowed.

The Killigrews flinched and drew back.

"That is better. Your lady is being tended to—"

"How is she?" someone shouted.

"Will she live? What of the babe?"

"These matters are in God's hands." Hugh eyed them with stern disapproval. "Whilst yours are idle. Whatever happens to your lady, life here must go on. Why has the fire been allowed to die down? Why do I not smell dinner cooking in the kitchen?"

Emmeline plucked at his sleeve. "Milord, go easy. They love Mariot and are worried about her."

"Softness will not move them." Raising his voice, he asked, "How can your lady rest easy when the work lays undone? How will she thrive if there is no food for her to eat?"

"I will see the meal started," offered one woman.

"Are you the cook?" Hugh demanded.

The woman stiffened. "The housekeeper."

"Ah." He looked down his nose at her. "Then we will leave you in charge of these...laggards."

Around them, the crowd shifted, people muttering to each other in Cornish and glaring at Hugh.

Hugh crossed his arms over his chest and glared right back. "Your lady will be most disappointed when she learns you have let worry over her get in the way of your responsibilities."

One by one, the Killigrews turned away and went about their tasks. A group of women disappeared behind the screen that led to the pantry and, thence, to the kitchens. Others began to tidy the tables, while two men tossed a great log into the fire. They were working, yet their wretched expressions tore at Emmeline.

"Did you have to make them feel so guilty?" she asked.

"Guilt is a powerful motivator and far kinder than the lash," Hugh muttered. "None of us can shirk our duties. If the lord fails to protect his people, they are vulnerable to attack. If the servants fail to serve the lord, all will starve."

Emmeline nodded glumly. Lord Hugh was clearly a hard worker, but humorless and insensitive. She understood the former. When their mother had taken ill, Emmeline had worked from dawn to dark trying to run the shop and had expected Celia to do the same. Celia had balked. Emmeline had called her lazy and shiftless. Watching Jamie with his men had taught Emmeline that people work better when urged by smiles and praise than by scowls and threats. Jamie would have gotten the Killigrews back to work without making them feel badly.

"Had you not best go upstairs and finish the potion you were preparing for Lady Mariot?" Hugh asked.

"You are right, of course." Emmeline lifted her skirts and nearly ran from the hall. Halfway up the stairs, she realized Hugh was behind her. "Where are you going?"

"You will have difficulty lifting that heavy pot."

True, but she had no desire for Hugh's company. "What of the servants? Are you not afraid they will laze about if you are not there to supervise them?"

If he heard her sarcasm, he didn't show it. "My squire is there. He'll make certain they keep busy."

Emmeline recalled the man, tall and burly, with black hair and sharp, canny eyes. "It may take an hour to boil down the infusion into a syrup," she warned.

"I have naught else to occupy my time. 'Twould give me a chance to learn something of my new sister." Though he stood below her, their faces were level with each other. Seeing his two good eyes made her wonder what was beneath the patch on Jamie's left one. Hugh would know. This was her chance to find out about Jamie.

"Very well." She led the way up to the solar. As they entered the room, she realized there was a slight hesitation in Hugh's step. "Did you injure yourself on the ride from Penryn?"

"Nay." He glared at her. "You must know I was wounded in the same incident that took Jamie's eye."

Emmeline wet her lips. "He did mention it, but he did not say how it came about."

"I am not surprised." Hugh walked away from her, his steps so controlled the limp was nearly invisible. "Shall I add more wood to the fire?"

Hmm. The mystery deepened. "Please do." She hurried over and knelt beside the hearth. The herbal infusion had not suffered from her brief absence, but it needed at least another hour of cooking. She grasped the handle to lift the pot.

"Allow me." Hugh took up the pot, effortlessly positioned it on the hook over the fire, then raked the coals and new bits of wood under the bottom of the pot.

Emmeline thanked him and busied herself grinding the rosemary leaves in a small mortar.

"That smell reminds me of home. Mama has the maids strew rosemary in the rushes to keep them fresh smelling."

"Your home is very grand," she said, though grand was inadequate to describe the vast, humbling estate.

"You've been there?"

Drat. "Jamie described it so lovingly."

"He did? I am surprised, since he has refused to take over the running of estate."

Now she was surprised. Jamie's yearning when he spoke

of his home had been so marked. "You can like a thing without wanting to possess it," she said slowly.

"Not something like Harte Court! But overseeing the most beautiful lands in England is too tame a task for Jamie," he snapped. His intensity was startling, so at odds with his former reserve. "He'd rather be off adventuring at sea or wenching with his low friends."

"Oh," she murmured, stricken.

"It was thoughtless of me to mention his other women. The only excuse I can offer is that I am not yet used to the idea of Jamie having a betrothed wife." He cleared his throat. "I—I should like to know you better. Hmm. Where did Jamie meet you?"

Now she was discomforted. "At a, er, festival."

"Your parents, where do they live?"

"I am orphaned." More or less.

"That explains why you are here with Jamie." He tisked. "'Tis not at all proper. We should engage a companion for you."

"Whatever for?"

"To safeguard your reputation." He rubbed his clean-shaven chin. She marveled that he'd not only washed and changed, but shaved upon their return from Penryn. "A nun would be preferable. To sleep in a pallet beside your bed," he added.

Emmeline struggled against the urge to laugh, imagining Jamie's surprise when he went to lie down on his pallet and discovered it occupied by a holy sister. "'Tis not necessary."

"Surely he has not already bedded you!" Hugh exclaimed.

"Nay." Her cheeks flamed hot as the kisses they'd shared. If not for Jamie's honor, hers would have been compromised.

Looking immensely relieved, Hugh cleared his throat. "'Tis none of my business, of course. I do not usually interfere in his affairs," he said stiffly. "But you will one day be a Harcourt, and thus your reputation is no small matter to the family."

He made it sound as if they were royalty. She was envious of such family pride and, anxious to learn more, asked, "Tell me of your childhood."

Hugh shrugged. "As the second son, I was preparing to enter the church. 'Tis a goodly calling, and I'd been assured of a rich post through my father's connections at court."

A rich post? She was disappointed to hear his calling was for profit, not religious devotion. "What happened?"

He looked at his left leg. It stuck out a trifle stiffly. "The church did not want a lame man as bishop."

"But you do not appear lame at all."

"At the time, 'twas not certain I'd keep the leg, much less ever walk again. They chose someone else."

"I am so sorry."

"I need no one's pity."

"Nor do I offer it." Sweet Mary, but he was touchy. "I understand what it is like to be denied something you greatly desire. I inherited my mother's apothecary shop and am good at herb craft...but I'd rather sing and play the lute."

"You are a merchant!" he exclaimed in horror.

She flinched, then raised her chin. "'Tis an honorable craft requiring great skill. I am proud to follow after her."

"Of course. I am just...surprised, for you do not seem coarse at all. Your speech is cultured, your manner polished."

"I clean my teeth each day and am relatively free of lice, as well," she couldn't resist adding.

Hugh's eyes widened, then caught the glint in her eye and frowned. "I meant to compliment you," he grumbled.

She supposed he did, but he was so...so unbearably stuffy. It was hard to believe he was Jamie's brother, much less his twin. "Forgive me, my lord. I fear I have a rather unfortunate sense of humor." To make amends, she told him a bit about the training an apothecary undertook, learning to read, write and cipher, in addition to memorizing the names and uses of hundreds of herbs. "'Tis vital that the right proportions be used in mixing a salve or potion and that the correct one be matched to the customer's ails. A plant that heals in a small portion, may kill in a larger dose."

"Indeed," Hugh murmured. He supposed it was too much to hope she'd poison Jamie in a fit of jealous pique. That his brother would stray was a foregone conclusion. Though passingly pretty, the little spice merchant couldn't hope to hold the interest of a jaded womanizer like Jamie. Could she?

Hugh studied her closely as she bent to stir the herbs steeping in the pot. Personally he preferred blondes, but there was something about Emmeline. A subtle blend of innocence and earthiness that was very appealing. Pity she was so lowborn. Why had Jamie betrothed himself to her? To coax her into his bed? Likely, knowing him.

Panic clawed at Hugh's vitals as a new thought intruded. What if Jamie wed her and produced an heir? A rival for Harte Court. Damn. He'd never expected his wastrel brother would marry. He'd assumed Jamie would one day be washed overboard in a storm or killed by an enraged husband. He'd become so complacent, he'd actually begun to consider Harte Court his. He'd accepted the betrothal contract with Neville's daughter because her property abutted his estate. Only it wasn't his...it was Jamie's.

"When did you say you were to wed Jamie?" Hugh asked.

"We...we have not yet set a date."

Hmm. Mayhap the betrothal *was* just a seductive ruse. "Well, I hope you will not let my brother lead you astray before the vows are spoken," Hugh said as forcefully as he dared. "He has ever been ruled by his, er, baser nature, but he will cease to respect you if you yield to him before you are wed."

"I will remember," she whispered, red with shame.

"Just to be on the safe side, I will speak with Lady Mariot about finding a nun."

"You are most thoughtful, my lord."

"Hugh." He took her hand and squeezed it gently. "After all, we are to be brother and sister."

The door to the solar flew open and hit the wall with a resounding thump.

"Well, isn't this cozy," Jamie snarled, stalking into the room like a tiger sizing up a rival that had invaded his domain, stolen his mate.

Hugh dropped Emmeline's hand and leapt up. "You are back."

"Obviously. What the hell is going on here?" Jamie demanded.

Jamie was jealous of him? Hugh could hardly credit it.

"We are preparing some medicine for Mariot," Emmeline said.

Jamie's lip curled. "You seemed most intent on each other."

"What?" Emmeline exclaimed. "Nay, I...we have been anxiously awaiting your return." She looked beyond him and frowned. "But where is Colan? Has he already gone—"

"Leave Colan out of this!" Jamie shouted. "I want to

know what my betrothed wife is doing alone with my brother.''

Hugh swallowed and stepped forward. "I am sorry, but—''

"You will not apologize," Emmeline snapped, swishing in front of him, fists on hips, eyes furious. "We have done naught wrong. Hugh was but helping me to brew a potion for Mariot.''

Jamie looked toward the hearth. "I think it's burning.''

"What?" Emmeline whirled around, spotted the plume of gray smoke and shrieked, "Imbecile. Look what you've made me do." She dropped to her knees, grabbed for the cooking pot and cried out again as the hot metal singed her fingertips.

Hugh was closer, but Jamie was quicker. Pushing her out of the way with one hand, he scooped up the leather pad and moved the iron pot off the coals. Without pausing to check the smoldering contents, he reached for Emma. "Let me see." He cradled her hands in his, turning them over to reveal angry red blotches on her fingers and thumbs. "Don't just stand there, Hugh, get the herb woman. Or a leech. Bring salve and—''

"I am fine," Emma said softly.

"Only look at your poor fingers. They are burned," Jamie said in an appalled whisper.

"A bit singed, no more. I've suffered worse sticking my fingers into hot water.''

Jamie touched her cheek. "I do not like seeing you hurt.''

Frozen in place, Hugh stared at the pair of them in dawning horror. Never had he seen his brother act so around a woman. First jealousy, then this…this panic over a few blisters. Panicked himself at what this might mean, Hugh opted for retreat. "I will go and make certain the servants are about their work.'' He left quickly, needing time to think this through.

"Jamie, whatever has gotten into you?'' Emma asked as the door closed after Hugh.

Jamie had no idea. Nay, that was not so. He knew full well why he'd made a fool of himself. He loved her. He shouldn't. Unfortunately, knowing that did not ease the longing he felt whenever he was near her. Or thought of her. Dredging up some of his scattered control, he asked, "What can I do for you?''

"Stop shouting. And stop jumping to unfounded conclusions,'' she softly added, with a rare, teasing grin.

"I cannot help myself. We Sommerville males are notoriously protective of our ladies.''

"But our betrothal is just a ploy—''

"Aye, so it is,'' Jamie said softly, regretfully. Then he turned his mind to safer ground. "Why is Hugh going to check on the servants?''

"Things are in a muddle because Mariot was taken ill while we were in Penryn. Did Colan return with you?''

"Aye. He stopped in the stables. Is Mariot all right?''

"She is resting and the pains in her belly have stopped, but she lost a babe last year. I'm doing all I can to save this one.'' She poked a spoon into the gummy residue at the bottom of the bowl, wincing as the wooden handle scraped her burned flesh.

"Let me be your hands.''

"Really? You would stoop to doing woman's work?''

"Healing is everyone's work. Tell me what I should do.''

"If you will get the wine pitcher from yonder sideboard, I will see if I cannot save this potion.''

They worked together for several minutes, the silence

broken only by her mumbled instructions. He followed them exactly, stirring wine into the dark paste at the bottom of the bowl.

"Why did you shout at us?" Emma asked as he raked up the coals and hung the small iron pot over them.

"I was jealous."

"Of your brother?" She looked utterly confused.

"He's the sort of man you would prefer...sober, honorable and as dependable as a rock."

Emma giggled. "I thought him rather pompous."

"You did?" He felt dizzy with relief.

She explained about Hugh's lecture to the servants. "He was right to chide them for standing about, but 'twas out of worry, not laziness. He hurt their feelings, but what could I say without making it seem I condoned their behavior?"

"Hugh has a way of doing that. He means well, but he sees things as all good or all bad. And, I fear, he thinks me the most black hearted of wretches, incapable of being redeemed."

"He suggested I have a nun for a companion."

"To pray for your soul?"

"To safeguard my virtue from you till we're wed."

"Oh." Jamie blinked. "What did you say?"

"I did not tell him the betrothal was a sham."

A sham. He didn't want it to be. He wanted—

"Lady Emma!" Colan skidded to a halt in the doorway. "Hugh said Mariot was ill. Where is she?"

"I have put her to bed. Wait!" Emmeline called when Colan made to run out again. "Let me speak here of what happened rather than upset her by talking in her presence." She went on to tell of the pains that had struck whilst they were shopping and of the hurried journey home. "We rigged a blanket between two of the horses, and Lord Hugh walked beside it the whole way. She is resting comfortably, but should stay abed for several days.''

"I thank you." Tears glinted in Colan's eyes. "If anything happens to her I don't know what I'd do."

"Is Mariot all right?" Bran asked, coming in behind his brother. "Jesu, if she should die..."

"She will not," Emmeline said firmly, though she was by no means positive she'd keep the babe. "She is strong, and the cramping produced no bleeding." She shouldn't have said that, for all three men blanched. Here, she thought, were men who cared for their womenfolk.

"Can I go to her?" Colan asked.

"Of course, providing you say naught to excite her. I will come with you and give her this infusion. After she drinks it, she will sleep until the morrow."

"Shall I carry that pot for you?" Jamie asked.

"Colan had best take it. The fewer people we have in the room, the better." She was all brisk efficiency now, intent on her patient, but she paused at the threshold. "You and Bran look as though you could use a bit of fortifying. There is wine in the pitcher on yon table." She was gone in a swish of woolen skirts, but her thoughtfulness lingered.

"What about tonight?" Bran murmured.

Jamie shrugged. Restless, he poured himself a cup of wine and drank without tasting it. "We could not change the arrangement even if we wanted to." Simon DeGrys would be waiting for him off Flushing Point. The proper lantern signal would bring him in and the dance would begin. If he wasn't there, DeGrys would likely assume he'd changed his mind or been captured. Either way, his plans would be ruined.

"Has your brother explained his presence here?"

"Nay. There hasn't been time for a private word."

"Mayhap it's a sham. You said Hugh supported this peace treaty of Oxford's. Could he be here to spy on you?"

"Hugh?" Jamie snorted. "We've had our differences, but to Hugh, family loyalty is everything. He proved that by nearly getting himself killed trying to save me."

"Save you from what?" Emma asked, coming back into the room.

"Myself," Jamie replied, not untruthfully.

Emma blinked. "What is it? You both look so...grim."

"We were worried about Mariot," Jamie said smoothly.

Bran scowled. Switching to Cornish, he said he'd go and check on Hugh's movements. But he stopped beside Emma before he left. "Thank you for helping Mariot. She is a good woman. One of the few." The words sounded as though they'd been torn from the private hell inside him.

"I was glad to help," Emma replied.

Bran grunted, shot Jamie a warning look and stalked out.

"What a strange man he is," Emma said.

"Not so strange when you consider he blames himself for his mother's death. Guilt turns a man bitter."

She tilted her head, considering this for a moment. "You speak from personal experience...something having to do with Hugh. That is part of the strain between you."

Jamie nodded, no longer questioning how she seemed to know his inner feelings. Reflexively he touched the patch. "Sometime, when I'm feeling particularly brave, mayhap I will tell you the tale...or what I recall of it." He stood, uncomfortable with the notion her growing respect would be shattered when she learned what had happened that terrible day. "Speaking of Hugh, I'd better find him and see what brought him here."

"I suppose I had best go down and make certain all is in readiness for dinner," she said glumly.

"Why do you grimace? Do your hands pain you?"

"Nay. I dread the task, is all."

"Why? 'Tis surely far easier than curing the sick."

"That, I am at least trained for. 'Tis a good thing you are not really contracted to wed me, my lord, or you'd find yourself shackled to a woman who has no idea how to manage a household."

Jamie tucked her hand into the crook of his arm, careful not to touch her fingertips, which were smeared with salve. "With the exception of my Aunt Gaby, the Sommerville wives are not much interested in such things. Aunt Arianna is a goldsmith. My mother concerns herself with the land and welfare of the peasants."

"They are unusual women, then."

"So are you, Emma." Jamie released her hand and gestured for her to precede him, as the stairway was too narrow for them to walk side by side. He studied her thick braids and the straight spine they beat against, the gentle sway of her hips as she negotiated the winding steps. She was unusual and special. If only he'd met her earlier...or later, when this was all over...

They found Hugh in the hall arguing with the steward over the placement of the trestle tables for dinner.

"The lords of Arwenack have always sat with the people. What would Lord Petrok think if he found his table set off by itself on a dais?" the steward muttered.

"He would thank you for bringing civilization to the benighted corner of Cornwall," Hugh said, tight-lipped and stern.

"Benighted!" cried the steward.

Emma tugged on Jamie's arm. "Quickly, get your brother away before his scolding starts another quarrel."

"Your wish is my command." Jamie kissed her and waded through the crowd of tense Killigrews, thinking how well he and Emma worked together. "Hugh," he called, just as the steward turned an unbecoming shade of purple. "Did you not say you had something you wished to tell me?"

Hugh glowered at the steward. "'Twill keep till I've..."

"Nay. I have to go out in a few hours and would know what trouble is brewing."

"Out?" Hugh seemed to come alert, like a hound scenting game. The expression was so fleeting it could have been a trick of the light. "Is there somewhere we could be private?"

Jamie nodded and hustled his brother back up the stairs to the chamber he shared with Emma.

Declining both the offer of a chair and a cup of wine, Hugh posed before the empty hearth, arms crossed over his chest in the manner of a parent about to lecture. "Lily has been murdered."

"Lily?" Jamie frowned, thinking back of the women he had known over the years. He prided himself on recalling all their faces, but a few of the names eluded him. "Should I know her?"

"She was Celia's maid."

Jamie paused, wine cup suspended halfway to his mouth. A shiver of foreboding crept down his spine. "Celia's maid...I do not believe I ever saw her. Celia's and my acquaintance was brief. I helped her out of a bit of trouble...she was grateful." Jamie shrugged negligently. "A swift coupling in her chamber, and I went on my way." Celia had several times invited him back, but he'd made excuses, having found her tedious and clinging. The invitations stopped abruptly, and he'd supposed she'd found someone else. "I never saw the maid at all."

Hugh's disapproving scowl deepened. "If you take up with women you barely know and treat them so cavalierly, 'tis no wonder you find yourself embroiled in such a dreadful business. Lily apparently remembered things differently. According to Sir Thomas Burton, she claims you were a regular visitor to her lady for many months. Her only male caller. Her lover, in fact."

Jamie sighed and raked a hand through his hair. "She is mistaken or lying. I had not been in London for months, and the crew of the *Lady* told Sir Thomas so."

"Lily was murdered the night after Mama's fete. Do you have an alibi for that night, too?"

"Why would I need one? I didn't know the girl. Has Sir Thomas sent you to arrest me?"

"Hardly," Hugh exclaimed. "I am your brother. I am on your side in this."

He certainly didn't sound like it, but then, Hugh's manner was always brusque and censorious...especially toward his wayward twin. "Then why did you come so far to tell me this?"

"To warn you. Oxford has taken an interest in the case. He has sent Giles to Cornwall, supposedly to collect the tin tax. In reality, Giles is to find proof against you."

"How Giles must relish that!" Jamie slammed the cup on the table; wine sloshed over the rim, scattering across the mellow oak like droplets of blood. "I think 'twas he who murdered Celia and tried to frame me. It makes sense. I first met Celia while saving her from Giles's unwanted attentions. He was furious at me for interfering and at her for refusing him. What better way to repay us both than to kill her and implicate me in the crime?"

"Indeed." Hugh cleared his throat. "Do you have proof?"

"Proof of what?" Emma asked from the doorway.

Jamie's fears shifted suddenly. If Lily had been eliminated because Celia's killer thought she knew something, Emma could also be in danger. "'Tis nothing, love."

"Another woman has been murdered," Hugh said.

"Murdered?" Emma entered slowly, looking from one of them to the other. "And you think Jamie did it?" she asked of Hugh.

"Not I, but—"

"I did not even know the woman." Jamie wrapped a protective arm around Emma. "Were you looking for me?"

Emma was not deterred. "Who has died?"

"A maidservant," Jamie said quickly.

"When?"

"The night following our mother's fete," Hugh replied.

"Oh." Emma relaxed. "He has an excellent alibi. He was tied up, from the moment he left Harte Court till three nights later."

Hugh scowled. "Sir Thomas checked with the harbormaster. The *Lady* was in port then, though she had been expected to sail."

"He was not aboard ship, he was at my shop."

Jamie tightened his grip on Emma and shot her a warning glance. "I don't think Hugh will be interested in our courtship."

She glanced up at him, smiling. "But 'tis such a fascinating tale. If I had not kidnapped you."

"You kidnapped him?" Hugh asked, shocked. "Why ever—?"

"She was captivated by my charms. Were you looking for me, love? Did you need something?" Jamie asked.

Emma frowned. "I came to change my gown for dinner." She gestured toward the bed, where the maid had laid out a blue cotehardie. Beside it lay Jamie's second-best tunic.

Hugh gasped. "You two are sharing a room?" he cried.

"'Tis not so strange," Jamie countered. Many a betrothed couple slept together.

"Appalling." Hugh launched into a diatribe on the necessity of preserving Emma's good name.

Jamie accepted it with good grace, glad to have the subject of Lily's death forgotten for the moment. When they were private, he'd tell Emma about it and warn her to say nothing about being Celia's sister. He even agreed to move out into one of the lesser wall chambers. But he chose the one closest to this room. Not because he hoped to sneak in a visit to Emma, but so he'd be nearby to defend his lady.

"Yer brother is up to something," Hollis grumbled in Hugh's ear as he bent to refill his cup.

Hugh glanced across the table and down a few places to where Jamie sat with Emmeline. He was attentive enough to his lowborn betrothed, but under the flirting and banter was an air of suppressed tension Hugh knew only too well. Jamie was bent on some mischief. "Agreed," he whispered.

"Shall I send word to Lord Giles?" Hollis and Roger, posing as his squire and page respectively, were Giles's men.

"And tell him what? That Jamie's gaiety seems forced? We do not know what is about to happen or where." Hugh glanced about, careful to hide his censure of the Killigrews' castle. "For the moment, we must bide our time."

Hugh settled back to enjoy the meal. The food was surprisingly good, if simple—fish in a cream sauce, stewed hare, meat pies and plenty of wine. Bordeaux, his palate told him. His conviction that Jamie and his cohorts were involved in smuggling, grew, and with it, his determination to catch his brother.

Dieu, how I hate him, Hugh thought, watching Jamie preen before his betrothed. She laughed at something he said, her face glowing. Her gaze flicked to his patch and softened even more. Damn. Why did women find Jamie's disfigurement romantic while his limp repulsed them? It was not fair. Not fair at all. Hugh intended to see that Jamie paid this time...for every past slight.

"Will we sing again tonight?" Hugh heard Emmeline ask as the servants removed the gravy-soaked trenchers.

"Nay, I fear I must go out this evening," Jamie replied.

Out of the corner of his eye, Hugh saw the girl blanch.

Jamie took her hand and kissed it, murmuring something that made the color flood back into her cheeks. She looked down, her manner shy and virginal. Jamie smiled and touched a lock of her hair, his manner protective and reserved. But his gaze smoldered when he looked at her, and he was as finely drawn as a stallion around a mare in heat.

Hugh pursed his lips. Jamie claimed they'd not shared a bed, and watching them together, Hugh was inclined to believe him. But 'twas only a matter of time before they became lovers. The fact that Jamie had agreed to move out of her chamber increased Hugh's worries instead of easing them. Jamie had never before been so solicitous of a woman's reputation.

Jamie stood and gently touched Emmeline's shoulder. "I must go out, Hugh. Would you mind bearing Emma company?"

"'Twould be my pleasure. A chance to get to know my new sister better," Hugh said. She was a clever girl who knew more than she let on. But he was far more canny than any mere girl. One way or another, he'd trick her into betraying Jamie's plans.

200   *Scandal's Daughter*

... intimacy anymore. Either way, he risked losing Emmie's love.

Chapter Twelve

"**I** am worried about Jamie," Hugh said. He and Emmeline sat at the table while Jamie went to arm for his mysterious errand. "I feel he is involved in something dangerous."

Emmeline shivered. Her nerves were still raw from the discussion she'd had with Jamie just before dinner. Lily was dead. Strangled to death, like Celia. Coincidence? Jamie didn't think so, and neither did Emmeline. The news that this Giles Cadwell was now in Cornwall had greatly disturbed Jamie. Why? He had an alibi for the night Lily was murdered. But he was hiding something else from her. Something to do with the fleet?

"We were not close as lads, but I always knew when Jamie was up to some mischief. Only now he is a man grown, and the mischief is far more serious. Did he tell you where he was going?"

"Only not to worry if he was not back before dawn." She turned to Hugh. "I am afraid, too."

He patted her hand. "I do not think it is another woman. Not when he looks at you so warmly."

Emmeline gritted her teeth. Did he think her so shallow that all she cared about was Jamie's regard?

"I think 'tis smuggling." Hugh's expression hardened as he glanced around. "If so, 'tis the Killigrews' influence. Not that Jamie is a saint, but he has grown wealthy on legitimate trade. He has no need to resort to smuggling, but these Cornishmen dislike the king and seek to cheat him of his revenue."

Smuggling no longer seemed the crime it had before she'd met the Killigrews. "The king would only spend the coin on luxuries."

Hugh looked at her aghast. "That is beside the point. The revenues are King Richard's by law, and if Jamie is dealing with the French, the penalty could be stiff indeed. I tried to warn him earlier this evening, but he refused to discuss it, insisted he was in no danger, but I know when he is lying."

"How stiff a penalty?"

"For trading with the enemy, the charge could well be treason. The penalty for that is drawing and quartering."

Emmeline gasped. "But...but how could they catch him?"

"Giles Cadwell," Hugh replied. "He is Jamie's enemy. He thinks, and I agree, that Giles may have murdered Celia and tried to frame him. I cannot help but think Giles has gotten wind of Jamie's smuggling and come here to ruin him."

Not smuggling. She knew this had something to do with the fleet. Emmeline's heart sank. "What can we do?"

"I must find out where Jamie is going and help him."

She hesitated, wondering whether to trust Hugh or not. What if Jamie had received word the French knew about the ships and were planning to burn them? He and Bran would do everything they could to stop that.

A stir at the far end of the hall delayed her decision. Jamie strode toward her, his mail and armor gleaming in the torchlight, his cape flowing out behind him. How strong he looked. How invincible, but the eye patch was a silent reminder that he was only too human. Too vulnerable.

She stood at his approach, longing to fling herself into his arms and weep. Instead, she laid a hand on his chest. The thud of his heart echoed beneath the metal links. "Please don't go."

"I must." He caught hold of her hand and drew her into the relative privacy of a recessed window. "Why so glum? Shall I ask Enyon to fetch Mariot's lute so you can play for Hugh? He is no great lover of music, but your playing could charm even—"

"I am afraid for you."

He smiled faintly. "'Tis flattering to have you fret over me, my lady," he drawled in that smooth courtier's voice of his. "Will you give me a token to carry with me?"

Emmeline cuffed him in the arm. "'Tis no laughing matter."

"Hold, you will bruise yourself." He took her fist and kissed the red spot. "My life is not worth one mark—"

"To me it is."

His smile faltered. "Emma...do not care. You will end up being hurt, and that I could not bear."

She lifted her chin, desperate enough to throw away her pride. "Your warning comes too late. I started out hating you, but somehow...somehow you have made me care—"

He covered her mouth with his, as though stopping the words would change what she felt. The kiss ran through her like strong wine, dulling her senses to everything save the feel of his warm lips and strong arms, but when he lifted his head, she saw the regret in his gaze. "God help me for wanting what I should not...cannot in all good conscience...take."

"Jamie, what is it? Where are you going?"

"I cannot tell you."

"Promise me you will come back unhurt."

"Ah, now you have confused me with a gypsy fortune-teller." He kissed the tip of her nose. "Knowing he has a woman such as you waiting for him is the strongest reason a man can have for wanting to survive. I care for you, too, Emma. God help us both." He was gone before she could recover her wits or her breath.

"What did he say?" Hugh demanded.

"He..." *He cares.* Joy swelled inside her till she thought she might burst with the wonder of it. A week ago she'd despised the man she had *thought* he was. Then he'd showed her how deceiving appearances could be. He'd given her a glimpse of the way things could be between a woman and an honorable man.

God help her, she *was* falling in love with him.

Hugh gave her a little shake. "Do not stand there like a moonstruck calf. Did he say where he was going?"

Going? Reality sobered her. "H-he skirted my questions."

"He is good at that." Hugh glanced around. "Well, I guess there is no hope for it. I shall have to try and follow him."

Emmeline caught hold of his arm. "You'd become lost in the woods. Jamie knows what he is doing."

Hugh snorted. "He thought the same on the day he lost his eye. Did he tell you his reckless disregard for his own safety nearly cost him his life, too?"

"Nay. He refuses to speak of what happened."

"He rushed headlong into trouble, and would have died had I not disregarded his command to the contrary and rescued him. 'Tis my sworn duty to do so again. I could not live with myself or look my parents in the eye again did I let him die."

Again Emmeline hesitated, weighing the risks of crossing Jamie against the danger. "What could the two of us do?"

"We could follow and see what happens. Giles does not dare kill him in coldblood, else he'd have done so before now. He wants to discredit Jamie, expose him to disgrace and ruin. We will bear witness to what goes on and sound the alarm if we see Giles in the area. Do you know where Jamie is going?"

"It sounds a chancy plan."

"It could save Jamie. I will go alone if you don't—"

"Nay. I will help." She considered her options. What harm if they rode to the shipyard and took a look around? Bran and a dozen Killigrews were going with Jamie. Colan was remaining behind, but he'd be unlikely to tell her anything. Men stuck together. But... "Mariot might know. Colan tells her everything."

"Go and question her, dammit," Hugh demanded.

Emmeline frowned, disturbed by his insensitivity. "I will ask, but I dare not press her without endangering her health."

"My brother's life is at stake," Hugh hissed.

"I love him, too," she murmured.

Hugh's expression grew darker. "All women do...even those who should have better sense. Go and see what you can learn. Remember, Jamie's safety, his very life, may rest on this."

With those ominous words ringing in her head, Emmeline went up to the master chamber. Mariot was awake and glad to see her.

"Oh, Emmeline. How can I ever thank you for saving my babe?" She held out her hands.

Emmeline took them, feeling like a fraud. "I'm so glad you are feeling better, but you must not get up."

"As if I could. Colan glares at me if I so much as lift my hand. He has gone down to get a warm brick for my..." She frowned. "What is it? You look worried. Is there something you haven't told me about the babe?"

"Oh, nothing like that," Emmeline rushed to assure her. "'Tis just that Jamie and Bran have gone out."

"More bands of spies sneaking around?"

"I don't think so. No alarm sounded, and they've only taken a dozen men with them." She swallowed, but the lump still stuck in her throat.

Mariot smiled. "Likely they've gone to check on something at the shipyard."

"Is it a long ride?" Emmeline asked, fishing cautiously as she plumped up Mariot's pillows.

"Six miles or so, just the other side of Penryn."

"Is the trek wild and dangerous?"

"Nay. The pass that leads down from the hills to the shore is steep, but not overly so."

"I wish Jamie had taken more men with him. He thinks he is invincible, but he's far, far too vulnerable."

Under cover of checking on her patient, Emmeline asked questions here and there till she knew enough to find the harbor.

Dark clouds crowded the sky, blocking out the moon and stars. A stiff wind, heavy with the promise of rain, ruffled the waters of Carrick Roads as Jamie watched a boat set out from the French galley and row toward shore. He waited alone on the narrow strip of beach. He'd ordered Bran and the others to patrol the hills two miles to the west, safely out of the way in case something went wrong and he was taken.

Predictably, Bran had objected. "If DeGrys doesn't live up to his part of the bargain, you'll have need of us."

"Simon has no reason to double-cross me. I'm giving him what he wants most. You are the only person in Cornwall who knows what I'm about. If this goes sour, you must get word to Harry. And…and tell my family I—I did what I thought best."

The grating of rocks against the boat's hull pulled Jamie from his reverie just as the sailors shipped their oars.

"The red rose smells sweetest," whispered a male voice.

"Yet is not without thorns," Jamie replied. He wondered if the Frenchman appreciated the jest on Lancaster's symbol.

"*Bien.*" A tall man stood up in the middle of the small boat and was lifted by his men onto the beach. Lord Simon DeGrys inclined his silvery head. Despite his haughty manner, the Frenchman was a shrewd old fox. A cagey opponent, Lancaster had dubbed him, but a realist, which was why John of Gaunt had approached Simon with this delicate matter.

"You are prompt," Simon DeGrys murmured.

"'Twould not do to dally here." Both were aware the business they had undertaken was fraught with risks. If Simon was caught snooping around on English soil, he'd be hanged as a spy. If Jamie was found helping him, he'd die a traitor's death—hanged, then drawn and quartered.

"You have mounts?" DeGrys asked.

"Not as grand as you are used to, milord, but hardy beasts well suited to this terrain."

Simon looked up at the jagged cliffs and the thick foliage cresting them. His aristocratic features showed a glimmer of respect for the impressive natural defenses. "Our ships have sailed these waters, but we could tell naught of the land beyond these cliffs. 'Twill be interesting to see what you have been hiding within all these years."

"I hope to make the ride worth your while." Jamie showed Simon's men where they could conceal the boat in the natural cut formed by a small stream. Four of them were to remain here, two others would travel inland with their lord.

Whipped by the oncoming storm, the Cornish woods lived up to their reputation for wildness. The wind howled through the treetops, making them writhe like tortured souls. The deeper they went into the interior, the darker it got under the towering pines, and the more apprehensive the Frenchmen looked.

Good, Jamie thought. He hoped they'd come away from this with a healthy respect for Cornwall. By his order, there was no talking, but when he called a halt and dismounted, Simon stepped near, scowling fiercely.

"By God, you had better be leading us truly, for I swear we could have circled back to the beach and I'd not have known."

Jamie grinned. "The way would be easier if we dared take the road, but we cannot risk running into my patrols or the king's."

"Perish the thought." Simon glanced nervously around the inky woods. "Is it much farther? I'll not rest easy till I'm back aboard my ship."

"The harbor is below us." Jamie took a deep breath. It did little to relieve the knot in his chest. Betraying your country, no matter your reasons, was a grim business.

The ride from Arwenack to Penryn on the wide, hard-packed road had been easy, the stretch from Penryn on-ward, hell. Here the path was narrow, the woods thicker and darker. The storm made the trees twist about so it seemed an assailant lurked behind each one. Emmeline's nerves were on edge, her hands ached from gripping the reins of her skittish horse.

Twice they'd been accosted by patrols of Jamie's men. But each time, the story Hugh had concocted had gotten them not only leave to pass, but better directions than Mariot's. Emmeline had told Hugh only that it was a shipyard, nothing more. Not that she didn't trust him, but the less said, the better. Hugh assumed it was a smugglers' haven.

Emmeline gasped as a man leapt from behind a bush.

"Who goes there?" demanded a gruff voice.

"Lady Emmeline. J-Jamie Harcourt's betrothed," she said through her chattering teeth. She went on to tell this man the same thing she had the other two. "M-my lord was injured at the shipyard and has sent for me…to help. I'm an apothecary."

The man grunted and stepped closer. "Who's with ye?"

"M-my guards. Jamie would not let me travel alone."

"Humph." The shaggy man whistled, and three others dropped out of the trees.

Emmeline's mare took exception and balked, but before it could bolt, the man who seemed to be the leader grabbed the bridle and held her firmly in place. "Thank you…"

"Dewy," he replied, tugging on his forelock. "The trail's a bit tricky from here on, so the lads and I'll go with ye."

Hugh lifted his visor. "Is it far?"

"Ten minutes on foot." Dewy began to lead her horse forward. "Is Jamie bad hurt, milady?"

"I will not know till I get there." How she hated betraying these people's trust. What was it Jamie had once said about the end justifying the means? She didn't see how it could.

"Hmm. Strange we didn't see anyone going to fetch ye."

"Ah…" Emmeline glanced at Hugh.

"There's the harbor, Lady Emmeline." Hugh pointed ahead and urged his mount into a quick trot. The rest of them scrambled to keep up.

"Oh, my…" Emmeline looked down on the harbor. It resembled a mirror set in the bowl formed by the surrounding hills. Dotting its surface were hundreds of ships, their masts swaying in the wind. The small fires on the opposite hill likely marked the workmen's camp. Below them on the shore rested the hulking skeletons of several more ships. An awesome sight. A wonderful sight. England's salvation.

"Who would have thought to find so many ships concealed so far inland," Hugh murmured.

She nodded. The site had been well chosen, the harbor safely hidden away, protected by the rugged land. A narrow black ribbon of water led away from it toward the sea.

Hugh exclaimed, "This is Jamie's smuggling fleet? The rogue must be king of the pirates."

Emmeline bristled, fed up with Hugh's slurs. "Nay, he is not. He's a hero. This fleet is England's. Jamie oversaw the building of it to repel the French invasion," she added proudly.

"Really?" Hugh sounded astonished. "Are you certain that isn't a fable he concocted to earn your respect?"

Calmer now, Emmeline turned back to look at the fleet. Pride swelled inside her, strong as the intensifying storm. She wished Jamie here so she could tell him how wonderful she thought he was. "Nay, for he did not tell me about this himself."

Lightning chose that moment to arc across the sky. In the wash of brilliance that followed, she saw four men step out of the woods to their right, perhaps three hundred yards away. More guards? Their silhouettes stood out against the gray bulk of the hill, their movements seemed…stealthy.

Dread prickled down her spine. "Dewy, who are those men?"

Another bolt of lightning struck. The four men were bathed in its white backlash. The distance was too great to make out their features, but the black patch one wore stood out clearly.

"Jamie…" Emmeline murmured.

"How can he be there if he's injured?" Dewy asked.

"There's someone else coming up the trail," one of his men called out. His warning ended in a gurgle. He fell to his knees, an arrow sticking from his back. Behind him, mounted men poured out into the clearing like a swarm of malicious ants.

"What the hell!" Dewy grabbed for the horn hanging from his belt, but he was struck before he could sound the alarm.

"As you can see, there are nearly eight hundred ships completed." Jamie gestured toward the harbor. "Most are already fitted and supplied, ready to sail at a moment's notice." Or so it looked from this vantage point. Only Jamie, Bran and a few others knew how deceptive the vessels' appearance was.

DeGrys nodded and closed his mouth, which had sagged open when he'd seen the fleet. "How many routes in?"

"Two land roads, a dozen lesser trails through the woods and the estuary." He pointed to the river. "It's been dredged so the larger vessels can pass through, but…note those fires burning on either side, back where the river is narrowest? Fifty men guard each bank, day and night, with another hundred at the main camp. Men are posted along the shore, at twenty-foot intervals, with orders to blow their horns at any sign of trouble.''

"How, then, do I destroy the fleet?'' Simon grumbled.

Jamie shrugged. "I do not know. I agreed to tell you where the ships were being built. I've done more. I've shown them to you. The rest is up to you.''

"If I could land enough men…''

"Without rousing every soldier in Cornwall?''

"Hmm.'' DeGrys rubbed a hand over his face. "I will think of something. I must. If our invasion should fail, King Charles will have my head.''

"If we're discovered here, King Richard will have both of our heads.'' Jamie turned away from the harbor. "We had best le—''

A scream ripped through the silence. A woman's scream, followed immediately by a jagged streak of lightning. It illuminated a scene straight from his worst nightmare.

A woman ran down the hill toward him. Emma, her hair streaming out behind her, her mouth open in a cry that was drowned out by thunder. After her charged a knight on horseback. Behind him streamed a trio of foot soldiers.

Drawing his sword, Jamie shoved Simon toward the woods. "Begone. Follow this trail back to the beach or hide and I will find you later.'' Without waiting for an answer, he spun around and raced toward Emma. His feet seemed made of lead, and he knew he'd never reach her in time. Emma!

He prayed for a miracle to save her, because he couldn't.

His miracle whistled out of the woods. A slender, white-fletched arrow that struck the knight in the throat, drawing a gurgle of pain before he pitched from the saddle.

'Twas all Jamie needed. Darting forward, he grabbed Emma's hand and dragged her up the hill, away from the carnage, toward the safety of the dark woods. He dared not take the time to look at her, but heard her labored breathing, felt her falter as she struggled to keep up. "Come on. Just a little farther..."

"I..." She stumbled, tripped and would have gone down had he not caught her around the waist. "Leave me," she cried.

"Never. Just hang limp." Tucking her under his arm, he made for the crest of the hill and the woods. So near, only a few feet, now, but behind him he could hear heavy footsteps beneath the steady rumble of thunder. He dug deep inside himself for the burst of speed that took him into the trees.

The darkness swallowed them up, but he knew this land nearly as well as he did Harte Court. Veering to the right, he plunged into a thicket and swung around a large oak. These hills were dotted with caves. If he could last till—

"Jamie...here." Bran popped out of the darkness and motioned him toward a pile of rocks.

Jamie ducked behind them, setting Emma gently on the ground. "You're not supposed to be here," he gasped out in Cornish.

"Damn lucky for you I am not one to follow orders," Bran snapped. "What the hell is going on? How did Cadwell get here?"

"Giles?"

"Aye, 'twas his troop that attacked us," Bran growled. "I think she led them here." He glared at Emma.

"Nay." Jamie leaned over her and stroked the tangled hair from her face. "Emma, are you all right?" he whispered.

She opened her eyes, gasping for breath. "What happened?"

"Are you all right? Were you hit?" He skimmed his

hands over her, feeling for broken bones or bleeding wounds.

"Nay. Jus…just winded and frightened. What—"

"Shh. There's no time for answers now." Or for his own questions about how she came to be here. He stroked her damp, grimy cheek and glanced back at Bran. "Our lads?"

"Keeping Cadwell's men busy."

Jamie nodded. "I want you to go after Simon DeGrys."

"What of you? If Cadwell should catch you—"

"A problem, I grant you, but if he captured Simon, 'twould ruin all we've worked so hard to accomplish. And if he talked…"

Bran groaned and scrubbed a hand over his face, streaking the charcoal he wore to hide his skin. "But…"

"Go, and quickly. Last I saw them, Simon and his men were headed south, darting through the woods like scared hares." Lightning scored the sky, baring Emma's ashen face and haunted eyes. Desperate as he was to put distance between himself and Giles, she could not go far. He drew Emma closer, touched by her trembling. "We'll skirt the harbor to the north and shelter in the caves. With Giles occupied here, the way should be clear."

"Why not go to the camp?"

"Nay. If Giles should break through, I don't want him to find me there and connect me with tonight's events." Their gazes locked, bleakly reflecting the disaster they now faced. "When we are rested and the way is clear…we'll go on to Carn Brea. 'Tis well away from here, and we'll be safe there." As safe as anywhere, though after tonight, his future looked even grimmer.

Chapter Thirteen

A loud noise jerked Emmeline from sleep to murky darkness. Disoriented, she whimpered and tried to sit, but something weighted her down.

"Easy," murmured a familiar voice.

"Jamie?" She clutched at the heavy band about her waist and realized it was his arm.

"Aye, love, I'm here." His hold on her tightened.

"Good." She burrowed further into his embrace. The thud of his heart beneath her ear, the solid feel of his body wrapped around hers was reassuring, but some niggle of worry penetrated her cozy nest. "The soldiers!" she cried.

"Far away. We're safe in a cave."

"How did we get here?" In truth, she recalled very little after the attack.

"I carried you," he said simply.

She looked up at his face and realized his patch was gone. Squinting against the gloom, she struggled to satisfy her curiosity about his eye. The left socket held something dark, but was it shadow or substance? Tentatively she reached out. Her fingers barely grazed his brow before he jerked back.

"Nay!" He grabbed her hand and held it at bay.

"Your eye." She'd felt the ridge of scar tissue along his brow and seen his lid close. Over what?

He cursed and turned his head away; when he looked back, the familiar black triangle was in place. "The patch was wet."

Please don't shut me out, she wanted to cry, but he held himself so tensely she knew he not only expected the plea, he'd resist it. "I am sorry. I didn't mean to pry."

His grin was a white blur in the smothering darkness. "You have more right than anyone, but—" But he wasn't ready to trust her. "Are you thirsty?"

She sighed and accepted the diversion. He sat up, and she felt chilled, bereft of more than just his heat. There was desire and, aye, respect between them, but would there ever be trust?

"Take a small sip," he cautioned, putting the spout of a drinking skin to her lips. "All Bran had with him was whiskey."

Emmeline took a gulp, gasped and choked as the fiery liquid burned a path down her throat.

"Another?"

"Nay," she rasped. "I may never swallow anything again."

Jamie chuckled. "The burning will pass. It takes a bit of getting used to, but 'twill warm you up." He pressed another sip on her, and this time it went down easier. The third and fourth gulps slid down…and lit a fire in her belly. "No more," he said, pulling the skin away. "Wouldn't want you drunk."

"I never overimbibe."

"You've never had whiskey before, either." He drank deep himself, then set the skin on the ground. "What were you doing at the harbor?" His voice was darker, steel cased in velvet.

"We came to warn you and make certain you were all right."

"We?"

"Hugh and I. He thought Giles Cadwell had come to Cornwall to catch you at smuggling, but I feared 'twas the fleet—"

He gasped. "What do you know about that?"

"Mariot told me you were building ships to repel the inva—"

"Damn. I warned Colan not to tell her. 'Tis a secret."

"It slipped out. She meant no harm."

"Bloody hell!"

"I did not say anything to Hugh about it."

"You didn't have to…he saw it with his own eyes. Damn. What in hell did you hope to prove by following me?"

"To keep Giles from falsely accusing you of treason for trading with the French."

"Of all the harebrained schemes…"

"It did not seem so at the time," she said defensively. "We feared you'd come to some harm, and so you might have had we not been there to warn you of the soldiers skulking in the woods."

"'Tis possible you two led Giles to me."

She gasped. "So, it *was* Giles who attacked us?"

"It was," he said in a hard voice.

"Do you really think he followed us here?"

"I do not know. 'Tis certainly possible," he said slowly. "But 'tis also possible Giles trailed the workmen to the site or bribed someone to lead him there."

"I am truly sorry," she said in a small, choked voice. "They…they shot Dewy, and another man, I think. And Hugh…oh, what of Hugh? Do you think he escaped?"

"Bran's men got him clear. They'll take him back to

Arwenack and make certain Giles leaves the area." He sighed and looked out toward the gray square that marked the entrance to the cave. In spite of his outward confidence, he was worried about the others.

"Why didn't we go with them?"

"I wanted you clear of the fighting."

There was more to it than that, but if she pressed, he'd only close up like a clam. "You are upset that Giles saw the fleet. Why is the fleet being kept a secret? It would reassure people to know we aren't defenseless against the French."

"Things are not that simple."

"Do you think I am too simple to understand?"

He covered her hand and squeezed gently. "You are too clever and too impetuous for your own good." He sighed. "But I suppose part of the blame for this fiasco is mine. I knew you and Hugh were worried and should have guessed you two would try to save me from myself." He cursed under his breath.

"You still haven't told me why the fleet is a secret."

"Because...hell, I cannot fob you off with another excuse. Mayhap if you understand what we are up against, you will more readily follow my orders." He exhaled sharply, then began to describe for her the complicated workings of the court.

The king's foibles were not news. His pettiness, excesses and acts of favoritism to men such as the Earl of Oxford were common knowledge. 'Twas fascinating to hear Jamie speak of what went on behind closed doors at court, to realize he knew personally so many powerful influential people. Yet it underscored the differences in their stations.

"Do you really think the French will use a peace treaty to gobble us up?" she asked when he'd finished speaking.

"Most definitely. France was beaten and humiliated by us for years. They long for retribution, and for profit. King Charles has doubtless made promises to Oxford and those who help arrange the treaty...land grants here or in France. Mayhap even the throne itself, for he can't afford to let Richard live."

Emmeline gasped, shocked the earl would stoop to treachery against his own king. "So your fleet is a threat to Oxford because if England wins, he'll have less than if she loses."

"I knew you had a quick mind."

"For a woman."

"I appreciate a canny woman. All the women in my family are quick-witted and nearly as clever as the men."

Emmeline realized he was steering her away from the political intrigue, but could not resist learning more about his family. "Nearly?" she asked, pretending to bristle.

He chuckled. "Well, there have been a few times when the ladies had to help us Sommerville men out of desperate situations."

"You call yourself Sommerville, but your name is Harcourt."

"Harcourt is my mother's name."

"Your father never married her?" Emmeline gasped, thinking of the handsome Lord Alex with his roguish reputation.

"Of course he did," Jamie replied indignantly. "Three times, in fact. They betrothed themselves to each other when they were stranded on an island. Wed again when they were rescued to make certain 'twas legal because by then Mama was carrying Hugh and me. They wed a third time so my father could take her name. She was the last of the Harcourts, her father and only brother having died, and Papa wanted the name carried on for her sake."

How ironic, his parents were thrice wed and hers not at all. "What a romantic thing to do."

"Hmm." He lay down beside her, elbow bent, his head propped on one hand. His other arm he draped across her waist, a caress as warm and intimate as his voice. "So the balladeers thought, for many a verse did they dedicate to my sire's grand gesture."

She reached up and brushed his stubbled chin with her knuckles. He looked wild and disreputable with his tangled hair, black patch and insolent gaze. She was no longer deceived by his outward appearance. It felt so right lying here with him in the dark. "You are something of a hero yourself."

He tensed. "I am the furthest thing from it."

"What is it? What happened to make you think that?"

He shook his head. "Enough talk for now. You should rest. In an hour or so we must leave."

"Why? Are we not safe here?"

"For now, but the ground is hard, and there's no fire."

"We need none. Your body radiates nearly as much heat as a brazier." She snuggled closer, sighing as her chilled body soaked up the warmth of his.

He groaned and inched back. "Emma, this is not a good idea."

"Why? I am cold. Will you not share your warmth with me?"

"If we stay like this much longer, I'll share a good deal more of my body than just its heat," he growled.

Belatedly she realized that he'd removed his armor and her boy's clothes. Only her thin linen shift and his woolen hose came between them. The discovery caused a queer little lurch in the pit of her stomach. 'Twas like the time she'd stood on the edge of a gorge and realized that with one step, she'd tumble over the edge. Only this was a precipice of her own making. For so long she'd held herself aloof from every emotion save duty and responsibility. Yet he made her want to give in to the tension that seethed between them, to seize this moment.

"Jamie. I—I feel so strange. Hot and muzzy."

"'Tis likely the whiskey." His voice was lower, huskier; his breathing suddenly as ragged as her pulse.

The emotions warring inside her crystallized suddenly. She knew what she felt for him went far beyond a simple yearning of the flesh. She loved him. "I—I think it is you...us."

"Emma. We cannot. If something should happen—"

"We will always have this moment." She ran her hands up the furry expanse of his chest, pleased by the feel of his sleek muscles rippling at her touch. "I need you."

"And I you. But I care for you, too. More, with each passing moment. Which is why I will not take you here, in this dark cave with the danger closing in around us."

This was the second time he'd told her he cared. The declaration fell short of what she longed to hear, yet behind the words he uttered she sensed the ones locked inside him. *He loved her.* He loved her and wanted to protect her...even from himself. The conviction that this was right grew inside her. "I love you," she whispered, sliding her hands up his neck to frame his face. "I need to touch you, to hold you, to show you how much..." She brought his mouth down and matched it to hers.

She loved him. Jamie groaned, his good intentions shattered by the intensity of her response. Her lips parted before the questing sweep of his tongue, welcoming him in a prelude to the more intimate joining to come. Raw, hot sensation rushed through him. No one had ever matched him as perfectly as she did. The small whimpers coming from her throat as he took the kiss deeper tore at his control.

Dimly he realized he must slow down. Wrenching his mouth free, he buried it in the fragrant silk of her hair and struggled against the assault on his control. "Emma...love, I do not mean to frighten you, but I've never wanted anyone as I do you."

"I am not afraid...not of you." She wrapped her arms around his neck. "I want to feel your skin against mine."

"'Twould be my pleasure to oblige you, my lady." Jamie stripped the shift from her in one swift, practiced move, but nothing in his experience equaled the jolt of pleasure when Emma's breasts brushed against his chest.

"Oh, Jamie." She gasped as his hands slipped up her back and around to cup her high, full breasts.

"Soft...you are so soft." He stroked and caressed her breasts, drinking the sighs of wonder as they fell from her lips. When his fingers plucked the nipples into hard buds, she cried out and arched her back. 'Twas an offering he could not refuse. Lowering his head, he took one thrusting peak in his mouth.

"Jamie!" Emma cried, his name dying to a whimper as his warm, wet mouth drew down, suckling the sensitive nipple. The unexpected intimacy should have shocked her. Instead, her senses came vividly alive. Her skin tingled, her blood turned to molten fire. When he lifted his head, she whimpered again, this time in protest, and tunneled her hands into his hair to urge him back.

"You like that," he whispered against her heated flesh.

"Aye...more than I can put into words," she muttered, frustrated because no other description had ever eluded her.

"Love needs no words," he murmured, and bent to suckle the other breast.

Shivers rushed through her, and she became a creature of pure sensation, glorying in the spell he wove. Instinctively she arched her body, pressing herself against him, her hands tangling in his hair as she urged him. Her pulse beat in thunderous counterpoint to the rhythm he set, but nowhere more tumultuously than at the juncture of her thighs.

He seemed to know, for his hands moved over her with possessive familiarity, coming lastly to the most sensitive of spots, where the need had built to a sharp, grinding ache. His fingers brushed over her, grazing her with fire.

"Oh," she cried, twisting restlessly, not knowing if she wanted to escape or linger.

"Easy." Jamie lay beside her, his breath coming in ragged gulps as he fought the crushing need to bury himself in her heat. He kissed her gently, stifling the small cry of alarm raised as his finger slipped inside to touch and test. Her body wept for his, but she was so small, so tight. So precious. "Are you frightened? Shall I stop?"

"Nay." Her voice was shaky, and he wished for light so he could read her expression. "'Tis all so new...but I like it when you kiss me. And when you touch me, my insides draw so tight I feel as though I'll...I'll explode. If you stop, I'll die."

He chuckled. Her openness charmed him. Her honesty humbled him. How far they had come in such a few short days. "If we stop, I know I shall die. I want you more than my next breath."

"Will you touch me then?"

"Where? Where would you have me touch you?"

Embarrassed, Emma ducked her face into his shoulder. "H-here." Taking his hand, she guided it to her hip and then down. She drew in a sharp breath as his fingers grazed the hidden bud that was the focus of her desire. She sobbed his name as he gently stroked her there, bursts of pleasure radiating through her like shards of lightning. Her hips began to move of their own accord, rising and falling in time with his long, clever fingers. When he rose up over her, she instinctively parted her thighs, relishing his solid weight and the taut strength of him pressed hotly against her belly.

"Open your eyes, Emma," he coaxed.

Anticipation sizzled through her as she saw his face above her, blazing with emotion even in the dimness. "You love me."

"With all my heart and soul."

"And I you!" she cried, reaching to draw him to her. The cry became a soft moan as she welcomed the hard, plunging edge of him, the stab of pain nothing compared to the surge of pleasure as he filled the void inside her. "Jamie...oh, Jamie."

"Now we are well and truly joined," he murmured. "Forever."

"Forever," she echoed as he began to move, slowly at first, then more swiftly, setting her afire from the inside out.

Jamie had never known such joy, such a sense of completeness as they moved together. Two halves of one whole. Emma matched him perfectly, following where he led, then forging ahead. She took him so deep inside her he no longer knew where he left off and she began. He wanted to tell her, but just then her eyes flew open, glittering in the darkness, shining with such love, such wonder that no words were necessary.

Forever, he pledged.

As if in answer, her body tightened around him, and she cried his name. He buried himself in the heart of the storm convulsing her, utterly consumed by the fire, yet he felt reborn as he poured his love into her. "Forever," he cried. She whispered the word back to him. Their gazes locked in silent communion. A solemn pledge.

You should not have taken her, Jamie's conscience chided. 'Twas the truth, yet as she slept in his arms, Jamie felt contentment seep through him, not regret. That would come later, if his scheme was exposed and he was forced to pay the ultimate price for his treachery...and mayhap taint her with the same black brush. The thought of Emma standing beside him on the scaffold was intolerable.

The storm had moved off, and 'twas light enough for him to see her face, pillowed on his shoulder. How heartbreakingly lovely and innocent she looked. Yet her softness hid a will of iron and a bravery few men could match.

She was a complex woman, this slender termagant who'd captured his heart. She was witty and wise, bold and impetuous, yet wary where men were concerned. The fact that she'd given herself to him outside of wedlock humbled him and shamed him. He should have waited till they were married. If only he hadn't come so close to losing her tonight, he might have found the strength to resist. But the danger they'd escaped, combined with her declaration of love, had swept away his reason.

The wonder of their newfound love surged through him, momentarily driving out fear and remorse. There was so much he wanted to show her, share with her. He wanted to take her home to meet his family. He wanted to come home each day to find her waiting for him. He wanted to fall asleep in her arms each night and wake each dawn to find her pressed close to his heart.

As though sensing his regard, she stirred and opened her eyes. "Jamie?" she asked hesitantly. Her uncertainty tore at him.

He masked it with a smile. "How do you feel, love?"

The endearment made her eyes glow. "Fine. And you?"

"Hmm." He stroked her back, glorying in the shivers that raced through her as she arched against him. "I feel like the most fortunate man in the world. But I hope you realize that last night sealed your fate...you are stuck with me forever."

"I am?" She tilted her head back and stared at him. Emotions flickered across her expressive face: disbelief, joy, hope.

"We'll be wed when we reach Carn Brea," said the man who'd escaped more marriage traps than he could count.

"You do not have to," she murmured. "I—I didn't expect you would, you know. I...I made love with you because I wanted to."

"I'd wed you because I love you."

"You do?" Her eyes glittered with hope and tears.

"Did I not tell you so last night?"

"I—I thought I had dreamed it."

"Or that I was carried away by lust?" he asked knowingly.

"Well..."

Silly love. Yet he knew her fears weren't unfounded, given his past...and her past experiences. "Mayhap you found my loving lacking in some way and would look elsewhere," he teased.

"Nay. 'Twas the most wonderful..." Her face flamed. "You said that just to wring a compliment from me."

"Alas, my confidence is such a fragile thing it needs all the praise it can—ouch!" He rubbed the arm she'd pinched.

"You are impossible."

"I know. 'Twill likely take you forever to mend my ways."

"Forever?" she whispered.

"Aye, so we pledged last night...with our hearts and souls as well as our bodies...and I'll not let you cry off now that it's light and you can see your lover is a scarred rascal—"

"Nay." She looked at his patch, and for a moment he feared she'd try to touch it again. "I love you, warts and all."

He exhaled. Someday he'd be ready to bare his secrets, but not now. "Ah, she accuses me of having warts."

"'Tis possible...I've yet to see all of you in the light." She grinned, her humor new and very becoming.

It struck him again how far they'd come, how much they'd taught each other in a few short days. He hoped they'd have a lifetime...forever to...

"What is troubling you?" she asked.

"Naught, I—"

"It does no good to try and keep things from me," she chided. "I know you must be worried about Hugh and Bran and what Giles will do now that he's found the fleet. You must have a hundred things you'd rather see to, yet you are stuck here protecting me."

Damn. She was coming to read him far too well. "There's nowhere I'd rather be than with you." He hugged her close and hid his face in her neck lest she see his other fears. "I love you, Emma-mine. Never forget that."

"I won't. I love you, too. So very, very much."

A nightingale called just outside the cave. Jamie sat up, felt around for his clothes and began pulling them on.

"Jamie...?"

"Shh. There's someone outside. Stay here." Clad in

hose and tunic, he picked up his sword and crept out of the cave, keeping to the shadows. The call sounded again, to his right and a hundred yards away, he guessed. Silent as air, he slipped from the mouth of the cave and blended into the predawn gloom.

Jamie came up behind the bird caller, and nearly got a belly full of cold steel when the man whirled. "Easy," Jamie growled, jumping back out of range.

"Sorry," grumbled Feok, sheathing his blade. "I've been creeping about the woods, whistling at every cave I came to. Makes a man a mite jumpy."

Jamie nodded. "Bran sent you?"

"Aye." Feok shook like a hound, his droopy garments spraying water in all directions, then sat down on a rock. He was a skinny little man, as comfortable in the woods as any of the animals. "We had three men wounded... including Dewy and his brother...but they're all likely to live."

"What of my brother?"

"Wrenched his leg when his horse fell on him. The wound is not severe but he'd hurt that leg before."

Jamie swore softly. It seemed Hugh was always getting hurt because of him.

"It hasn't stopped him from shouting at Bran and Colan about sending out more search parties to look for ye and yer lady." Feok frowned and peered about. "Is she well?"

"Hmm. I left her in the cave...but knowing her, she won't stay put for long. Tell me quick what's been happening."

The news was mixed. Giles and his men had retreated to Truro to lick their wounds. It wasn't known how much Giles had seen or if he'd send for reinforcements and try to take the shipyard. "Oh, Bran said to tell ye that of the three hares ye sent him after, two got safely to their burrow. One's gone missing."

Jamie's stomach rolled up into his throat. "We have to find out what happened to him. Take as many men as you need. Search the woods. Stop at every farm..."

"Who are they?"

"Giles's men," Jamie lied. No one knew about the plan with DeGrys except himself, Bran and the Lancasters. So it must stay.

"Bran's already got the lads out beating the bushes. Be he dead or alive, if he's in the forest, we'll find him."

And if he isn't. If Giles has him. Disaster.

"Bran sent a horse and supplies to see ye on yer way to Carn Brea. I'm to go along...in case of trouble."

"Trouble is something we seem to find plenty of," Jamie said morosely.

Hugh hobbled into the inn using the stout stick Colan had given him for support. Easing himself into a chair, he called for ale and scanned the room. If this wasn't Penryn's meanest tavern, he'd be surprised. The low ceiling and plaster walls were black with soot from the hearth. Smoke hung thick in the humid air, yet couldn't mask the stink of sour ale and overripe bodies. It was mid afternoon, but the place was crowded with drunken sailors and surly tinners, all doing their best to out shout each other.

A plump woman sidled up to Hugh out of the gloom and set a chipped pottery cup down on the table. Her face was filthy, her teeth yellowed, and her hair a tangled mess. The drab gown she wore strained to contain her billowy flesh. "Care to step upstairs with me?" she murmured.

Hugh's lip curled. "Not if you were the last wom—"

"Sir Giles says ye're supposed to come," she hissed.

"Why did you not just say so." Hugh struggled to his

feet, tossed a coin into the cup and limped through the crowd.

The whore hurried after him, tucking the ale-soaked coin into her bosom. "Just this way."

Hugh looked up the narrow, crooked stairs and groaned. But he pressed on. By the time he entered the appointed room, he was drenched in sweat and his wrenched knee throbbed like a bad tooth. "Why did we have to meet here?" he demanded.

Giles looked up from the map he'd been studying. "Because I can hardly come calling at Arwenack, and you told Roger you were in no condition to ride to Truro."

"Perish the thought." Hugh sank into a rickety chair and reached for the ale pitcher. Giles's coin had bought a better grade than was being served below, but the cups were just as filthy. He pulled a handkerchief from his sleeve and wiped the cup before filling it. "What went wrong?"

"Everything. We'd managed to elude their patrols while we followed you and the girl, but the moment we reached the harbor, dozens of the heathens fell on us from ambush. If that cursed woman hadn't cried out, we might have caught Jamie."

"He was there, right enough. I saw him a distance away, talking with three men. But I do not know what they were doing, for they scattered at the first sign of trouble."

"We caught one of them," Giles said.

"Jamie?"

"Nay. A soldier or sailor, by his dress. We think he may be French, for he speaks like one."

"French," Hugh breathed, eyes round with wonder and something that delighted Giles. Satisfaction. Hugh claimed he was doing this out of patriotism, but he wanted his brother eliminated as much as Giles did. "Did you question the man? Has he implicated Jamie in the smuggling?"

"Not yet. He was wounded and has been fevered these past two days. I've engaged the best physicians in Truro. They say he'll live. 'Tis just a matter of waiting till the fever subsides. Then we'll see what he knows. What of your brother and the girl?"

"They still have not returned to Arwenack. The Killigrews have search parties out looking for them, but thus far they've not found them. Are you certain you do not have him?"

"Nay, dammit, I said I did not."

Hugh nodded. "I've learned something about the ships in the harbor. Emmeline told me they were being built to thwart the French invasion. 'Tis supposed to be a secret, of course, but I led Colan Killigrew to think Jamie had confided in me. Colan confirmed the fleet is indeed ready to repel the French."

Ships to stop the French! Damn, Giles had not thought of that. He'd assumed...bloody hell, he hadn't actually given them much thought. He'd been too busy trying to get away from the Cornishmen, then too excited about the mysterious French sailor to give the ships much thought. Oxford would pitch a fit when he learned of this. It would ruin his schemes...and Giles's, too.

"Well, that is that, then," Hugh said glumly. "Obviously you were mistaken and Jamie is not involved with the French. I will be returning home as soon as I can arrange transport."

"Nay!" Giles cried. He itched to lunge across the table and slap the sanctimonious prig, but it would take time to plant another spy in Arwenack...especially one as valuable. He'd send word to Oxford about the ships. Doubtless the earl would order them burned...and cast blame on the

French. In which case, the Frenchman he'd captured would come in handy...dead or alive.

More important, somehow, he had to implicate Jamie, as well. The coin and lofty titles Oxford had promised Giles would mean nothing if he couldn't bring Jamie down...once and for all. Then it came to him. "Jamie may have sold that secret to the French."

Hugh's head came up. "I do not know. Jamie has done many unsavory things, but betray his country...?"

"All men have their price. We must remain vigilant till we know what is going on. Will you continue to help by providing me with information on your brother and the Killigrews?"

"Of course," Hugh replied at once, nearly giddy with relief. If Jamie was a traitor, he'd hang. And Harte Court would come to Hugh. "Anything I can do to save England."

"A toast, then," Giles proposed, raising his cup. "To the two things we want most...England's safety and Jamie's ruin."

Hugh straightened in his chair. "See here, Jamie is my brother. I do not *want* him harmed."

"Really?" Giles's eyes narrowed to canny slits. "You may fool others with your act of brotherly concern, but I know you hate him as much as I do. Together, we can make certain he receives his just reward for making our lives hell all these years." He extended his cup toward Hugh in silent challenge.

Hugh hesitated, torn as always between the love he should have felt for Jamie—his twin—and the animosity that had grown inside him like a canker from their earliest days. The dark side won. Slowly, grudgingly, he lifted his cup. "I will do what I can, but my family must never find out I helped you."

Chapter Fourteen

They were wed three nights later, in a wooded glen at the foot of a great brooding hill known as Carn Brea, site of an ancient Celtic fort. The ceremony was as pagan as their surroundings, Emma thought, pale moonlight filtering in through the canopy of leaves, an eerie mist rising from a nearby stream.

"If you have doubts, we need not do this," Jamie murmured as he led her into the clearing. He looked like a Celtic prince, in a knee-length white tunic, embroidered at the neck and hem with swords and fire-breathing dragons, his legs bare except for low leather boots.

"I do not doubt our love," she replied, "but this all seems...unreal, like a passage from some Druid tale."

"Does it, now? Well, you make a most beautiful priestess." He unpinned her long cloak and drew it from her shoulders. Air hissed from between his lips.

Self-conscious, she smoothed a hand over the gown given to her by Marta, wife of the village headman. Made of some gossamer white fabric, it fell from shoulder to ankle in supple folds. Oak leaves, mistletoe and silver wheels were worked into the embroidery at the throat and hem, to ensure fertility and long life, she'd been told. Her hair was loose, caught only by a silver circlet at her brow. "'Tis so sheer I feel...naked."

Jamie stared, robbed of speech by her sensual beauty. The wisp of cloth, so thin it must have been woven by fairies, was more provocative than blatant nudity. Even in the moonlight, 'twas obvious the only thing under the gown was Emma. He could plainly see the dark tips of her breasts thrusting against the cloth, the supple line of her waist, the curve of her hips and the intoxicating lure of the shadowed vee at the juncture of her long, shapely legs. For a variety of reasons, he'd slept apart from her since that night in the cave, and now his celibacy came back to haunt him...a surge of desire so overpowering he swayed as he fought to control it.

"Jamie? Say something. Are you disappointed?"

"Disappointed? Nay. You fair take my breath away."

She smiled faintly. "I am glad, for you make me feel a little dizzy, too. I...I was afraid when you did not come to me these past few nights that you no longer desired me."

"If the priest is not here in one minute, you will find out exactly how mistaken you are."

"Sorry to have kept you waiting," Father Bernard called, walking into the glen from the direction of his small chapel. He smiled pleasantly at both of them, but looked a little too long at Emma for Jamie's peace of mind.

"What is wrong?" she asked as he bundled her into the cloak.

"I do not want you to catch a chill." Jamie affixed the brooch to her shoulder, withdrew her left hand and arranged the woolen folds so naught else showed.

Father Bernard grinned. He was nearly forty, squat and balding, and had known Jamie for many years. "I'm glad to see you so solicitous of your bride's, er, health. Do you want to change your mind and wed in the warmth of the chapel?''

Jamie shook his head. Religion in Cornwall struck an odd balance between Christian and Celtic beliefs. Couples who clung to the old ways were often wed in the wood, sometimes by a Druid who might also be the village blacksmith, sometimes in a ritual of their own making. 'Twas unusual to ask a Catholic priest to conduct such a clandestine ceremony, but Father Bernard had heard Jamie's confession...the whole sordid truth. The priest had been shocked and dismayed, but in the end he'd agreed to keep the marriage a secret to protect Emma. If Jamie was arrested and charged with treason, he didn't want her tainted by association.

Less easy to justify were his reasons for wedding her. Partly, it was to prove he loved her and that he was better than Cedric. But in his heart, he knew he wasn't. He was a selfish bastard, unable to control his desire for her. Nay, if it had been simple lust, he'd have managed to walk away. He'd wanted women before and done so. But he loved her...so very, very much. More than he'd thought it was possible to love anyone.

If you'd truly loved her, you'd have left her alone, his conscience chided. A good and noble man like Hugh would have saved her by denying his own feelings.

Jamie looked deep into Emma's eyes, dark pools of love and compassion, the other half of himself, and tried to make amends. "Are you certain you want a rogue for a husband? 'Tis not too late. I will understand if you—''

"Nay." Her hand shifted within his grasp, linking their fingers together. "I will love you forever and ever."

"And I you." Pray God they didn't both regret it. "Proceed, if you please, Father."

Emma barely heard the words of the ceremony that

bound them in marriage. Her entire being was focused on Jamie, standing so tall and strong beside her. She loved him with all her heart and believed he loved her, yet something troubled him deeply. She only hoped it was concern over the fleet and not second thoughts over tying himself to one woman.

Though she'd told him it didn't matter if they wed, it did. His insistence on it had touched her and frightened her. They came from two different worlds, and despite his assurances his family would welcome her warmly, she had serious doubts that the Harcourts, with their noble lineage, would be pleased with their son's bastard wife. Worse was the fear she'd not be woman enough to hold the interest of a man as experienced and worldly as he.

Emma started as something cold was slipped onto the third finger of her left hand, a gold ring set with a large cabochon ruby, the one he usually wore on a chain around his neck.

"My Grandmother Sommerville gave it to me years ago for my bride. 'Tis a perfect fit," Jamie whispered. He lifted her hand and kissed the ring. "Just as we are." When he gazed at her like that, as though she were the center of his world, she believed everything would work out. It had to, because to be separated from him would be like losing herself.

"Are you going to kiss your wife, or merely devour her with your eyes?" the priest asked, chuckling.

Emma raised her lips, expecting to be swept up and crushed in an embrace that reflected the hunger in Jamie's gaze. Instead, he cradled her face in his palms and kissed her with such care, such gentleness it brought tears to her eyes.

All too soon, he lifted his head. "I have never loved before," he whispered, his breath warm on her mouth. "I will never love anyone as I do you. Whatever comes, remember that.''

"Keep your eyes closed. No peeking, now. 'Tis only a few more steps," Jamie coaxed.

Emma laughed, struggling to keep her gown up with one hand while he led her along by the other. She'd been surprised when, after thanking Father Bernard, Jamie had taken the path away from the village. She'd tingled with anticipation, thinking he was so eager for her he couldn't wait. But they'd passed several cozy-looking bowers without stopping. When she'd asked where they were going, he'd told her it was a surprise and ordered her eyes shut.

Deprived of her sight, Emma soaked up other clues, the tinkle of the stream to their left, the rich scent of damp loam and herbs, wild parsley, water betony, chives. An owl called overhead; an animal scurried through the brush, but she felt no fear of their surroundings, only curiosity.

Jamie stopped. "Don't look yet," he commanded. A latch lifted, followed by the rasp of rusty hinges.

A cottage, she guessed, half expecting to be met by the dank smell of dust and mildew as he helped her step over the threshold. Instead, the smells of candles and greenery eddied in the unseen room, along with a whiff of food...hot bread and something savory with meat and herbs. Her stomach growled.

Two warm hands covered her eyes. "I'd say you ate no more today than I did. Feast your eyes." He lifted his hands.

Emma opened her eyes, blinking against the sudden dazzle of candlelight. The room was small and low ceilinged, with dark walls and a cheery fire crackling in the hearth. As her gaze adjusted, it moved from the fireplace to the low table set for two. There were flowers on the table, covered dishes warming on a flat rock by the fire.

"Oh, Jamie!" She turned to find him watching her with an uncertainty that tugged at her. "This is wonderful. Marta and the other women were with me all day. Who did this?"

Jamie ducked his head. "I did all but the cooking."

"You are a man of many talents, my lord." She went up on tiptoe, looping her arms around his neck and drawing his head down for a kiss. A quick kiss. When their lips met, they clung, tasting and savoring, but when Emma's tongue crept out to search for his, Jamie drew back.

His breath was raspy, his face flushed. "Much more of this and I'll have you on your back on the doorstep," he muttered.

"I would not mind. I've missed you," she added shyly.

"And I you. These last few nights were the most difficult and lonely I ever passed."

"Then why did you not come to me? I'd have welcomed you."

"I'm glad, but I wanted to give you some time to consider whether this was what you wanted, and to let you, er, heal."

"I'm healed now...."

"Good, because I plan to make up for lost time tonight." His words made her senses hum. He kissed the tip of her nose and gently turned her toward the hearth. "Food, first. If you swoon, I want it to be from passion, not hunger."

"I am far too excited to eat," Emma said, pouting prettily as he led her to the table.

Jamie chuckled, but his good intentions nearly went up in smoke when he removed her cloak. Moonlight had turned the gown translucent; firelight made it seem to disappear altogether. He looked away, at the two plump cushions he'd placed side by side on the floor. How would he last through the meal with Emma sitting inches away in her cobweb-thin gown. "Mayhap you'd be more, er, comfortable on the other side of the table."

"Too far away." Emma sat on the cushion nearest the fire and patted the seat to her left, gazing at him through her lashes.

Jamie groaned and sank down onto the cushion. It was going to be a long meal. He stared fixedly at his plate as she served slices of venison in wine sauce and a ragout of wild mushrooms.

"Jamie?" she said.

He turned toward her, startled when she slipped a bit of mushroom between his lips.

"Good?" she inquired.

Jamie fought to keep his gaze from straying down into forbidden territory. "Better than when I sampled it earlier. I should eat all my meals from your fingertips." He basked in the warmth of her smile. How wonderful it was to see her happy, free and easy of the strictures she'd imposed on herself. Passion could wait till she'd had her wedding supper and the surprise he'd planned for afterward.

He filled their cups with sweetened mead, a potent local brew, and lifted his. "To my wife, the most beautiful woman I've ever known."

She stiffened. "You've known so many. What if you grow tired of me? What if you meet someone else who—"

"Hush." He grazed her cheek with his knuckles. "I know exactly how lucky I am to have found you. There have been other women in my bed, but never in my life or my heart. 'Tis said that the Sommerville men fall in love only once, but it is for life."

She bit her lip, eyes filling with tears. "Oh, Jamie..."

"None of that on our wedding night." He kissed away her tears, knowing only time would convince her of his consistency. "Will you drink to us?" He lifted a silver cup embossed with ancient symbols, silently pleading for her trust.

Emma studied him, thinking how unbearably handsome he looked in the firelight, like a golden god or a pagan warrior. The intensity of his gaze was tempered by love. His crooked smile was engaging, the lure of a man bent on seduction. Make no mistake, she'd married a rogue. But he was hers, and she'd never give him up. "To our love." She accepted the cup and drank. The mead was thick, rich and as sweet as the promise glowing in Jamie's face as he matched her gesture.

"I love you, Emma-mine," he said when he lowered the cup.

She chuckled. "Must you ever twist my name about?"

"Emmeline is far too stiff and stuffy a name for my little firebrand. Do you truly object to being called Emma?"

"I confess, you've worn me down. I've come to think of myself as Emma." Her laughter and the kiss she blew him set the tone for the rest of the meal. They fed each other bits of food, interspersed with sips of mead and gentle teasing. Their lighthearted banter covered the current of passion flowing between them, subtle as a summer breeze, yet needing only a look or a touch to explode into a full-blown storm.

Emma's senses were so finely drawn by the time they'd cleaned their plates that she could barely sit still.

"Cheese and fruit?" Jamie asked.

"I couldn't eat another bite."

"Mead? Honey? Music?"

"Music?" She stared as he drew a lute from beneath

the table and handed it to her. "You want me to play now?"

"Is there something else you'd rather do?"

She blinked. "Are you trying to drive me crazy?"

"I'm trying to make a special memory for you."

"Oh, Jamie...I love you."

"And I you."

"But if you don't kiss me soon, I swear I will expire."

"Your wish—" he cupped the back of her head and drew her toward him "—is my command." Her mouth was warm, slick and provocative, melting under the pressure of his. She kissed him as though she were starved for his touch. Her sensual forays met his stroke for stroke. His control slipped further and further. He fought for sanity and found it by wrenching his mouth free.

"Jamie?"

"Not here." Breathing hard, he stood, swept her into his arms and carried her the few steps into the next room.

She gasped, her hands tightening around his neck as she saw the canopied bed that filled the small chamber. The bower was washed with the soft light of a dozen candles, set on pikes in the corners and on the table beside the bed. "It...it looks like something from a dream...a fantasy."

"I want to make this night as fantastic as any dream." Jamie set her on her feet, keeping his hands on her arms to steady her.

"You already have." Desire brought a becoming flush to her cheeks, made her eyes gleam like polished emeralds. Her hair had fallen forward, concealing what the gown did not behind a fall of gleaming chestnut silk.

Like a man in a trance, Jamie brushed the hair back over her shoulders. The candlelight gave her skin a pearly sheen beneath the gossamer gown that revealed every provocative curve of her slender body. "Jesu, you are beautiful," he murmured.

Emma gasped as one hand reached out to trace the line of her shoulder. She felt naked, exposed, yet strangely neither ashamed or afraid. Despite the fierce hunger in his face, she knew he'd treat her gently. His touch burned her through the thin fabric, leaving a trail of fire over her collarbone and down the valley between her breasts. They tingled, the nipples peaking in anticipation. When he hesitated, she leaned toward him, wanting to press herself against him to ease the ache.

He growled her name, his voice as rousing as the feel of his hands slipping down to cup her breasts, massaging and caressing them in his wide, callused palms. "You are so soft..." He drank the throaty moans from her lips, his tongue teasing her with light parries, an erotic parody of the joining to come. She was not aware he'd loosened her gown until it slid from her shoulders and the cool air rushed over her.

Before she could feel chilled, his mouth raced over her skin like licks of fire. "You smell like wildflowers," he murmured, skimming her collarbone. "And taste like honey. Especially here..." His lips settled on one breast, sending a shock through her. The swirl of his tongue moved closer to the nipple, circling it before his mouth closed over the waiting peak.

"Jamie." She arched up, pressing her breast more fully into his mouth, her hands tangling in his hair as she urged him on. He obliged by suckling her with devastating thoroughness. The air backed up in her lungs and shivers raced through her, tightening the sensual coil at the top of her thighs.

The feel of Emma trembling in his arms, the soft whimpers coming from her throat as he pleasured her other breast, roused Jamie's desire to a fever pitch. He lifted his head from her sweet-scented flesh and took her mouth in a blistering kiss while he stumbled the few steps to the bed. Laying her down on the coverlet, he toed off his boots, grabbed the hem of his borrowed tunic and dragged it over his head.

"Oh, my...!" Emma exclaimed. Her eyes were wide, shocked.

Jamie followed the line of her gaze and flushed, holding the tunic in front of him. She matched him so perfectly, he forgot how innocent she was.

"Nay. Do not cover yourself. I was only...surprised." She levered herself up on her elbow and tugged the tunic from his grip. Her eyes widened further, and he hoped it wasn't revulsion. "You are so beautiful...sleek and powerful as a stallion. I just had no idea 'twould be so...huge."

His flush deepened with a mix of pleasure and chagrin. "I am made no different than any other man."

The knot of longing inside Emma tightened. Her whole body thrummed with the need to feel him over her, to writhe and squirm against him. "Come...lie with me." She reached for him, sighing when he stretched out beside her on the bed and drew her into his embrace. Relishing the feel of his hard chest against her aching breasts, she wriggled closer. He responded with a low growl and rolled till she lay half under him. She ran her hands down his back, loving the way his muscles rippled beneath her palms, wanting more. "I want to touch you."

"You will." His breath was ragged and shallow, as though he'd run a great distance. "But not just now. Damn." Air hissed through his teeth; he shuddered. "I am no green lad, but you make me feel as urgent and hungry as though this was my first time."

She looked up at him in wonder, noting how passion drew his features taut, the way his neck corded as he fought for control. The force of his passion sparked an answering urgency deep inside her. "I can wait no longer," she murmured, her legs parting instinctively, her hips rising in mute appeal. "My body aches for yours, so empty inside I feel I'll shatter if you don't fill me with your heat, your strength, your love."

He groaned, gripping her rump and lifting her. She tingled with anticipation. Then she was the one groaning, sobbing his name as he slid into her, slowly. There was no pain this time, only a sense of completeness, of being linked with the man who held her. Their hearts pounded in concert, their bodies aligned in perfect harmony. She knew there was more, a golden pleasure she searched out with a subtle flexing of her hips.

Jamie shuddered, swept by wave after wave of the most intense pleasure as Emma rose beneath him. She was so hot and tight, the feel of her straining to reach that sensual peak so exquisite, he knew he'd not last long. Determined to take her with him, he quickened the pace. She moaned softly, her hands greedy as they clutched at him, her body opening to take him deeper, fueling his masculine hunger with her own subtle brand of feminine aggression. They soared together, higher and higher.

Emma's eyes flew open, and she cried his name, her silky heat clenching around him, drawing him with her over the crest. He followed her willingly, filling her with his love.

Some time later, Jamie's mind began to function again. Afraid of crushing Emma, he rolled onto his side but kept her close, their bodies still joined.

Her lashes lifted, eyes luminous with love, smoky with

passion. "I did not think it could be better than the first time, yet this was. Is it always so?"

"Nay." He stroked the damp curls from her forehead. "There is always a certain amount of pleasure...for the man, at least. But the joy...the wonder, the sense of connection? Those are as new to me as to you. I've never felt their like before."

"Truly?"

"Truly. We are bound together by more than desire, more than the vows we exchanged tonight. I know you felt it, too. Our hearts and souls are linked forever."

"Forever," she echoed, but as she stared into his loving gaze, the eye patch seemed to mock their closeness. She reached up, brushing her fingers over the black leather. "Your eye..."

He shied away from her touch. "'Tis an old wound, and I'd not taint this night with the scars of my past."

Emma nodded, not wanting to ruin the night, either. "It pains me to think how you must have suffered."

"Not half as much as I should have." He kissed her and cuddled her close. "Sleep, now, you must be tired."

She was, but as she drifted off to sleep, she wondered if he'd ever trust her with his secrets.

A rush of cool air invaded Emma's warm nest, pulling her from sleep. "What?" She opened her eyes, recoiling as she spotted a tall figure bending over the bed.

"Easy." Jamie's voice was low, soothing. "'Tis just me." He blew out the candle he held, plunging the room into near darkness. The only light was a faded wedge coming in through the door to the main room.

"It can't be morn."

"Nay. Dawn is still some hours away." The mattress sagged as he climbed into bed.

She snuggled against him, wincing as she came in contact with his icy skin. "Brr...where have you been?"

He moved away. "Wait till I've warmed up. I've been outside, making certain all was quiet."

She shivered, but not from the cold. "Do you think Giles could find us here?"

"Nay. The men from Carn Brea are on watch."

"I'm glad." The specter of danger moved her up against him. "You warm up quickly."

"Hmm. Only because you are near." He shifted her so she lay in the lee of his body, her back nestled against his chest, his arm draped protectively across her waist. "I'm sorry I woke you."

"I feel curiously rested." She wriggled further into his embrace, enjoying the novelty of their position.

"So I see." His arm tightened, fitting her more closely against him. The solid wall of his chest brushed her back as it rose and fell; his heart hammered against her shoulder blades. "I should be tired, but you've a way of...reviving a man." His lips drifted down her neck, kissing their way to the spot where it joined her shoulder. He gently nipped her there, sending hot shivers rushing down to her breasts. The heat pooled in her nipples, hardening them in a heartbeat. His hands swept up from her waist, resting lightly on her ribs below her breasts.

Emma came fully awake, senses screaming in sensual anticipation, waiting for him to move the last critical distance. When he didn't, she shifted, pushing the swells into his waiting palms. He cupped her breasts, shaping and massaging them till her blood boiled and her breath came in ragged pants.

"You have the most beautifully sensitive breasts," he murmured in her ear. He plucked gently at her nipples, turning them into aching beads. He played her like a lute in the hands of a master minstrel. Some invisible wire seemed to run from her nipples to the hidden core deep inside her, for it tightened and throbbed in time to his erotic melody.

One of his big hands drifted away from her breast, settling over the flat plane of her belly. "Can you feel how much I want you?" he murmured, drawing her tight into the curve of his body. The hard, naked length of his manhood pressed into her buttocks.

"Aye." The pulsing heat of him drove her wild. She wriggled against him, delighted by the trembling leap of his flesh and his throaty groan. Her own desire burned hotter and hotter. She tried to turn in his arms, aching for him.

"Not yet. Let me pleasure you." His hand moved down her belly. His fingers sifted through the curls at the top of her thighs, gentling probing the slick folds, finding buried treasure. Fiery heat speared through her as he lightly pressed on the tiny bud ripening there.

Emma cried out, arching against his hand. Stinging pricks of pleasure were her reward, like lightning scorching her sensitized flesh. Driven wild by the exquisite rush of sensation, she twisted restlessly, half wanting to escape the sensual torment.

"Easy, love, easy. There's naught to fear. Let me show you how beautiful it can be." He bathed her neck in kisses, one hand teasing her nipple, the fingers of the other creating a riot of unspeakable delight.

"Jamie," she sobbed, desire so taut she could hardly breathe.

"Aye. Open for me, love." His groan mingled with hers as he slipped into her from behind, filling her with a single plunge that made them both cry out again in relief and wonder. A heartbeat later, he began to move. "That's it, take me deeper,'' he murmured. Cradling her hips in his big hands, he drew her into the swift, sure strokes that carried them higher and higher.

With each thrust, Jamie burned hotter, until the core inside him splintered on a wave of ecstasy so pure and bright it chased the darkness from his soul. Dimly he heard her call his name, felt her body convulse, drawing him over the edge with her, out of the night and into the light. "Forever, love," he whispered.

Chapter Fifteen

"Why did you leave Harte Court?" Emma asked.

Seated beside her on the ground, Jamie stiffened. They had climbed up to the top of Carn Brea, explored the stone fort built by the Celts and now sat enjoying the view of the Cornish countryside and the remains of their lunch.

"I shouldn't have asked," Emma said when the silence became unbearable. "But we've shared so much this past week." She'd told him her deepest secrets, about her parents' non-marriage, the book of verses hidden in her money chest...she'd even confessed to feeling ambivalent about running the apothecary shop and terrified about meeting his family. In return, he'd regaled her with tales of his misspent youth, days at court and life at sea. But there were holes in his stories...gaping sores he kept carefully hidden.

"Did you wed me hoping to be the mistress of a great estate?" he growled, still not looking at her.

"Oh! That was unfair and untrue. 'Twas you who insisted we marry." Exasperated, Emma punched him in the arm. "Ouch!" The blow hurt her more than it did him. Though he wore only a simple tunic, his flesh was as hard as armor.

He whirled and grabbed her hand. Cradling it, he stroked the reddened skin. "I am sorry, Emma. That was mean and spiteful of me." He looked at her, finally, expression remorseful. "My only excuse is that I fight to hide my scars." He glanced away, absently touching the patch. "And not always fairly."

She understood. In the same way a cornered animal sought to protect itself, Jamie lashed out when his inner self was threatened. How to make him see she was not his enemy? "'Tis all bound up together, isn't it?" she guessed. "Your wounded eye, leaving Harte Court and Hugh."

He smiled faintly, ruefully. "I should have known that you would divine that, close as we are." He sighed, looking down on the peaceful Cornish landscape. The yellowed grasses of the moors lay to the right, to the left and ahead of them, the dark green of the forests stretched out to meet the pewter wash of the sea. "Do you recall the other day, when we walked to the coast?"

Emma nodded. "I wanted to splash my hands in the water, and from here, it seemed as though the land and water were on the same level. But once we reached the coast, I found that was an illusion." She shivered, recalling the steep, dizzying drop down a sheer cliff face to the sea churning against the rocks.

"Life is like that. Little is as it seems on the surface."

She searched his profile, beginning to understand what he was telling her. "I know you are not the selfish wastrel you pretend to be. You are intelligent, compassionate, kind to others, a protector of the weak and quite likely the most honorable man I've even known. What I do not understand is why the pretense was necessary."

"Emma. Emma. You cannot know what your faith in me means." He put his arm around her and hugged her, his single eye suspiciously moist. "But I am not nearly as good a man as you think me. I have seduced more than my share of women...though no unwilling ones...and left more than a few broken hearts in my wake. Most grievous of all, my parents' among them. I have disappointed my mother and father at every turn, save Papa is somewhat proud I am a fair ship's captain. I was a wild, irresponsible fool, thoughtless and uncaring of the heritage they'd bequeath to me. Worse, it is my fault Hugh is a cripple."

Ah, at last they came to Hugh. Emma wrapped both arms around Jamie to counter the tremors shaking his big body. "Go on."

He hesitated for so long she thought he'd say no more, then he dragged in a shaky breath and continued in a voice scarcely above a whisper. "We never got along. My fault. I was born with a cursed need to excel. I strove to be the best in swordplay, the first across the line in a footrace or a horse race. In my youthful arrogance, I couldn't see what always being second was doing to Hugh, how it turned him from pursuits he enjoyed."

"'Tis a failing we share, I fear," Emma soothed. "Because I envied Celia's beauty and popularity, I taunted her with my accomplishments, my singing, my knowledge of herbs, my ability to earn a wage without depending on a man."

Jamie smiled faintly. "Petty stuff. I went off to court and became the shining star in Lancaster's tail while Hugh studied for the priesthood. But I ruined even that for him." He squeezed his eye shut, and she braced for the worst. "When I turned twenty, my parents ordered me home to assume my station as heir and learn the running of the estate. The prospect of counting bushels of grain and settling the vassals' disputes bored me. What I really wanted was to go to sea. The three of us argued long and bitterly over it. Hugh made the mistake of thinking he could preach to me. I challenged him to fist-fight. My own twin. A priest three weeks' short of taking his final vows.''

"Hugh accepted, and we tore out of the castle to settle our differences in the woods, away from prying eyes and interfering parents. I reached the glade first, of course, dismounted, unbuckled my sword and threw it on the ground. Filled with seething passion and righteous indignation, I scornfully watched my brother ride toward me. He was halfway across the meadow when a trio of brigands attacked me.''

Emma gasped, her gaze flying to the patch.

"Aye.'' He fingered it, mouth set in a grim line. "The first blow caught me here. 'Twas aimed at my neck and would have taken my head off had not some whisper of movement or instinct for survival warned me. I ducked, but not quite quickly enough.''

"Sweet Mary. How did you avoid being killed?''

"Hugh.'' Jamie sighed and tilted his head back, shivering in the grip of that terrible memory. "He leapt to my defense with only an eating knife. They ran him through, nearly severing his leg, and left him to bleed to death while they turned to finish me off. Neither of us would have survived had not my father ridden up with two of his men. He'd learned of my challenge and had followed us to keep me from beating Hugh senseless.''

"'Twas a dreadful thing, but why do you blame yourself?''

"If not for my cursed randiness, we'd not have been attacked. The three men were the brothers of a woman I'd bedded some months before. They'd learned she was no longer a maid when she refused to marry the man they'd chosen for her and insisted she wanted me. Her brothers wanted my blood in retribution for ruining their sister's chance at a rich marriage settlement.''

"Oh, Jamie. 'Twas not your fault.''

"It was. My father carried us back to Harte Court, and my Aunt Gaby, who is accounted a great healer, stitched us back together. Hugh first, for he was losing blood...''

"By the time she got to you, your eye—''

He shook his head. "The scars I bear are no more than my due. The mark of Cain, a sign of my evil for all to see.''

Emma took his face between her hands and turned it so their gazes met. "You are not evil. Thoughtless and arrogant in your youth, mayhap, but such is the folly of youth. You have made up for those mistakes a thousand times over.''

He leaned down and kissed her, a quick brush of the lips, yet she tasted his pain and remorse. "The strange thing is, that whilst I was healing at Harte Court, I realized the life was not boring. Mayhap not as thrilling as going to sea, but there were challenges and rewards aplenty. I saw, too, that it had become too vast for my father to oversee alone. I'd have stayed, and gladly, if not for Hugh.''

"You could not bear to stay and see him limp?''

"That was a part of it, but the crippled leg had also ruined his chance to become a bishop. The church didn't want a man who could barely hobble about. Other doors were closed, as well. He couldn't earn his way as a mercenary nor would a great lord want a castellan who couldn't fight to protect the land. Though his leg is much improved now, at the time he was doomed to live out his life at Harte Court, a useless, purposeless hulk. So deep was his anguish, I feared he'd take his own life.''

"Oh, Jamie.'' It was hard to imagine the haughty Hugh

reduced to such straits, but her own mother had sunk into a decline when she learned how Cedric had betrayed her. "What changed him?"

"I turned my back on Harte Court and gave it to him." He said it bleakly. "I knew how much he loved it, and hoped running the estate would give him a reason to live. I tried to sign it over to Hugh, but 'tis entailed to the oldest son." He grasped Emma's hands. "I should have told you this before. Doubtless you expected to be chatelaine of Harte Court one day."

"Perish the thought!" Emma exclaimed with such horror it made him chuckle.

"I promise we'll not want for anything." Then he remembered the fleet and DeGrys and shivered with foreboding.

"What is it?" she cried.

"Naught." He folded her close so she wouldn't read the lies and half-truths. "Are you happy here, Emma?"

"Aye." She burrowed into his chest, making his heart lurch.

"Good. I will arrange for you to stay here when I go—"

"Go?" she said, popping up so quickly her head bumped his chin. "I will go wherever you go."

"Much as I'd like that, you cannot always go with me."

"Why not?" she demanded, scowling, chin thrust out.

Concerned for her safety, Jamie fell back on an old habit. "How can I take you with me to the jakes?" he teased. "Or into the barracks at Arwenack where the soldiers sleep?"

"Humph. You cannot divert me with silliness. When you leave Carn Brea, so will I…either riding beside you, or scrambling along afterward, prey to every brigand and wild animal—"

"Vixen," Jamie exclaimed. "Crafty, manipulative vixen."

"I had an excellent teacher."

"Nay, you are the one who has taught me." She looked so adorable, with the sun on her face and the wind in her hair, that he had to kiss her. Their lips met and clung, the air between them suddenly charged with passion.

Emma's anger melted. 'Twas impossible to stay angry at him for long. Jamie exuded warmth and charm. Being with him was like being sucked up into a storm, chaotic but exhilarating. Their stay in Carn Brea had been a revelation to her. Though they occasionally visited the village, mostly they were alone together. By day, they'd roamed the countryside hand in hand. Nighttime brought a more sensual exploration. Their lovemaking had taken them from raw, burning passion to an exquisite tenderness so sweet the memory made her eyes mist over. Never had he made her feel anything but cherished.

Now, her heart still aching from the bitter story of his youth, she wanted to use her love to heal him. Drawing on all they'd learned...together...she set out to seduce him.

Jamie groaned, his senses spinning as Emma turned aggressor. Her lips were wickedly enticing, her hands supple and clever as they raced past his belt and brushed him intimately. "Emma!"

She withdrew her hand, face flaming. "Am I too bold?"

"Never."

"Because you have already done everything?"

"Nay," he said quickly, seeing doubts turn her eyes from sparkling green to dull brown. He'd never be bored with her. "Because you are my wife," he reminded her. "And whatever we do is done for love. You may do with me as you will. Anything." *Anything but look under my patch*, he amended as she gazed at it. He held his breath, waiting for her to ask.

Mercifully she didn't. Cocking her head, she grinned at him and reached for the buckle on his belt.

"Here? In the open?" he asked his prim wife, intrigued when she flushed and nodded. Still he looked around, assessing, for this was not his first tumble in the wood. The grass was soft, their position shielded by low brush. Why not? Their time might be perilously short if Giles learned about DeGrys. "'Tis a novel idea," he murmured. True. Everything they did seemed new because he was with her. "I am yours to command, love."

Giggling, she pushed him down onto the grass, sprawling across his chest as she attacked his mouth.

"Jamie!" A voice called from below them.

Scrambling to his feet, Jamie saw Colan striding up the trail from the valley, and his heart sank.

The news must be grave indeed, if Colan had come himself instead of sending a message.

"We're here, love," Jamie whispered.

Emma jerked upright in his arms and blinked, instantly alert. They'd traveled all night to reach Arwenack before daylight. "I don't see the walls."

"They are ahead...through the trees." His arms tightened briefly, crushing her against his mailed chest. "Colan will take you to Penryn and put you aboard a ship bound for London."

"He'll have to bind and gag me."

"Think, love. Think with your mind, not your heart. Giles's reinforcements will arrive today or tomorrow. They'll fight to gain control of the shipyard...there will be casualties."

"All the more reason for me to stay. Mariot is not strong

enough to nurse the wounded..." Her voice and her heart stumbled, thinking Jamie might be hurt. "I'll be needed. And you said Giles could not take Arwenack except with a long siege."

"He'd try it to bring me down."

"Surely the king won't let Oxford destroy our only hope of defending ourselves from the French."

"I doubt Oxford has told the king about the fleet. Or if he has, he'll make it seem that I burned the ships."

"Traitors," Emma hissed. "They deserve the most foul of deaths for betraying us all." She felt Jamie stiffen and turned her head. "Surely you do not disagree."

"Nay. A traitor deserves exactly that."

Colan trotted down the trail toward them. "The way is clear, the postern gate opened to admit us."

Jamie nodded, dismounted and helped Emma onto her own horse, abandoned when she'd become so sleepy he'd feared she'd topple headfirst onto the trail. The three of them rode in silence, not speaking till they'd reached the edge of the woods. An open field lay between them and Arwenack's stout gray walls.

"We've had no reports of enemies in this area," Colan whispered. "But the archers—" he pointed to the dark figures moving along the wall's walkways "—will cover our approach." He started across the meadow.

Jamie hesitated. "Emma. Remember your promise to say naught of our marriage...not even to Mariot."

"Aye." Grudgingly. "But I still do not care if being your wife puts me afoul of Giles and Oxford."

"I do. Giles is vicious and cunning. If he thought it would hurt me, he'd kill you in an instant."

"He would murder a woman in cold blood?"

"'Tis very possible he killed Celia," Jamie reminded her grimly. "And he might have spies inside Arwenack."

"Does this mean we will not share a room?" she asked slyly.

Jamie cursed. "Mayhap we can find a way around that." He snapped a lead rope on her horse and drew her with him across the dark meadow.

Emma's neck prickled the whole way, but they arrived safely, to find Mariot and Colan embracing. The pair broke apart at once, and Mariot hurried over to welcome Emma with a warm hug.

"Is Jamie as angry with you as Colan is with me?" Mariot whispered, peering over at the two men.

"Aye. He was most wroth with me for following him to the shipyard and causing so much trouble," Emma said, though she wanted very much to share her good news with Mariot. "If not for me, Giles wouldn't know about the ships."

"You mustn't think that." Mariot kept an arm around her shoulder and steered her toward the keep. "Colan says 'twas inevitable once Giles came to Cornwall, but they all wish it had not happened for a few weeks."

"What difference can so short a time make?"

"By then, the autumn storms will be upon us, and the weather in the small sea 'twixt France and England will be so foul the French will not dare venture across."

"Oh." Despite her promise to hold herself aloof from him, Emma glanced back, looking for Jamie. He'd mounted up again, and was preparing to ride out. "Where is he going?"

"Ah, you do still care," Mariot said, smiling. "I expect he's going to the shipyard to talk strategy with Bran. They've stripped Arwenack bare of fighting men, save the bare minimum required for defense, and done the same to every village and keep loyal to the Killigrews. But there's no way of knowing how many men Oxford will send against us.''

Emma shivered, terrified by the grievous odds they faced. ''Why do they not attack Giles first?'' she asked as they passed through the entryway and climbed the stairs to the upper floor.

Mariot opened the door to her solar and ushered Emma in before answering. ''Bran was all for that, but Jamie wouldn't hear of it. At the moment, we're in the right, he said. But if we struck the first blow against men loyal to Oxford—''

''He'd have the perfect excuse to wipe us all out.''

''Exactly.'' Mariot took one of the chairs before the fire.

Emma sank into the other. ''This is all my fault...and Hugh's. Speaking of which, where is Hugh?''

''Asleep in his room, as far as I know. The knee he wrenched heals slowly, and he's still using a cane.'' Mariot poured them each a cup of wine, then uncovered a small platter containing bread, cheese and cold meat pies.

Emma accepted the wine, but barely nibbled at the food. ''I—I am sorry I tricked you into telling me where the shipyard was.''

''Hmm. Bran holds us both responsible, of course, but that's because Rosalind's perfidy soured him on women. Colan blames Hugh for having coerced you into it.''

''I probably wouldn't have gone if he hadn't...nay, I'll not blame him for my mistake. We both acted out of concern for Jamie. I just wish there was some way I could set things right.'' Tears blurred her vision, spilling hotly down her cheeks.

''Oh, Emma. You are exhausted. Come, your bed is ready. The best thing you can do right now is get some sleep.''

''I must be tired. I never cry.'' Emma dried her eyes

and went with Mariot. She asked after her friend's health and the babe's, delighted to hear there'd been no more fainting or cramping. But when Mariot finished tucking her in and crept from the room, Emma found sleep elusive, her mind whirling with fear and regrets.

If only there was something she could do....

Chapter Sixteen

Bran was waiting for Jamie by the time he reached the hill overlooking the shipyard. The woods looked black against the pewter light of coming dawn. Fog covered the surface of the harbor, thick as clotted cream. Only a few ships' masts protruded through the billowing mass, eight or ten of the hundreds that had filled the harbor. No campfires burned along the shore; the workmen's tents had been struck and carted off.

"The men are all safely back in their homes," Bran said.

Jamie nodded, swept by an emptiness that was only partly relief. Overseeing the shipbuilding had consumed him for months. "And the fleet?" he asked.

"Beyond Giles's reach." The struggle to accomplish that had etched deep lines of fatigue into Bran's face.

"You've done a fine job, my friend."

Bran snorted and looked toward the harbor, the furrows around his mouth tightening. "Aye, well, the lads and I were all for making a fight of it."

"Giles would have loved that…a chance to declare you all traitors and hunt you down like animals, burn the villages, rape the women and girls."

"If 'twas only just myself, I'd have chanced it," Bran grumbled. He'd been spoiling for a fight ever since his mother's death. "But I'd not want the innocent to suffer." He paused. "I'd like to see Giles's face when he realizes the ships are gone. Do you think he'll run back to his master like a whipped cur?"

"Defeat is something Giles doesn't take gracefully. And there's DeGrys's missing man. Have you found him?"

"Nary a sign." Bran scrubbed a hand over his face. "He could have been wounded, crawled into a hole and died, but we searched carefully. We'd have seen some sign. I don't like it."

"Nor do I. But if Giles had captured him and forced him to talk, there would be a warrant out for my arrest."

"Depending on how much the man knew."

"He stood there whilst I showed DeGrys the fleet and described each ship. He is Giles's proof that I betrayed England to the French, and he won't hesitate to use it."

Bran groaned. "Giles is holding him at Robertsons' in Truro. I'm trying to get a man inside the keep."

"Good." But Jamie could feel the ax poised to fall on his neck. "Damn, we were so close. We just needed a little more time for DeGrys to return to France and tell Charles about the fleet."

"What do you propose we do?"

"We wait. We see what we can learn about Giles's plans, and we wait to see what DeGrys will do. And we pray."

"Will you return to Carn Brea?"

"Nay. If Giles has sent for more troops, we'll be safer behind Arwenack's stout walls. The longer I can keep Giles wondering where I am, the better 'twill be for everyone. He'd not hesitate to cut down anyone who stood in the way of getting me." Jamie recoiled, thinking of Emma.

"I have a favor to ask of you, Bran. If I'm arrested, I want you to see Emma safely back to her home in Derry. I'll give you money to get her settled."

"Colan would be better suited to comforting your bride."

"If I'm charged with treason, not a soul, including your brother, would help me or mine." Because no one would understand why he'd done it. "I am sorry to saddle you with a task you find onerous, but you are the only one I can trust with my Emma. She is everything to me, my heart, my soul, my other half. If I am imprisoned or dead, she will want to live no more than I would if she were gone. Much as I regret having to leave her, I will face death more easily knowing she has you to help her."

"What is this talk of death?" Bran said gruffly, his eyes suspiciously moist.

"Promise me."

Bran nodded. "I will guard her with my life, but—"

"Nay, I have not lost heart or hope. It must be this place." Jamie wheeled his horse away from the skeletal remains of the shipyard and the ghostly beauty of the harbor. "Come, let us return to Arwenack and leave our morbid thoughts here."

Even as he crested the hill and entered the protective cover of the woods, Jamie knew he could not dismiss his troubles by simply riding away from them as he'd done when he'd left home.

Hugh could scarcely believe his eyes when he hobbled into the hall to break his fast and saw Emma sitting with Mariot at one of the tables.

Jamie must be back!

Hugh lurched toward the women, cane thumping, trying to ignore the sharp pains in his left knee. Harder to ignore were the sympathetic stares of the Killigrews. Jesu, how he hated this. The pitying glances, the doleful words he knew were being whispered behind his back. Cripple. Half-man. It reminded him of the first year after his laming. Everyone had been kind and solicitous. No one had really understood what it felt like to have your strong, dependable body reduced to a weak husk.

Hugh hated being dependent nearly as much as being pitied. If not for Jamie, he'd have been neither. 'Twas Jamie's challenge that had sent them to the woods that fateful day, and the brothers of Jamie's lover who had lamed him.

"Hugh!" Emmeline jumped up and rushed to meet him. "Mariot was just telling me what she's been doing for your leg, and I—"

"Where is Jamie?" he asked.

"Gone out somewhere." Emma took his arm. "You have worked yourself into a fever trying to do too much."

Hugh gritted his teeth over a curse, well aware of the sweat dripping into his eyes and trickling down his spine to dampen the fresh tunic he'd put on. "Where has my brother gone?"

"I know you are worried about him, Hugh, but Jamie is well able to look after himself. Let me see to your leg."

"I am just as capable of looking after myself as he is."

"Normally I am sure that's true," she said. "But your leg—"

"My leg is none of your affair." Condescending bitch. He tried to shake her off, but she clung as tenaciously as a tick, nor did words dissuade her summoning two burly menservants to carry him upstairs to Lady Mariot's solar. He found his voice again when she instructed the men to remove his hose. "I will not lie here naked before you!" Hugh shouted.

"Your modesty does you credit, milord." She giggled. "Jamie would be only too happy to shuck off his clothes for any woman. Of course, that was before. If he tried it now, I'd scratch his eyes out." She giggled again.

When had the prim Lady Emma taken to giggling? He'd thought her a sober, responsible lady. Hugh stared at the woman kneeling beside his chair. Her hair was loose, tumbling about her shoulders and down her back in shiny chestnut waves, a perfect foil for skin the color of fresh cream. There was a becoming flush in her cheeks, and her eyes sparkled with such vitality it seemed she'd swallowed the sun. She was beautiful.

Hugh frowned. He remembered her being only passably pretty.

"Forgive me," she murmured. "I didn't mean to tease you. Jamie's wry humor seems to have rubbed off on me."

Hugh knew then what had caused the transformation in the plain, somber Lady Emma. *Jamie.* He had a way of doing that to women, like a sort of sensual magician, whose touch turned even the most sensible into mindless slaves to his towering passion. Aye, she did look like one of his whores, all ripe and dewy. "He has bedded you, has he not?" he exclaimed. It would ruin everything if Jamie bred an heir on her.

Emma flushed and stammered a denial, but he knew she lied.

"He'll never wed you now that he has what he wanted."

She stiffened, her chin rising in response to his challenge. "That is really none of your affair."

Aye, it was. But Hugh knew better than to press. "You are right, of course," he said smoothly. "I'm sure he'll honor his pledge to you." He doubted Jamie knew the meaning of the word, but he had a soft spot for this woman. Emma had proved useful once, she'd do so again.

How much did she know about Jamie's activities? He looked at his knee and realized the best way to regain her goodwill was to become her patient. Steeling himself for the coming ordeal, he said, "I would appreciate your looking at my knee, if you do not think Jamie will mind."

She cocked her head, staring at him intently. "Jamie would make any sacrifice for you, Hugh. As I'm sure you would for him."

"Hasn't he told you, I already have."

"He told me."

"He told you about the attack?" Hugh asked, aghast. Jamie never spoke of that day, even with their parents. Now he really was worried. If Jamie wed her and bred up a child, an heir to Harte Court, it would ruin all Hugh's plans.

Emma stood and turned away to poke in Mariot's medicine chest while the servants helped Hugh off with his hose. She liked Hugh less and less. He was bitter, sulky and said insulting things about Jamie. 'Twas on the tip of her tongue to set him straight about why Jamie had left home, but she didn't want to violate Jamie's trust. Besides, it might only make matters worse.

"You may turn around," Hugh said.

Emma sighed. She was exhausted and worried about Jamie, not the best of moods in which to try and deal with Hugh. Girding herself with what patience she could muster, she marched over to Hugh, the medicine chest before her like a shield. Her patient wore an equally grim expression and a blanket over his lower body. Setting the chest on the floor, she knelt and lifted a corner of the blanket. Despite her annoyance with him, the gnarled mass of purpled flesh made her gasp.

Hugh twitched the blanket over it. "You are repulsed."

"Nay." She steadied her nerves and folded the blanket

back. "As a trained healer, I've seen worse." Once the initial shock was over, she was under control, able to assess the damage. A long, jagged scar extended from his hipbone, around the front of his thigh to his knee. It was old and thickly corded with white scar tissue. The pain must have been excruciating, the convalescence long and arduous. The damage to the muscles was so extensive she marveled he'd been able to walk again. That he did so with hardly any limp was a tribute to his determination.

"Well?" he demanded.

She swallowed. "Though the swelling and bruising are painful, I cannot find anything broken or misplaced. Mariot said you were thrown from your horse when we were attacked."

"My horse took an arrow and went down, pinning my leg."

"You were fortunate not to have been captured by the enemy."

"As were you. Where did you and Jamie go?"

Emma bristled at his tone. "We hid in a cave."

"For five days?"

"Part of that time."

"It must have been primitive and uncomfortable."

Emma's face flushed as memories of wild passion and incredible tenderness filled her. "We, er, made do."

"I am sure you did." His voice was ripe with innuendo. "What did you do for food? Or did you live on love?"

Oh, the man was too exasperating. "You do not believe in love?" she snapped.

"I believe in duty and honor...they last far longer than the heated gropings between two people in the throes of passion."

"You confuse lust with love," she said, more furious by the moment.

"Do I?" he murmured, considering her closely. "And I say one body is much like another in the dark. If I came to you in the night, you'd not know the difference between us." His gaze glittered, not with the brilliant heat of Jamie's, but with a coldness that sent a shiver down her spine.

"I would know," Emma exclaimed.

"You fancy yourself in love with him," he said, voice silky again. "Very foolish. Women are drawn by his lazy charm and do not realize until too late that he is a dangerous man to know."

Emma ground her teeth together. "Jamie is one of the most gentle men I've ever—"

"Celia de Vienne found that out...to her sorrow."

Emma gasped. "What do you know about her?"

"Only that she was unlucky enough to prefer Jamie over Giles Cadwell, and was murdered...mayhap by one of them."

"Jamie did not kill her," Emma said firmly.

"No doubt you'd like to believe that."

"What are you trying to say?" Emma cried. Trembling with emotion, she grabbed hold of his tunic and shook him. "Celia was my sister, if you know something, tell me straight out."

"Your sister..." Hugh's eyes rounded.

Belatedly, she recalled Jamie asking her to keep their connection a secret, but what was done was done. And Hugh was family. "Aye. Celia was my sister. If you know something about what happened to her, please, please tell me," she begged.

Hugh continued to stare at her as though she'd grown two heads. Or spit on her sister's grave.

Unable to bear his censure, Emma stood and turned toward the hearth. The goodly fire crackling there did nothing to drive the chill from her bones or the ache from her heart. "Please tell me what you know," she said, more calmly.

"N-naught. I am surprised to find you with a man who was accused of her murder. A man who was your sister's lover."

Emma flinched. She'd tried not to think about that, tried to pretend it had never happened. Jamie claimed it had only been the one time. She believed him...because she loved him. Whirling, she employed Jamie's favorite tactic, diversion. "Jamie didn't kill Celia. He wasn't even in London at the time. He thinks 'twas Giles Cadwell. He had a grudge against Jamie, and Celia once repudiated his advances."

"I see." Hugh had recovered his color and his composure. "Does he have proof Giles is a murderer?"

"Nay. But that doesn't mean Jamie is guilty."

"Agreed. How do you come to be with him?"

Emma seized the change of subject like a lifeline. "The tale is most unusual." She bent to the medicine chest again to hide her nervousness and selected the ingredients for a poultice for Hugh's knee. When the herbs were crushed together in a bowl, she steeped them in boiling water. All the while she worked, she told Hugh what had happened from the time she'd kidnapped Jamie till their arrival in Arwenack. Of the marriage, she said nothing.

"You have had quite an adventure," Hugh remarked.

She shrugged noncommittally. "There, I think this is cool enough." She soaked a cloth pad in the infusion then bound it to his knee with a length of linen.

"I hope he doesn't hurt you as he has so many others," Hugh said. "I do not mean to speak ill of him, but Jamie is, after all, a rogue with wandering eyes, better to—"

"Eye. He has only one, and 'twill not stray," she snapped.

"Well said, my love," Jamie drawled, strolling in through the open doorway.

Hugh's lip curled as he watched the stupid chit leap up and run to greet Jamie as eagerly as though they'd been parted for years, not a few hours.

"I can't say I like coming in to find my betrothed bending over a half-naked man," Jamie growled.

"'Tis just Hugh," the girl replied, dismissing him with a wave of the hand. "I was seeing to his leg."

As though he would ever again be satisfied with Jamie's leavings, Hugh thought, glaring at his twin. Jamie looked back at him over the top of her head. He wore that smug smile Hugh hated. The one that hinted he knew secrets the rest of the world did not. For once, Hugh smiled back, thinking Jamie did not know how close he skated to the brink of disaster.

"They what?" Giles roared.

The captain of his troop retreated a step. "The ships have vanished from the harbor," the man repeated.

"Where did they go?"

"Out to sea. Our scouts saw the last of them clearing the mouth of the estuary just before dawn this morn. There are a few vessels left behind, but they appear to be unfinished."

"And they did naught to stop them?" Giles waved off the question. Of course they couldn't stop them. Damn. Damn. The whole fleet was likely out to sea by now, lying in wait for the French. Charles would be unlikely to conclude a treaty while he was fighting for his life. Giles paced the length of Lord Robertson's withdrawing room, furious as any predator robbed of its prey. The troops he'd sent for should arrive in a day or so, but to what avail? Oxford would have his hide for this, and it was all Jamie Harcourt's doing.

Giles turned on his captain. "When the reinforcements arrive, we'll lesson these arrogant Cornish bastards. A few burned villages and severed heads should get us Jamie Harcourt."

"What charge, milord?"

"Charge! On my orders."

"The earl said we were to draw as little notice to ourselves as possible," Walter reminded him.

Giles gnashed his teeth, but nodded. Oxford was not above bending or breaking laws to suit himself, but with public sentiment running against the royal favorites just now, he was treading more carefully than usual. "Let us see how the Frenchman fares. I was told his fever broke this morn and gave orders that he was to have no more of the opiate. Mayhap he has regained his wits and can tell us who Jamie was meeting."

With Walter trailing after him, Giles crossed the hall to the wall chamber where the sailor or soldier, whichever he was, lay on a field cot. A maidservant sat with him at all times, and the physician lurked nearby, preparing an endless stream of noxious-smelling concoctions to restore the injured man's blood and reduce his fever.

"Well?" Giles demanded.

The physician, a tall, gawky man, bolted up from his stool, his black gown flapping like the wings of some great crow. "The fever broke this morn. He took a goodly bit of the elixir—"

"When will he be able to talk?"

"Well…" His beak of a nose twitched as he regarded his patient. "He lost a goodly amount of blood, and is very weak, but he spoke a few moments ago, thanking the maid—''

"You have done fine work," Giles said. "Walter, see he is paid and provided with an escort back into Truro."

"But...but Jean may need me."

"Jean?"

"Jean le Peque. He said that was his name."

"Excellent. He is not only alive, he has his wits about him. Walter, pay our good friend twice his usual fee."

The physician hesitated, then shrugged and began to pack up the tools of his trade. Lucky for him. Giles didn't want him spreading rumors of torture about town, but an accident could have befallen the quack had he refused to leave.

After sending the maid on her way with a suitable bribe, Giles waited with barely concealed impatience until Walter had seen the old man out and returned with the tools of *his* trade. In many ways, they were not so different.

"Lock the door," Giles commanded. He bent over the cot, noting Jean's pasty color and raspy breathing. "This will require skill and delicacy," he said, warming to the task. "Our guest is not in the best of health. Jean," he called, shaking him gently.

The sunken lids fluttered up. Jean's eyes were dazed with pain and confusion, but he seemed to perceive the danger. "Wh-who are you?" he rasped.

"Lord Giles Cadwell. 'Twas my men who found you, wounded in the woods. Do you remember why you were there?"

Jean shook his head, but sweat beaded his upper lip.

"Ah, I see we must do this the hard way. Actually, I am glad to get in the practice. It has been some time since I've had the pleasure of *questioning* anyone. I want to be in top form when I arrest Jamie Harcourt. I see that name is familiar to you.''

Jean moaned and shook his head, eyes darting wildly about in search of escape. There was none, of course. He was far too weak to even get out of bed. Not much sport, really. Pity, Giles hoped Jamie would be more entertaining.

In short order, Giles knew who Jamie had been meeting and why. All he needed was to locate Harcourt and take him into custody. That plum fell into his lap as he was cleaning Jean le Peque's blood from his hands.

''Roger, what do you here?'' he asked, surprised to find Hugh's page on his doorstep.

''Milord is still not able to ride so far, nor did he want to trust his message to paper.''

''Well, I hope no one saw you coming here.'' Giles gestured the boy into his chamber, but offered neither refreshment nor a seat. ''What news?''

''Jamie Harcourt is at Arwenack. He returned this morn.''

''Ah.'' Giles rubbed his hands together. For a day that had begun in disaster, it was ending rather nicely.

''Milord said to tell you Jamie had returned in secret. Also, the Killigrews are provisioning to withstand a siege and bringing all the villagers and their livestock inside the walls.''

''Damn.'' Giles slammed his fist into his palm. '''Twill be nigh impossible to pry him out of there in time. We shall have to apply a bit of pressure.'' He grinned, relishing the task.

Chapter Seventeen

Jamie was unusually silent as they climbed the stairs to their chamber, and Emma feared something had gone wrong, but when he opened the door and saw the tub set up by the hearth, he smiled. "A bath. Did you smell me coming?"

"I thought you might be cold and tired, so I bade the servants keep water hot and bring it up the moment you arrived."

A knock at the door announced the arrival of a string of menservants bearing steaming buckets of water, which they immediately emptied into the huge oaken tub.

"You are a woman to be valued above all others." Jamie kissed her lightly and made for his bath, leaving piles of filthy clothes in his wake. She had only the briefest glimpse of his naked backside before he settled into the water. "Ah..." He leaned his head back against the rim, eye closed, mouth slack with bliss. "A wife is a very handy thing to have."

"Clod! What of your other women?"

"My *former* women were more interested in their pleasure than my comfort." He opened his eye and grinned. "Speaking of pleasure, are you going to wash me, too?"

"I might." She put aside her dour thoughts and drank in every detail, savoring the quiet joy of this private moment, for she suspected they'd have few. There were too many people with claims on Jamie's time and talents. The fire leaping behind him turned his hair into a golden nimbus and gilded the sculpted planes of his chest and shoulders. Wide shoulders, unbowed by the burdens they'd borne. His cocky smile and the intelligence gleaming in his dark eye hinted at other facets of his complex personality.

How wonderful he was, how dear and precious. Foolish tears, joyful tears prickled. Thank you, Mary, for sending him to me.

"Emma, are you all right?"

"Of course." She blinked away the moisture and busied herself getting a linen cloth and bowl of soft soap. But when she knelt beside the tub, he knew.

"I can't bear to see you cry, Emma." He stroked her cheek, his fingers were warm and slick. "Undress for me."

"Now? But what if someone comes in?"

"Bar the door. We will pretend we are alone on a deserted island like the one where my parents were stranded."

"But you haven't had your bath, and you must be hungry." She gestured toward a covered tray on the table by the window.

"I can see you'll be a most capable chatelaine," Jamie said, knowing she worried about it. "You've thought of everything. And we'll get to it all...eventually." He rubbed a wet finger over her mouth, captivated by the way her gaze turned smoky. "Bar the door, and while you are about it, close the shutters, too."

"Why? Usually you like the light."

"So I do, but today I've a yen to make love by firelight." The intimate rasp of his voice was as seductive as his words.

Emma rose and hurried to the door, tingling with anticipation. Behind her, she heard a flurry of splashing water and imagined him rushing to complete his bath. She made quick work of fastening the hide-covered shutters over the room's single window and raced back to the tub just as he was rinsing the soap from his chest.

"Now douse the candles," he whispered.

"The candles." There were three, two on wrought-iron pikes at either side of the hearth and one on the bedside table. When she blew it out and turned, the room was dark, Jamie only a black shape against the glow of the dwindling fire.

Water sluiced down his body as he stood and picked up a towel to dry himself. Like a statue come to life, or a pagan god rising from the sea, she thought, transfixed by the fascinating play of light and shadow over his corded muscles. The wet plop of the towel hitting the floor broke the spell.

"Undress for me, love," he softly commanded.

Emma hesitated, feeling oddly shy. 'Twas foolishness, really, given all they'd done together. But she was exposed to the firelight, while he stood concealed by the shadows.

He lifted a hand to his head, tugged and threw something onto the crumpled linen. The patch.

Her doubts melted in a wash of love and gratitude. "Oh, Jamie." She began to tug on the laces at the side of her gown, tangling them hopelessly in her rush. His hands were there to conquer the knots and, finally, to slip the cotehardie over her head. The shift followed with breathless speed. Naked, her body gilded with firelight, she raised her arms to the lover whose face she could not see yet trusted with all her heart.

His hands slid down to cup her rump, lifting her against his warm, damp body, his mouth slanting over hers in a kiss as ripe with hope and promise as his gesture. He'd removed his patch, bared himself to her. Not in daylight, true, but if he'd taught her anything, 'twas that the journey toward love and trust was made up of many, many small steps.

Jamie raised his head, but kept her firmly against him. "Someone should paint our portrait thus...the golden lady seduced by a dark lord."

Emma kissed his chin, wishing she could see more of his eyes than two black disks in the pale blur of his face. At least there were two. Could he see? "You are a worse romantic than I."

"I do not count it a failing."

"Nor do I. Not any longer." She stroked the side of his face, daring to let her fingers brush his left temple, and felt the furrow cut by the patch's thong. "Because of you, my love."

He trembled, but didn't shy from her touch as he had before. "I thought I knew everything there was about love, but till I met you, I was blind." He swept her into his arms and carried her to the bed, laying her back amid the pillows.

Trembling herself, she lifted her arms in mute appeal. Instead of stretching out on the bed, he bent to kiss her. His tongue slid past her parted lips to slip within and steal her reason. Desire ran like hot wine in her veins. She clung to his neck, legs milling restlessly on the coverlet as she sought to ease the tension building inside her.

"Tell me what you want," he murmured.

"You. Only you." She swept a hand down his body and brushed the jutting proof he wanted her as badly. "Love me."

He evaded her grasp. "I do. I will. But slowly." He kissed her again, his hands tracing the line of her ribs, swirling up to gently cup the swelling weight of her breasts. His thumbs grazed the nipples with fire. She gasped, then moaned and arched off the bed as the wet heat of his mouth closed over one sensitive peak.

Emma tunneled her hands in his damp hair and pressed him closer as he suckled at first one, then the other, breast. She cried his name, sang it in need and wonder. The sweet, dark rhythm he created with his mouth echoed inside her, setting off the most incredible avalanche of feelings. His lovemaking had been hot and tempestuous, languid and teasing, but never had it reached this intensity. Never had she wanted him more.

"Jamie." She tugged at his hair. "Please..."

He lifted his head a fraction, his breathing as ragged and rapid as the clamor of her pulse. "Your skin tastes like spring."

"Oil of gillyflowers." She grabbed his shoulders and tried to urge him over her. 'Twas like trying to budge rock.

"Did you put it all over? Even here..." He eased her thighs apart, his long fingers gently teasing the petals of her womanhood. They opened in a heated rush, like a spring runoff. Then suddenly his mouth was there, where she'd never imagined it.

Emma gasped in shock. "Jamie! Nay, you cannot."

"I must. I am drunk on the taste of gillyflowers and Emma. I pray you, let me drink my fill." His mouth was persuasive as sin, hot as fire, and clever beyond belief.

Her objections melted. She quivered with anticipation, hot shivers coursing through her as he took her higher and higher. She was held in thrall by the spell he wove, yet never had she loved or trusted him more than now, when he demanded her complete surrender. She gave it willingly, freely. The coil inside her tightened, then burst into a shower of stars. "Jamie!"

"I am here, love." And he was, joining their bodies in a swift, sure stroke that stole her breath again. Before she could catch it, he was moving inside her, linking them in a ritual as old as time, soaring with her back to the stars.

They dozed afterward in each other's arms, roused finally by an ominous growl.

"What was that?" Emma asked, sated and disoriented.

"My belly."

"You're hungry. I knew we should have eaten first." She threw back the blanket he'd put over them.

"Stay. I'll get it." The bed creaked as he climbed out. On his way to the table, he detoured by the fire long enough to light one of the candles.

Peering out from between the bed curtains, she waited to catch her first real glimpse of his face, but when he turned, she saw he'd put the patch back on.

Jamie set the tray down on the bed and removed the linen towel with a flourish. "A veritable feast." He made a great show of smacking his lips and rubbing his belly, starkly aware of Emma's disappointment. *I am new to this. Give me time.*

She smiled, and the knot in his chest eased. 'Twas all right. She understood. "Silly man. 'Tis only bread and cheese."

"Eaten from your hand, nectar of the gods."

"Now he expects me to feed him."

Amid much teasing and giggling, they fed each other, sipping wine from a single goblet. They put on neither clothes nor pretext, which made him feel all the worse when occasionally her gaze strayed to the damned patch. If ever he could put it aside, 'twould be for her, but the patch was such a part of who he was, what he was, he didn't know if he had the courage to risk it.

Jamie stretched the meal out as long as he could, but eventually the food was gone. The castle bell sounded, warning the dinner hour approached, and he knew time had run out.

"Has something happened to the fleet?" she asked suddenly.

"Nay, why?"

They lay sprawled on the bed, propped up by mounds of pillows. "You are so tense, and you were quiet earlier."

"The fleet is safely away." He told her only what the world would soon know, that ships had been sighted leaving the harbor and sailing down the river into the sea. "Most have not yet been commissioned, so they're flying King Arthur's Pendragon pennant."

"What a whimsical touch. Do you sail after them to London? Will the king be there to honor you?"

"Actually, I am going to stay here…at least till I see what Giles will do about this."

"He'll be livid," she said with relish.

"Emma…" He took her hand. "I want you to go home."

"Home? To Harte Court?" She shivered and pulled a blanket over her. "I suppose, but I am a bit apprehensive about meeting your parents. What if they don't think I am good enough…?"

"I thought you might like to go to Derry…to check on the shop and your people."

"That is kind. I'd like that." She grinned. "Anything to postpone the inevitable. When will we leave?"

"Well…" He laced his fingers through hers, but already he could feel her slipping away from him. "I have to stay here and make certain Giles behaves himself. Hugh can take you.''

"Hugh! I'm to go alone...with Hugh?" She shook her head, burying her face in a cloud of hair. "Nay. Firstly, I will not leave you. Secondly, I do not like him when he says disparaging things about you."

Jamie grinned. "And here I feared you'd prefer my perfect brother to me."

"He is not perfect. He is cold, stuffy and judgmental."

"That he is, but he is also one of the few men I'd trust to see you safely home."

"What are you not telling me?" she demanded.

A pox on clever women. "Everything is fine."

"Then there is no reason for me to leave."

"Emma..."

A loud pounding at the door cut off his protest. "Jamie! Jamie! 'Tis Colan, let me in." He hammered on the door.

Jamie leapt from the bed, grabbed the coverlet from the floor and crossed the room. Cold fear gripped his belly as he wrenched open the door.

"We've had a message from Giles." A grim-faced Colan pushed past Jamie, followed closely by Bran. "A warrant, actually."

"A warrant?" Jamie asked, quietly closing the door. But he knew, God, he knew, this was the moment he'd been dreading.

"For your arrest." Colan looked worried, puzzled. "He claims to have proof you betrayed the fleet to the French."

"We'll get you away," Bran said. In his eyes was the same wild terror that iced Jamie's veins. Giles had De-Grys's man.

Colan swallowed. "There's something else..."

"What?" Jamie glanced between the two brothers.

"His reinforcements arrived this afternoon. They've surrounded Penryn and vow to burn it to the ground, and the people with it, if you don't surrender by tomorrow noon.''

''Nay!'' Emma exploded out of the bed in a welter of slender limbs and dark hair, the blanket barely covering her. ''I won't let them take you.'' She wrapped both arms around him and clung.

''I have no choice.'' Heart breaking, Jamie hugged her close. ''I love you, Emma. No matter what happens, remember that.''

''What do you mean you are not going to rescue him?'' Emma demanded, glaring at the Killigrews assembled in the solar.

''Quiet, or I'll lock you in your room again,'' Colan snarled.

Emma held her tongue and looked to the others for support. She had not given in gracefully when Jamie agreed to surrender. She had cried and threatened to follow him to prison. Jamie had soothed her, made love to her and tricked her into drinking a cup of opiate-laced wine. When she'd awakened, he was gone. ''Bran?''

''He made us promise not to attempt a rescue,'' Bran growled. He, at least, looked as wretched as she felt.

''He betrayed us,'' Petrok said, bewildered and hurt.

''Jamie is not a traitor. He is not.'' Enyon's lower lip trembled. ''He would not do such a thing.''

Emma put her arm around the boy and hugged him. They clung together, firm in their conviction, but what could a woman and a boy do? She didn't even know where Giles was holding Jamie. ''How can you be so certain he is guilty? You have only the word of that sailor. Likely he was tortured to reveal—''

''Jamie admitted it.'' Colan's face was rigid as carved stone, stark with disbelief. ''I was there when Giles brought forth this Jean le Peque. I heard him say that he'd come ashore with Simon DeGrys and Jamie had taken them to the harbor...showed them the ships we had slaved to build."

"But the ships are safe...they sailed away," Emma said.

"They've not been seen since. Doubtless they now fly the French flag," Colan cried.

Petrok sighed. "To think I treated him like a son."

Emma cast about wildly for more ammunition. "What could he hope to gain? Jamie has money and—"

"DeGrys promised him the admiralty," Colan said. "He admitted it freely."

"But..."

Hugh stirred in his chair, a silent, nearly forgotten spectator in a corner of the room. "Your loyalty does you credit, Lady Emma, but Jamie did admit he was guilty."

Emma stood firm. "He is not. I know he isn't."

"Jamie would not have confessed to so serious a crime if he was innocent," Colan said. "I—I did not want to believe it, either, at first. I tried to defend him, but Jamie named dates and places when he had gone to France and met with DeGrys. He gave details of their conversations. He...he boasted of how he had used us to further his ambitions." Colan spat the last.

Emma flinched. "Why would he do it?"

"Who knows," Hugh said sadly. "I gave up trying to understand what drove him years ago. No doubt Jamie thought this a grand adventure." He sighed and shook his head. "I must go home and somehow break the terrible news to my parents that their firstborn son has disgraced them again. Let me escort you home."

"To Harte Court?" she asked fearfully.

"Nay, when I bid him farewell Jamie said you had better return to Derry and put this unfortunate incident behind you.''

Our love is not an unfortunate incident. Emma looked around at the others and realized that none of them, with the exception of young Enyon, supported her. So it would be in Derry if the townsfolk learned she'd wed a traitor. This would be worse even than when it had gotten out that she was a bastard. This time, she was not cowering and running. Not only for her sake, but for Jamie's. She didn't know what was going on, but she did know he was no traitor. ''I cannot leave Cornwall while Jamie is here.'' She was going to see him and find out what was happening.

Being Giles's prisoner was not as bad as he'd expected—it was worse. Jamie tried to recall how long he'd been here, but time had blurred together. Bouts of torture blended into waiting for the next round of beatings to begin.

Jamie hung by his arms from shackles in a windowless cell that would make hell pale by comparison. A fire burned in the central pit, glinting off a gruesome array of instruments laid out on the floor: barbed lashes, thumbscrews, thin knives sharp enough to peel a man like a grape. He already knew which ones were Giles's personal favorites.

They had deprived him of his clothes, his patch and his dignity. He'd been burned, branded and beaten to the point of breaking, yet he hadn't. Not yet. There was a trick he'd learned when he'd been a guest aboard that Spanish galley, a way to turn his mind inward and escape the worst of the horrors being done to his body. Every round of abuse left his body weaker and his resolve stronger. Giles would not break him.

He had readily confessed to showing DeGrys the fleet.

He'd elaborated and expounded—it gave him something to scream besides God's name when the pain got too bad. But he had not given Giles what he wanted—the names of his confederates. Principally, Harry and Lancaster. Giles wanted them so badly he fairly drooled.

The door grated open and the devil waltzed in, his dark cape swirling, his smile chillingly smug. "Are you ready to tell me what I want to know?" Giles demanded.

Jamie glared at him. "Nay."

"Pity. I thought you might like to spare your betrothed the, er, rigors of my hospitality."

Emma! His heart stopped. "I have no betrothed."

"Emmeline. Does the name not ring a bell?"

A whole chorus of them. Images of Emma laughing and loving rose to haunt him. He shook them away. Denial was useless. He wondered how Giles had come by the information. "If you had her, she'd be chained beside me." The pain of that image was worse than all the torture he'd endured.

"I will have her soon. Then we shall see." Giles whirled back out the door, leaving Jamie alone with his fears.

Chapter Eighteen

Something was wrong.

Emma stared out the window of her bedchamber, but she didn't see the dawn light stealing across the verdant countryside beyond Arwenack's walls. Her thoughts were turned inward.

Something was very wrong.

Why would Jamie confess to a crime he didn't commit?

To protect someone. But who? None of the Killigrews had been implicated in his treasonous act. In fact, they were outraged to have been taken in by Jamie's scheme.

Why could they not see he was incapable of such an act?

Emma clasped his book of verse closer to her chest. She had no need to open it, for the prose was etched in her mind and heart. Stirring words of love and honor. The man who wrote them could not have betrayed his country.

She had to see him, talk with him.

Emma spun away from the window and crossed to the chest. Carefully placing the book inside, she withdrew Peter's clothes, washed and mended now. Hugh had learned where they were keeping Jamie and had agreed, after considerable argument on her part, to escort her there. He was certain Giles would not refuse to let Jamie's brother and betrothed see him.

The thought of seeing Jamie in prison, chained like an animal, sent a shiver through her. If they'd hurt him, how could she bear it? If he told her, to her face, that he had done this terrible thing, could she bear that?

Steady. You know he is not guilty. This was Giles's doing. She had to believe that. In the dark hours of the night, she'd worked out the sequence of events. Giles had murdered Celia and tried to pin it on Jamie. When that had failed, he had set up the business with the French. Why had Jamie confessed? Because Giles had some hold over him or had threatened someone he loved. The Killigrews or mayhap his own family.

Emma drew in a deep breath, and with it came the subtle scent of leather and Jamie from the open trunk. Bitter tears burned in her eyes. Oh, my love, I have to save you. But how? How?

If their situations were reversed, if she was in trouble, Jamie would find a way to save her. She could do no less.

Stronger now, Emma dressed, buckled on the long knife Jamie had left behind and crossed the room. The corridor and stairway beyond were empty, but when she reached the entryway, she heard the servants setting up the tables in the great hall. Keeping to the shadows, she crept along the wall and out the door, praying no one would see her. Hugh was meeting her by the back gate, and he'd stressed the need for secrecy.

"Convinced as they are of his guilt, the Killigrews may try to stop us from going to him," Hugh had told her.

Emma had allowed that was true, but she felt uneasy about going with Hugh. He'd been kind and solicitous since Jamie's arrest, but he didn't believe his twin was innocent. She most certainly didn't want him standing about making caustic remarks while she was trying to speak with Jamie.

She reached the back of the stable without encountering anyone. Nearly there. She must cross an open yard to reach the curtain wall. A hundred yards along it was the metal-banded door set into the stone. Just as she stepped away from the building, a hard hand grabbed her around the waist and dragged her into the bushes. Her scream was cut off by a wide, callused palm, her struggles subdued with ridiculous ease.

"Where the hell are you going?" Bran scowled down at her in the gloom.

Emma pried loose one of his fingers. "None of your affair."

"Tell me, or I'll shake it out of you." He looked furious enough to do just that.

"I'm going to see Jamie."

Bran's frown deepened. "They've taken him to London."

"London?" Emma squeaked. "But Hugh said he was at the Robertsons' castle in Truro."

"Did he now?" Bran's grip eased, but not his expression. "They took him away by ship...two days ago."

"Two days... Hugh's information must have been old." Her eyes filled with foolish tears. "I will go to London, then. I have to see him."

"They're taking him to the Tower. You'll never get in."

And Jamie would never get out. "Do you...do you know what they intend to do with him?"

Bran looked away. "Aye. As soon as the king's signed the writ, Jamie will be hanged, drawn and quartered."

She closed her eyes on a wave of anguish so strong it nearly swamped her. "We have to save him," she whispered.

"Save him?"

Frightened and exasperated, Emma grabbed hold of his arm and shook him. "Jamie is innocent. *He did not do it.* I must find a way to prove Giles framed him. Failing that, I must free him. I must." Her frantic words were cut off by his hand again.

"Hush. Do you want to rouse the whole castle."

I do not care, Emma said with a glare.

Bran sighed. "He said you'd be trouble."

"Who?" she mumbled into his palm.

"Jamie." Bran looked off into the distance, but his gaze seemed focused on some inner pain. "He asked me to look out for you...make certain you didn't do something foolish."

Emma snorted and lifted his fingers away from her lips. "He is a fine one to talk."

"Aye, well..."

The hedge in his voice put her senses on alert. Carefully she searched his face, her mind swirling over the conversations and confrontations since Jamie had been arrested. Bran had been present at all save her chat with Hugh about visiting Jamie. Each time, he'd hung back, neither defending nor condemning. But his eyes had grown more haunted with every passing hour.

He knew something. "Tell me," she demanded.

"What?"

"I am accounted a bad liar, but you are surely worse. You know what is going on, and if you do not tell me, I will kick and scream and thrash till they hear me in Penryn."

"I could slit your throat."

"Fraud." Emma wriggled free...only because he let her go...and sat up. Crossing her arms over her chest, she glared at the surly giant. "Talk."

Bran sat down beside her and shook his head. "'Twill do no good. Jamie's caught fast this time." His eyes held no glimmer of hope. "He did it, you see, met with DeGrys, told him about the fleet, then brought him to the harbor to see it."

"Nay." Emma put her hands over her ears to stop the terrible words, but they rang over and over in her head till she thought she'd go mad. "Why?" she whispered.

Bran shrugged. "For the admiralty, I expect."

Emma thought she'd cried herself dry these past few days, but her eyes filled again. "Something is wrong. Very wrong. You say he did it, and I must believe you, though I didn't before. But…but there must be some other reason. Some good reason. Either Giles forced him to it or… Henry of Bolingbroke!" Emma grabbed hold of Bran's arm. "Why did I not think of him before. Jamie met him in London." She tried to stand, but Bran pulled her back down again.

"Where are you going?" he whispered.

"To London. I would be powerless to accuse such an important man, but Sir Thomas Burton is an acquaintance of mine. I will tell him about Bolingbroke. He'll arrest him for questioning."

Bran groaned and covered his face.

"What is it?"

"Jamie was right," Bran mumbled, raising his head. "You are one woman in ten thousand, but you will be our ruin."

"Nay, I will be his salvation."

Bran caught hold of her hand, his expression deadly serious. "You must not tell anyone about Bolingbroke. 'Tis true we are in this together, Jamie, Bolingbroke and I, but Jamie has endured days of torture without breaking to keep that secret."

"Torture…" The blood rushed from Emma's head. She swayed, black dots dancing before her eyes.

Bran swore and put an arm around her. "Bolingbroke and his sire, the Earl of Lancaster, are trying to save England from Oxford and his ilk. If they are accused of treason, the whole country is doomed."

"But Jamie…"

"He knew it might come to this when he agreed to the plan."

"What plan? What is really going on?"

"That, I cannot say. There's too much at stake, too much to lose if the information falls into the wrong hands."

Emma nodded slowly, but she was not resigned to letting Jamie pay the ultimate price. "Then we shall have to rescue him."

"From the Tower? How?"

"I do not know, but I know someone who will."

Hugh waited for over an hour past the appointed time. Finally, his leg stiff and aching from the dampness, he hobbled back inside the keep.

"I assume Emma is in her room," Mariot replied when he approached her in the hall. "She has taken her meals there since…since…" She began to cry softly. "I just don't understand how Jamie could have done this."

"My brother has been a disappointment to us all," Hugh said. But not for much longer. They'd taken Jamie to London in secret for fear the Cornishmen might either try to free him or kill him before he could implicate his cohorts in crime. It was up to him to get Emma there, too. When Jamie saw they had her, he'd quickly name the Lancasters as his accomplices. Then he'd hang.

Soon Jamie would be gone, and he would have it

all…Harte Court and the respect he'd been cheated of all his life. How nice Jamie had turned traitor. If he'd died in battle, he'd have been revered as a hero. If he'd been lost at sea, their parents would have mourned him all their days. But a traitor… Likely they'd scrub Jamie's name from the family records like the blot he was.

Hugh's euphoria faded when a maid came back to report Emma was not in her chamber. Nor was she found after an extensive search of Arwenack's grounds and buildings. Lady Mariot cried buckets, fearing Emma had gone to Truro to visit Jamie and gotten lost. An army of men went out to comb the woods, but turned up no trace of her…alive or dead.

Rather hoping for the latter, Hugh decided to wait a few more days to see if she could be found. Thus he postponed the unpleasant task of telling Giles that Emma was lost to them as a weapon against Jamie. Remaining at Arwenack had the added benefit of sparing him from trying to appear suitably glum while he told his parents what Jamie had done.

If he was patient a little longer, he'd have what he wanted.

Harte Court was larger and grander than she'd remembered. The sitting room, where they'd been left to wait by a haughty servant, was twice the size of her solar at home, the carved chairs and wall tapestries fine enough for a royal palace.

"I should have taken time to change," Emma murmured, trying to smooth the wrinkles from her tunic. Three days of hard travel by sea and land had left their mark on her, but she had no other clothes. They'd left Arwenack that very morn, with naught but what they wore and the coin Bran had in his pouch.

"This is a waste of time." Bran paced before the cheery fire like the caged wolf he greatly resembled.

"Wait outside, then, and I'll confront the high-and-mighty Lord Alexander myself," Emma snapped.

"Confront him with what?"

Emma whirled toward the door, groaning as she saw the man framed in the opening. Lord Alexander himself, looking so much like his son she wanted to cry.

"My steward said you craved an audience." His cold haughtiness, so like Hugh's, undercut her confidence. He'd never believe her. He'd never help her.

Still she had to try...for Jamie. "Aye, your lordship. I...I have come to ask a favor," Emma stammered.

"Indeed?" He entered the room with that same graceful, catlike glide he'd passed to his son.

Emma wet her lips. She was so wrung out with exhaustion and worry her legs were limp. Taking hold of the back of a chair to brace herself, she began, "'Tis...'tis about Jamie."

"Jamie?" He looked her up and down, disapproval clear. "How do you come to know my son?"

"I...I am his wife."

"Wife!" he thundered, driving her back a foot. Before she could recover, a woman appeared in the doorway.

"Michael says we have guests." Lady Jesselynn was less elegant than at her birthday fete, dressed in a green woolen gown, her hair confined in a fat red braid. Behind her came Johanna, Jamie's beloved sister.

"This...this woman claims she's Jamie's wife," Alex said, sounding as much confused as angry.

The lady's mouth opened, but no sound came out. Johanna uttered a faint shriek.

"I—I know this is a surprise," Emma said. She wanted to run away from their censorious eyes, but if she couldn't make them believe in Jamie, who would? "I have his ring." She opened her hand. She'd been clutching it so tightly her flesh bore the imprint of the Sommerville crest. "I swear I have not come to make any claims on you...except a few moments of your—"

"Jamie's wife." Lady Jesselynn crossed the room with a swift, decisive stride. She barely glanced at the ring, her sharp green gaze intent on Emma's face.

"You were at Mama's fete," Johanna exclaimed. "You're the minstrel Jamie fought over."

"The one Jamie left with," Alex added in a shocked whisper.

Emma nodded. "It seems my sins have come back to haunt me. I left with him so I could kidnap him and force him to confess to my sister's murder, but that is not important, now."

Alex's eyes turned flinty. "What have you done with my son?"

"I haven't done anything, but he...he is in trouble and—"

"Take me to him." Alex grabbed her arm and shook her.

Bran cursed and sprang from the corner where he'd been lurking. He wrenched Alex away from Emma and shoved him up against a wall. "Touch her again, and I'll break your arm."

"Nay, Bran." Emma tugged on his sleeve. "Let go. He meant no harm." Actually, Alex's concern for Jamie gave her hope.

"He had no call to hurt you, and you half-dead on your feet," Bran growled. But he did let go of Lord Alex. "I told you it was a mistake to trust outlanders. We'll get him out of the Tower ourselves."

294 Knights Divided

"What tower?" his lordship demanded, rubbing his arms.

"*The* Tower...London Tower," Emma said.

"*Dieu.*" The change in Alex was lightning quick, fear tightening the lines in his handsome face.

Lady Jesselynn gasped. "What happened?"

"He has been accused of treason," Emma said softly.

"Treason!" Jesselynn swayed, clutching at her husband for support. "Nay."

Alex wrapped an arm around his wife. "That's impossible. He has not always led the life we wanted, but treason..." He shook his head. "Jamie would never do such a thing."

"Thank God." Emma tottered over to one of the chairs and sank into it. "Thank God, you believe in him."

"Of course we do," Jesselynn said. "He is our son. But please..." She left her husband's side and knelt at Emma's feet. "Please tell us about Jamie."

Johanna followed her mother. "Is he all right?"

Emma wiped the tears from her eyes with the back of her hand. "Aye, well, nay. So much has happened... I did not know where else to turn. Now that I am here and you've not thrown me out, I scarcely know where to start."

"Poor thing. You look exhausted." Jesselynn turned to Bran. "From whence did you come?"

"From Cornwall...in three days."

Lady Jesselynn's eyes rounded. "You need food and rest."

"All that can wait till we've spoken of Jamie." Emma gratefully accepted the cup of wine Alex offered her, noting the silent thread of communication that ran between him and his wife as they stood together, arms linked, ready to support each other. So it was between herself and Jamie.

So it would be again when they got him free. If they did. Nay, she couldn't give up hope.

Emma was safe. He had to believe that, or go mad.

Still every time the cell door opened, Jamie feared to see her standing there in the flesh and not just a figment of his imagination. Conditions had improved in the two— or was it three—days since they'd brought him to this cell in the bowels of the Tower. Giles had gone off to consult with Oxford and, until he returned, they'd given him back his clothes and…more important…the patch. He was no longer subjected to physical torture, but he hadn't eaten in so long he was dizzy and light-headed.

His mind wandered, reliving past glories, regretting old mistakes. He longed to see Harte Court once more and his parents, and Jo. Ah, Jo. He knew she would be someone special when she grew up, and wished he could be there. It comforted him to think that Hugh would make certain Harte Court prospered, care for their parents in their dotage and find a good man for Jo.

But who would look after Emma? Who would tease her from her serious moods and appreciate her gift for music? Who would sing with her after supper and laugh with her and love her?

The door to his cell creaked open and the guard ducked in under the low lintel, shoving a torch ahead of him into the gloom. Blinking against the sudden glare, Jamie saw a slight figure in a hooded cloak trailing after the guard. A priest come to hear his last confession?

Oddly, the idea the end was near seemed more blessing than curse. He'd tried not to dwell on the hopelessness of his situation, but there truly was no way out. The sooner it was over, the better.

"Wait here," the guard growled, and the priest stopped

just inside the door. The guard, an ugly brute with a pock-marked face and broken teeth crossed the few steps to Jamie's cot. Settling the torch into a ring in the wall, he bent and unlocked the shackle on Jamie's left leg. "I'd best leave yer other leg fettered and yer wrists, too," he mumbled. "I'm taking enough of a chance as it is."

"What?"

"Yer friend's compliments." The guard jerked his head in the direction of the priest. "Half hour's all I can give ye. But I expect a man who's been without as ye have'll be quick about it."

Jamie shook his head, trying to clear it. "My friend's sent the priest?"

"Priest! Ha, that's a good one." The guard stood and shook the pouch on his belt. It gave off a sweet, metallic clink. "It's a whore...young and right pretty, she is."

"Send her away."

"Are ye daft, man? Ye'll not get another chance like this. Lord Giles is due back this evening. Likely he'll have the writs and ye'll be bound for the gallows in a day or so."

"I don't need a woman."

The guard snorted. "I heard different. Heard ye'd futter anything in skirts."

"That was before I married."

"Please, sir." The whore threw herself at his feet, her forehead pressed to his knee. "Please let me stay. His lordship won't pay me otherwise. I promise I don't have the pox."

"That's the least of my worries," Jamie snapped. "Run along. I could not rest easy in my grave if I broke my wedding vows."

"Please, sir. I'm accounted ever so talented." The girl

tilted her head back, grinning out at him from the shadow-draped depths of her cowl.

"Oh, God!" Jamie gasped as he recognized her face.

"I'll take that as permission to stay." She peered back at the guard. "Thirty minutes, you said."

"Aye." The guard wiped a hand over his face, eyes bright with lust. "When ye're done here, come see me." He lumbered out without a backward glance.

"Emma!" Jamie breathed when the door had closed.

"Oh, my love." She cradled his face in her hands and kissed him ever so gently. "You are so thin... Papa said they wouldn't feed you." From beneath her cloak, she pulled a small sack.

Jamie watched with a sense of detachment as she unloaded a flask and several wrapped bundles from the sack. In a moment he'd wake up and find this was all a dream. "Cedric sent you here disguised as a whore?"

"Not very likely. 'Twas *your* father who thought about the food and wine." She unstopped the flask and held it to his mouth. "Watered wine. 'Twas Mama's idea...your mama's...that I play the whore. Bran and Papa were none too happy, but..." She shrugged and handed him a hunk of bread. "There's hard cheese, sausage and five apples." She loosened the top of her gown, bent forward and the latter thumped out onto the bed.

Jamie touched one of the apples. "It feels real."

"Of course it is."

He reached out and ran a finger down her cheek. "You are softer than I remembered...and so much more beautiful. Are you real, too, or another of my fantasies?"

"Oh, love." Emma's smile dissolved into tears. She hugged him, and he tried not to wince. "Where are you hurt. Let me see." She cried harder when she lifted his tunic and saw the furrows in his back and chest. "I need salve and needle and thread and a poultice for these deeper ones," she muttered, poking and prodding with gentle care.

Jamie kissed her hands. "Now I know you are real. In my dreams, you are intent on pleasuring me, not torturing me with your noxious potions and sharp needles."

She blushed. "I'd do that, too, but not here." She looked around at the dank walls running with slime. "We will have you out of here in a day...two at the most."

"Impossible. This is the Tower."

"We can do it...we will. Your Uncle Gareth is seeking an audience with the king to plead your case. If that comes to naught, Papa...your papa...and Bran have worked out a plan to get you out of the Tower. Should that fail, your Uncle Ruarke is gathering an army to waylay you on the way to the gallows and—"

"Have they not heard the charges against me?" Jamie asked.

"Of course." Emma's lower lip trembled, but she stilled it quickly. "I...I do not know why you confessed to treason—"

"Emma. Did Bran not tell you that I brought DeGrys ashore and showed him the fleet?"

"He did. But...but I know you did it for a good reason."

Jamie bowed his head over their linked hands. Her trust and faith humbled him. "What news of the French invasion?" he asked.

"None that I know of." She was puzzled by the question. "The Earl of Oxford's peace treaty has not been signed, but neither have the French called off the threat. We did hear rumors that the Duke of Lancaster has set sail for England. Why?"

"No reason." Every reason. Until he knew what the

French were going to do, he must remain silent…even to the grave. If Lancaster arrived before they hanged him, the duke could not, would not, step in to save him. "Emma." He held her hands and looked deep into her eyes. "Your coming here has meant more to me than you can know, but I want you to go back and tell my family there is to be no escape attempt. No plea to the king, no midnight assault on the Tower's walls, and especially, no battle at the Smithfield gallows."

"But…but, Jamie. We love you. I love you. I cannot let you go without a fight. I do not know what is going on, but—"

"Exactly, you do not know. You are wrong about me, Emma. I am guilty. I sold my country to the enemy for the price of a glorious title and a king's ransom in gold. But I overplayed my hand and got caught." He forced himself to let go of her hands, to speak coldly and callously. "I regret you were embroiled in this. I regret you made the mistake of falling in love with me and got hurt."

"Jamie…"

"Nay. I am not worth saving, I tell you. And I will not have my family or you risk everything to try. If a rescue attempt is made, I will not go. Tell my father and uncles that."

"Time's up," the guard called from the door.

Emma stood, drawing the cowl back over her head. "Loving you was not a mistake." She turned and started for the door, her spine stiff, shoulders square.

"Remember what I said," he called after her.

She looked back over her shoulder. "I remember everything you have ever told me…everything."

Chapter Nineteen

It was an ugly day to die.

Jamie had hoped to feel the warmth of the sun on his face and smell the flowers one last time before he bid the world farewell. But one of the fierce storms that so often came in October had swept in from the channel during the night. Thunder growled overhead, and an icy rain pelted down as the guards hustled him from a side door and into the waiting cart.

The foul weather hadn't deterred a crowd from gathering. He anxiously scanned their faces, torn between hope he might see a friendly one and fear his loved ones had ignored his warnings and come to free him.

"Traitor!" screamed a toothless crone.

"Hangin's too good fer him!" a man cried.

A hail of stones and rotted vegetables mixed with the rain.

Jamie winced and tried to duck out of the way as a rock struck his back. The shackles bit into his barely healed wrists. The weight of the chains and metal collar drove him to his knees. Panting, he paused to marshal his strength. Without the food and wine Emma had brought him four days ago, he might have been too weak to stand for his own hanging. Nay, he'd not give Giles and Oxford the satisfaction of seeing him bowed.

Struggling to his feet, Jamie stood still while the guards tied his arms to the wooden cross in the center of the cart, a device designed to hold him upright and give the spectators a clear shot at him while he was transported to the gallows.

Giles watched from atop his horse. True to the guard's prediction, he had returned the day of Emma's visit. "The king has signed the writ ordering you drawn and quartered in four days' time. I'd as lief kill you myself, but Oxford has promised me an earldom if I can get you to implicate Bolingbroke and Lancaster before then," Giles had growled. He'd then proceeded to raise torture to an art form. Nothing he'd done had loosened Jamie's tongue, which had only made Giles more furious.

"Ready, my lord," the guard said to Giles.

"One final chance, Jamie. I have yet to give the executioner his final instructions. Tell me what I want to know, and I will see your death is swift and painless."

"I'll see you in hell," Jamie snarled. "And pray you are not long in joining me."

Giles swore, then gave the order to leave.

The cart lurched into motion, bouncing and swaying on its crude wooden wheels. An added bit of torture for the condemned, Jamie found. White-hot agony scorched through joints abused by lengthy sessions on the rack. He ground his teeth together to keep his cries locked inside. Tilting his head back to pray for strength, he received an unexpected bit of solace. Cool rainwater splashed onto his face and dripped into his mouth. He swallowed eagerly, parched after days without water, his throat raw from screaming.

Something slimy and noxious smelling hit his chest, fol-

lowed by a chorus of jeers. Opening his eye, he saw the
spectators who lined the road, a seething mass of angry
men and women shrieking for his blood. They'd have it
soon enough, he thought, and blocked them out by thinking of Emma and his family.

Mama and Papa, she'd called his parents, and referred
to his uncles as though they were hers, too. What a relief
to know she'd found the courage to go to them and that
they'd obviously made her welcome. His was the most
wonderful family in the world. He found solace in the
knowledge they'd care for Emma when he was gone and
could not.

The cart stopped with a jolt that made Jamie groan
aloud.

"Bow your head to His Majesty, you insolent bastard,"
Giles snarled at him.

Squinting against the rain, Jamie saw the king had come
to see him punished. He sat on his throne beneath an oiled
canopy, surrounded by his court. Their gaudy silks and
glittering jewels were a bright spot in the otherwise grim
landscape of Smithfield.

"Your majesty," Jamie said, his voice like gravel.

Richard's handsome face ruffled with regret. He was tall
and fair as his sire and grandsire had been, but he had not
their good judgment or ability to rule. "You have disappointed us, Jamie. We played together as boys. Your verse
and your prowess on the tourney field are fond memories.
You were ever the prankster, but never maliciously so. Had
I not read the confession you wrote and known it to be
your own hand, I—"

"He has admitted his guilt, sire." Oxford lurked behind
the royal shoulder like an evil wraith, thin, dark and malevolent.

Richard sighed, slender, beringed fingers toying with the

huge ruby that hung around his neck. Its worth would have fed a small town for a year. "I wished you had told me you wanted an admiralty," he said petulantly. "I'd have granted you one." And he would have, too, dealing it away as he had countless other even more valuable prizes till the treasury was bankrupted.

This is what I give my life for? Jamie thought sourly.

"If I might be allowed a moment with my brother." Hugh stepped from the shelter of the canopy and approached the cart.

"Hugh. You shouldn't have come. Please tell me Emma and the rest of the family are not here, too," Jamie whispered brokenly.

"I arrived at our London house yesterday and did not find them there. They must be at Harte Court. I stayed in Cornwall to look for Emma." Hugh's expression grew more glum. "I am sorry to tell you this, but she has been missing for over a week."

Jamie opened his mouth to tell Hugh she was alive and at Harte Court, then he saw Giles watching and realized the only thing that had saved Emma from Giles was her supposed death. The longer she stayed missing, the safer for her. "Thank you for what you did. I will see her soon enough."

"Aye." Hugh cleared his throat, then leaned close to whisper, "I spoke with Oxford earlier. He vowed that if you gave up the names of your cohorts, he would try to arrange for clemency...exile, mayhap."

A lie. But poor Hugh couldn't know that. Even now, at the last moment, he was trying to save his disreputable twin. "There is nothing to tell. I acted on my own."

Hugh sighed and nodded. "Well, that's that, then."

"Promise me you'll do nothing rash to try and free me."

"What?" Hugh blinked. "Nay. That is, I want to, but—"

"The risks are too great."

"Exactly 'tis only because you've been estranged from us these past few years that we were not all arrested with you."

"Get on wi' it!" shrilled one of the spectators, and the cry was taken up by the others.

Giles stepped forward. "Time is up."

"I've done all I can," Hugh said sadly, turning away and going back to his place in the stands.

"Take care of Harte Court and the family," Jamie called.

Hugh looked over his shoulder. "You can count on that." He smiled, his eyes glowing with an odd, zealous light.

The guards moved in, undoing the ropes and dragging Jamie from the cart. As he lifted his head, he saw the horror that awaited him. Robed and masked, the executioner stood in the shadow of the noose. To one side was the table spread with the tools of his trade and the block. Jamie's stomach turned and rolled up into his throat. They'd stretch him out on that great stone slab and carve him into four pieces. He prayed for the strength to endure, to die without giving up what he knew.

The piercing wail of the pipes cut across his morbid thoughts and silenced the crowd. They parted to make way for a procession dressed in green and gold. The sound grew louder as the pipers approached the gallows, till the very air reverberated with the stirring cry of a dozen Highland bagpipes.

Music, how fitting. Jamie wondered who had arranged it. When the musicians stopped before the pavilion, Jamie belatedly recognized the man bowing to the king.

Alford le Trompour. Old and wizened, his steps stiff, but his aristocratic face and mane of white hair unmistakable.

His heart pounding wildly, Jamie looked at the rest of the players. Markham was there, looking even more sullen than usual, and several other men who'd performed at Harte Court. But no Emma. No Bran. Thank God. This must have been arranged by the mayor as London's contribution to the event.

"The presentation I promised is ready, your majesty," the old man said gravely.

"What the hell is this?" Oxford shouted.

Richard raised his narrow chin. "We agreed that this must be done, but I will say when. And I say 'twill not be until I've given my friend a send-off."

Oxford's curses were drowned out by shouts of approval from the onlookers as a line of wagons moved into view and began to snake through the crowd. The first one carried a dancing bear, decked out in crimson steamers and pawing the air...to the horror and delight of the spectators. In the second, a bare-chested man swallowed and disgorged a shiny sword.

After them came what must be the largest troop of entertainers ever assembled anywhere. Legions of tumblers pranced into view, each trying to outdo the other in the complexity of their jumps and rolls. Rows of knife throwers marched in, their knives tracing shiny arcs as they tossed them into the dark, wet sky. Lewd shouts greeted the undulating waves of dancing girls, their veils rendered transparent by the rain. There were wedges of acrobats, wagon loads of contortionists, and hordes of jugglers tossing about apples and small red pouches. Lastly came the mummers, a hundred strong at least, dressed in armor and performing the "Sword Dance" with mock weapons.

The king's soldiers pushed back the crowd to make room for the groups of entertainers to mass before the royal pavilion.

"Well?" the king called out to Jamie.

Jamie grinned in spite of himself. It was the sort of lavish spectacle for which Richard was known. "I am glad you did not save this for my funeral, sire, I'd have been sorry to miss it."

Richard inclined his head; the gems in the royal crown winked softly in the gloom. Jamie realized this was what he was dying for. For *what* Richard stood for, not *who* he was. For England. For his family and these players and, aye, even for the mob that had come to watch him die.

Jamie straightened his shoulders, scarcely feeling the manacles on his ankles and wrists. He'd done it so they might live free of French rule. And it was well worth the sacrifice. His only regret was that he didn't yet know if he'd succeeded. If only there had been some word from France.

A howl of outrage sounded the first sour note. The bear had taken exception to something...the crowd, the rain, the pirouette his handler wanted him to make for the king. Snarling, it lashed out with one mighty paw, caught his master by the shoulder and sent him flying into one of the poles supporting the canopy. The pole cracked and bowed, drenching guests and guards alike in the water that had been pooling in the canvas, then collapsing altogether, trapping the king and the royal hangers-on.

Like glass shattering, the trouble splintered and spread. Deprived of his master, the bear charged about, terrorizing horses and people alike. The dancing girls screamed and fled into the arms of the king's guard, who were only too happy to carry the poor women to safety. The knife throwers lost their grips on their weapons, sending people to their knees in panic. The panic spread to the jugglers. The sacks flew every which way, splitting open in a hail of silver coins. Caught in the frenzy between fear and greed, the crowd became a seething mass, half scrambling to get away, the other half grappling for the money.

Jamie stared in disbelief at the chaos. Was this all a dream? Would he wake up in his cell and find it hadn't happened?

"Keep hold of the prisoner!" Giles shouted above the din. The hay in the wagons had been set afire by a jugglers' torch, and smoke began to roll across the field.

"Shall I take him back to his cell?" A mailed figure wearing Oxford's colors and an iron helmet appeared out of the pall.

"Aye. I must see to the king and Oxford." Giles started toward the pavilion. Outraged screams rose from beneath the canvas, which humped and writhed like some hideous monster. "Take the horses and go around. The cart will never make it."

"He can't ride with his legs fettered."

Giles swore, then dragged the key from around his neck and tossed it at the guard. "Don't free his hands. And mind he gets there safely, or you'll take his place on the block."

"He'll not get away from me, and that's a promise." The guard removed the manacles from Jamie's ankles, then took his arm and led him through the choking smoke.

The idea of escape flickered briefly, but Jamie knew he was too weak to get far. So he staggered along beside his taciturn escort. When they started down the knoll behind the gallows, his bare feet slipped on the wet grass.

"Easy." A muscular arm went around his back, steadying him. "Not much farther now."

Indeed, a score of mounted men waited at the bottom of the hill. The horses were huge destriers, their black coats blending with the flowing cloaks of their riders so it seemed man and beast were one.

Jamie blinked. "Ah, this is a dream, and you are the devil's henchmen come to claim me at last."

"Oh, Jamie," one of the riders exclaimed. The voice sounded so like Emma's he wanted to weep.

"Pay him no mind." The guard stopped before the riderless horse, opened a saddle pouch and withdrew a black cloak. "He's about reached the end of his tether."

The feel of warm, dry wool settling over his shoulders seemed so damned real. Jamie watched a drop of rain bead on the surface, then sink in. His brain was doing the same, falling further and further into madness. "If this is a dream, I hope I never wake up." He swayed slightly.

The guard caught him. "I'd better take him up before me. I think Nero will carry us both."

"Nero?" Jamie's head snapped up. "Nero is Papa's horse."

"Aye." The guard dragged off his helmet. The face revealed in the half-light was Alex Harcourt's. "Bran, better give me a hand getting him into the saddle."

"Bran?" Jamie watched in horror as his friend dismounted and came toward him. He looked wildly around at the others, gasping as each in turn pulled back the cowl to show their faces, seven men from Harte Court and Emma. "What are you doing?"

"Rescuing you," his wife said calmly. "And I must say I resent having to stay here when it sounded as though you were having much more fun up there."

"Alford's plan worked perfectly," Alex said. "You should have seen the bear...and the jugglers. Emma's idea of using the coins was brilliant. The Londoners will scratch the grass off of Smithfield trying to get it all."

"You can't do this." Jamie turned to his father. "When

Giles realizes I am missing, he'll ride straight to Harte Court.''

"And find it locked up tight.'' Alex motioned for Bran, and together they lifted Jamie into the saddle.

"Oxford won't let this rest. He'll have us all declared outlaws and lay siege to the keep,'' Jamie said.

"We pray it won't come to that.'' Alex swung up behind him. "Lancaster sailed from Spain a week ago. We are buying time till he returns.''

Lancaster! Jamie's heart leapt, then fell. Lancaster would not dare speak in support of him.

"What do you mean he is not here?'' Giles took a second look into the miserable cell that had held Jamie. "He has to be. I sent him back here hours ago.''

"Who with?'' asked the constable of the Tower.

"I do not know the name of every man here. He wore Oxford's colors. Assemble your men and I'll pick out the miscreant. He must have lost Jamie in the melee…or taken a bribe to let him go.'' Giles struck his palm with his balled fist. "By God, I'll see the bastard strung up beside Harcourt when I catch them.''

"Where is he!'' Oxford's bellow preceded him into the room by only an instant. He ducked into the cell, looking fit to chew steel. "What happened? Where is Jamie Harcourt?''

Giles retreated before the hot words, till his back hit the slimy wall, and he could go no further. "I—I do not yet know, my lord, but I have men searching—''

"You mean you have lost him?''

"Not I.'' Giles rushed to explain, stumbling over his words like an errant lad. "'Tis the fault of the players. I will have the entire troop arrested and thrown in the Tower.''

Oxford glared at him from reddened eyes, his face streaked with soot, his clothes torn and rumpled. "Oh, you will? Beginning with the bear who started it all, I presume." He leaned in, pressing his grimy nose against Giles's. "I am sick to death of your whining and lame excuses. You lost the fleet. You lost Jamie Harcourt...you've even lost the thrice-cursed bear, who has taken to the hills along with the rest of the players. I've a mind to throw you in the Tower. In this very cell. I—"

"Giles! Giles!" Hugh raced up the narrow stairwell and skidded to a halt by the open door. "I know where they've taken Jamie. Oh, pardon, your grace." He bowed to Oxford. "I—"

Oxford turned away from Giles. "Where have they taken him?"

"To Harte Court...the estate I was to get when—"

"I know what it is, you dolt." Oxford began to pace, muttering to himself as he stroked his sooty chin. "What of the fortifications? Is it built to withstand a siege?"

"Siege!" Hugh cried. "Nay, you cannot. I've spent years—"

"Stop sniveling," Oxford roared. "And do not tell me what I can and cannot do," added the man who had the king dancing to his tune. "I will inform His Majesty that the traitor has been located and request troops to pry him from his hiding place."

"I'll bid the men prepare to march," Giles said.

Oxford glared at him. "If you want to keep your head, you will stay out of my sight."

"You...you cannot dismiss me!" Giles exclaimed, aghast.

"I can...and I do." Oxford swiveled toward the door, where a pair of guards lurked. "You, there...take this miserable cur below and escort him out of London. He's to be barred from my homes and from the royal residences, too. Let it be known that any man who gives him shelter or aid is my enemy.''

''Your grace.'' Giles fell to his knees. ''Please do not cast me out. I have nowhere to go. Let me stay...I promise I'll—''

Oxford glared at him. ''If there's anything I hate worse than a failure, it's a sniveling failure. Get him out... now.''

The guards leapt to their duty, snagging Giles under the arms and dragging him, whimpering and protesting, from the cell.

''It is not my fault,'' Giles screamed, his voice echoing in the corridor. ''''Tis Jamie Harcourt's...curse him. Let me go, and I will kill him myself.... I will sneak into that castle and kill him while he sleeps, I will...'' The slamming of a door abruptly shut off his increasingly frantic ranting.

''Your grace?'' Hugh touched Oxford's sleeve. ''What of me?''

Oxford turned, lips curling in a snarl of rage, then he thought better of it. ''Do you know this keep? This Harte Court.''

''Of...of course, I was born and raised—''

''Good. You will come with me and advise me how best to take the place,'' Oxford commanded, starting for the door.

''Your grace, I could not destroy my own castle.''

Oxford's eyes narrowed to flinty slits. ''Then you will find some other way to deliver up your cursed brother or you will find *your* head separated from your neck.''

''Of course,'' Hugh said, his mind whirling for a way to save Harte Court and himself. ''I might convince him to surrender.''

"Hah! Only a fool would do that, and he is clearly no fool."

"Nay, he is not," Hugh said slowly. "But he is sentimental and protective of our family. I will think of something, never fear. Have I your leave to go to Harte Court and speak with—?"

"Go to hell, for all I care, just bring me Jamie."

It had been years since Harte Court had been called upon to withstand a siege, though defense had been its original purpose. The outer walls were twelve feet thick, joined by a series of round towers, culminating in the main gate house, twin towers containing the drawbridge that spanned the moat. Just inside the towers, the entryway slanted sharply to the left, cleft by a series of portcullises, which could be lowered to entrap an invading army while the defenders poured hot oil and arrows down on them from above.

Jamie's mouth was set in a grim line as he watched barrels of oil and baskets full of arrows being hauled up to the wall walk. The outer ward was a patchwork of tents for the hastily assembled Harcourt troops and pens filled with livestock brought in to feed them. On the tiltyard, squads of men received last-minute training in the art of siege warfare. A skill they'd soon be putting to the test.

Swinging his head, Jamie stared at the army assembled outside the gates. A thousand strong, they made no attempt to hide their activities as they went about the business of building scaling ladders, and assembling the catapults they'd dragged over the hills.

"Do not lose heart, son." Alex laid a hand on his shoulder. "We are well prepared to withstand whatever they throw at us. Though I'm surprised they came so quickly." Scarcely a week had passed since the fiasco at Smithfield.

"If Richard had moved half as decisively against Bruges, the French wouldn't have taken the wool market."

"'Tis Oxford's doing. He was humiliated by my escape." And doubly infuriated because there was no one to blame it on, thank God, but an irate bear run wild. The players' timing had been impeccable. It had taken great skill to make the whole thing look like a colossal accident. "Oxford wants me badly, and he'll not leave till he's got me." Jamie turned to his father. "Let me go out. I will offer to surrender if the king will overlook your part in freeing me."

"I am not giving you up."

"Think of Mama and Jo."

"I'm thinking of my own hide. They'd skin me if I let you go out," his father teased. "And your wife would hold me down."

"Papa…" The rest of his plea was cut off by the thunderous crash of the battering ram hitting the main gate.

It had begun.

While the ram pounded at the gates, bands of men rushed forward with scaling ladders, then paused on the bank of the moat, trying to decide how they might get across. Harte Court's walls rose straight out of the moat. Except in summer, when the water was low, there was no bank upon which to set the ladders. Still the men ran up and down like mice in a maze, looking and gesturing and arguing amongst themselves.

Alex laughed. "Neither Richard nor Oxford is much of a military leader, thank God."

"That may be so, but they can still starve us out," Jamie reminded him. "Oxford will not give up till he has me."

"All we need do is wait for Lancaster."

"Papa," Jamie said in exasperation. "Lancaster can do naught. I have told you time after time, he will not, can not, save me. I am guilty. I did lead Simon DeGrys to the ships."

Alex's expression hardened. "So you say, but you have not told me why, and do not mention that foolish bit about the admiralty, for I'll believe it no more than your wife does."

Emma.

Weak still from his imprisonment, Jamie turned and leaned against the solidity of the battlements. Emma, who had coerced an army of minstrels and players to stage a huge diversion to free him. Emma, who had cried over his wounds as she tended them and steadfastly refused to leave his side or his bed, in spite of his fury at her. "She has deluded herself into thinking I am a hero."

"Her loyalty is but one of her fine virtues." Alex braced his shoulder against the wall. "I must admit when she arrived and announced she was your wife, we were…skeptical." He smiled faintly. "She looked more like someone's squire…a grubby one."

"But she cleans up rather well."

"Emma has the kind of beauty that will last…the kind that goes beyond the surface to her heart and soul."

"Aye, she does." Jamie smiled for the first time in days. "I am glad you've made her welcome. She has no family left except for Cedric."

"From what you've said, she's better off without that worthless piece of c—"

The slur was punctuated by the whine and crash of a huge boulder sailing over the wall. It landed in the bailey, scattering dirt and panicked sheep.

"And so it begins," Hugh grumbled, limping up the steps to join them. His leg was still not completely healed. "They'll keep at this till Harte Court is reduced to rubble."

"We've little to fear," their father replied. "The inner walls and keep are set so far inside the outer defenses that no stones will reach them."

Hugh sniffed. "Time is on their side. They'll batter down the outer walls, then move the attack within. We are doomed."

"Do not say that." Alex gave Hugh a little shake. "Richard will grow bored with this and abandon the siege."

"Oxford will never give up," Hugh grumbled.

Jamie agreed. Shivering, he looked back across the inner ward to the keep where the women had stockpiled food, bandages and medicines. He would not be the death of his loved ones, Jamie vowed. Before it came to that, he'd steal out the postern gate and give himself up.

Chapter Twenty

His body wedged into the upper branches of a tall pine at the edge of the woods, Giles gauged the progress of the siege. Four days had passed since the arrival of the king's army, and thus far little headway had been made. The battering ram pounded away at the metal-banded front gate, leaving a few dents, but no gaping holes. The catapults continued to lob rocks at the walls, which shook but didn't crumble.

By day, bands of Oxford's knights rode around the keep and jeered at the defenders, offering mercy to those who surrendered, promising a hideous death to those who didn't. The only reply was an occasional hail of arrows from the archers on the walls.

"A pox on them all," Giles mumbled, grinding his teeth in frustrated rage. His hatred of both parties was so great it twisted inside him like a writhing flame. He scarcely noticed that his gaudy finery was stained and tattered, or that his belly rumbled with hunger. His burning gaze was focused on the green and gold banners proudly flying from Harte Court's highest tower. If he could get inside, he'd find Jamie and kill him.

No waiting for him to divulge the names of his cohorts.

No waiting for the hangman to carry out the king's writ. Just Giles's knife or sword or bare hands, settling an old score.

When Jamie was dead, King Richard would reward him personally. Giles knew what he wanted.

Harte Court, and everything else that had belonged to his rival. For once, Jamie would come out last. Smiling grimly, Giles settled into the crook of the tree. When the castle fell, he'd find Jamie and kill him.

Jamie was up to something.

Emma felt it in the increased tension of the body lying beside her in the bed, his back to her, not touching hers at all. He hadn't touched her since they'd ridden in from London. His refusal to kiss her or speak to her any more than was absolutely necessary hurt, though she knew why he was doing this. Not to punish her for planning his rescue...though he was furious about that...but to put distance between them.

Foolish, gallant man, he was preparing her for the worst. He was trying to draw away from her, thinking it would make things easier in case they were parted again. Well, she was not giving him up. She was fighting to keep him. "Jamie?" she whispered.

"Aye." Cool and impersonal. The night candle burned on the bedside table, casting pale light over his head and shoulders.

"I have finished the verse...the one I began in Cornwall. I thought you might like to hear it."

He started, but didn't turn. "'Tis late and you are tired."

"Oh, but I'm not a bit tired." Emma leapt up and rushed to open the chest at the foot of the bed. The roll of parchment was right on top. It did her heart good to see the passion flare in his eye when she carried it to him clad only in her hair.

"Emma." He levered himself up on one elbow, nostrils flared, breath quickening. "This is not a good idea."

Stubborn man. "Nay, 'tis an excellent one." The bombardment of ram and catapults had stopped for the night. He could not use duty as an excuse to avoid her. She sat down beside him and handed him the parchment. "I want you to read this now."

Jamie swallowed, struggling for control. The subtle veil of her hair was more seductive than mere nudity. Bathed by the soft candlelight, her breasts rose and fell with every breath she drew, her nipples playing hide-and-seek between the dark, shiny strands. He longed to push the silky curtain aside, to touch her gently flaring hips and taut belly, to mold their bodies together...one last time.

"Are you not going to read it?" she asked nervously.

Dazed, Jamie nodded and tipped the paper toward the candle. He'd thought to skim the words and get this over with quickly. The sooner she slept, the sooner he would leave. But her prose caught his attention and held it fast, for the story she told was of her own journey from darkness into light. The light of his love. Their love. The stanzas ended with, "When true love dwells in two hearts so pure,/ Never can it be banished!"

Jamie lowered the paper, unaware he was crying till she leaned forward and kissed the tear that trickled down his cheek from beneath the patch.

"I know you are wroth at me for putting your family in jeopardy, but I swear I did not force or coerce them. We all love you and could not just let you die."

"Emma." Overwhelmed by the depth of his love for her, Jamie gathered her into his arms. "I love you, too. So very much." It was heaven to feel her soft body sliding against the hard planes of his, her mouth opening to the questing edge of his tongue. His self-imposed control shattering, he kissed her with all the longing pent up inside him.

"Oh, how I have missed you," she murmured, when he let her up for air. "Love me. Fill me with your love."

Groaning her name, he clutched her to him, hands and mouth greedy as they raced over her warm, sweet flesh. It seemed like years instead of weeks since he'd last loved her. He'd thought to make the eventual parting easier for her by holding himself aloof, but realized it made no difference. There was no diminishing the love that bound them together.

She shared his urgency, trembling in his arms, her nipples already hard before he suckled them. Crying his name, she reached down to guide him home. She was hot as fire when he thrust into her, so lush a haven he knew he'd not last long. Already he could feel the silken tremors begin inside her. She arched beneath him, her hands grasping at his flanks, her hips rocking against his.

"Aye, Emma. Take me with you, love." He sank into the molten core of her, buried so deeply it was impossible to tell where one ended and the other began. Together they raced toward the summit, and then they were soaring. Free.

"Forever," Emma whispered as she tumbled over the brink.

"Forever," he echoed.

A moment later, or was it an eternity, Jamie drifted back from the heights to find he'd moved to his side and taken her with him, their bodies still joined. Her head rested on his chest, over his heart. Her eyes were closed, her breathing slow and measured.

"Sleep, love," he whispered, gently stroking the hair back from her face so he could engrave the image on his heart and mind. He wanted to remember her thus, her lips rosy from his kisses, her features soft in the candlelight, washed free of cares by their loving. In a few hours, he must leave.

The agony of parting from her ripped at him like giant claws, the pain so sharp he could scarcely breathe. Yet he knew he had to go...to save those he loved.

Last night the watch had reported that the king's men had managed to create a ford across the moat by filling in a section of it with rocks and debris. Come morn, they'd push the siege tower over the rubble and the assault would commence in earnest. Thus far, there'd been no deaths, but there soon would be. Each death would scar the hearts of attackers and defenders alike. The gulf between them would widen, filled with hatred and the thirst for revenge. Even if Harte Court did hold out, his family would be outlawed for making war on the king.

Better to surrender himself than to be the instrument of their downfall.

Jamie waited as long as he could, the joy of holding Emma balanced against the ache of knowing this would be the last time. There would be no brave band of minstrels come to create a diversion for his rescue, no hope of reprieve this time. It would be him, alone, facing Oxford and the king. Only Hugh knew he planned to surrender, and Hugh would tell no one because he agreed it was necessary. Odd that in this final act the two of them should be in harmony.

Eventually the sky began to lighten with the coming dawn, and Jamie knew he could put off the inevitable no longer. His heart heavy, he slipped from beneath the covers and began to pull on the dark clothes he'd laid out in the chair. He left behind his sword, the one his father had given him at his knighting. If by some chance their union last night bore fruit...he didn't know whether he hoped or feared it might...and Emma quickened with their son, he wanted the boy to have something of his.

Drawn to the bed one final time, Jamie adjusted the blanket around Emma's shoulders and brushed her lips once...twice. *Farewell, my love. God keep you.*

Despite the early hour, the great hall was filled with mailed knights, hastily breaking their fast before going out to take up their posts on the walls, Jamie saw as he glanced inside. He'd known most of them from birth and didn't want to be the cause of their deaths. The fear someone would spot him and try to prevent him from leaving hastened his steps through the entryway and out across the bailey.

Careful to stay clear of the guards patrolling the castle grounds, he approached the postern gate and rapped three times. From the other side, someone knocked back, twice. Taking a steadying breath, Jamie unbarred the door and eased it open.

Hugh stepped in through the opening. He looked haggard and nearly as wretched as Jamie felt.

"Have you been to bed?" Jamie asked gently.

"How could I sleep at a time like this? While I was in their camp, I got a look at the siege tower. Whoever built it knows his business. 'Tis large enough to hold at least fifty men and covered with sheets of metal...impossible to set afire."

Jamie nodded. "If you were successful, they won't use it."

"You trust Oxford to keep his word and pardon the rest of us once he has you?"

"I trust Richard for that. You have his pledge?"

"Aye." Hugh handed him the leather document case he wore slung over his shoulder. "'Tis all there...just as you asked."

Jamie unrolled the parchment. There wasn't sufficient light to read the decree, but he saw Richard's seal on the bottom, and he trusted Hugh. "My thanks for doing this. It took courage to go out alone to their camp."

Hugh shrugged uneasily. "As you predicted, Richard respected my flag of truce. And, too, neither he nor Oxford has any grudge against me."

"Even less now." Jamie rolled up the royal writ and handed it back to Hugh. "I've left letters for Mama, Papa, Jo and Emma in the strongbox. Will you see they get them?"

Hugh nodded, then cleared his throat. "How can you be so calm, knowing…knowing…"

"Knowing I am going to die?" Jamie managed to smile. "I was prepared to die ten days ago. This has been a…reprieve. A chance to make my farewells to Emma and the family and ensure they won't be blamed for my scheming." Brave words, but Jamie's legs went weak as he recalled the horrors he'd been through. Would they torture him? Or would Richard grant him a swift death? "I'd best go," he whispered. "They are likely waiting."

Hugh nodded. "I…I am sorry."

"I, too," Jamie said. For so many things. For having let his parents down. For having failed Lancaster. Most of all, for having to leave Emma. "Take care of things for me." Without waiting for Hugh to answer, he tugged open the heavy banded door and stepped outside.

Into the waiting arms of Oxford and his men.

"Seize him," Oxford snarled.

Jamie offered no resistance as they clapped him in irons and dragged him across the grassy field to their camp. He was already drawing inside himself as he'd done in prison, dulling his senses to the physical pain and his mind to the mental anguish of knowing his life had come down to a few moments.

Alex Harcourt sat alone at the high table, already wearing his mail and armor. He stared glumly out over the hall, noting the set faces of the men chewing on their bread and cold meat. By tonight, some of them might be dead. A grim thought reinforced by the distant pounding of the ram. It had done little damage, but the constant reminder they were under siege cast a pall over the keep's defenders. More alarming was the threat of the siege tower. Today the dying would begin.

A stir at the back of the hall heralded Hugh's arrival. His limp was a bit more pronounced, his expression inscrutable. He mounted the dais, slid into his customary chair and accepted a cup of ale from a serving maid. All perfectly ordinary, but there was an air of suppressed tension that jangled.

"Are you all right?" Alex asked.

"As much as can be expected with Harte Court besieged."

Alex sighed. One son cared too little for the estate, the other too much. He faulted neither. "They'll likely bring up the siege tower in a short while. I've ordered more rock and barrels of pitch moved to the spot, but if they come in great numbers, we may run out of missiles to hurl down on them."

"They will not come," Hugh said flatly.

Some paternal instinct caused Alex to straighten. "Why not? What has happened?"

Emma hurried into the hall just then, clad in her bed robe, her hair flying about in wild disorder. "Papa, have you seen Jamie?" she demanded the instant she reached them.

"Not since last night." Knowing things had been strained between them, Alex asked delicately, "Did he...was he with you?"

"Aye." Her faint blush hinted at a reconciliation, but it faded quickly. "He must have left me some time ago. But...but he didn't take his armor or his sword. He's not in the stables or the jakes. Jo is still sleeping, and Mama hasn't seen him."

Jesselynn raced in just then, her face ashen with fear, her clothes askew. "Alex, we cannot find Jamie anywhere."

Alex looked to his second son. "Where is your brother?"

"He went out through the postern gate...an hour ago."

"You knew and didn't stop him!" Alex roared, surging up from his chair in a rush of rage and anguish.

"Stop him? I helped him." Hugh stood slowly. "He did not want anyone to die for his sake." He withdrew a parchment roll from his belt and handed it to his father. "The king agreed not to proscribe us or to continue the siege once he had Ja—"

"Saddle my horse!" Alex bellowed. Shoving his chair out of the way, he hurried from the hall.

"Where are you going?" Hugh called out.

"To get Jamie back!"

Emma scrambled after him. "I'm going, too."

Jesselynn was right behind her, followed by a stream of alarmed Harcourts, all shouting their willingness to fight for the return of their lord.

"But...but the king has promised to spare us," Hugh cried over the din. No one paid any attention to him.

The Earl of Oxford rubbed his hands together in anticipation as his men made ready to hang James Harcourt. The king had insisted the bastard be well treated...as befitted a man who'd surrendered...but he'd also agreed to a speedy execution.

The victory had cost Oxford nothing. That fool Hugh had refused any payment save Harte Court, to which he'd be heir in any case...as soon as Jamie was dead. Moreover, Harcourt was now in Oxford's debt for having agreed to lift the siege and exact no reprisals on the rest of the family. It had been amusing to see the proud lord beg for his estate and, almost as an afterthought, the lives of his parents and sister. Amusing, because Richard had already decided not to punish the rest of the Harcourts.

"What of your brother's wife?" Oxford had asked.

"The amnesty must extend to her, also, I suppose. My parents are fond of her," Hugh had mumbled.

"What if she carries his child? Would it not inherit instead of you?" Oxford had asked.

Hugh's expression had hardened. "There will be no child."

Oxford speculated that, pregnant or no, the wife would not outlive her husband by long.

"My lord. We are ready," called his captain.

Indeed they were. Jamie sat atop a borrowed nag, his arms bound behind him. The noose lay lax around his neck. Two men held the horse's bridle, lest it take fright and carry out the sentence prematurely. The king's own priest stood to one side, fervently muttering prayers for the soon-to-be-departed soul.

"Tell His Majesty we await his pleasure," Oxford muttered. It displeased *him* that Harcourt seemed unaware of his impending doom, staring off into thin air as though he were miles away instead of here, about to hang.

Oxford frowned. He wanted Harcourt cringing in terror as punishment for all the trouble he'd caused with that fleet of his. The French had flatly refused to sign any peace pact till they knew where the ships were. The bumbling fool, Giles, had been unable to find out anything about the ships or connect them to the Lancasters. What a waste. No treaty with the French and Duke John due back in England any day.

Oxford stalked over and looked up at his young nemesis. "Where are those damned ships?" he demanded.

Harcourt didn't move or respond.

Oxford covertly drew his eating knife. A jab or two in the leg should jog his memory.

"Ready, are we?" Richard asked, coming up behind them.

"Aye." Oxford resheathed the blade and turned a suitably somber face toward the king. "Whenever you are."

Richard looked at Jamie and sighed. "I suppose—"

"Milord!" One of Oxford's men raced up, dirt scattering as he drew rein. "Riders approaching, your grace."

"Harcourts!" Oxford hissed. "Keep them away till—"

"Nay. They have a right to be present," the king said.

"So they can pull off another trick to free him!" Oxford turned toward his men. "Hang—"

"Hold!" roared a voice that brooked no argument.

Oxford whirled to see his worst nightmare riding up on a lathered white stallion. John, Duke of Lancaster, followed closely by Bolingbroke and fifty men in blue and white livery.

The duke swung down with a speed and grace that belied his years. "What passes here, Oxford?" he roared, tugging off his helmet. His face was red beneath a shock of gray hair. "What are you doing to my foster son?"

"Hanging him, as befits a traitor," Oxford said, smiling.

The sound of Lancaster's familiar voice roused Jamie from his daze. "Leave it be, my lord," he said. "You cannot help me." Dimly he was aware of the rope chafing his neck, and the people grouped around him. Lancaster and Harry looked stricken. Oxford's mouth flapped wildly as he threatened them with dire consequences if they tried to interfere. "Leave it be," he repeated.

"He did confess," the king said unhappily.

Lancaster puffed up like a wet hen. "I don't care—"

The clearing erupted into chaos as a troop of Harcourts charged in, followed closely by the king's soldiers. No weapons were drawn, but there was a great deal of shouting and pushing as the royal soldiers tried to keep Jamie's family from him.

In the confusion, Emma slid from her horse and ran over to grab hold of his boot. "Help me get him down," she pleaded.

Jamie's gut rolled with fear for her. "Emma, get back before you are hurt."

"Nay!" Oxford darted forward and slapped Jamie's mount on the rump. The creature reared, then bolted.

Jamie felt the saddle slip from beneath him and tensed, waiting for the rope to tighten around his neck. Instead, hard hands grabbed hold of his legs, hoisting him up. Lancaster and his father...one on either side, supporting him.

"Cut the rope! Cut the rope!" Emma sobbed.

Harry did just that, the sharp edge of his sword making short work of the hemp. As the rope fell slack, his two fathers lowered Jamie to the ground. He lay there for a moment, conscious of Emma kneeling beside him, her face buried in his chest, crying softly. His mother was on the other side, praying, he thought. Dimly he heard other voices, arguing.

"Does your uncle rule this land?" Oxford snarled.

"Nay, he does not. What is the meaning of this intrusion?" the king demanded.

"My lord." Jamie turned his head and sought Lancaster with his gaze. "Please do not do this. I am—"

"A hero." Lancaster threw Oxford a smug, triumphant look, then smiled at the king. "The French have called off their invasion. Bad weather, they say, but the real reason is that they fear our mighty fleet."

Jamie laid his head back down, tears of relief burning behind his lids. "It worked. DeGrys believed me."

"He did, my boy." Lancaster laughed. "He did, indeed."

Chapter Twenty-One

"You mean the ships were not real?" Jo asked, perched on the edge of a stool at Jamie's feet.

"They were not." Lancaster stretched his legs toward the fire leaping in Harte Court's great hearth. "When I proposed the idea of a fleet of ships, young Jamie told me there wouldn't be time to build enough of them to drive off the French."

"So you built empty hulls," Jo said.

Jamie nodded and repeated the story again, for the benefit of his sister and the flock of avid Harcourts. "We cut the wood as thin as we could and still have them float. The masts were hollow, the decks nonexistent."

"But I saw men aboard some of them, and you said they sailed out of the harbor." Emma's chair was as close to Jamie's as she could get it, her right hand still laced with his left. She had not let go of him from the moment they'd stopped the hanging. Though she didn't begrudge his family this time with their hero, she couldn't wait to get off alone.

"A few were real ships," Jamie said, "to fool Colan and those workmen who didn't know the truth. And in case the French spies got a close look."

"Why was Colan not told?" Emma asked.

"For two reasons," Jamie replied. "Firstly for his own protection. Secondly, if I was caught, Colan's outrage would help convince everyone I was a traitor. You see," he added, "if the French had any doubts about my story— if they'd guessed I wasn't betraying my country, but seeking to trick them into believing us stronger than we are— they'd have attacked."

"Where is the fleet now?" Richard asked.

"The real ships are off Carrick Bay with *Harcourt's Lady,* awaiting word it's safe to make port. Bran sank the hulls in the harbor of the shipyard." Jamie sighed and shook his head. "We hated to do it, but once DeGrys had seen our floating armada, the false ships became a liability. If word got back to the French that they were not seaworthy, our ruse would have failed."

"But surely you could have told me," the king complained.

Jamie dropped his gaze, and through their joined hands, Emma felt him tense. "I am sorry, your majesty, but—"

"'Twas on my orders he kept silent," Lancaster interjected. "Some of your ministers resent my suggestions, and might have rejected this one simply because I put it forth." He smiled, no doubt referring to Oxford, who had gone off in a fit of temper upon hearing that Jamie was no traitor. "The plan was a chancy one, greatly dependent on secrecy."

"And Jamie's bravery," Bolingbroke added. "He was willing to sacrifice himself to convince everyone the fleet was real. If he'd revealed our plans, and word got back to the French that it was a hoax, they'd have known we were vulnerable and attacked."

Lancaster nodded. "We owe Jamie more than we can repay for twice putting his neck in the noose, literally. 'Twas imperative DeGrys believe Jamie would sell out our one hope for salvation. 'Tis why I chose a man with such a...colorful...reputation. The French would have been skeptical if someone like...like young Hugh had approached them with a scheme to betray his country.''

Richard laughed at that and peppered Jamie with questions. The crowd hung on every word of the exchange, hungry for details of their lord's heroic deeds. Jamie's parents and sister especially, were beaming with love and pride.

How wonderful to see their faith in him confirmed, Emma thought. Glancing around at their shining faces, she felt the happiness swell inside her. Her imagination wove bright fantasies of staying here always, of building a life here among these wonderful people who'd accepted her...bastardy, low birth and all...without a qualm. Then her gaze found Hugh, and her soaring spirits faltered.

He stood apart, as usual, in the shadowy recess of a window embrasure. His attention, like most in the room, was riveted on Jamie, but instead of respect or admiration, his features were twisted into a mask of naked hatred.

Alarm raced down Emma's spine, coiling into a knot of fear deep in her belly. Hugh's animosity was not the petty spite of a sibling resenting his brother's moment of glory. Nor was it a recent thing. She sensed, with chilling insight, that Hugh had hated Jamie all his life. But never more so than now.

Because Jamie's victory had snatched the prize from Hugh's grasp. *Harte Court.*

Hugh shifted suddenly, lowering his head to look at something he'd removed from the pouch at his belt. Craning her neck, she tried to see it. Firelight caught on what he held, a flash of silver, nothing more, before his fist closed over the object. What was it? Something of Jamie's he'd taken when he thought Harte Court was his?

While she struggled with the mystery, Hugh turned and

moved along the edge of the crowd, heading out of the hall. Was he going to his room to sulk? Nay, he took the stairs that led up to the third floor and the apartment she shared with Jamie. He must be returning what he'd taken. When long minutes passed and Hugh did not reappear, she assumed he'd gone down the back stairs and outside to work out his rage in private.

"Why so tense, love?" Jamie whispered in her ear.

Emma started. Confessing she did not like Hugh would only cause more trouble. "I am tired, is all." She looked up and realized how ashen he was. "Come up to bed."

"Gladly. Eagerly." He kissed her temple and murmured, "Last night I was too hungry to linger over you as I wanted, but when I get back, I intend to—"

"Where are you going?"

"The king has asked to speak with me privately in Papa's counting room so he can give me some reward or other." He grinned at her. "Knowing England is safe and we will have a lifetime together is all the reward I need, but..." He shrugged.

"'Tis difficult to dissuade the king in a generous mood. I will anxiously await your return so I can reward you, my lord." Emma stood, curtsied to the king, kissed her new Mama and Papa, hugged Jo and left the hall. She felt a moment of trepidation when she opened the door to their chamber, but if Hugh had been here, he was gone now.

Humming to herself, she picked up the clothes she'd scattered about in her rush to save Jamie. Was it only a few hours ago? It all seemed like a dream, a nightmare, banished by the truth. Jamie had not betrayed them, he'd saved them. The relief of knowing the ordeal was behind them and their whole lives ahead of them was dizzying.

She lifted the lid on the clothes chest and bent to place the folded garments within. Behind her, she heard the door creak open. Turning, she saw Jamie standing just beyond the threshold in the dark hallway.

"Well, that didn't take long." She started toward him, wondering if he'd think her too bold if she suggested they bar the door and while away the afternoon in bed. "What prize did His Majesty bestow on you? A title or some bauble...?" She stopped, voice trailing off as she drew near enough to recognize the tall, blonde man lurking in the shadows. "Hugh!"

"Aye." He slipped into the room and closed the door, leaning back against it as he stared at her.

"What are you doing here? Has aught happened to Jamie?"

"Nothing bad ever happens to my brother. He leads a charmed life." Hugh pushed away from the door and stalked toward her.

"What do you want?" she asked, alarmed and retreating before him. Not only was he acting strangely, there was an odd, almost frantic look in his eyes. "If you've come to speak with Jamie—"

"I intend to do more than speak with him. I intend to settle something we started long ago. And you are going to help me."

"Of...of course." Her legs bumped against the clothes chest, forcing a halt. Her mind raced. What did Hugh want? He hadn't threatened her, yet her skin crawled with apprehension. Leave, her intuition urged. "But I fear it will have to wait. I...Jamie is with the king. They expect me down immed—"

"Nay. They are speaking privately. No doubt Richard is heaping riches on my brother. An earldom, at least."

He deserves it, Emma thought, but she kept silent, frightened by Hugh's sullen, hostile mood. "What did you want me to do?" she asked, stalling. How long before Jamie returned?

"Ride out with me."

Ride where? And more importantly, why? "I fear I am not an experienced horsewoman. If you wait for Jamie—"

"We will." He bent down, snatched her cloak from the top of the trunk and thrust it at her. "Put this on."

"But I don't want to go for a ride. I want—"

"I do not give a damn what you want." He grabbed hold of her arm and twisted it behind her back so violently she cried out. His other hand closed over her mouth. "Quiet. We are going to ride out to the glade and wait for Jamie," he snarled in her ear. "The glade where it all went so horribly wrong."

The glade. Emma's stomach turned as she realized what he meant. "Wh-why?" she mumbled into his palm, causing him to lift his hand a fraction. "What do you intend to do?" she asked.

"Fight…as we should have years ago. Only this time 'twill be to the death, winner takes all."

"Jamie won't come."

"He will when he knows I hold you, my dear."

"He may come, but he won't fight you, Hugh."

"He will if it means your life."

Emma's stomach rolled into her throat. Stay calm. Think of some way out. "You would not harm me, Hugh, and Jamie knows—"

Hugh laughed, an ugly, coarse sound that iced her blood. "You'd be surprised how far a man will go when he's cornered. I was. I never meant to kill her," he added, his voice low, musing. "But she pushed and pushed, demanding, threatening. The second time was easier."

"What are you talking about?"

Hugh looked down at her, his expression tight. "Never mind. Suffice to say I'd have no compunction about eliminating you if you stand in the way of what I want…what I deserve."

"But Jamie isn't sufficiently recovered from his ordeal in prison to fight."

"That is his hard luck, then," Hugh snapped.

"I won't go with you." Emma opened her mouth to scream.

He cut it off with his hand. "Silence, or I'll kill you now. Don't think I won't," he added. "I can still leave my note telling Jamie to meet me. He'll not know if you're alive or dead." Glaring at her, he released her arm, slid the knife from his belt and pressed it against her throat.

Emma glared right back at him, though her heart beat against her ribs like a trapped bird. He had to be lying about having killed someone. Mad. He must be mad. But while she was trying desperately to think of a way out of this, Hugh proved he was also an extremely clever and thorough planner.

Taking a strip of cloth from the trunk, he bade her tie it around her mouth. When she was gagged, he sheathed the knife, sat her on the edge of the bed and bound her hands and feet.

"There, that should hold you for a moment." He rummaged through the chest and unearthed one of Jamie's spare patches. "You were doubtless wondering how I intended to take you out of here trussed up like a goose for market." He tied on the patch and adjusted it before facing her. "I don't. You and I, my dear little wife, are riding out for a romantic tryst down by the river." He gave her a roguish grin so reminiscent of Jamie's that her rioting heart skipped a beat.

With the patch on, he looked exactly like Jamie. No one would stop them.

It was nearly dusk by the time Jamie climbed the stairs to his chamber, exhausted but exhilarated at the prospect of a few hours alone with his wife. He threw the door open, expecting to be greeted by warm hugs or at least to have the fun of sliding into bed beside her if she was sleeping.

The room was empty, the fire in the hearth reduced to a pile of cold ashes. Where the hell was she?

He found the note on the bed.

I have Emmeline. Meet me in the glade, and we will settle...as we should have years ago. Come alone and unarmed, or she dies. Don't think I won't do it.

It was signed with a solid black H.

Hugh!

Jamie closed his eyes against a rush of shock and disbelief. Had Hugh gone mad? What was he hoping to accomplish?

Settle this in the glade...as we should have years ago.

Then the quarrel had been over Harte Court. Likely it still was, but he couldn't believe Hugh meant to harm Emma. Still stunned, Jamie opened his eye and caught sight of something else laying on the bed. A silver pin in the shape of a unicorn.

Hand trembling, he reached out and picked it up. 'Twas exactly as Emma had described it.

Celia's brooch.

The one Sir Thomas's men learned Lily had taken and tried to pawn. Yet it hadn't been found on her body.

Because the killer had taken it when he murdered her?

Jamie groaned and dropped the brooch, unwilling to let his mind jump to the logical conclusion.

Hugh wasn't capable of murder.

Jamie clung to that as he slipped a long knife into the top of his boot and hurried from the room. Several people seemed surprised to see him back from a supposed ride with Emma. So, Hugh had left wearing a patch and posing as him. He'd obviously been good at it.

Good enough to fool a woman Jamie had once bedded?

Jamie didn't want to think about that, because if Hugh had killed once, he'd not hesitate to do so again.

Neptune's hooves pounded in time to the frantic beat of Jamie's heart as they galloped along the track and into the woods. Emma was all right. She had to be. Hugh would not harm her till Jamie arrived. But what about afterward? Facing the hangman had been far easier than this, Jamie thought.

A strong sense of déjà vu swept over Jamie as he crossed the meadow and saw Hugh step from the woods on the far side. Only their parts were reversed, and Hugh was waiting for him.

Jamie stopped a dozen yards away. "Where is Emma?"

"Here." Hugh tugged her from cover and shoved her onto her knees at his feet. Her hands appeared to be bound before her; a cloth covered her mouth. But she was alive...for the moment.

"Let her go, and you can do whatever you want with me."

Emma made a grunting sound behind her gag.

"Be still, Emma," Jamie called, terrified she'd say or do something to provoke Hugh. Now that he'd gotten Jamie here, Hugh had no reason to keep her alive. "What do you want? Hugh?" he asked, hoping to keep Hugh's attention focused on him. If only he could somehow signal Emma to crawl away.

"I want a fight...with swords, this time, and to the death," Hugh said. Bending, he lifted two swords from the ground.

Jamie nodded in agreement, even knowing he was too weak to wield a weapon for long. "Let Emma leave now."

"And bring back Papa? Nay." Hugh buried the blade of one sword in the earth in silent challenge.

"At least let her withdraw a safe distance," Jamie pleaded as he walked Neptune closer. His eyes moved from Hugh's hardened features to Emma's fear-filled ones. Did she suspect what he did about Hugh? Did she know Hugh couldn't afford to let her live? It was imperative she get away while they were fighting. "May I kiss my wife goodbye?"

"Nay. I'd not trust you...either of you."

Emma chose that moment to tear the gag from her mouth. "Run, Jamie, run. He means to kill you!" She screamed and launched herself at Hugh. Her shoulder caught him behind the knees and the two of them tumbled into a heap.

"Emma!" Jamie spurred Neptune forward, but he knew he'd never reach them in time. Already Hugh had regained his footing. He stood over Emma, sword raised above her sprawled body.

A guttural scream split the air, just as it had seven years ago when Jamie and Hugh had been ambushed. This time a single man jumped down from the branches of a huge pine. The fading rays of the sun caught on the weapon he held aloft, then it plunged downward in an ominous arch toward Hugh's back.

"Hugh! Behind you!" Jamie shouted.

Too late. Hugh went down beneath his attacker just as Jamie slid from the saddle. Drawing the knife from his boot, Jamie sent it flying...straight into the neck of his brother's assailant.

The man reared back. It was Giles Cadwell, his features contorted with a mix of fury and pain. "Nay. It can't be..." He looked down at Hugh, then at Jamie. "I can't have killed the wrong one. It's not fair that Jamie should win." He twitched, then collapsed sideways, sliding off to reveal the hideous, gaping wounds he'd carved in Hugh's back.

"Hugh. Oh, God, Hugh." Jamie knelt in the grass, hands trembling as he turned his brother over.

Emma crawled nearer, her hands still bound, the gag hanging loose about her neck. "Is he dead?"

"N-nay," Jamie said hoarsely.

"Untie my hands. Let me see what I can—"

Hugh groaned, his eyes fluttering open. "There's nothing you can do," he whispered, blood flecking his lips.

"Hush," Jamie said. "I won't let you die..."

"Why? I would have let you die...here...years ago..."

Jamie touched his shoulder. "You saved my life, then, Hugh, what has happened to change you?"

"Didn't mean to save you...heard Papa coming...had to make it look like I tried to help you." He coughed, liquid rattling in his lungs. "Nearly got myself killed...ruined everything."

Emma stuck out her hands. "Untie me. I'll try to help him."

"Fools, the pair of you," Hugh said in a raspy whisper as Jamie undid her ropes. "'Tis better...only hang anyway..."

"What do you mean?" Emma whispered.

Jamie looked at his brother, but the words stuck in his throat.

"I...I killed Celia...and Lily," Hugh said.

Emma gasped as the pieces of the puzzle clicked horribly into place. "You were Celia's lover?"

"She thought I was Jamie." Hugh laughed, or tried to; the sound ended in a strangled groan. "Told you all men...the same in the dark." He looked at Emma. "Didn't...didn't mean to kill her...shouldn't have tried to force me to wed her. But then...I thought you'd hang for it, Jamie. You escaped. You always do."

"Rest, Hugh. I'll go for help."

"Too late." Hugh lifted a hand toward Jamie's patch. "Too late from the moment...I was born." He ripped the patch away and stared at the scar that cut across his twin's face from above the brow to the cheekbone. "Ugly...not as hideous as I thought. Can...can you see?"

Jamie shook his head.

"Good...hate to think you always won." Hugh closed his eyes and breathed his last.

Epilogue

"You do not have to do this," Emma said gently. The bell had just rung, summoning them to dinner. They were dressed and ready, yet Jamie hesitated just inside the door of their chamber.

"I know." Jamie traced the ridge of scar tissue from his brow to his cheekbone. "Do you think I'll frighten the folk from the hall when I appear without my patch?"

"You will cause a stir, but fear, never." 'Twas as Hugh had said, a scar, but not a hideous deformity. The lower corner of Jamie's eye was raised in a permanent look of wonder, and his vision was blurred. But he was neither blind nor ugly.

"I feel naked without the patch, but I suppose I will grow used to going without it, as I did to wearing it."

"What will you tell your parents about this?"

"Not the truth," Jamie said. "Only you know that."

He'd done it for Hugh. The mark of Cain, Jamie had once called it, and that was exactly the way he'd seen it. Hugh had been lamed by an attack for which Jamie blamed himself. Unwilling to come away unscathed from the incident, he'd donned the patch. And he'd lied to Hugh about his sight.

The good brother, Jamie had called Hugh, but he couldn't have been more wrong. Envy and hatred had eaten away at him from the inside, twisted him into a murderer. Adversity had only honed Jamie's honor and bravery.

Her knight in shining armor. Emma put her arms around his lean waist and hugged him tight. "What will you say when people ask why you've taken if off?" she asked.

"I will tell them I feared 'twould curdle your milk."

Her gasp of mock outrage became a soft sigh as his hands skimmed up to cup her breasts. He fondled them as gently as though they were made of spun glass...which was exactly the way he'd treated her since this morn when she'd told him...

"Are you sure you are carrying our child? Your breasts are only a bit fuller, and your belly is as flat as ever."

"Not for long." By her estimate, she'd conceived on their wedding night, and would deliver in late July.

"Do you mind if I tell Mama and Papa tonight? They leave for Scotland on the morrow, and I know the news would...ease them."

Emma nodded. They'd buried Hugh two weeks ago and sent Giles's body to his cousin in Kent, but Alex and Jesselynn still mourned the loss of their son. Typically they blamed themselves for not seeing how deeply he resented Jamie. "If the babe is a boy, we could name him Hugh," she said slowly.

"Absolutely not. Mama blames Hugh's misdeeds on the fact he was named after her brother...the one who tried to wipe out Papa and the rest of the Sommervilles to gain their lands."

"Well, we're definitely not calling him after my father."

"I guess we'd best hope it's a girl, then."

Emma looked up, thrilled to see both his eyes gazing back. Since Hugh's death, he'd gone without the patch when they were private. A mark of his complete trust in her. "Would you be disappointed if 'twas a girl?"

"Nay, I'd spoil her as I intend to her mama." Jamie dipped his head to nuzzle her neck, whispering all the delicious things he planned to do with his babe's mother when they were private for the night. "Are you certain you feel well enough to go down to dinner? I could fetch us a tray." He waggled his brows.

"I never felt better." She'd not miss the Harcourts' reaction to their lord's unveiling for anything. She had hopes that seeing Jamie without his patch would please Alex and Jesselynn nearly as much as had the news Jamie would be staying at Harte Court and assuming his duties as heir.

There was a brief knock, and the door flew open.

"Mistress Emmeline!" exclaimed Molly. "Ye've got to come!" She glanced at Jamie, blinking rapidly. "What happened to yer patch, milord?"

"I lost it."

"Humph. Suppose 'tis only fitting, seeing as how you've given up yer pirating ways."

"Did you want something?" Emma asked.

Molly's mouth rounded. "'Tis Cedric...he's here."

"How did he find us?" Emma whispered.

"He went to the shop in Derry, and the new owners told him where we'd gone." Molly and Toby had both decided to join Emma at Harte Court while Peter apprenticed with the new apothecary.

"I think I feel faint after all," Emma murmured.

"Nay, love." Jamie put his arms around her. "Do not worry yourself sick over this. All will be well, I swear it."

"But...but he'll try to wheedle money from you, and he'll... oh, Molly, tell the steward to lock up the plate and—"

"Easy, love. I cannot bear to see you upset. All will be well, I swear it." Jamie took her hands and laced her fingers with his. "We will go down and face him. Together, there is naught we cannot brave...you have shown me that."

"But I...I am so embarrassed to be his daughter."

Jamie smiled sympathetically. There were times when he didn't like recalling his brother was a murderer, but then... "You are your own person and not accountable for his sins."

"What can we do?"

"Well..." Jamie winked at Molly, tucked Emma's hand into the crook of his arm and led her from the room. "Bran is returning to Cornwall in a few days. I could send Cedric with him...to look after my interests in the tin mines."

"You'd inflict Cedric on your friends?"

"On the tinners, who are twice as sly as Cedric and three times as bold."

Emma stopped Jamie at the top of the stairs, motioning for Molly to go on ahead of them. "Have I told you how proud I am to be your wife?"

"Not since yesterday, I think." The gleam in his eyes warmed her clear to her toes.

"Well, I am. Long ago I wrote about a man like you, a knight who was brave, strong and honorable, yet unafraid to be gentle." Stretching up on tiptoe, she framed his scarred face in her hands. "I did not really think such a man existed...till I met you. I love you, Jamie Harcourt. Forever and ever."

"And I you, Emma-mine," he said softly. "Twice as much, for I traveled through hell to find you." He kissed her tenderly. "Much as your love means to me, your trust means even more. Against all odds, you believed in me. Your love gave me the strength to come home again." He took her right hand, kissed it and placed it over his left eye. "Your love gave me the courage to overcome my scars."

"As you cured me of mine." His scar was nearly invisible in the gloom. In time, so too would be the horrors of the past. But the future...the future looked bright indeed.

Smiling, Emma lifted her face for his kiss. As his mouth closed over hers, her heart swelled with love.

Together. Forever.

*   *   *   *   *

Harlequin® Historical

A clandestine night of passion
An undisclosed identity
A hidden child

RITA Award nominee

Miranda Jarrett

presents...

THE SECRETS OF
Catie Hazard

Available in April,
wherever Harlequin Historicals are sold.

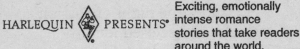

You are cordially invited to a
HOMETOWN REUNION
September 1996—August 1997

Bad boys, cowboys, babies. Feuding families,
arson, mistaken identity, a mom on the run...
Where can you find romance and adventure?
Tyler, Wisconsin, that's where!

So join us in this not-so-sleepy little town and
experience the love, the laughter and the
tears of those who call it home.

WELCOME TO A
HOMETOWN REUNION

Daphne Sullivan and her little girl were hiding
from something or someone—that much was
becoming obvious to those who knew her. But
from whom? Was it the stranger with the dark
eyes who'd just come to town? Don't miss
Muriel Jensen's *Undercover Mom,* ninth in a
series you won't want to end....

Available in May 1997
at your favorite retail store.

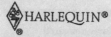

HARLEQUIN®

LOVE *or* MONEY?
Why not Love *and* Money!
After all, millionaires
need love, too!

How to Marry a MILLIONAIRE

Suzanne Forster,
Muriel Jensen
and
Judith Arnold

bring you three original stories
about finding that one-in-a million man!

Harlequin also brings you
a million-dollar sweepstakes—enter
for your chance to win a fortune!

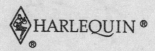 HARLEQUIN ®
®

HTMM

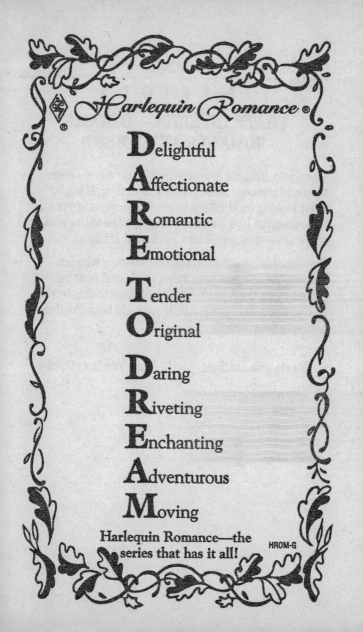

Harlequin Romance ®

Delightful

Affectionate

Romantic

Emotional

Tender

Original

Daring

Riveting

Enchanting

Adventurous

Moving

Harlequin Romance—the
series that has it all!

HROM-G